THE MORAL MAFIA

THE MORAL MAFIA

DAN REYNOLDS

RNR Publishing Company
Omaha, Nebraska

ISBN13: 978-0-9824125-6-5
ISBN10: 0-9824125-6-8
Library of Congress Control Number: 2010909723
Cataloging in Publication Data on file with publisher.

RNR Publishing Company
12335 Decatur Street
Omaha, NE 68154
www.RNRPublishingCo.com

Printed in the United States of America
10 9 8 7 6 5 4 3 2 1

ACKNOWLEDGEMENTS

I OWE A DEBT OF GRATITUDE TO SEVERAL PEOPLE WHO helped me turn the Moral Mafia manuscript into a novel. My wife, Pat, has read many versions of the Moral Mafia in manuscript form. Her input was always spot-on and we spent many hours discussing the characters and events in the book. I'd like to thank her for her support and common sense advice. In addition, I thank my children for their indulgence and understanding for the times I missed a life event in order to work on this project.

I have three editors to thank. All have contributed to the final quality of this text. Sandra Wendell did an early manuscript edit of *The Moral Mafia*. Mary B. Reynolds edited the manuscript in its final stages, and Pat Reynolds and I did the final edit. I'd like to thank all three of them for their keen eye and attention to detail. Also, many thanks to the members of my fiction writers group, *The Omaha NightWriters*, who have read and critiqued many of this book's chapters.

Lisa Pelto is the President of Concierge Marketing. She and her talented staff continue to advise me in ways that only they can. She and Gary Withrow are responsible for the incredible cover and layout of this book. Thank you both for everything you do. You have been a Godsend to me.

Eugene (Bud) Hartlaub is an acquaintance turned friend who has never failed to provide me with the much needed encouragement and resources to get my books to market. Thanks, Bud, for your support.

1

THREE MEN ENTERED THE THIRD FLOOR CONFERENCE room of Chicago's old Farm Credit Building on 42nd Street. The modern glass and steel décor did not fit with the rest of the building's marble floors and hand carved oak architecture, yet the technology-laden accoutrements made it grand in its own way. Such technology did not come cheap, but Tony Constantino had financial resources available to few men anywhere. No one knew his net worth. He preferred it that way. Two weeks ago, the *Chicago Tribune* had estimated his assets in excess of fifty million dollars. The article was neither flattering nor accurate, but Constantino smiled when he had read it.

Close, he had mused, *they're only two billion off the mark.*

The don took his customary position at the head of the table, facing the room's entrance. Constantino never sat with his back to a door. Leaning firmly against his seatback cushion, he exuded the air of a confident man, a man who was perfectly content with life.

Constantino was a devout Catholic, a family man adored by friends and feared by business associates.

For all his wealth, Tony Constantino lived in a modest home. He purchased a new car once every three or four years. If he had a weakness for spending, it was on technology. In sharp contrast to his father, a man who ran the family for thirty-five years, Constantino owned a host of high-tech gadgets. He found that dabbling in technology stocks was far more exciting than running the family's gambling casinos and brothels. His participation in the drug cartel was anything but glamorous, and it was becoming more dangerous every year. But this was the hand life had dealt him, and he gladly accepted it as his destiny.

The second man, a gargantuan figure known as John Henry, went straight to the bar and poured a drink. He then walked to Constantino, who was fondling a remote control, and handed him a Grappa, imported from the family's business in Sicily. Taking a small sip, Constantino savored his favorite brandy.

"Mmm, thank you John Henry." He reached in his breast pocket for a Cohiba Cuban cigar. "It's time to prepare for our meeting, gentlemen."

John Henry rolled his sweaty sleeves down around his thick arms. He put on the sport coat he had removed in the sweltering downtown heat. The third man, Mario Manetti, fumbled with something in his right hip pocket, and then he patted it and nodded. He reached to his opposite side to find his cell and called Mike Sloan, who was waiting outside for Constantino's guests to arrive. He spoke softly to Sloan as Constantino studied the conference room's bright and cheery surroundings.

Through the high-tech windows to his left, Constantino could see a row of stately old buildings reflecting the early evening sun. Through the glass in front of him, he could see Trina Mandolfo, his niece and secretary, and farther back, several cubicles that formed a path to his elite corner office.

Constantino clicked the remote, and every image beyond the glass disappeared from view under an opaque film of liquid crystal. A few canister lights illuminated automatically, but the room was transformed from eye-squinting brightness to near darkness. The display panels of three computers in the back of the room shone brightly from a distance. So did the numeral three above the elevator, which Constantino had installed for private use. It took a few seconds for the three men to adjust to the darkness. Shadows fell everywhere except on Constantino, whose figure seemed to radiate an eerie yellow glow under the incandescents. John Henry and Mario Manetti took positions near the room's entrance. Constantino raised the remote control once more and, like magic, an eighteen-inch swath of glass became clear at the top-most portion of the opaque gray windows. Light gushed in from the early evening sky.

"Perfect," Constantino said checking his watch with a brief smile, "The stage is set. Mike will be escorting our guests up here any minute. Are there any questions regarding this evening's meeting?"

Manetti's fingers tugged his thick black mustache and then he patted his pocket once more. Calmly, he answered, "Just one, Tony, is there any chance Mr. Lang will cooperate?"

The remaining glint of contentment drained from Constantino's eyes and they narrowed until they were slits. The corners of his mouth turned down and his grasp on the remote control tightened.

"None, the fool has already leaked the information to his shareholders. He should have kept it quiet until the project was further along. Anyway, we can easily discredit him; convince everyone that the memory chip was just a hoax. It shouldn't be too difficult, considering the improbability that such a technology even exists."

"What about his researcher?"

"Napierilla? He's a weak man. He has four children—he'll cooperate." Constantino changed the subject, "How is your mother, Mario?"

Manetti sighed as he leaned his shoulder against the closed door. "I saw her early this morning, Tony. She's doing much better. She asked me to thank you for the roses."

"She's a wonderful woman, Mario. No man could ask for a better mother."

3

Manetti tugged at his lapels, straightening his suit coat. "She still has some numbness on her left side, but the doctor thinks she'll make a full recovery."

"I've arranged for maid service for the next few months. A woman recovering from a stroke shouldn't be doing housework."

Mario's eyes softened. "You are too kind to us, Tony."

"Nonsense, you're family—and family is everything."

Constantino reached in his right pocket and produced an intricately engraved gold lighter. As he lit his cigar, there was a light knock on the door. John Henry opened it to face a gawking man who was no doubt, William Lang. John Henry shrugged off his stare. From where Lang stood, the conference room's door jam blocked a good portion of John Henry's forehead from view.

Jesus, how big is this guy?

Mike Sloan had escorted William Lang and his researcher, Keith Napierilla to the conference room. He stepped from the hallway in front of Lang, who hadn't moved, and waved his arm motioning Lang and Napierilla to move to the conference table. Lang made no attempt to hide his rudeness, and continued staring at John Henry. It was as though his eyes were powerless to do anything else. For the second time, Sloan motioned their guests toward the table. Lang still had his neck craned, looking up at John Henry, but he began to inch his way toward Constantino.

Constantino managed a weak smile, "Hello Bill, good to see you."

"Ahh—same here, Tony." Impeccably dressed as always, Lang extended a perfectly manicured hand to Constantino, who remained seated. They shook hands briefly. Constantino's voice took on a playful quality and he said, "I can see you are in awe of John Henry's dimensions. Just wait until you sit down—it's like looking up at a skyscraper."

Skyscraper nothing! He looks like Frankenstein's monster.

Lang swapped glances with Constantino, then John Henry, then Manetti, and again with John Henry. He never connected with Sloan's eyes before he was again transfixed on the man whose head was almost as flat as it was thick.

"Yes, he's a big man," said Lang, "probably played basketball in high school—right, Mr. Henry?"

The behemoth seemed to find no humor in the remark. He replied in a stoic voice, "It's John Henry."

Still unable to retract his stare, Lang answered, "Right, thanks for correcting me, John Henry."

"Gentlemen, please have a seat," Constantino said. Watching Lang closely, he glanced at the fourth man, Sloan. "Mike, will you tell Trina she can leave for the evening?" Sloan disappeared and closed the opaque glass door behind him. Constantino raised his glass, offering his guests a drink. "What will you have from the bar, Bill?"

"Do you have any scotch?"

"John Henry, please get Mr. Lang a scotch. What about you Mr. Napierilla?"

The pale, boney figure was studying his surroundings with great curiosity, "Water is fine, thank you."

Lang's attention finally drifted to Constantino. "It's good to be in this neighborhood again, Tony, I love the charm of these old buildings."

"There are a few for sale, Bill. I could make some inquiries if you're ready to escape the grueling gridlock of Oak Brook's rush hour traffic."

"You couldn't tear me away from the 'hustle and bustle,' Tony. Besides, we already have the perfect research facility. But enough of that, I've only got a few minutes and you said this was important."

"It is, Bill. I don't want Simmons' memory chip to go into production."

Lang turned an ear toward Constantino as though he wasn't certain he had heard correctly, "Excuse me?"

"You heard me, Bill. I want you to turn over the prototypes and all the design data you have on them. Mario will pick everything up around noon tomorrow."

"Wait a minute—hold on! I've already told the board—and our shareholders."

"A mistake you will have to rectify, Bill."

Lang leaned forward, unconsciously straightening the tie below his stiffly pressed collar.

There must be a misunderstanding of some kind. Surely he can't be serious? Not after all the trouble he went through to steal the design? For God's sake, he had Simmons killed for it.

Lang's face was drawn, "Is someone on to us?"

"Not at all, Bill."

"Then why do you want to stop production? We stand to make millions, even billions on these chips."

John Henry set a bottle of water in front of Napierilla, and a scotch in front of Lang. Sloan re-entered the room and took a seat at the far corner of the table. Lang glanced up through the smoky gray hue at John Henry, and then at Manetti and Sloan, and thought the situation looked a little clearer now. *I've heard rumors of Constantino's goons, they mean to intimidate us.*

Coolly, Constantino answered the question, "I have a personal use for the chips, Bill. I want them back."

Lang's sapphire-blue eyes possessed the same disbelief his voice now projected. "I can't do that, Tony. Besides, they can't possibly do you any good. We haven't completed the algorithm for compressing, storing, and reconstructing data. The chips are useless in this state."

"Not to me, Bill, I have a use for them exactly as they are."

Lang's face betrayed his disdain for the comment, as he strained to think of what possible use Constantino could have for the memory chips.

Andrew Simmons, a professor and research scientist at the University of Chicago, had developed two tiny memory chips that use complex mathematical algorithms to create thousands of terabytes of virtual memory. The problem was that the data then had to be compressed and stored on a hard disk before powering off the computer or all the data was lost. Lang knew the chip threatened to make obsolete every current design for memory chips, and bankrupt any company that did not license the new technology. But there was still work to be done.

There can't be a useful purpose for the chips in this state, Lang thought.

"Let's talk about this a little, Tony."

"There is nothing to discuss."

"If it's about money—"

"I could buy your company many times over; it's not about money."

"But we had an agreement."

Constantino didn't appear to comprehend Lang's predicament, "Listen Bill, I feel bad about this. I'll comp you two hundred thousand for your trouble."

"I don't want your compensation, Tony. I want the chips. I can't give them up, I—I'll lose all credibility with the board and our shareholders."

"Make up a story, Bill. Tell them it was all an elaborate hoax. You aren't out any money."

Only my reputation, ang thought, imagining the worst at next Tuesday's board meeting.

Lang was silent for a moment, and then his eyes filled with rage. He pounded the table with his fist. "WE HAD A DEAL!"

Manetti and John Henry stood behind Lang. They moved a little closer. Keith Napierilla stiffened. Lang was unaware of their current proximity.

"I can't do it, Tony, I WON'T DO IT!"

"So you're refusing to give them back to me?"

"You're damn right! My company's future is riding on these memory chips. It's just too late to give them up now, for any reason!"

Tony leaned back in his swivel chair, "I guess you're right, Bill—I suppose it is too late." He shifted his glance to Mario Manetti and nodded. Lang saw the gesture and shuddered.

The gangly, but astute Napierilla had been fidgeting throughout the conversation. It was as though he had sensed the impending trouble that Lang was too ignorant or preoccupied to see. Pale and sweating, Napierilla watched his employer intensely.

"I've got to go," Lang said curtly. He began to stand, but didn't rise two inches from the chair before John Henry's massive hand shoved his shoulder down. Napierilla went rigid and squeezed his water bottle so tight it overflowed onto the conference table. Like a surgeon, Manetti skillfully withdrew his chosen instrument from his jacket's side pocket. He placed the long barrel expertly behind the chair, below Lang's right shoulder blade and angled the line of trajectory to his heart. He squeezed the trigger. Napierilla convulsed at the shrill metallic sound of the muffled gunshot. No one outside of the room would have heard it. Napierilla stared at the man with the thick mustache and watched him withdraw the weapon. A waft of smoke drifted from the silencer that he used to stifle the deadly blow. Napierilla was paralyzed with fear as Lang's body slumped forward. So afraid was Napierilla that he didn't even twitch when Lang's forehead smashed against the table. Without moving a muscle Napierilla's eyes ticked like a second hand, moving from the table to the man who gave the nod.

Constantino's voice was calm, almost soothing, "I understand you have four children, Mr. Napierilla?"

"Please, p-please don't hurt them," he stuttered.

"I have no intention of harming your children, Keith. May I call you Keith?"

Pale, fearful, and unable to speak, Napierilla nodded.

"I want you to return the prototypes and research to us tomorrow." Constantino pointed at Manetti who was unscrewing something from the barrel of his gun. He continued, "Mario will meet you in front of your building at noon. While you are at it, pack any personal belongings you want to keep and bring them with you. From now on, you work for me. All your needs financial and otherwise will be taken care of. Mike—show our new employee to his office. And, Keith, welcome to the family."

2

THE KITCHEN DOOR FLUNG OPEN AND BOUNCED BACK from the door stop. Two figures carrying luggage pushed through the doorway laughing heartily. They turned to face a large table packed with children. Before Jim O'Brien could set his suitcase down, the screaming was well underway.

"Daddy's home!" six-year-old Molly shrieked. Eight-year-old Danny asked, "Did you bring us a present?"

"Hi, kids!" Jim said, "No presents, but I did buy a treat for later."

The hulking figure at Jim's side had a huge grin on his face. "I gotta tell ya, Peg, if you had seen that flight attendant from Kansas City making the moves on your husband, you'd be in divorce court tomorrow!"

Peg O'Brien got up from the dinner table and Scott Troia gave her his customary bear hug. She could smell the beer on his breath.

"Is that right? Perhaps I need to hear this story!" Peg gave Jim a playful frown while she waited for a response.

Jim's cheeks reddened a bit. "It was nothing, Peg—a flight attendant was flirting a little bit, that's all."

"And did you flirt back?"

"Of course not, I know better than to face the wrath of your cast iron skillet!" Jim smiled as he mimicked Peg hitting him on the head with a frying pan, then he grabbed her and pulled her close. "You know there's only one girl for me." He gave her a tender kiss and the youngest children giggled.

Scott gave the couple a look of admiration, "Well, Jim, it doesn't look like I'm going to get you into trouble tonight. I guess I might as well go home."

"Not so fast, Scott—who was this flight attendant anyway?"

"The prettiest blond I've ever seen, Peg, and the funniest thing, too. Jim told her he was married, but she just kept hinting that she was going to be at the Shelton Club tonight." Peg's eyes grew a little more serious now. "You mean she kept flirting even after Jim told her he was married?"

"Yup. Jim finally told her he wanted to go home and spend some time with his eleven children. You should have seen the look on her face!"

Peg's features softened again, "We see that look a lot, don't we, Jim?"

"Yes we do, Peg."

"Anyway, you don't have to worry about Jim. He's about the most devoted family man I've ever known."

"Don't go christening him for sainthood, Scott. Fidelity is supposed to be the norm in a marriage, but the nerve of that woman. What's happened to the morals of the people in this country?"

Jim spoke up, "Okay you two, let's not discuss morality any further. Scott and I have already worn out the topic, and it just gets everyone upset. I'm home, and it's time to enjoy the evening. What's for dinner?"

"There's a whiskey steak warming in the oven."

Scott laughed, "You shouldn't mix all that beer with the hard stuff, Jim."

"Very funny—care to join us?"

"No, but thanks. Joan probably has my dinner ready too. Maybe we'll have beer battered fish!"

Jim and Peg laughed. Jim shook his head side-to-side in mock disgust, and pointed his thumb over his shoulder, "Two days of Scott's corny jokes, Peg. Thank God I'm home." Scott grinned. He prided himself on telling simple jokes. Jim considered it his best friend's most endearing quality.

Scott addressed the kitchen table, stuffed as it was with kids. "Now your dad has had plenty of time to rest the past few days, so you kids make sure to keep him up late tonight. You know how he loves to play games." The children laughed and began to chatter about what games they could play. When he heard Danny mention "Candy Land," Scott gave Jim a sideways glance and started for the back door. "My work here is done."

"Thanks for driving, Scott. See you in the morning."

Ten minutes later, Peg noticed that Jim seemed more preoccupied than usual. His eyes hovered over his dinner plate with an absent gaze.

"Jim? Jim, are you listening to me? We have to be at the church by four o'clock tomorrow." His eyes remained on his untouched meal.

"No problem, Peg, I'll leave the office by two." Within seconds of Jim's comment, Peg was again engaged in a half dozen conversations at once. Without missing a beat she quipped at Molly, "Use a fork—not your fingers," then turned her attention to her oldest daughter, Erin, "Did you resolve the problem with the flowers?"

"Yes, but they want to charge us additional for the substitution."

"Don't worry. Your father will straighten things out with the florist, won't you dear?—Jim? Yoo hoo? Are you with us? Is something wrong?"

Jim returned from his daydream, "Sorry honey, I was just thinking about work. Hacker activity is way up, and we've received a new project from the FBI, a big one. They're under a lot of pressure to catch these guys—fast. I'm already understaffed, and Steve Wakeman just left for vacation. With the rehearsal dinner tomorrow, and the wedding Friday, I don't feel like I'm accomplishing much for our clients."

"Why don't you go to the office for a while tonight, Jim. Maybe you can catch up a bit."

"No, that's alright—I'll put in double duty next week. I'll get caught up eventually."

As if the small amount of attention he'd just received had a healing power, Jim suddenly felt much better. He forked a reddish piece of steak into his mouth, and chewed slowly savoring the sweet whiskey glaze. He listened to snippets of simultaneous conversations around the ten-foot-long picnic-style kitchen table. Erin and her mother were once again knee deep discussing the details of her wedding; Colleen was trying to convince Megan that they should swap groomsmen because hers was too tall. Jim sensed there was more to this story, perhaps something to do with the boy being cute. Morgan, Shauna, and Eileen were talking about volleyball— all three were accomplished athletes. The little ones, Danny, Katie, and Molly, were talking for the sake of joining in the merriment, or just to make noise—Jim wasn't sure. Kelly was at a movie with her fiancé, Kevin—a reminder of the next O'Brien wedding, which is set to occur in October, eleven months from now. Jim looked around the table and thought, what a wonderful sense of humor God must have. Nine girls! The good Lord had blessed Jim and Peg O'Brien with nine girls—and two boys.

The weddings alone will break me, Jim thought daydreaming again. I wonder if we'll ever be able to retire.

The recurring thought brought a look of concern to Jim's face, but did little to detract from his good looks. Jim appeared a good ten years younger than his age of forty-six. He was of average height and build. His dark hair was tinted red, and became lighter in the summer months. His emerald green eyes were set in a handsomely chiseled face. His demeanor was confident, and friendly, but Jim often appeared to be deep in thought. He was an intelligent man who found solace in solving problems of any kind. He owned a small but profitable computer consulting firm based in Omaha, Nebraska. His client geography had sprouted tentacles and now extended to both coasts as news of his expertise in computer forensics and Internet security spread. He had many more opportunities to expand his business than he could take advantage of, mostly due to difficulties in locating the high caliber of technical staff he demanded. The search for new talent consistently limited his efforts. Jim didn't complain much, but when he did it was always the same thing. "Why are most applicants either helpless geeks or prima donnas? Why is it so hard to find good people?"

Tonight, as typical of most evenings, Jim planned to retire to his recliner and reach for his notebook computer. Whenever he was home, he spent countless hours researching the latest internet threats or attempting to hack through the security measures of mock internet sites provided by industry organizations for that express purpose. These mock sites were responsible for Jim's recent notoriety in the field. The top minds in the security industry developed these sites using the latest ideas and technology, and Jim could invade them effortlessly. Jim's evenings were usually split between playing games with the children and honing his technical abilities. Playing games with the kids allowed Jim to know each of them intimately, to teach them problem solving skills, and to keep up with what was happening in their lives. Jim conducted his more serious work and research in the study.

"Who's on dishes?" Peg called. No one answered. "Guess I'll just have to check the chart! Let's see, Shauna—you're washing, Megan—you're drying, Danny—you sweep the floor. Now let's get going!" The O'Brien family owned a dishwasher, but it never seemed quite big enough to accommodate the evening's dishes. Unless a few of the children were missing at dinner, at least a handful of dishes were washed in the sink.

Jim sat down in his recliner. The leather was cold and made him shudder. November was typically chilly in Omaha, but tonight, the autumn temperature was unseasonably brisk. It was the second day of the month and pitch dark well before six o'clock. Just six weeks earlier it was still twilight by nine pm. The early darkness didn't yet seem natural to him. His internal clock said it was time to go for a walk, but Jim didn't like to walk in the dark—too dangerous these days—even in a suburban Omaha neighborhood.

The O'Brien's weren't wealthy, but Jim made a handsome income. Both he and Peg were very frugal. Jim's friends often joked about how far they could stretch a dollar. The O'Brien children had most of the same amenities as children from smaller families. However, most of their purchases, especially apparel, lacked popular name brand labels. Jim always claimed, *"Clothes are necessary—brands are frivolous."* At the start of each school year, Peg would shop for school clothes at discount stores. Except for the labels, even a keen eye would find the quality indistinguishable from clothes purchased from upscale department stores. On those shopping occasions, the front door would fly open and the kids would parade around the house and model their new wardrobe for Jim. This meant changing into all their outfits as well as dress and athletic shoes. Peg rarely failed to purchase twenty-two pairs of shoes for the same price her fashion conscious neighbors paid for three pairs of their designer brands.

The telephone rang. Jim could hear one of the children call for their mother. He got up from his chair and started in the direction of his bedroom to get a sweater. Faintly, he could hear Peg say, "Oh dear God!" He doubled back and headed for the kitchen. Peg had a beautiful complexion with naturally pale skin and auburn hair. She wasn't the slender girl he originally married, but she had a pleasing, even sensuously full figure. Meeting her for the first time, no one would guess she had borne eleven children. At this very moment, Jim thought she looked older than at any time he could remember. However, it was not her physical age that sapped some of her youth tonight—there was emotional pain, stress, and even fear in her expression.

"What's wrong, Peg?"

"That was the police."

"What did they want?"

"Tom has been arrested."

*   *   *

Attempts at conversation were futile between Jim and Peg on the way to the police station. Recently, any topic involving their oldest son usually put them at odds with each other. *The evening started off so well,* Jim thought, *I hadn't even realized Tom was absent from the dinner table... or did I?* Tom was seventeen and going through a rebellious phase. Funny, it didn't seem that his other children experienced the severity in mood swings, or general disposition at his age. *Was it because he was a boy?* Jim wondered, *Will little Danny be like this too—a disappointment—a black sheep?* Then Jim wondered whether he was responsible for the way Tom had turned out. It was the start of a very frustrating evening.

At the station, Officer Joan Sheppard escorted Jim and Peg to her desk. She was a short and stocky woman, pretty, but not beautiful. Jim couldn't help feeling Officer Sheppard could take care of herself in a scrap. She had nearly finished reviewing a long list of laws Tom violated just a few short hours ago.

"—fortunately, the damage to these cars is mostly limited to the bezels surrounding the stereo systems. I don't know what the owners will do, but you should be prepared for any one of them to press charges."

"Maybe that's what the boy needs ma'am," Jim said just a little too quickly, "maybe we should consider letting them press charges."

"Jim is upset, Officer Sheppard," Peg said apologetically, as she shot him a look that told him his comment was cruel. "Tom isn't a bad boy—he has a conscience. I'm certain he'll want to make restitution."

Jim couldn't look at Peg—he didn't believe a word she was saying, but he added, "Tom has had a difficult time the past few years. We need to help him get past some issues." In reality, some old suspicions were welling in Jim's mind. He kept them in check.

Officer Sheppard was exceptionally perceptive. "This is Tom's first offense, and he has been very cooperative."

Manipulative, Jim thought.

"If you are willing to pay for the damages and can assure me that you will get your boy some counseling, I will do the best I can to avoid any legal charges. No guarantees, of course."

"Can we put a little scare into him?" Jim asked.

"What do you mean, Mr. O'Brien?"

Even as Jim answered Sheppard's question, her penetrating eyes said she fully understood his intent.

"Too often kids screw up, and their parents get them off the hook. Tom committed some deplorable acts tonight. If we fix the problem too easily, the lesson learned will have little value. We should make this as painful as possible for him; make him feel fortunate he is not going to jail. In fact, let's make him beg a little—make him swear he'll never do it again."

"That's horrible!" Peg said, disgusted at the thought. "That's not very Christian of you."

"But it is, honey—it's the *MOST* Christian thing we can do. We've got to make certain this does not happen again, ever! For his sake and the sake of others, we've got to teach him a lesson!"

Officer Sheppard ignored Peg's frown and nodded as she picked up the telephone and said, "Bring in the O'Brien boy."

Moments later, a uniformed officer escorted the boy into Joan Sheppard's small, stark office. In a cold voice she said, "Have a seat next to your father, Tom." Looking more embarrassed than ashamed, he chose to sit by his mother instead. Officer Sheppard didn't notice. She appeared to be searching for something in his file. She hesitated a moment, scribbled a few notes, and then closed his file and folded her hands on her cold gray desk.

There was a long and unnatural silence. Jim lost the uneasy look he had just minutes ago. He tried not to be obvious as he watched his son for any sign of remorse. He saw none. Except for his slender build, Tom looked a lot like his father. His thick dark hair had the same unmistakable reddish tint that was a trait of all the O'Brien children. He was dressed in his usual attire—baggy cargo jeans that would certainly fall to the floor without a belt. His flannel shirt was untucked, and unbuttoned, revealing a white *wife beater* t-shirt. Jim deplored the slang name Tom used to describe the shirt style.

Finally, Sheppard broke the silence, "I have some questions for you, Tom. Do you realize the serious nature of your actions this evening?" He started to answer, but she cut him off. "Do you have no respect for the property of others? Do you have any idea how much trouble you are in? Just what were you thinking?"

Tom winced when he swallowed, as though his throat was dry. He appeared to be having difficulty responding to the question. "I don't know—I guess I wasn't thinking."

"Judging by the quantity of car stereos you've stolen and the list of charges against you, I would say that's pretty obvious. Why did you steal them?"

"We just wanted to make a little money, that's all."

"Who is *we?*" Jim asked.

"Matt and me."

"Anyone else?"

Tom avoided his father's eyes, "No."

Officer Sheppard leaned back in her chair and gave Tom a sharp look. "I don't suppose you've given any thought to getting a legal job?"

"Yeah, I've thought about it, but I don't want an eight-dollar-an-hour job working in some fast-food restaurant."

"Why not?" Sheppard asked. "Lots of kids your age work in fast-food restaurants. In fact, many college kids pay their way through school by working in fast-food restaurants."

Sheppard's eyes widened briefly and Jim knew why. She probably noticed how Tom leaned forward with clenched fists as though he was going to blurt something out. But instead, he suppressed his outburst and leaned back in his chair and frowned. "I don't plan to go to college."

Jim scowled, and Officer Sheppard raised her eyebrows, "Why not?"

"I can make just as much money learning a trade."

"I don't mean to argue with you, Tom, but that's just not true. The right college degree would allow you to make a much higher income than the average tradesperson. What kind of trade did you have in mind?"

Anything that doesn't involve my company. Jim thought.

Tom squirmed under his father's gaze.

"I don't know—something in construction, I guess."

"There is nothing wrong with learning a trade, Tom, but if your goal is to make a good living, you really should consider going to college." Tom was silent as he gazed across the room. It seemed evident that the subject of college was a sore spot between the boy and his father. Officer Sheppard changed the subject. "Well, regardless of what you decide to do about your education, stealing is just plain wrong—wouldn't you agree?"

"Yeah, I guess so."

Officer Sheppard leaned over her desk. "Listen carefully, Tom. As a result of the probable charges against you, you could be sent to a juvenile detention center for a period of six months to a year."

Tom's eyes grew large as though he was gripped with fear at the thought of such a punishment. "What if I return everything and pay for any damages—would I still have to go?"

"Regardless of the punishment Tom, you'll be required to make full restitution to the people you wronged. In addition, these people are going to be mad as hell. You stole from them—damaged their personal property. There is no doubt they'll want to press charges."

"Dad, can't we get a lawyer to take care of this?"

"I don't know if I want to, son."

Tom's features hardened. "What—what do you mean?"

"Well, you *did* the crime didn't you? I think you should accept whatever punishment you have coming to you."

"You mean you want me to go to jail?"

"It's not that I want you to go jail. But I feel people earn things, both good and bad. In this case, I think you should take whatever punishment you've *earned*."

Tears filled Tom's eyes, and he struggled to speak. "Look, Dad, I'm really sorry. This whole thing was stupid. I can't believe what we did, but you have to help me. I'll never do anything like this again—I swear!"

Officer Sheppard stood up and walked to the window. Jim sensed that she was going to add a touch of drama. It was difficult to refrain from smiling. This was exactly the scenario he'd hoped they could stage for Tom.

Somehow, Tom needs to be taught a lesson, but is it working? Is he learning a lesson? Is he contrite, or just sorry he got caught? Jim suspected the latter, but couldn't be certain. He knew Tom was frightened, but he was still unable to detect any genuine remorse.

"This is your first offense, Tom," Sheppard said as she gazed through the window. "I don't know if I can keep you out of the detention center or not, but if I can, I'll want some strict assurances from you. Will you give them to me?"

"Wha-what kind of assurances?"

"Your parents shall not be required to pay for any of the damaged vehicles. You will get a job and pay for the damages on your own. In addition, you will contact and apologize to each of the victims. Even if you avoid sentencing to a detention center, you will most likely be placed on probation for a minimum of one year. I cannot guarantee there will not be other conditions or punishments, but you can count on those I've already mentioned. If I go to bat for you, do I have your word you will do whatever we require of you?"

Tom answered quickly, "Yes, I'll do anything you want."

"Alright then, it's agreed. You will be released into your parent's custody tonight. Mr. O'Brien, I'll call you tomorrow to update you on my conversation with the county attorney. I'll have details as to how we should proceed."

Jim stood up, "Officer Sheppard, I cannot tell you how grateful I am for your help."

"You are welcome Mr. O'Brien. You and your wife seem like good people." She shot a look at Tom, "But I do have some genuine concerns about the path your son is currently taking. I suspect he needs some additional guidance to get through the adolescent phase of his life. You need to keep a very close eye on him. Please don't let us see him back here again."

Jim caught his son's gaze, "He won't be back, Officer Sheppard—I won't let him come back."

The ride home was painful for everyone. No one spoke for several minutes. Finally, Peg tried to relieve the tension in her typical, disarming way. "Thank goodness for Officer Sheppard. Another officer may have made it much more difficult for us."

"I knew we'd get off," said Tom.

Jim glowered, his voice sounded cynical. "What do you mean by that?"

"Well, I have friends who have done worse and never got into trouble."

Peg tilted her head back and closed her eyes as if expecting the worst.

Jim's knuckles turned white as he gripped the steering wheel. "That's the problem, Tom. You shouldn't have friends that do those things—PERIOD!"

"What I meant is, I know of people who have done worse."

"Let me ask you, Tom, do you enjoy tarnishing the family name? Do you like being a two-bit criminal?"

"Hey, I'm not a criminal. I just made a mistake—that's all!"

"You just made a mistake, huh? Well, I've got to hand it to you son, that's the worst politically correct crap I've ever heard! The prison system is full of people who just made mistakes, and if you don't watch it, you'll be one of them. Every time you get into trouble you say the same thing... 'I made a mistake'. Well, this mistake is going to cost you plenty! Consider yourself grounded!"

"For how long?"

"UNTIL I SAY OTHERWISE!"

Tom knew better than to irritate his father any further. He could work on his mother for a reduced sentence later. He folded his arms and stared out the car window.

3

MIRANDA PETERS' INTENSITY IMPRESSED JIM. IN THE three-week period since she joined Jim's company, he noted that when she was researching fraudulent web sites, or e-mail schemes, she often scrunched up her face, giving it an ominous, almost menacing quality that marred her otherwise beautiful features. Such was the case this Thursday morning. Miranda was deeply engaged in her work. She was somewhat startled when Jim spoke, "Good morning Miranda. How is our rising star this morning?"

"Oh! Good morning Jim. I didn't notice you come in."

"Yes, you seem to be deep in thought—anything I can help you with?"

Her eyes lost their intensity, and she smiled in a relaxed way that restored her remarkable beauty. Miranda wore a white silk blouse and upscale designer blue jeans that drew constant stares from the male employees at Computer Forensic Consultants, Inc.

"Maybe there is. I broke the codes on the password protection scheme and restored some missing data on the computer the FBI left us yesterday, but there is something I just can't figure out. There is no hint that this computer has ever been a host to a web site of any kind, no less a fraudulent one. There are no links, no software— no traces of anything out-of-the-ordinary. The FBI told me that this was without doubt, the same computer Tony Constantino used to defraud American Express, but I'm coming up dry. I can't find a single trace of anything suspicious. There's an old AOL account, but it looks like it was used only for personal correspondence, and there are no e-mails later than June. This computer looks clean."

Jim thought that there was an abundance of concern in Miranda's chestnut eyes. She did not wear much make-up, nor did her striking features require it. Her dark brown hair was slightly longer than shoulder length. It had an intense sheen which reflected the light in any setting. Her eyebrows and eyelashes were naturally dark too; a perfect match for her eyes. Her high cheekbones and full lips lent a movie star quality to her appearance.

Jim felt grateful to have a problem he stood a chance of resolving. His luck in working out his son's problems had been dismal. "Give me about a half hour to make some calls, and I'll give you a hand with it. I always welcome a challenge."

Jim smiled warmly and continued to his office, but Miranda's assessment gave him an uneasy feeling about the case. She seemed overly perplexed by the lack of information that materialized from her efforts on the project. Jim liked the fact that she had such high standards for herself, and there was no doubt that she was one of his most intelligent troubleshooters. In three short weeks she had successfully resolved four fraud cases, and identified the source of multiple viruses and worms that would certainly lead to arrests for the FBI. She inherited one of the projects from Steve Wakeman, one of Jim's best troubleshooters, who finally threw his hands up in despair and proclaimed a pass code could not be deciphered. Jim was anxious for Steve to return from vacation so he could give him the news that Miranda had solved the case and maybe rub it in a little.

Word of Miranda's achievements quickly spread throughout Jim's office and the FBI's regional office in Kansas City. She had quickly resolved every assignment he had given her so far, until now. Jim knew he had a winner when he interviewed Miranda last June. She was a graduate of Harvard with a degree in Computer Forensics. Miranda was the first employee Jim ever hired with a formal education geared toward computer crime. He was certain her abilities would elevate his company's performance to a whole new level.

Jim slipped into the chair behind his desk and went through his agenda for the week. He couldn't stop thinking about Tom's arrest. He finally pressed the phone's speaker button, followed by the top-left speed dial button. A few seconds later, Jim's youngest child, Molly answered the phone, "Hellooo?"

"Hi sweetheart, is Mommy home?"

"Know what Daddy? Mommy's taking us to the Henry Doorie Zoo!"

Jim laughed at her pronunciation of the Henry Doorly Zoo. "Isn't it a little cold to go to the zoo?"

"We're going inside to see the fishes!"

"Ahhh—you're going to the aquarium—sounds like fun."

"Yeah, and they got sharks too!"

"I'm glad honey. I hope you have a great time. Is Mommy home?"

Almost immediately Peg answered, "Hello?"

"Hi, it's me—I just wanted to apologize for last night. I know I was pretty negative, but I want you to understand why."

"Okay, why?"

Jim sensed Peg's challenging tone and spoke in a soft voice. "I've been observing Tom much more closely than in the past. I think he's using drugs."

"We've had this conversation before—what makes you such an expert at reading the signs?"

"You don't have to be an expert to notice his glassy eyes or his slurred speech. He used to talk to us when he came home at night. Now he avoids us completely and disappears into his bedroom."

"He probably doesn't want to have any more discussions about going to work for your company."

Jim ignored the comment, "It just doesn't make sense, Peg. He's stealing car stereos when he could make a decent hourly wage here while he learns the business. Does that make any sense to you?"

"That's what this is all about, isn't it? You are upset that he doesn't want to carry on the family business."

Jim frowned. *Jesus, how did I get put on the defensive end of this conversation?*

"Not at all, Peg, but until recently he had a genuine interest in doing just that. The boy is a computer whiz, he has real talent. He could go toe-to-toe with half of my staff. Why the sudden interest in learning a trade? Something has changed. I think he is taking drugs and needs to keep himself at arms length to avoid getting caught."

Peg's voice turned sour, "You're reaching for something that isn't there."

"No, Peg, I'm being brutally honest. His grades have taken a nose dive, and two nights ago, I could swear his eyes were rolling up into his eyelids."

"Why are you always ready to believe the worst about your son?"

"Peg, we've discussed this before—I know you've seen his glossy eyed look, and you certainly can't miss his slurred speech."

"He said he was swimming at Lifetime Fitness—his eyes were red from the chlorine in the pool and he was very tired. You really need to stop looking for the bad in him."

"NO ONE IS LOOKING FOR THE BAD IN ANYONE! I haven't mentioned these things in weeks, but I can't ignore it. It's getting worse—something has changed. I think he's moved on to harder drugs!"

"That's ridiculous!"

Its like talking to a brick wall, Jim thought. "You've got to open your eyes to this, Peg!"

"You just can't stop picking on your son."

"THAT'S NOT TRUE—NOT TRUE AT ALL! Why can't you believe for a moment that one of your children may have a problem! What makes us so perfect?"

"We have raised good kids, and Tom is as good as any of them!"

"Do your other children steal car stereos? Don't you see how it all fits? He can't work if he's stoned, and he needs to steal to support his habit. Peg? Peg?"

Jim closed his eyes as he hung up the phone. When he opened them, he was staring at Miranda in the doorway. She was holding a stack of diagnostic reports. "I'm sorry, Jim—I was just going to leave this on your desk. I didn't mean to intrude."

How long was she there? What did she hear? There is nothing like a family scandal to change an employer/employee relationship. Shit!

"It's okay, Miranda—come on in." Jim realized his voice was wavering. He was noticeably shaken as he said, "Let's get to work on the Constantino case." There's hundreds of thousands of cardholders depending on us for this one." The two of them moved to a small round work table in the corner of Jim's office. He always used this table when reviewing cases with his employees. A voice interrupted them.

"Don't tell me Miranda needs help!" Scott Troia's head was protruding into the doorway, his body unseen around the corner. "This must be some tough case if she needs your advice."

"Come in, Scott, maybe you'd like to hear some details of the Constantino case."

"You bet I would, Jim." I heard on the news this morning that this is the biggest credit card fraud in history. They're calling it the *Great Cyber Robbery.* Whoever solves this one is going to make a name for himself—or herself."

"I'm not in it for fame, Scott," said Miranda with a contrived smile, "I just want to solve the case."

Jim knew she was sincere. Already forgetting about the conversation with Peg, Jim said in a calm, confident voice, "Tell us what you know so far. Let's take it step-by-step."

"I have run all of our diagnostic software," Miranda said, with a sigh, "and some of my own as well. I recovered the NTFS file system artifacts, including the swap file, file stack, and spooler files. I have restored all of the prior data that had been deleted from the computer's hard drive. There is no doubt that Constantino's family is involved in some minor illegal activities, but I have found no clues to connect this computer to anything significant. There is no mention of American Express anywhere and no trace of malicious applications or programs capable of intercepting point-of-sale transactions. I have checked all of the e-mail accounts and retrieved all correspondence. Unless I am just overlooking something obvious, I'd say this computer is clean."

Jim noted her serious tone; her cheeks had gone pink. "There's nothing to say it isn't clean, Miranda. It's clear that the FBI came up empty too. Their best people have been scratching their heads on this case. That's why they finally decided to ask us for help."

"I can tell you that they're right about one thing," said Miranda, "it is Tony Constantino's computer. In addition, it was once configured as a server. The baffling part is this—there is no evidence that it was ever used as a server. It may as well have been used for playing video games."

Jim's eyebrows furrowed, "You said earlier, there were no e-mails past last June. Were there other files created since then?"

"Yes, loads of spreadsheets and word processing files. This computer was used right up to the date it was confiscated by the FBI." Miranda looked at Troia, "There is an old AOL account, but it looks like it was used only for personal correspondence. This computer is clean."

"Scott—care to give it the once over?"

"You know it, Jim—that is, if I can get my head to stop pounding!"

"Too much beer on the plane?"

"Too much beer in the airport!"

Miranda perked up, "Oh, I forgot to ask you. How was your speech at the conference?"

"Out of six hundred attendees, only five hundred and ninety-nine fell asleep," Jim joked. "I'd say that's okay."

Scott interjected, "He knocked em' dead, Miranda, and thank God too, or we might have had to spend another grueling hour in that airport lounge. A few more beers and he may have surrendered to that pretty flight attendant." Miranda still felt too new to tease the boss, but she was a little curious about the flight attendant.

"No kidding? Flight attendants aren't usually the aggressor," she said.

Jim didn't reply.

Troia didn't hesitate to comment for him, "Yeah, women flirt with Jim all the time, but the man's a rock."

He is a doll, Miranda thought. *Sounds like he's a gentleman too.*

"It's good to know that there are still men out there who are faithful to their wives."

Jim's cheeks were pink; he cleared his throat. "Okay Scott, I think we wore the flight attendant thing out last night too. What do you say we get some work done?"

Scott gave Jim a sly grin, "Slave driver."

"Miranda, don't share anything else with Scott. Let him take a fresh look at this, and for God's sake, don't feel like you failed us in any way."

Miranda's eyes fell to the floor, "I should have been able to find something more."

Looking sympathetic, Scott interjected, "Look, Miranda, you've been a star player with this company since you came here. If you couldn't find anything, there's probably nothing to find. And contrary to popular belief, some computers are clean, ya know. But since its Jim's policy to get a second opinion on cases of this magnitude, I'll take a peek and see if anything turns up."

"Miranda," Jim said, "Howard Beekler is having some difficulty with his current project. Can you give him a hand?"

An undertone of disappointment betrayed Miranda's smile. "A day with Howard? This should be interesting."

"I know Howard's a little geeky, but he's been doing this for years. You might even learn something from him."

Scott started laughing, "Yeah, like how to color coordinate a pocket protector with your favorite outfit."

Jim tried hard not to laugh, "That's enough Scott. Like all of you, Howard is a valued employee." Jim smirked, "A little different perhaps, but valued nonetheless. Now let's get going, we've got a lot to do this week." Miranda left to find Howard. Scott stayed behind.

"She's wounded," Scott said.

"Our egos get hurt every day, Scott. It's part of the job. She'll get over it."

"She's different than most, Jim. I've never seen anyone take it as personally as she does."

"She's determined."

"She has a killer instinct for this stuff. Someday, you may be working for her."

Jim smiled, "Great! Then she can have all the headaches that go with this business."

"How are Erin's wedding plans coming along?"

"Everything's set, but I can't wait for it to be over. The first O'Brien wedding is causing a little tension at home."

"I'm sorry to hear that," Scott said

Jim grew somber, "In addition, I think Tom is using drugs, and Peg won't even entertain the possibility that it could be true."

Scott's eyebrows arched, "Little Tommy, our computer wizard? You could have knocked me out with that punch."

"I know—it was hard for me to believe at first, but I've been watching him closely and I'm certain of it. He's using! And he's not so little any more. He's nearly eighteen, a senior."

"Any idea about what kind of drugs he's using?"

"No, but I think it's more than marijuana."

"Jesus Christ, Jim! You've gotta get a handle on this, but quick!"

"I know, but without Peg's backing it's going to be difficult."

"You know what that drug commercial says—'Do whatever it takes to get between your kids and drugs.'"

Jim nodded, "As much as I hate to do this, I'm going to search his room. I need some proof."

"Let me know if there is anything I can do to help, buddy."

Scott appeared more wounded than Miranda. Having no children of his own, he admired and was very close to Jim's family. Scott had been Jim's best friend since their college days, and had always looked up to him. He not only admired Jim's intelligence and good business sense, but his honesty and integrity as well. Scott Troia was a large man of Italian heritage, and stood at least three inches taller than Jim. His coal black hair was starting to show a peppering of grey. At forty-seven, he had developed quite a paunch from sitting behind a desk. His gigantic hands had a smooth, almost feminine quality, but Scott possessed an incredible degree of physical strength. In their younger days, he had helped Jim out of a couple of scuffles at the college tavern they frequented on the weekends. After twenty-eight years of friendship, and fifteen years of working together, Scott and Jim were inseparable.

After college, Jim and Scott had planned to start a software development company. As much as Scott wanted to join Jim in business, he lacked the confidence to go through with it. Instead, Scott went to work in the IT department for Union Pacific, a large railroad company. For years Jim's software company survived on his reputation as a brilliant programmer. Although his business didn't thrive, he didn't starve either. Over a period of nine years, Jim's company changed directions several times. His initial experience led him to write software code on a sub-contractor basis for banks, where security issues were critical. Jim got a break when a giant anti-virus software company utilized his team to add security features to their software products. As the internet grew in popularity, so did the need for his experience in security issues. Jim began tracking the source of viruses but took a particular interest in white collar crime. He realized he had tapped a lucrative market and changed his company's course one more time. Capitalizing on the opportunity to become a leader in cyber crime, Jim's company literally eventually owned the insurance fraud industry in Omaha. In addition, most of the local law firms utilized his expertise to uncover digital evidence to prosecute computer criminals. CFC was now on retainer for three anti-virus software companies, a handful of big corporations, the U.S. Postal Service, and most recently, the FBI.

Nine years after Jim started his original company, he again asked Scott to join him as a project manager. Scott did not hesitate this time. He was well aware of Jim's success and realized that he was quickly becoming the most sought after consultant in the cyber crime industry. Most of the time, Jim insisted that his employees match his own knowledge of the industry, but he made an exception for Scott. Although there were more talented software engineers in the field, he trusted Scott more than anyone. Jim knew that Troia had a great work ethic and he needed an honest, principled man to manage his growing staff.

"I appreciate that, Scott. I may run home after lunch. Tom is at school, and Peg is taking Molly to the Zoo."

"What'll you do if you find drugs?" Jim's eyes looked uncertain.

"Find out where he's getting them and cut off the source."

"You know I have connections."

Again, Jim smiled in a teasing way. "You mean your MAFIA friends?"

"I mean my uncle's family. You know they are there if you ever need them."

"Thanks Scott, but I've been getting by for twenty-five years without their help."

"Twenty-eight, but who's counting?"

Jim grinned, "Do you really believe they're affiliated with the mob?"

"I'm positive of it, Jim. You know that I would never do anything illegal, and I've never asked for their help in the past, but they do have access to information you and I simply can't get. Maybe they can find out where Tom is getting his drugs."

"What would your uncle say if he knew you were analyzing the computer belonging to their mafia kingpin?"

"Well for starters, I'm pretty sure they don't have any affiliation with Tony Constantino. The Omaha organization is miniscule and their mafia ties are distant, but Constantino controls one of the most powerful mafia organizations in the country."

"Well, you can be sure I'll keep your offer in mind, Scott. Meanwhile, the Constantino case—excuse me, I guess it's now called the *Great Cyber Robbery,* is the hottest thing we've got going. Can you get to it this morning?"

"I'm already on it, Jim," Scott said, walking to the door. Seconds later, Jim heard Scott yell down the corridor, "I'm gonna need aspirin Linda—lots of it!"

At eleven o'clock, Jim called Linda Simmons into his office. "I'm leaving for the day, Linda. Have you had any luck tracking Vince down?"

"No I haven't. No one at the Bureau has seen him today, and I've left him three messages. Still no luck with the *Great Cyber Robbery*?"

Jim rolled his eyes, "I sure would like to know who decided to give this case such a comic book name."

"It's the number one story in the news—kind of exciting, don't you think?"

"Yeah, I suppose, but we aren't making much progress on the case. I need to see if Vince has uncovered any more details that can help us unravel the mystery. Constantino's hard disk appears to be clean as a whistle. They may have confiscated the wrong computer."

"Are you going to look at it yourself, Jim?"

"No, I've reviewed Miranda's reports, and Scott's taking a fresh look at it now. I don't think there is anything I would have done differently. If Vince calls back, have Scott speak with him. I'll brief him as to what questions to ask before I leave. If Scott comes up empty, we'll just have to ask Vince what he wants us to do with the computer."

Linda Simmons was a slender woman with sky blue eyes and blond hair. Jim thought she must have been a breathtaking beauty in her youth. But at forty-nine, she looked ten years older. Her deeply tanned skin was leathery from excess exposure to the sun. Her blond hair showed long streaks of gray and she still wore it at shoulder length. Linda answered the phones, kept Jim's appointment calendar, and the company books. Even though Scott was the project manager, Linda knew more about the details involving each project than anyone else in the office. She was a valued member of Jim's "trust network."

"You go home to your family, Jim. We'll take care of everything here until Monday."

"Thanks, Linda. I have a lot to do before the prenuptial dinner tonight," *including searching my son's room for drugs.*" Jim quickly briefed Scott as to what he wanted him to ask Vince Mitchell, the

FBI's Director of Computer Forensics, when he called. With the day's laundry list of action items complete, Jim made his way through the busy office toward the front door. He caught Miranda's glance as she was explaining something to Howard. She rolled her eyes and smiled as if to say she'd rather be working alone. Jim returned the smile, thinking to himself as he approached the door; *she's a great asset to the company.*

4

JIM SHOOK HIS HEAD IN DISGUST AS HE WADED through the dirty laundry on the floor of Tom's basement bedroom. He rarely entered any of his children's bedrooms. He trusted them and believed in respecting their privacy. Perhaps that is why he felt so uneasy now. He was about to break one of his own principles by rummaging through his son's room. He stood motionless in the center of the room for several minutes. His heart raced with mounting intensity as he contemplated what he might find. His hands were clammy and he felt sweat trickle down his forehead. *Should I do this? I'm about to break a confidence I worked hard to establish with Tom. Oh, quit lying to yourself, Jim—you're just afraid of what you're going to find.*

A minute passed, and then another. Jim realized he was daydreaming. If he was going to do this, he couldn't waste any more time. He studied the room. His eyes were drawn to an expensive looking stereo system. *I don't recall Tom having such a nice stereo system. How could he afford to buy such a thing?* As he moved toward the stereo he saw other expensive items, most of them electronic games and gadgets. *Surely a boy whose only income has consisted of an occasional lawn mowing or sidewalk shoveling, couldn't afford such luxuries.*

Jim opened Tom's top dresser drawer. He found more gadgets, a digital voice recorder, a gold butane lighter, an MP3 player, and a small tin box that jingled with the sound of coins when shaken. He opened the box and exposed a handful of coins and a diamond ring. Three of the coins were gold, the rest were silver. All of the coins were in mint condition. The silver coins were dated from the eighteenth century. The gold coins were Kruggerands.

A seventeen year old with Kruggerands? The diamond appeared to be at least a full carat or more in size. *Where did he get these things? He had to have stolen them.* There was no other explanation, but Jim knew he would soon find out. Now he would have to confront him—there was no turning back.

Jim fished in his shirt pocket for a piece of paper and pen. He wrote the denominations and dates of the coins on the paper. He knew he could quickly research the value of the coins and diamond on the internet. He continued his search, but found nothing else in the room. He carefully pondered, *If I were hiding drugs where would I put them?* He eyed the bed and mattress, the bookcase, and the armoire as possible candidates. There was no closet in either of the basement bedrooms. Jim and Scott Troia finished the basement eight years ago, when the five bedroom house could no longer accommodate sleeping quarters for all the children. He looked up at the suspended ceiling—*Bingo!* There was a chair by Tom's study desk. *I might as well begin at the top.*

Jim stood on the chair in a crouched position until he could slide one of the panels to the side. Rising to his tiptoes his head protruded into the area above the ceiling. In the shadows of the recess, he could barely see the silhouette of what appeared to be a shoe box. He slid the box toward him, and then grasped it with both hands. Stepping off the chair, he placed the box on Tom's desk. Although all the lights were on, Jim felt as if he was in a dimly lit room. Sweat dripped from his forehead and splattered on the lid of the box. He was certain that whatever the box contained would change his relationship with his son forever.

Moments later, Jim realized his worst fears. Inside the box he found a Playboy magazine, a brass marijuana pipe, a small bag of marijuana, matches, a crusted spoon, and a syringe that appeared to have been used several times. Jim could hardly breathe. He quickly stuffed everything back into the box and placed it where he found it. Dragging the ceiling panel back into place, he turned out the lights, and darted upstairs. He met Peg and Molly coming in the front door and whisked by them. "Jim, where are you going? We have to leave for the church in a few hours."

Jim never looked back. He jumped into his Honda Accord and tore down the street. Peg called his cell phone, but he didn't answer. Fifteen minutes later, Scott Troia met Jim at Clancy's Pub. Scott saw two empty beer glasses on the table and had already guessed what that meant.

"So I gather the news is bad."

Jim didn't speak right away; he looked at Scott with unmistakable fear. Scott thought for a split-second he was looking into someone else's eyes. He took a seat across the table from him. Jim reached out and grabbed Scott's thick wrist and said, "It's the worst scenario I could have imagined." He put his glass to his mouth and emptied it.

"Let me buy you a beer, Scott. If you are going to listen to this— you're gonna need one too."

Jim ordered two beers. When the waitress left the table, he hung his head low, and then began to roll it from side to side. Scott waited patiently for Jim to continue. Finally, he spoke, "I don't know the drug, but I know the method. I found a rather badly beat up syringe in Tom's room, along with a crusty spoon, a pipe, and some marijuana."

"Jesus, Jim!"

"There's more. He's got all kinds of expensive toys and gadgets in his room,—not to mention a diamond ring and Kruggerands."

"Kruggerands! Where do you think he got all that stuff?"

"There's no question, Scott—it's got to be stolen merchandise. My son is a thief!"

Jim filled Scott in on the rest of the details, including last night's trip to the police station. When he was finished, Scott asked, "What'll you do next?"

"I don't know. I need to identify the coins and the diamond ring—see if there are reports of them missing. I need to find out where he's getting his drugs. I need to talk to Peg—tell her what's been going on."

"You don't plan to tell her tonight—not with the prenuptial dinner and all?"

Jim didn't answer.

"You'll wait until after the wedding, won't you?"

"Yes, yes, but until then, how can I look Peg or Tom in the eye without tipping them off that something is wrong."

"You've got to, Jim. This is the sort of thing that could completely ruin Erin's wedding—you only get one wedding!"

"Yeah, I know."

"So you'll wait?"

"Sure I'll wait, but when I do tell her she's going to go ballistic. She won't be able to handle this. I'm not certain I can handle it either."

"You'll do what all parents do Jim—you'll find your own way to cope with the situation. You'll do whatever it takes to get through another day, another week, and another month."

"You don't understand, Scott; I really don't think Peg can deal with this. She has a mental picture of our family as a slightly bigger "Brady Bunch." She has been in denial about Tom's stealing, and she doesn't even see the obvious signs that he's using drugs. When I mention it, she gets defensive and shuts me out. I get this eerie feeling she somehow blames me for what he is doing. The fact is—I don't know how I will even bring up the subject again."

"All right Jim, let me give you some advice."

"That's why I asked you here, Scott—I can't think straight."

"The first thing you should do is call that your last beer."

Jim nodded, "That's easy enough to do."

"Now, the second thing you need to do is change your mindset so you can survive the rest of the evening. Think about having your whole family together at the prenuptial dinner. Think about toasting the bride and groom. Think back to your own wedding day, and what you and Peg were feeling just before you took your vows. Your daughter is probably feeling the same things right now. Put everything else out of your mind."

Jim was still nodding, gathering his thoughts, "Right."

Scott could see that he was making some headway. He continued to focus on the wedding. "How well do you know the groom's folks?"

"I've only met them once. They're coming in from Boston."

"Oh, that's right; they're from 'Bean Town.' How did your daughter ever meet a boy from Boston?" Scott knew the answer, but he was taking Jim farther away from his anguished state.

"They met in school. Trent's a law student at Creighton University. I suspect the kids will move to Boston after he finishes school in May. His father is the CEO for a newspaper publishing company."

"Smiling wryly, Scott said, "I smell money."

"Yes, they are quite well off. At least Erin will get a good start financially."

"Do they come from old money?"

"It's funny you should mention 'old money'. The Wilshire's have been in the newspaper business for three generations. They own forty-two papers. I couldn't even begin to guess their net worth."

"I'm impressed, Jim. What's the old man like?"

"It's really hard to know. Preston and Elizabeth have been very warm and accepting of our family, but you can tell they are people of great wealth. They don't flaunt it, but they seem very proper."

"You aren't exactly a pauper, Jim. You're well educated, you make a great income, and you are a self-made man."

"I appreciate the kind words Scott, but you can tell they are used to spending money in ways we could only dream of. Every time we try to economize on some extravagance for the wedding, Trent immediately speaks up and says his parents can pay for it. At first I wouldn't hear of it, but after a while I just gave in. It's gotten completely out of hand. If Peg and I had only two kids instead of eleven, we'd feel much differently about spending so much money on the reception. The fact is, I still have ten more weddings to go, and when the kids see how elaborate this wedding is, we'll have set a precedent, an unrealistic expectation for all the weddings to follow."

"I see your point. Sounds like this won't be your typical buffet dinner."

"Oh there will be a buffet alright. We'll have hors d'oeuvres from a buffet just before the sit down dinner. And you can enjoy your meal while listening to a fifteen piece orchestra."

"Gosh Jim, just knowing you makes me feel like I'm moving up in the world!"

Jim finally cracked a smile and said, "Yes, it's a dream come true, isn't it?"

"You're gonna' be alright, pal."

"Thanks for meeting me here, Scott."

"You're my best friend—what else could I do?"

Their eyes locked and the two clasped hands with a firm handshake. Jim held his grip a little longer than usual. The gesture said everything that needed to be said.

5

THE SMALL BANQUET ROOM AT THE OMAHA HILTON Hotel was abuzz with the gossip and laughter of young people. The wedding rehearsal was at St. John's Church, on Creighton University's campus. It went quickly and without mishap. Even the youngest O'Brien's—Danny and Molly, were on their best behavior as they walked down the aisle with the ring pillow and flower basket. At the prenuptial dinner, Jim quietly observed the members of the wedding party. They were telling stories and anecdotes about Erin and Trent. The room was charged with energy. He could hardly recall a more exciting moment in his life. His disposition had recovered from the depressed mood he was in just hours ago. He had not given Tom's predicament a single thought since they arrived at the hotel.

The older teenage girls, Colleen, Megan, Eileen, and Morgan, were feeling right at home in their roles as bridesmaids. Even considering the age differences, they had developed a special kinship with the other members of the wedding party. Colleen was quite taken with David Jergensen, another Creighton law student and Trent's best friend. She had convinced Erin to swap David with her original groomsman because he was too tall. The ploy was obvious, but it worked. Megan didn't mind accompanying the taller groomsman. She had a steady boyfriend and had no emotional ties with anyone in the wedding party.

Kelly, the second oldest O'Brien child, was also the Maid of Honor. She was engaged to be married next October. She stood next to her fiancé, speaking to the room about her childhood escapades with Erin. Jim became a little emotional as she concluded:

"Erin possessed a keen sense of justice. She always stood up to the neighborhood bullies when we played kick the can or tag. She was skinny as a rail, and must have weighed all of forty pounds, but she wouldn't let anyone push me around. She could stop an argument in an instant, and she always knew how to work out a compromise. In Erin's mind there was never time for fighting—there was just too much fun to be had. Like the time when we performed "Grease" in our back yard. We sold sixteen tickets. We didn't know it at the time, but Dad bought them all and gave them to the neighbor kids. Erin's friend Janie insisted on playing the part of Sandy Olson, but Erin didn't mind. Even though she had practiced the part of Sandy for a week, and Janie couldn't carry a tune in a bucket, she found other things to fill in the gap." She glanced at Janie who was chronically blushing, just to make certain she wasn't too offended, and then continued:

"Erin settled for the part of Rizzo. She was great, too. She picked out our costumes, choreographed our dance steps, and made each skit a lot funnier than any of us could have. She was the creative genius behind most of the goofy skits we performed as kids. She has been and continues to be a great sister, a great mentor, and my best friend. I know she's going to make Trent a great wife. Although I know we will always stay in touch, somehow I already miss her." Kelly raised her glass and said, "So here's to Erin who is moving from childhood actress, to adult director—may your children have as much fun as we did."

There was heavy applause. Jim had listened to several of the bridesmaids and groomsmen speak. When the noise subsided to a level where he thought he could be heard, he found his champagne glass, stood up, and walked a few steps closer to the soon-to-be bride and groom. He spoke with great sincerity and emotion:

"I love all of my children very much," Jim said smiling. "As you all know—there are a lot of them to love. Although each of them has traits that are similar, they are all quite different. I think parents always develop a unique bond with their oldest child. I know this is true of Erin. She has always been a leader, not a follower. Being the oldest, she was kind of a guinea pig for Peg and me. We learned a lot about parenting from her. We always believed that her kind nature and accepting disposition were gifts from God. She has been an ideal role model for all of her siblings, and for this, Erin, I thank you."

Erin was tearing up, Trent handed her a tissue. His pockets were stuffed with them. Jim turned to Trent and locked eyes with him. He cocked his head, raised an eyebrow, and intentionally hesitated before speaking. This drew some subdued laughter. Then he continued:

"When Erin told me that the two of you were getting serious, I was elated. You had only been dating about six months at the time, but I was comfortable in hearing the news. I watch my children closely and I have been diligent in observing your relationship. It warms my heart when I see the way you two look at each other. But even more than that, I can see that the core foundation of your relationship is built on mutual respect. It is the single quality I hope all of my children can find in their eventual soul mates. Trent, you are an intelligent, hard working young man, and I am certain you will be everything Erin could hope for in a husband. We are all so proud to have you join our family." Jim raised his glass above his head, "Please join me in a toast to Erin and Trent—may they enjoy lifelong happiness."

Again, there was heavy applause. Erin came around the table to hug her father. Trent followed and shook Jim's hand vigorously. Peg joined them and within seconds they were surrounded by all their children, most of them sobbing. Jim stood motionless. His eyes welled up with tears as he savored the close bond his children had established with one another. *The Brady Bunch,* he thought. He finally told them to return to their seats so that Trent's father could say a few words.

Preston and Elizabeth Wilshire rose from their table in unison. Elizabeth stood perfectly poised at his side as he spoke.

"Thank you, Jim. That was spoken eloquently. In all my life, I have never witnessed a family so close and so loving. If this is a direct result of having eleven children, maybe Elizabeth and I should consider having nine more." There was laughter. Jim and Peg were used to jokes relating to their large family. They laughed as well. "We have also been blessed with wonderful children. Trent and Adam have never failed to make me proud. They have—"

Jim could see Tom sitting just to the left of Megan and the tall groomsman. He appeared to be attentive, listening carefully to Preston's speech. *Is he high on something?* Jim tried to return his attention to Preston's talk. "—a wonderful young woman like Erin. I cannot tell you how fond we are of her."

Where did he get the money to buy all of the expensive things in his room? What kind of drugs is he using? Where is he getting them from? Is he in trouble?

Tom noticed his father watching him—he smiled and bobbed his head as if to acknowledge the festivity of the occasion. *I can't tell if he is under the influence or not,* Jim thought, as he smiled and returned the gesture.

"—you have been everything a man could want in a son, and you have found a perfect match in Erin. Here is to your success and happiness." Preston raised his glass, "To the future Mr. and Mrs. Trent Wilshire." Referring to the couple with their future married name got everyone out of their chairs. The room erupted in cheering, applause, and whistling. Jim held on to a line Preston Wilshire had just spoken, *"You have been everything a man could want in a son."* For a moment he was filled with envy. Peg came to him and took his arm, "Look at the wonderful family we have raised."

"Still raising," Jim said with a forced smile, "still raising."

The commotion was beginning to mount as dessert was served. The young adults appeared to be getting restless and were beginning to move around the room. Preston was genuinely intrigued by Jim's business. The two men were engaged in a detailed discussion regarding Jim's clientele, while Peg and Elizabeth talked about the children. "So did I hear correctly that the FBI has you working on the *Great Cyber Robbery*?"

"Yes, it's true." In a light-hearted spirit Jim added, "By the way, who in the world named it the *Great Cyber Robbery*? It's a little dramatic, don't you think?"

"I do, but then again the CNN reporters that coined the phrase have always been a little too dramatic for my taste. How is the case going? I understand several million dollars were siphoned from American Express card holders."

"That's correct, Preston, but before I tell you anything more about the case, I need to ask your indulgence."

"Certainly Jim, what is it?"

"I have sworn to keep the details of this and all FBI cases confidential. Because of your position in the newspaper business, I have to ask that we speak off the record."

"I admire your professionalism, Jim, but remember, I just own the business—I am not a reporter."

"I understand, and hope I haven't offended you, Preston. No matter how much I respect or trust someone, I always make my position clear regarding confidentiality. I have learned how easily information can get into the wrong hands."

"You have my word, Jim; I will repeat nothing I hear from you regarding this case. So—how is the investigation going?"

"Not well at all. The FBI claims to have confiscated the actual computer used in the crime. We have been analyzing it for two days now, without even the slightest clue as to how the crime was committed. Either they acquired the wrong computer, or we are chasing the world's brightest computer criminal. It's my opinion that they confiscated the wrong computer. We solve quite a handful of extremely difficult cases every day. We have some of the best minds in the field of computer forensics working on this, and they have found nothing."

"Fascinating. At some time in the future, would you be open to letting us do a general interest story on your company?"

Jim looked surprised, "Well, as long as I can establish some guidelines for the story—I guess I'd be honored."

"Let's plan on it! Who knows, it could be good for future business."

For a moment, Jim wondered why he would want to do anything that would promote his business. He already had more work than he could handle. The company could desperately use three or four more employees like Miranda right now. But then he had a wonderful thought. He wondered if a promotional story might just attract the kind of employees he was looking for. The possibility was intriguing.

Jim's eyes darted to his cell phone—it was vibrating. He looked at the caller ID and saw the name Vince Mitchell on the display. "Excuse me, Preston, it's the FBI." Preston smiled, and nodded his approval.

"This is Jim. Hi Vince, how are you? I'm at my daughter's prenuptial dinner, why? Chicago? I can't do that—I told you I'm at my daughter's prenuptial dinner. What? When?" Jim listened intently for a few minutes. "HE ASKED FOR ME BY NAME? How would he know that?" His face grew solemn. "How long does he have? I'll make you a deal—I'll meet your plane at the airport, but not until ten o'clock. You need to promise me you'll fly me back immediately after the interview, regardless of the time. Alright—I'll be there. Goodbye."

Peg and Elizabeth were silent as they had heard the last portion of the conversation.

"What's the matter, Jim?" Peg asked. "What's going on? Where are you going?"

"I'm flying to Chicago to interview a mob boss."

6

JIM MET THE FBI'S CONTRACTED PILOT AT A SMALL hanger just south of the Omaha airport. "Are you Mr. O'Brien?"

"Yes, are you Sam Kellogg?"

"Yes, Sir. I have instructions to take you to Midway Airport in Chicago and wait for you. An escort will meet you and take you to your final destination. Do you have any idea how long you'll be?"

"An hour or two, but no longer, my daughter is getting married tomorrow, and I'm going to need some sleep."

"Congratulations, Mr. O'Brien."

"Thanks, Sam. Let's get going!"

"Certainly, climb aboard."

During the flight to Chicago, Jim had plenty of time to contemplate the evening's events. The prenuptial dinner went without a hitch. It concluded at nine o'clock, and most of the wedding party continued their celebration at the O'Brien house afterwards. Preston and Elizabeth Wilshire remained at the Hilton where their room was reserved through Sunday. When he arrived home, Jim had gone straight to his study to get some notes and his briefcase. He then proceeded to his bedroom where he retrieved a small leather pouch containing a set of undergarments and essential travel toiletries for occasions just like tonight. Although he planned to be gone for only a few hours, he was always prepared to spend the night if necessary. He then found Peg and led her to the study so he could explain his plans for the evening. She knew he was leaving for Chicago to meet with the mafia boss alleged to be responsible for the *Great Cyber Robbery*, but she knew nothing more.

Jim repeated what Vince Mitchell had told him. The FBI had followed Tony Constantino to a small Italian restaurant in Chicago. While he was having dinner, the FBI approached him for questioning regarding the *Great Cyber Robbery* case. When he refused to cooperate, one of the agents threatened to take him to the local FBI office. Vince said that Constantino turned his back on the agent and mocked him with a laugh. A rookie agent took a sudden step toward him, a move misinterpreted by one of his body guards. The agent was shot in the stomach. The other agent opened fire on the body guard and killed him. A cousin of Constantino's who worked at the restaurant fired several shots at the agent killing him. Unfortunately, Constantino was in the line of fire and took two bullets. An ambulance rushed him to a nearby hospital, but he is not expected to live through the night. Peg pleaded with Jim not to go. He assured her that he was in no danger. He was simply going to question Constantino about the computer allegedly used in the *Great Cyber Robbery*. A conversation with him might help to put the pieces of the puzzle together. Jim couldn't help dwelling on one fact, *he asked for me by name.*

There was an FBI agent waiting by a large black car when the Learjet 60 taxied into the small private hangar at Midway. The man was very tall, about six-foot four. His figure was cut like a decathlon athlete. He had strong broad shoulders and thick arms that complemented a waist that tapered to a size that Jim hadn't worn in years. Even at eleven fifteen in the evening, the man with coal black hair wore dark sunglasses and the stereotypical black FBI suit. Jim frowned as he picked up his brief case and walked to meet him.

"Hello, Frank," Jim forced a smile.

"Hello, Mr. O'Brien, I trust you had a comfortable flight?"

"Considering I had two hours notice and had to leave on the evening of my daughter's prenuptial dinner, I'd say it was great."

"Vince appreciates your situation, Mr. O'Brien, I'm sure he will be very grateful for your efforts."

Jim thought he detected a slight bit of sarcasm in that statement. It fit perfectly with the traits of the man Jim had met only twice before. Frank Saunders accompanied Vince Mitchell almost everywhere he went. During Jim's prior meetings with Vince and Frank, he found him to be extremely rude and aggressive. While it was clear that Vince was in charge, it was obvious that Frank wanted to give the orders.

"Where is Vince—is he at the hospital?"

"No, he was called away about a half hour ago—something to do with a lead on another case."

"Oh? That's too bad; I wanted to speak with him while I was here. I won't be able to talk to him again until after the wedding."

"You can talk to me, Mr. O'Brien."

"I'm sorry, Frank, I can't—Vince gave me explicit instructions that I cannot share the details of this case with anyone but him."

Frank's face was emotionless, but his tone of voice said what he was thinking, "Of course, Mr. O'Brien, shall we go?"

The ride to The University of Chicago Hospital was awkward at best. Frank Saunders lacked both social graces and communication skills. Although Jim didn't like him much, he attempted to strike up a conversation a few times. During the fourteen minute drive, all Jim was able to learn about Frank was that he had no family. Frank wouldn't let Jim dig any deeper into his personal life. Once they arrived at the hospital, it was a quick trek to the second floor, where they were greeted by two additional agents outside Tony Constantino's room.

"This is Mr. O'Brien," Frank said in a cold, subdued voice. "He's here to question Constantino."

The agents propped the door open to reveal a small private room. They stood in the hallway facing the door so they could clearly see Constantino lying in his bed. A third agent was standing over him, making small talk. *There seems to be quite a few agents present to watch this man die,* Jim thought, as he entered the room.

7

TOM O'BRIEN PACED THE CONVENIENCE STORE PARKING lot, shivering in the cold. The boy he was waiting for approached from a distance. He was a short, black teenager of about seventeen. As he drew closer, Tom recognized his broad shoulders, a physical feature he didn't share. Deacon Reynolds wore baggy blue jeans, while Tom still wore the dress slacks and shirt from the prenuptial dinner.

The black boy said, "Where's your coat dude?"

"I left it at home."

"Thas' crazy man, ain't you cold?"

"Yeah, but I had to sneak out of the basement and my coat was upstairs. Can we do this fast? I've gotta' get home."

"No problem, got the money?"

Deacon Reynolds could see the hesitation in Tom's face. He anticipated a problem.

"Yeah, I got it, but I can't find it—can I pay you tomorrow?"

"Whas' wrong wich you boy? You know I don't deal on credit!"

"I know, but I can't find my money. I thought it was in a metal box in my dresser drawer. I must have misplaced it. But I can get it to you tomorrow, I swear!"

Tom was unaware that his father had discovered the box this afternoon. After meeting with Scott Troia at Clancy's, he made a return trip to confiscate the tin containing the Kruggerands and diamond ring. Jim came to the conclusion that at one time there were a lot more coins in the box. He suspected that Tom had been pawning them to buy drugs.

"How many of those gold coins you got left?"

"Three."

"I don't know man. I sure don't like the sound of this."

"Come on Deacon, you know I'm good for it. I've never let you down yet, have I?"

"No, but you's using 'bout three times more 'n you use to. For all I know, you runnin' outta money."

"That's not it Deacon. I got it—I swear!"

Deacon had only been selling for about a year, but what dealer couldn't spot a desperate customer. Tom was irritable and beginning to come unglued. He needed a fix, and soon. A golden opportunity had just presented itself.

"Sorry Tom, no money, no honey. Gotta protect my own self, ya know."

"Look Deacon, I'll pay you extra, instead of four hundred, I'll pay five."

Deacon looked up at the dark sky as if he were pondering. Tom bit his lip hard.

In a soft and whiney voice, Deacon asked, "What's them gold coins called again?"

"Kruggerands."

Deacon liked Kruggerands. He especially liked these because they were from South Africa. The one ounce coins were worth almost five hundred dollars.

"Two coins, or seven hundred dollars—your choice."

Tom groaned, "That's almost double what I normally pay."

"Thass right, I ain't no bank, ya know. You want to pay me now; I'll take the regular amount, otherwise, two coins or seven hundred."

Tom's head hurt. His stomach was tied in knots. Voices inside him were saying *Just do it, pay him tomorrow.* He succumbed to his powerful vice, "All right—just this once."

Deacon must have felt commanding. He had just earned several hundred dollars he didn't have to pay to his supplier. Deacon held the small cellophane bag an arm's length away and asked, "What time you wanna hook up tomorrow?"

"Aww shit! My sister's getting married tomorrow. I don't know if I can get away."

Tom noticed that Deacon began to withdraw the bag. "Wait! Meet me at the DC Centre tomorrow night at nine o'clock."

"What the hell is the DC Centre?"

"It's a social hall a few blocks from here. That's where the wedding reception is going to be." Tom scrutinized Deacon for a moment; *He sure is ugly—dirty too.* "Meet me in the parking lot at nine. I'll be watching for you."

Deacon had just made one of the shrewdest deals of his life. He smiled his ugly smile and then he slapped the bag into Tom's hand and said, "You better be, I don't like to be kept waiting."

8

AGENT SAUNDERS POINTED AT JIM O'BRIEN, "MR. Constantino, this is Jim—"

"I KNOW WHO IT IS, YOU BUFOON—NOW LEAVE US!"

Raising his voice was too much for Tony Constantino; he began coughing violently. Jim winced with each successive cough, as he could clearly see Constantino arch his back and convulse in pain. Wanting to help, Jim reached for the water pitcher on his table.

"Let me get you some water, Mr. Constantino." The coughing continued while Jim poured some water into a Styrofoam cup. "Here, drink some of this."

Constantino took the cup but held it for a moment while he gathered his composure. This gave Jim an opportunity to study the notorious mafia leader he had only read about in the newspapers.

Tony Constantino appeared to be less than average height, although it was difficult to gauge as he lay in bed. His profile revealed thick arms, large hands, and a pot belly. On his right hand, he wore a massive gold ring with an enormous diamond set in its center.

His hair was completely gray and judging from the age spots and wrinkles on his face, Jim determined that he was in his late sixties. His head was enormous. It did not seem to match the rest of his physique. His small brown eyes held a menacing quality that gave Jim a sudden shiver. He was feeling nervous as Constantino looked at Saunders and continued:

"I said leave us!"

The third agent, who was talking with Constantino when they arrived, had already instinctively left the room.

Saunders said, "I cannot do that sir."

"You can and will—or you can send this man home right now!"

Frank was still wearing his sunglasses, his face stony and expressionless. Reading body language was difficult for Jim, but years of handling customers on the telephone allowed him to gauge a person's emotional state from the sound of their voice. The voice he heard now told him volumes about Frank's state of mind. "This goes against FBI regulations—we must have someone present at all times!"

"It was nice meeting you, Mr. O'Brien. Have a pleasant journey home."

Touché, Jim thought, trying hard not to smile. Constantino looked weak, but there was no question that he was a strong man, strong of body and spirit.

Saunders piped in and said, "I need to get approval to do this!" Then he looked at Jim and said, "Let me talk to you in the hallway for a minute." Jim followed him out the door and down the hall, beyond earshot of the other agents.

"Listen up, Mr. O'Brien—this is without a doubt, one helluva bad idea!"

Jim couldn't help the small grin that appeared on his face. Saunders noticed. "It's your call Frank."

"You want to speak to him alone, don't you O'Brien? Does it make you feel important?"

Jim shook his head, "Look Frank, I could care less whether you're present or not. However, it would be a good idea to speak with him while he's still alive."

Smart-ass. Jim could almost hear Saunders thinking those exact words as he jeered at him. So much for making friends.

Jim continued, "We are completely baffled by what we have learned so far about this case."

"So you don't know anything?"

Jim regretted what he just revealed, "That's right—and the only way we stand a chance of solving this case is to talk to Constantino BEFORE he dies."

Frank broke character and smiled with ferocity. "I'll let you speak to him alone on one condition—"

Here it comes, Jim thought. "What's that?"

"—you must agree to fill me in on all the details before you leave."

"I told you already, I am not supposed to share the details of this case with anyone but Vince."

"And I am not supposed to let him speak with anyone privately."

It was obvious that Frank felt he had the upper hand. He undoubtedly saw a chance to get a leg up on everyone who was trying to solve the case. In his mind, he saw some kind of glorious victory in his future.

"Alright Frank, I'll do it, but only because he could die at any moment."

Frank escorted Jim back to the room. With an air of authority he said, "I'll allow the two of you to visit alone."

"Mighty kind of you, Mr. FBI man," Constantino said mockingly.

"I'll be back in twenty minutes."

Jim thought he saw a tinge of pink in Frank's cheeks as he turned to leave the room.

"Bet he's back in ten."

Jim chuckled, "You may be right, Mr. Constantino."

"That man is no good—no good at all."

"He makes me uneasy," Jim confessed.

"Whatever you do, don't trust him; he'd turn on you in a minute if you let him."

54   *What an ironic warning,* Jim thought.

"I'll watch myself, Mr. Constantino."

"For God's sake, man, call me Tony."

"Okay, I will." With a serious look, Jim said, "I'm not exactly sure where to start, Tony. Why did you ask me here?"

"I know all about you, Mr. O'Brien. I know you are world renowned for your expertise in computer forensics. I also know that you have my computer, the one those FBI bastards took from my office. You haven't made any progress with it, have you?"

Jim answered no, by shaking his head. *How would he know that?*

"I asked you here, Mr. O'Brien, because I need you."

Puzzled, Jim began to formulate questions in his mind. Then he thought, *I'd better let him take the lead.* "Call me Jim."

A weary but genuine smile swept across Constantino's face. "You are exactly as I predicted you would be. Tell me about your family."

"My family?"

"Yes, I never do business without knowing something of a man's family."

Do business?

"Well, to begin with, I have eleven children, nine girls and two boys."

"Capital! So you are a family man!"

"Yes, we are quite close, actually."

"Good! A man is nothing without a family. Like old Saunders there—he's empty—there is nothing good in him. He will spend his entire life trying to get ahead for his own selfish motives."

"I'm afraid you're right about that."

"I know I'm right. I know his kind inside and out. You are Catholic, aren't you?"

"Yes, how did you know?"

"Just an assumption—but it's good to know."

Jim sensed that Constantino was not the type to assume anything. He was certain Constantino knew his complete biography and was simply making small talk.

"What do you know about me?" Constantino asked.

"Well, for starters, they call you the most powerful man in the country Mr.—er, excuse me, Tony. They say you are a don for the mafia, a ruthless man to be feared."

"Just who 'is they', Jim?"

"The newspapers, the media, and I suppose, the FBI."

"Do you really want to know who I am?"

"That's not why I came here, Tony, but Yes, I'm curious."

"Why?"

"I guess it's the inquisitive side of me, Tony. I'm a troubleshooter, a problem solver—I like to know what makes things tick. In order to do that you need to collect information."

"So, do you want to know what makes me tick?"

Jim felt uncomfortable. *Use caution, Jim old boy.* Flatly, he replied, "Yes, I'm interested."

"Then you are a fortunate man. One of my gun wounds is inoperable. I'm bleeding to death—and since I can die at any moment, nothing I say or do now will have much impact on the remainder of my life. For that reason, I may share some things with you I have never told another person."

"I am flattered, Tony."

"Don't be, the information I am about to give you is going to cost you."

Jim swallowed hard, "What do you mean?"

"You are probably the last person I will ever speak to—besides those fucking FBI agents. I have some last wishes, some personal errands I need to have done. You are my only hope of having them carried out. If you help me, I'll not only give you the information you want, I'll make you a wealthy man as well."

O shit! Watch out, Jim.

Jim looked visibly upset, he felt trapped. "I'm not interested in the money, but tell me—these things you need to have done—are they legal? I won't do anything illegal."

It was as though Constantino held Jim's gaze in a vice, "Listen to me closely, Jim. I won't ask you to do anything illegal. All I need you to do is deliver a few personal belongings to one of my associates, and to my attorney, and give them a message. You see, I wasn't exactly planning on dying this week. I just have to wrap up some loose ends, some things for my family, that's all. I'll give you more details in a minute, but tell me this much right now—if I can convince you there is nothing illegal about what I am asking of you, will you do it in exchange for the information you came here for?"

At that precise moment, Jim had a premonition that what he was about to learn would be too sensitive to share with Frank, Vince, or anyone else tonight. In addition, he might need some time to ponder whatever it was Tony wanted him to do, before going ahead with it. For now, he would agree to Tony's terms, and if he decided any part of it was illegal or immoral, he simply wouldn't do it. After all, who would ever know?

"Okay, Tony. If there is nothing illegal about what you want me to do, and it doesn't endanger my family or me, I'll do it."

"Good. You look like an honorable man, Jim. Are you an honorable man?"

"Yes."

"And I have your word of honor that you will do what I request?"

"Yes."

"Okay, here is what I want you to do." Constantino wasted no time. His demeanor grew quite serious. "I own the old Farm Credit building on 42nd Street. My attorney, Michael Lanza, has an office on the second floor. Across the hall, in the second floor restroom, there is a shower area where you will find a row of old metal lockers. The items I need you to deliver are in the last locker on-the-right."

"You mean I just need to walk these items from the restroom, out the door, and across the hall to your attorney's office?"

"Yes. Deliver all of the items to my attorney—except for one."

Jim frowned, *Here it comes.*

"There are several folders. They all go to Lanza, except for the thick folder that contains an address book. I need you to deliver this entire folder to Jimmy Bonaiuto. You'll find his address in the book."

Address book? Constantino has a little black book? I wonder if all his cronies are in there too. "Who is Jimmy Bonaiuto?"

"Number two in the family—my successor. You must deliver this to him in person. No one else can see it. No one else can know you ever touched it. Never speak of it—ever!"

Jim's mouth was dry. His eyes darted back and forth. "I have to say, Tony, I am not comfortable with this. How can you assure my safety?"

Tony removed the diamond ring from his right hand. "Give this to Jimmy Bonaiuto. Tell him I gave it to you from my death bed. Tell him that you want to keep your identity confidential, and it is my wish that he do so. Make no other conversation with him. He will be so happy to have the address book; he won't even give you a second thought. Can you do this?"

Jim felt as though his left hand were on a bible as he solemnly stated, "Yes."

"You only have a few things to remember. The Farm Credit Building on 42nd Street, the last locker on the right in the second floor bathroom, the padlock combination, my attorney's name, Michael Lanza, and my successor's name, Jimmy Bonaiuto. Do you think you can do it?"

"Yes, and we can review it once more before I leave."

"The combination is simple to remember. Seven right, four left, and six right, it corresponds with Independence Day. Just remember July Fourth, 1776, and use only the last digit of the year."

"Thanks Tony, I can remember that."

"Now—tell me the names of my attorney and my successor."

"Michael Lanza and Jimmy Bonaiuto."

"Good Jim, now you can ask me anything you want."

Jim tried to compose himself, "You already know I own a computer forensics consulting company."

"Yes, you have my computer in your Omaha office."

Jim continued, "The FBI claims you used it in the *Great Cyber Robbery*."

"We did."

Jim's eyes flew open wide. Attempting to contain his excitement, he bent over Constantino and whispered, "How long have you known that we had it? And how come we can't find any data on it? How does it work?"

"Calm down Jim. This will all make much more sense if I tell you the whole story. Let me start from the beginning. I am not a technical person by any means, but I have heard the overview a hundred times. I can describe how it works, but only from a layman's perspective. You will have to fill in the technical details later."

"That's fair, Tony." Jim's feet were getting tired. He dragged a chair from the window over to Constantino's bed and leaned in close to him. One of the agents heard the noise, and bobbed his head around the door. In a calm and confidential tone, Jim said, "Tell me everything as best you can."

"A research professor at the University of Chicago, by the name of Andrew Simmons, made some incredible discoveries in virtual computer memory."

"I've read some of his white papers," Jim said.

"Then you may or may not know he was on the verge of changing the entire computer chip industry."

Jim looked surprised. *I thought he had some pretty far fetched theories. I had no idea he was even close to a discovery, let alone taking a product to market.*

"Go on."

"He was already talking to the big three chip makers. He stood to make millions from his discoveries as soon as he completed his work. He developed two small chips that use a mathematical algorithm to simulate a hundred terabytes of virtual memory. From what I am told, neither chip contains more than a single megabyte of physical memory. His discovery would have made memory so cheap that it would surely put some of the chip makers out of business. This is where we came in. One of my associates introduced us to the CEO of a small chip maker, LSI Industries. They specialize in making chips that are no longer in production by the original manufacturers. He offered us a royalty for all future sales of these chips if we could steal the design from Simmons before he could apply for a patent. We knew Simmons was still months away from perfecting his process.

You see, even though the two chips could create a huge virtual memory, all of the data is lost when the computer is powered off."

I don't understand the significance of what you just told me, Tony, most physical memory works that way. As soon as you power down, you lose everything that hasn't been stored on a hard disk. That is the way computers are supposed to work."

"But Simmons was also working on an algorithm to compress, encrypt, and dump all of the data to the computer's hard disk so it could be reconstructed when the computer was again powered on. His algorithm can reduce terabytes of data to a file size of about half a megabyte."

Impossible, Jim thought. "I find that very difficult to believe Tony. And why doesn't he just use non-volatile memory?"

"What is that?" Tony asked.

"Non-volatile memory is not erased when power is removed from the circuit. The digital data is retained in the exact state it was in when power was applied. Nothing would have to be compressed or reconstructed."

"You mean like flash memory, right, Jim?"

"Right, Compact Flash Cards, Secure Digital Memory, USB Flash Drives, they're all non-volatile memory."

"I don't know the answer to that, but I have seen a demonstration with my own eyes. Except for the long amount of processing time it takes to reduce the file size, it works flawlessly. Simmons was working on speeding up the efficiency of the process. Unfortunately, he will never finish his work."

"Why not?" Jim asked.

"He's dead."

Jim hesitated, and then realized he had nothing to lose by asking, "Did you kill him, Tony?"

Constantino shifted his head on his pillow, "It became necessary. One of the big chip makers was about to give him a royalty contract and fund the remainder of his research. Once that happened, we might never have succeeded in obtaining the design data we needed."

60   "So you stole his research and killed him?"

"He had an automobile accident last June."

Jim's eyes fell. He raked his fingers through his auburn hair. *This man, Constantino, seems to be a likeable fellow. But how can he be so heartless? How can he kill for his own personal gain? He is indeed dangerous.* Jim wanted to leave, run as far as possible from the hospital, but he couldn't. His curiosity proved to be a stubborn flaw he had difficulty controlling. His inquisitive nature would never allow him to leave without getting the facts and solving this mystery. Secondary thoughts flashed through his mind. *Should he keep his word and make the deliveries he'd promised to make for Constantino?* He decided to think about that later. Time was too precious—he needed to forge ahead.

"So who is completing his work, Tony? Who is going to refine the algorithm required to speed up the reconstruction and storage of the data?"

"No one."

Now Jim was making the transition from nervousness to shock. "You mean you would steal someone's life's work, and murder them for something you aren't even going to use?"

"Oh, we're using it. We decided the chips suit our needs just as they are."

Jim's compressed lips formed a slit. "Now I am totally confused."

Constantino knew that Jim was many times his intellectual superior in subjects of a technical nature. For that reason, he was somewhat amused watching him squirm in mental agony before him.

"There is one final piece of the puzzle, Jim. What we took from Simmons yielded a much more valuable prize. While he was a genius in virtual memory development, he was also an accomplished programmer. Simmons was working on a secure internet browser and e-mail program."

Jim wondered, *How could that possibly compare in magnitude to the virtual memory chips?*

"That is how I stumbled across his white papers on virtual memory. I was reading about his concepts on security issues in operating systems. There was a lot I found far fetched with regard to his conclusions, but considering what you've told me, I will definitely read them again."

"Listen carefully, Jim. Simmons's program allows me to browse the internet inconspicuously and send untraceable e-mail correspondence." A weak smile appeared on his face as he locked his eyes with Jim's. "You can imagine why this would be useful to a businessman like me, right?" This program literally punches a hole in cyberspace and attaches my e-mail to hundreds, maybe thousands of random, in-transit communications, piggybacking on them until it reaches the recipient. Web sites are accessed using the same concept. There is no known point of origin to lead you to the sender. Any correspondence, regardless of your location, is untraceable."

This is unbelievable, Jim thought, *a stealth communications program!*

"That explains why an e-mail recipient can't track you down, but that doesn't explain why we couldn't find any evidence of correspondence on your computer."

"That's part two, Jim. I'll get to that in a minute."

Jim nodded, "But if there is no known point of origin, can the recipient reply back to you?"

"You're every bit as intelligent as I've been told, Jim. The answer is no. But if you knew the recipient's e-mail address in the first place, you'd just send a new e-mail. Can you imagine a network of these configured specifically for my organization? You see, the program chooses from millions of in-route e-mails, randomly attaching to them, snaking its way to its destination. Since most e-mails are reaching their destinations every few seconds, no two e-mails can use the same path. The e-mail looks like an ordinary message, except for one thing. The *From:* box contains gibberish where you would normally see the sender's e-mail address. The minute the e-mail is sent, it starts collecting these funny characters until it reaches its destination."

This technology has somehow abandoned the standard Internet Protocol, Jim thought. *It works, but how?* Jim considered how data is typically assembled into packets and how they can travel out of sequence and still be reassembled on the other end. *It's got to be similar technology. It just takes a few twists and turns, that's all. But, if no one is aware of the technology, it is surely a stealth method of communication. Undocumented, undiscovered, and invaluable to anyone requiring anonymous correspondence. The gibberish must be some kind of short-hand abbreviation for the path the e-mail took to its destination. I wonder if it could be deciphered?*

Unconsciously, Jim closed his eyes and began to massage his forehead as he concentrated on what was just said. *Return correspondence cannot latch on to a reverse path, because the random e-mails providing the initial path have already reached their destination and are no longer in transit. The return path is broken!*

There were few people in the country as technically adept as Jim, yet he struggled for a few moments to comprehend how this worked. Then he got it.

"Wait a minute—you are using the secure communications software in conjunction with the virtual memory chips, aren't you? That's why we never found any e-mails past June, or the little bits of trash left behind when surfing the internet. The correspondence, cookies, URL addresses, and all the other clues that are usually stored on the hard disk, and absolutely necessary for us to track cyber criminals, were stored in the memory chips—right?"

"You're a wizard, Jim."

"When the computer is powered down, all the data is lost—right?"

"Correct again."

"But we never found the software on the hard disk either."

Constantino's smile was weak as he closed his eyes and said, "The software was written to an e-prom chip."

Erasable Programmable Memory Chips, Jim thought. "I haven't heard that term in years, but that explains why it went unnoticed!"

"Where are the chips located?"

"All three chips are *piggybacked* to the Ethernet communications board."

That's an odd place for the chips to be located, Jim thought, but he was mentally spent, and simply too tired to contemplate whether there was any significance to their location.

"The chips are on the Ethernet card in the PC you currently have in your possession. I have a duplicate Ethernet board in my locker. As part of your compensation for helping me, you may keep it when you deliver my will to Michael Lanza."

Jim was dizzy. He rolled his head back looking up at the ceiling, *We never suspected hardware modifications.*

"I've got to know Tony, why didn't you just sell it? The military and government intelligence applications alone are probably worth billions."

Jim's thoughts drifted for a moment. *Imagine a messaging system with untraceable origins. It would be a powerful tool for the Secret Service and CIA to communicate in a completely anonymous atmosphere. Not only would correspondence be difficult to intercept, but it would be impossible to tell whether it came from a high school kid or the Pentagon. A perfect environment for sending top secret information.*

"I originally intended to do just that," Constantino confided. "God knows I could have sold the technology and supported the family for generations to come, but then I considered the effect that would have on the family."

Effect on the family? What possible negative effect could that have on the family?

"You see, Jim, for over seventy years my family has controlled or heavily influenced several industries. Every member of the family has a valued job, a special purpose in the organization. To simply give them money and watch them wither away with no purpose or goals, would destroy their value system and our way of life."

Value system? So profiteering and killing is better? Jesus, this guy's logic is a little flawed.

"Okay, Tony, let me see if I understand this correctly. The secure software creates a random point of origin for both e-mail and web surfing, making the user untraceable, correct?"

"Correct."

"Tidbits from correspondence, URL's, and cookies are stored in the ram memory chips and are accessible for reuse, until the computer is powered off, correct?"

"Correct."

"The software exists on E-Prom, but why do you need so much memory?"

"The memory chips are definitely overkill for these applications, but this software still requires more memory than you can stuff into a typical computer."

"You know, Tony, the computer chips provide the perfect failsafe since the computer is cleaned up once it is powered down. It really is brilliant."

"I told you, the chips suit our needs just as they are."

"Yes, you did."

Jim made his next request respectfully, and in a low voice. "I will want to acquire all of the research documentation you have on this, Tony."

"Then you will need to contact Keith Napierilla. He came to us from LSI Industries. He is the only man who knows how to use this technology to the fullest."

"Is his contact information in your *little black book?*"

"You *are* a quick study Jim."

"Forgive me, Tony, but this is all too much for me to comprehend in such a short period of time."

"I think you've comprehended everything quite well. What do you propose to do with the computer?"

Jim hesitated, "Pardon me for saying so, but this kind of power doesn't belong in the hands of anyone, not even the FBI!"

"Did I hear our organization's name mentioned?"

Jim turned around to see Frank Saunders. *How long has he been standing there?* Just the sight of Saunders seemed to irritate Constantino.

"WE'RE NOT FINISHED FBI MAN!"

"Don't take offense, Mr. Constantino. I said I'd check back in twenty minutes, and that is what I am doing."

"It's been fifteen minutes," Constantino tried to say sharply.

Jim noticed that Constantino's physical condition had changed for the worse. He was growing pale and noticeably weaker by the minute. Frank noticed as well. He cocked his head toward Jim, "Are you getting the information you need?"

"Just a few bits and pieces so far. Mr. Constantino has no technical background, so I need all the time you can give us. Can we get back to our conversation?"

Frank said nothing more, but simply disappeared from the doorway. "Do you think they are listening to our conversation, Tony?"

"I don't think so, Jim. Saunders had planned to join our conversation, and I had the room checked for bugs."

"How did you do that?"

"Standard protocol—there is a young orderly that comes in from time to time to check on me. The Feds think he is a hospital employee, but he's the son of one of my associates. David Manetti is a surveillance and communications expert. He can spot cameras and listening devices a mile away. He's given me the thumb's up each time he's left the room."

"So your people are in the hospital?"

"What do you think, Jim? I'm sure they are all over the place by now. David has done this before, in fact, every time I have checked into a hospital. You can't be too careful, you know. If the FBI made no attempt to bug the room, they either didn't have enough time to prepare, or they trust you, Jim."

"We have worked together on several cases; I have given them no reason to doubt my integrity."

"And I'm sure you never will."

"I have one final question, Tony."

"What is it?"

"How do you access the software?"

"From a DOS window. The user has to type a rather complex string of ASCII characters that opens a pipeline of communication to the chips on the Ethernet board. Once this is done, the software opens on the computer screen automatically. The software is simple. It does little more than allow you to view web sites or send basic e-mail—except for one special feature. It can tap into and redirect FTP or POS data."

Redirect point-of-sale data?

Jim stood up, walked a few paces away, and then whirled back, "Is that how you scammed, er, sorry, Tony, is that how you obtained the money from American Express card holders? You redirected point-of-sale credit card transactions into your own account?"

"Exactly. The news reports say the damages were several million, but they are lying. We captured almost two billion consumer dollars into a Swiss bank account. American Express doesn't know what to do, or say. They are simply at a loss for words, and much too embarrassed to disclose the actual amount. And who could blame them? That is why the FBI is under so much pressure to solve the case. We can do this to any credit card company—over and over again. And now, you have the means to do it yourself."

"I could never—"

"I didn't mean it the way it sounded, Jim. Besides, it was a very complex procedure. We had to obtain a lot of secret information from American Express—from the inside. I doubt many people besides me could have made it happen."

Mr. Napierilla and I are going to have a long, rather, several long discussions, Jim thought. His heart began to race. There were three issues he was burdened with. He would soon have to face Frank, with whom he'd promised to share the information he learned from Constantino. He did not want to share anything—not tonight. Then he thought about delivering the items to Constantino's lawyer. That was not so bad, he thought, but meeting Jimmy Bonaiuto, Constantino's successor frightened Jim more than he wanted to admit—even to himself. Then he thought about what Constantino said earlier, "I'm sure my people are all over the hospital by now." He didn't want to be seen. He didn't want his identity to be known by the mafia for any reason.

Jim realized he was day dreaming. He hadn't spoken in minutes. A glance at Constantino revealed that his eyes were closed. His skin had turned a gray, pasty color. He looked so helpless now. Jim had the information he came for. He could slip out and go home. But something kept him there. He placed his hand on Constantino's wrist.

"Tony," he said in a calm soothing voice. "How do you feel?"

Tony opened his eyes and slowly they focused, "I don't feel anything. No pain, no pleasure. I guess this is a good way to die, eh?"

"Can I get anything for you?"

"Nothing, you should be going home."

"Tony, are you sorry?"

"Sorry for what?"

"Sorry for the things you have done—for the people you have killed?"

Tony's eyebrows furrowed, "You really do need to know what makes people tick, don't you? Let me tell you something, Jim. I too, am a family man; only my family is much larger than yours. It spans blood relatives, God children, friends, and business associates. I have fed and clothed these people for many years. I have provided them with a livelihood through the family business. We sometimes took what we needed to survive—maybe thrive is a better word. Sometimes, we killed for the greater good, but whatever I did, I did for the family. God will forgive me for my sins."

Suddenly, Jim tilted his head back. "I almost forgot to ask—What ASCII string do you enter from the keyboard to establish communications to the Ethernet board?"

"I don't know, it's very long and I never memorized it."

Jim felt brief tinges of defeat seeping into his thoughts before Constantino added, "It's in the black book."

Constantino lost his intensity for a moment. "You look troubled, Jim. Is all that concern for me?"

"Some of it—but I do have a problem, Tony."

"Tell me about it, maybe I can help."

"I need to figure out what I'm going to tell Saunders about this case. I don't want to tell him anything at all, but he made me agree to repeat everything you told me in exchange for permission to speak with you alone. I want to destroy the software. I think it poses a temptation to anyone who uses it."

"You are indeed a man of honor. Tell you what you should do—give him a few pieces of information, and withhold the rest. Tell him there is nothing special about the computer at all. Tell him that the technology we discussed is on a USB flash memory drive. Tell him that they were not smart enough to find it when they took the computer. Tell them it's still in our possession. When you get back to your office, swap the Ethernet board with one just like it and be done with it. Then it's on to the next case, right, Jim?"

There was a moment of silence as Jim contemplated Tony's recommendation. "That's good advice, Tony. I may just use it. Thank you for that, and for answering all of my questions so thoroughly."

"Don't forget, you owe me a favor in return for what I have given you."

"I won't forget, Tony. I'll deliver the items we discussed to Michael Lanza and Jimmy Bonaiuto as soon as I can. Now I have to go. I'll keep you in my prayers."

Constantino seemed pleased that Jim would pray for him. He closed his eyes. In a weak voice he mumbled, "On your way out, tell that idiot Saunders I want to see him."

Jim couldn't help but smile, "I will."

Jim took Constantino's hand and gave it a gentle squeeze. His hands had grown cold. "God bless you, Tony."

He picked up his brief case and walked to the doorway. Giving Constantino one last glance, he was glad he would not be present to watch him die. He knew that this man had committed terrible crimes beyond his imagination, yet there was something noble about him. He knew it didn't make any sense at all, but in a perverse way he respected him.

In the hallway, Frank nearly pounced on Jim, "You're finished. Let's talk."

"Mr. Constantino asked to see you before we go, Frank. I don't think he has much longer to live."

Frank said nothing, but darted into Constantino's room. Jim stood in the hallway repeating two names in his mind. He was sure he had committed Michael Lanza and Jimmy Bonaiuto's names to memory. It was half past midnight. He felt like he had just run a marathon.

He was nervous and felt weak, mildly shaking. The interview had taken a toll on him.

A little sleep will do me a world of good.

He glanced down the hall and noticed someone dressed in white clothing studying him. *An orderly?* The tall, lanky young man with dark, neatly combed hair appeared to be in his early twenties. He was leaning against a hospital gurney. When he noticed Jim staring back at him, he walked down the hallway and disappeared. Moments later Frank emerged from Constantino's room. He wasn't wearing his sunglasses. After the disdainful look he gave Jim, he wished he was.

"COME ON, O'BRIEN, LET'S GO!"

"Is there a back way out of here?" Jim asked nervously.

"Why do we need to take a back way out of here?"

"Constantino said several of his men may be posted around the hospital, and—"

"What's the matter, O'Brien—scared the boogie man's gonna get you?"

Jim grabbed Saunders shoulder and spun him around, "I HAVE A FAMILY FRANK! I DON'T NEED TO TAKE UNNECESSARY RISKS!"

Frank had a demented look in his dark eyes, "You wasted my time, O'Brien—wasted it!"

Jim looked confused, "What do you mean?"

"Constantino—he told me that he fed you some cockamamie, bullshit story, and that you believed every word! He scoffed at all of us, saying a professional would never have wasted their time on such tripe. We had one chance to get the facts from him and you blew it! Now, we are going to the car, and we're going right through the front door! And by the way, if you ever touch me again—I'll kill you!"

Saunders took off at a brisk pace. Jim trailed behind him, bewildered and in shock. As they approached the hospital entrance, Jim kept a watchful eye out for Constantino's men. Even as he scrutinized the many faces, Jim was filled with joy at what Constantino had done.

70 *He removed the whole burden from my shoulders .By telling Saunders* *that he manufactured the whole story, Frank didn't even want to hear the details.* The somewhat perverse respect Jim had for Constantino became a little stronger just then.

9

PEG WOKE JIM AT TEN O'CLOCK ON FRIDAY MORNING. As he made his way to the kitchen for a cup of coffee, he reveled in the mixture of chaos and good cheer emanating from every nook of the house. The little kids were running wild. Their excitement was heightened by all the young adults in the wedding party coming and going. From the aroma coming from the kitchen, Jim assumed Peg rose early this morning to bake. Kelly and her fiancé Kevin were just sitting down at the kitchen table.

"Good morning, Dad."

"Good morning, Kelly. Hi, Kevin. How are the maid of honor and her fiancé doing this morning?"

"Fine, Mr. O'Brien."

"Kelly, do you think Kevin will ever call me Jim?"

She laughed and took his hand in hers, "I don't know, Dad, maybe in a year or two."

Kevin's cheeks turned pink. He was without a doubt the most polite young man Jim had ever met. He stood exactly Kelly's height of five foot-seven. He had light brown hair, which was always perfectly trimmed in a crew cut style. Jim figured that he saw a barber every two weeks. In the five years they had been dating, he had never seen his hair grow beyond its current length. What Kevin lacked in height, he more than made up for in other physical attributes. Although Kevin was an accountant, he more closely resembled a young, stocky, police officer. He was not very talkative, but after five years, Jim felt like he knew him well. As a couple, Kelly did most of the talking.

"So, Mom told me you had to go to Chicago last night. What was that all about?"

"Just a minute—I want to hear this too!" Peg said as she entered the kitchen.

"Okay, let me get a cup of coffee, and then I'll tell you what I can, but this case is confidential, so don't get upset if I don't answer all of your questions."

Peg started for the coffee pot. "I'll get the coffee—go on about your trip."

Jim reached for a freshly baked cinnamon roll. His eyes were filled with anticipation as he used a finger and thumb to peel a gooey roll from the pan. Peg only made her homemade cinnamon rolls on Christmas and Thanksgiving mornings, so this was an unexpected treat.

"First thing first," he said, as he took an enormous bite of his roll. He leaned back on his chair with his eyes closed. "God this is good. I may skip dinner tonight."

"With the money this dinner is costing us, Jim, I think we should all eat twice. Now—about your trip?"

There was more than curiosity in Peg's voice as she set Jim's coffee mug in front of him. Kelly sensed her concern and shot an uneasy glance her way. Jim noticed and began his explanation by setting expectations.

"Okay, first of all, everything is fine. I interviewed Tony Constantino, but I don't think I obtained the information the FBI wanted." He continued the lie. "Nor do I think we have the computer that was actually used in the *Great Cyber Robbery*."

"Constantino, the mob boss?" Kelly asked.

"Yes."

Peg looked relieved. "So is that the end of it, then?"

"There are a few loose ends to clear up, and if they do find the right computer, we'll pick up our investigation right where we left off."

Peg looked relieved, but Keith and Kelly only looked confused. Jim quickly provided them with the details which led to the reason for last night's trip.

"What was he like Dad?"—referring to Constantino. Did he look like a gangster?"

Jim shook his head, no. He looked like a helpless old man about to meet his maker. I felt sorry for him."

Peg gave him a puzzling look. "How could you feel sorry for a man who dealt in drugs, prostitution, and gambling? What's more, they say he killed several people."

"Don't ask me, Peg. I couldn't even begin to explain it. You just had to be there. Whatever he has become over the years, whatever he had done in the past, seemed to be stripped away last night. I saw only a man who loved his family more than anything. I asked him if he was sorry for the things he had done. He said that he did what he did for his family, and that God would forgive his sins. I, for one, will pray for him."

Peg gave Jim a look of admiration, "Was he Catholic?"

"A fervent Catholic, from what I could tell."

"I wonder if he saw a priest before he died."

Jim was caught off guard, "He died?"

"Oh that's right; you haven't heard the morning news. He fell into a coma last night and died at about six thirty this morning."

Jim knew he shouldn't have been surprised. Constantino was fading fast even before he left the hospital, but he was still saddened by the news. He picked up his coffee cup and started for his study.

"Do you want a roll to take with you?"

"No thanks," Jim said softly.

10

JIM SAT DOWN IN HIS LEATHER DESK CHAIR. UN-consciously, he swiveled from side to side. He was tired, but thinking clearly enough to know he had some important errands to run this morning. He opened his brief case, unzipped a small pocket, and retrieved a tiny item about the size of a postage stamp. He held it at eye level with care, and thought for a moment about what a technical marvel it was. The label read, *64GB Secure Digital Memory Card.* His left finger released the snap to the holster on his belt and then he slid his Smart Phone out. Locating a small slot on the edge of the phone he inserted the minuscule memory card into it, and the phone came to life, opening a software program. The screen revealed two command choices, *Backup* and *Restore.* With his finger, he selected the *Restore* command. Immediately, the Smart Phone began transferring data from the memory card to the phone's memory. Jim had erased the data last night, after making a backup copy. It took no more than a few seconds. He then touched the *Notes* icon followed by the selection of his latest entry. He read the newly restored notes he made last night during his flight back to Omaha. He checked them for accuracy:

- Farm Credit Building on 42nd Street in Chicago.
- Second Floor restroom – last locker on the right.
- Combination – seven right, four left, six right/ Independence Day.
- Constantino's attorney, Michael Lanza, second floor office
- Deliver folder containing address book to Jimmy Bonaiuto – address in the book
- Find ASCII code to activate stealth software – in the book
- Locate Keith Napierilla – in the book
- Search book for other data/information relevant to case.

Jim felt much better knowing that the data was still intact. He was afraid he might forget some of the details before he could make a trip to Chicago to carry out Constantino's final wishes. Jim connected the Smart Phone to a full-sized keyboard, and spent the next fifteen minutes writing notes about his conversation with Constantino. When he finished logging his thoughts, he backed up the file to the memory card. Confident that he could again restore the data if needed, he deleted the file from the Smart Phone.

After placing the memory card into the zippered pocket in his brief case, he reached into his pants pocket and retrieved Constantino's diamond ring. The stone was much bigger than Jim recalled. In the mid-morning light, it proved to be a dazzling, flawless diamond. Jim thought the value of this ring must be in the tens of thousands. For a moment, he admired how beautiful the ring itself was. He usually found diamonds of this size distasteful, especially in men's jewelry, but the massive gold setting complemented the stone's size. What he noticed next surprised him. There were three words boldly engraved on each side of the ring. On one side, the words scooped from the gold in vertical columns read: GOD, FAMILY, and WORK.

That pretty much describes how Constantino pictured himself, Jim thought. The three words on the other side read: HONESTY, RESPECT, and INTEGRITY. These words confused Jim at first. He certainly wondered how Constantino could envision himself as honest. But as he placed the ring in the zippered pocket with the memory card and closed the brief case, the words made more sense. The word respect was easy. A mafia don could not operate without it. But honesty and integrity, how do these words relate to Constantino? Jim pondered for a while, and concluded that within his limited world, Constantino was a man of integrity, at least as far as the family was concerned. Whatever he did outside that world didn't count. He loved his family, and protected every member from his children, to his favored business associates. With his financial resources, he created jobs for them, treating them fairly in the careful way he positioned their talents within the organization. He compensated them in a just and honest fashion. If nothing else, he gave them a sense of satisfaction and self worth.

As he stood up and started for the den door, Jim recalled the image of another diamond ring, the one he found in Tom's bedroom. Peering high from atop of his bookcase, he could see the tin box that contained the ring and Kruggerands. He still planned to see if he could identify the ring and locate the rightful owner, but not today. With Erin's wedding less than eight hours away, Jim wanted to run his errands and return home. There were too many things pulling him away, and he desperately wanted to enjoy some time with his family before they left for the church.

11

JIM'S EMPLOYEES WERE SURPRISED TO SEE HIM ARRIVE at work. He didn't say a word, but went straight to his office. In his desk, in the third drawer down on the right side, he removed a small tool kit. He quickly headed for his door and nearly collided with Scott Troia.

"Whoa there, Jim, I didn't mean to run you over."

"That's okay, Scott, I guess I'm in a little bit of a hurry."

"That's understandable—you have a wedding to attend tonight. In fact, I have a wedding to attend tonight. How is everybody doing? Has Erin gotten cold feet yet?"

Jim didn't have time for idle conversation, but he was never rude to Scott, or anyone else, for that matter. "Everyone is fine, Scott. I look forward to seeing you and Joan at the reception tonight. Is everyone else coming?"

"As far as I know everyone will be there, except for Steve, of course."

Jim nodded, "Steve was apologetic about not coming, but I told him months ago not to change his vacation plans. I think he still feels bad though. He even delivered Erin's wedding gift in person last Saturday."

"What brings you here, Jim? If there's any business you need me to take care of, just say the word and it's done."

"I appreciate that, but I just stopped in to pick up something I forgot. I'll be out the door in five minutes. I'd be grateful if you could keep everyone out of my hair for the few minutes I'm here."

"Say no more. I'll keep everyone in the office busy. Oh, before I head up front, did you hear about Constantino?" Scott was unaware of Jim's trip to Chicago last night, and Jim didn't want to bring it up now. It would just start a conversation he didn't have time for.

"Yes, I heard he passed away. I hope it doesn't affect our ability to resolve this case."

"To be honest, Jim, I don't believe this case will ever be solved."

Knowing full well that he intended to destroy the chips and software, Jim said, "You could be right, but I plan to take a personal look at it next week."

"Okay, Jim. Well, I'm headed up front now, so you can do what you need to do and get going—I'll see you tonight."

"Thanks, Scott."

Jim quickly walked to the end of the hall and turned left into a storage room. There he could see rows of shelves, a well organized layout of computers, hard disk drives, and PC related hardware. He went right to Constantino's computer. The CPU tower was wrapped in a large, silvery antistatic bag. It was properly tagged and contained a log sheet with the dates it was in the possession of anyone who attempted to troubleshoot it. He slid a screwdriver from his tool case and began to work quickly. Within two minutes he had removed the computer's Ethernet card from its slot. He put the CPU back in the cellophane bag, and placed the unit on the shelf. Aware that the smallest spark of static electricity could wipe out the chips on this board, Jim found a small antistatic bag and carefully placed the circuit board inside. Backtracking to his office, Jim opened his brief case and placed the circuit board inside. He did not speak to, or even glance at any of his employees as he left the building.

Jim drove to a Best Computers store in Central Omaha. There was another store closer to him, but Jim knew that this location had a better selection of computer hardware. He went right to the networking hardware aisle. In the car he had written down the make and model of the Ethernet card he removed from Constantino's computer. He was searching for that exact model now. There were none on the shelves. The card had been replaced by a new model. He swore under his breath. He knew he had to replace this card with the same model. There was no way to know whether the FBI had cataloged the contents of Constantino's computer. For that matter, they may have photographed each board. Jim was willing to bet they didn't, but at the very least, he needed to swap it with the same model.

He went to the computer repair counter and asked for the manager. He explained that he had to have a *CompuComm 3820 Ethernet card*. Since there were none on the shelves, he asked the manager to check the inventory of the other stores to locate one. The manager tried to be helpful. "The new model is really a much better card, Sir."

"I appreciate your help, but I must have the same model."

"I can't help you there. The only thing I could do is sell you a used one from one of these returned computers."

Jim's smile was so big, all of his teeth showed. "Do you have two of them?"

About ten minutes later, Jim slammed his car door, and opened his brief case. He held the Ethernet card he removed from Constantino's computer next to one of the two he had just purchased. They were identical, except for a piggybacked board containing three tiny chips. He identified two of the chips as ram memory. The third chip had a tiny glass window on top. Jim immediately recognized it as an EPROM chip, an erasable, programmable, read only memory chip.

He could hear his own sigh of relief as he realized that Constantino had not lied to him! Ever since Saunders told Jim that Constantino manufactured the entire story to waste the FBI's time and his own last precious minutes of life, Jim had been uneasy. After all, Constantino's story did seem a little far fetched. But it wasn't a dream; Jim's first guess was true. Constantino lied to Saunders, so that Jim would not have to tell him what he had learned. He felt a great deal of satisfaction as he shifted the car into Drive, and headed for the bank.

Jim kept a few life insurance policies, stock certificates, and a backup hard disk drive in a safety deposit box at the First National Bank of Omaha. He now added the postage-stamp-sized memory card, diamond ring, and Ethernet card to the box.

I'll replace Constantino's Ethernet card on the way home. Then I can enjoy the day. My daughter's wedding day.

12

JIM COULDN'T REMEMBER HAVING MORE FUN WITH his children. They were bursting with wedding-related small talk, joking, and laughing. Jim had a great sense of humor, but he couldn't tell a joke to save his life. He did possess an incredible sense of wit, which allowed him to embellish on a story someone else had told. He had been doing so for nearly two hours while the family relaxed, recalled old times, and enjoyed each other's company. As usual, Peg was in the thick of the crowd, which was a mixture of their children and three of Erin's bridesmaids.

Peg looked at the time and said to Erin, "Its two o'clock. We'd better get you girls to the hair salon." Erin's friends Janie, Chris, and Brianna, went to the hallway to get their coats, followed by her sisters, Kelly, Colleen, Megan, Eileen, and Morgan. Jim noticed that Shauna, who was twelve, stood up as well. Her face fell as the others got ready to leave. Jim understood why. Shauna was not asked to be a bridesmaid. As the girls made their way to Peg's fifteen passenger van, she watched out the window. Jim approached her from behind and put his hand on her shoulder. Shauna turned around, revealing her eyes, which had welled up with tears.

"Your time will come Shauna."

"I know Dad, I just thought I was old enough to be in the wedding."

"It's not your age, honey—it's just the sheer number of people in the wedding. Erin wanted another of her friends to be in the wedding, but she asked your sister Morgan, instead. If she had asked you too, she would have had to eliminate another one of her friends. Can you understand that?"

"Yes—but it still hurts."

Jim grabbed his daughter in his arms and squeezed her tight. She sobbed for a minute, and then wiped her tears away. "I love you, Dad."

"I love you too, kiddo. I love all of my wonderful girls. I don't know what I would do without all of you in my life. I am truly blessed."

And with that said, he felt a trickle down his own cheek. "Let's go get a snack—something Mom would get mad at us for."

In the kitchen, the four youngest O'Brien's were sitting at the table brandishing their own kind of youthful humor. Jim had lined up five bowls in which he had sliced bananas down the center. He was vigorously scooping vanilla ice cream into the bowls when Tom walked in.

"Hi, Dad."

"Hi, Tom, where have you been?"

"I had to exchange the shoes that came with my tuxedo, they were too small. But even the shoes that fit me are crap. They kill my feet."

"I know. Finding good rental shoes can be a nightmare. That's why I bought my own tux and shoes. With the number of weddings we have ahead of us, they'll pay for themselves in no time. Do you want a banana split?"

"No thanks. Matt and I got something to eat."

Jim frowned. He did not like Matt. He always appeared to be overly polite to adults, but Jim had heard too many snippets of his conversations with Tom. He had an uneasy feeling about him.

For one thing, he was dishonest. Matt worked at several fast food restaurants. He gave Tom free food almost daily. Jim had asked Tom to stop accepting free food many times. He said that it was wrong, and that it was no different than stealing, because the food wasn't Matt's to give away. Tom argued that kids from all the restaurants did the same thing, and that somehow, this was an accepted practice. Jim's argument was that it may be accepted among teenage kids, but not among restaurant managers. Matt would be fired if his boss found out.

Matt was also a "wheeler dealer," a trader, of sorts. He was always swapping goods for favors, or vice versa. Jim was afraid he was seeing the same traits emerge in his son, a trait that did not complement what he discovered in his room yesterday. But Jim held his tongue, *No disagreements today—nothing can ruin this perfect day.*

"Well, sit down with us anyway, Tom. We've been having a great time today."

"I will in a little while, Dad. I've got to make some phone calls."

Another frown. Tom was spending more time on the phone than Jim felt was normal, even for a young man of seventeen. He always used a cordless phone, and went to unusual lengths to find privacy, often stepping outdoors. Jim found that very suspicious on these cold autumn days.

Tomorrow we will have a long talk, Jim thought, as he placed the ice cream scoop in the sink.

After adding chocolate syrup, he handed a bowl to each of the children, beginning with Molly, the youngest. She shrieked, "Thanks, Daddy!"

The others gave him a more subdued thank you. He took a seat next to Danny, who always chose to sit by his father whenever possible. He didn't say a word, but ruffled his hair, as he did many times a day as a sign of affection. Listening to shrill voices and child-like banter might be irritating to some parents, but not Jim. He hung on to each word they spoke as if what they were saying held some great significance. And in his mind, indeed it did.

13

THE WEDDING CEREMONY WAS AN EMOTIONAL MARAthon. Everything went as planned, but there was so much crying throughout the service that the priest finally paused to remind everyone that this was a wedding, not a funeral. The comment drew some laughter and helped to relieve some of the tension. From that moment, the ceremony was slightly more upbeat.

Erin was a beautiful bride. When Jim first saw her in the dressing room, he couldn't believe his eyes. Gone was the little girl he chased around the back yard. He was taken aback not only by her physical beauty, but her transformation into the mature and graceful woman that reminded him so much of Peg in her youth.

Trent doesn't know how lucky he is.

From the reception line at the DC Centre, Jim cocked his head slightly, to see her greeting guests just a few feet away. He was told repeatedly by friends and family how striking his daughters were. They spent an hour and a half at the hair salon, and it appeared the investment was well worth it. Jim had never seen all of his girls with their hair professionally styled. Nor had he ever seen them all dressed in formal gowns. Peg had even purchased matching dresses for Shauna, Katie, and Molly, and curled their hair an hour before they left the house. Jim asked his brother David to take extra photographs of them. The reception line, which had been enormous, was now dwindling. It was nearly time to sit down to dinner. The family members alone packed the banquet room. Jim had five brothers and three sisters. Peg had six sisters and four brothers. Including grandparents, aunts, uncles, nieces, nephews, and cousins, there were one hundred-thirty Irish family members attending the reception. The inclusion of friends drove the number to well above two hundred-fifty.

Peg looked radiant in her emerald green silk evening gown. It was a few shades darker than the bridesmaids' dresses, and complemented her brown eyes and auburn hair.

"You've never looked more beautiful," Jim said as they started across the dance floor toward the dining tables.

Peg took his arm in hers, "Careful big boy, flattery just might get you somewhere tonight."

Jim smiled. "You don't think either one of us will have enough stamina for that, do you?"

"I recall you had the stamina for that several times on our wedding night."

Jim's smile broadened, "Ah, yes."

The trip to their table was a long one, or so it seemed. They were stopped a half dozen times by guests who wanted to congratulate them. When they finally reached their table, they sat next to Preston and Elizabeth Wilshire.

"Hi, Jim, how are the bride's parents holding up?"

"Pretty good, Preston," it is just as I remember our own wedding— that is to say, everything is a blur." Jim couldn't stop smiling. Things seemed perfect.

"More so for you, I suppose. Liz and I are simply spectators at this event. We are in awe watching the interaction between your children and their extended family. You must be so proud."

Jim looked out over the sea of red haired guests. "We are, Preston, but no less proud than we are of Trent. He has become as much a part of our family as any of our own children. It appears your son, Adam, comes from the same mold."

"Yes, he is following in his brother's footsteps. I have high hopes for both of them."

"You know, Preston, its unfortunate we didn't have more time to get to know each other. Perhaps we can make plans to get together for a visit this summer."

"That's a great idea, Jim—you come see us. We have a summer home at the Cape. You can stay with us for a few weeks."

Jim had heard Trent speak of their summer home in Hyannis, not far from the Kennedy home. "In fact, if you will do an interview for a general interest story on your company, the paper will pay your travel expenses."

Jim had never seen Cape Cod. The idea excited him. "Great! Let's iron out the details tomorrow."

Jim realized he was almost yelling over the roar of the guests. Although the noise was a little unnerving, he could see this was going to be a festive evening. Servers were already bringing baskets of bread to the tables.

Jim turned around to see if the reserved table behind him was occupied yet. There he saw Scott Troia and his wife, Joan, talking to Linda Simmons and her husband, Edward. Seated between Joan Troia and Howard Beekler, he saw Miranda Peters. She was listening intently to Scott and Edward's conversation. Had Steve Wakeman not been on vacation, Jim would have seated him and his wife, Julie, with Scott and the others. In their absence, he moved Miranda and Howard to the table closest to his. For some reason, he was glad they were close by.

Jim wanted to say hello to his employees. "Excuse me for one moment, Preston," he said as he rose from his chair.

Jim had never seen Miranda dressed in anything but upscale casual wear. Tonight, she wore a low cut burgundy evening gown. As Jim approached their table, he could see that it revealed the fullness of her breasts. But something else was different about

Miranda, *She's wearing lipstick.* The color was somewhere between red and the color of her dress. Jim was amazed that so few changes could make such an incredible difference in one's appearance. She was an incredibly striking woman, but tonight, she was absolutely breathtaking. Jim lifted his gaze to see that she was watching him. He smiled at her, and then quickly shifted his attention to Scott, as he realized he might have been staring at her breasts. *Oh my God,* he was certain of it now! Jim felt a tinge of embarrassment, but never lost his composure. He took a step toward the table as if nothing had happened and placed his hand on Scott's shoulder.

"Welcome to the first of many free dinners I will be sponsoring during the course of my lifetime."

Scott laughed and patted Jim's hand, still on his shoulder. "Better you than me, Jim."

"The ceremony was just beautiful," Joan said in a sentimental voice.

"It was one of the most beautiful weddings I have ever seen," said Miranda. "Your children are just gorgeous."

So far, so good, Jim thought. He couldn't detect any hint that Miranda was uncomfortable with what just happened. Perhaps she had caught his glance only a split second before he had caught hers. Maybe she didn't notice his uncharacteristic stare at all.

"I fully agree, but I'm afraid they get their good looks from their mother."

"Don't be modest, Jim, they all have your beautiful eyes and hair. The family resemblance is just incredible."

Miranda's comment made Jim blush and Scott pause, "Yeah, but a couple more of these receptions and that beautiful hair is gonna turn gray."

"Okay," Jim chuckled, "enough of that kind of talk! By the way, I have something for your table." Jim withdrew an envelope from the breast pocket of his tuxedo. "You are all very special to me. I want to show my appreciation for everything you do by making certain you don't pay for a single drink all night."

"I didn't know you were charging, Jim."

"We weren't going to, but then we heard you were coming."

Joan piped in, "Will you two stop!"

Jim was laughing heartily, "I can't help it, Joan, your husband is such a little boy. Anyway, beer and wine are on the house, but they are charging for mixed drinks." He handed the thick envelope to Scott. "Just have our people give the bartender one of these tickets whenever they order a mixed drink. It will be on my tab. Will you make certain everyone has all they need?"

"You don't have to ask me twice."

"That is very sweet of you, Jim," Miranda said as she locked her eyes with his.

Miranda was in on the joke. So was everyone else from the office. There was no need for drink tickets. In fact, all drinks were on the house.

"Passing those tickets out ought to keep him busy for a while," Jim said, with a grin.

Her admiring gaze held him hostage during a brief period of small talk, and the confident tone in his voice began to ebb. It returned quickly after he redirected his eyes out across the dance floor.

"Miranda, will you excuse me? I need to say hello to some of our guests before we eat."

Jim walked to another of the tables reserved for his employees, and began to make small talk. As he spoke, he couldn't rid himself of Miranda's image. An inner voice was asking him, *What was that all about?*

The entire evening belonged to the young members of Erin's wedding party. Some of the groomsmen had a premonition that the reception was going to be a dull affair, so they formulated a plan to liven things up. The best man, Owen Cooper, and Colleen's escort, David Jergensen, hatched most of the ideas, but all of the wedding party agreed to them. From the moment dinner began, they were in complete control. Owen even asked Jim and Preston if they planned to give a toast, and how long they planned to talk. He introduced them like an emcee. During the meal, the groomsmen presented a hilarious slide presentation, doing their very best to embarrass Trent. Kelly and some of Erin's friends performed a skit on Erin's behalf. *A skit,* Jim thought, *imagine that.*

Jim and Preston were surprised when at the conclusion of dinner, the fifteen member orchestra packed up their instruments and left. Some of Trent's wealthy friends hired a DJ, who had set up his equipment during the wedding ceremony. Within a few minutes, he began playing songs from a long list of rock and roll music. Jim was glad he hadn't paid for the orchestra, but he was a little embarrassed for Preston. The entire hall now echoed with blaring music, and the young members of the wedding party were dancing like there was no tomorrow. The little children soon joined them, and within minutes, they were being swung in every direction by the older ones.

Jim searched for Preston. He thought an apology was in order. He found him at the bar getting a drink. "It looks like the kids had their own plans for this evening, Preston."

"It does indeed, Jim."

"I apologize for what they did. Although the DJ seems to be a hit, it was rude of them to dismiss your orchestra."

"Nonsense, Jim, these young men knew what they wanted and they made it happen. I have a lot of respect for that. Besides, the music during dinner was a perfect fit. It allowed us to talk without raising our voices. Now, it's time to let the kids have their fun."

"Thank heavens," Jim said with a sigh of relief. "I was afraid they may have offended you."

"You always show concern for the feelings of others, Jim. You're a good man—a man of compassion."

"Thank you for saying so, Preston. Mind if I join you?"

"I think we can probably find a dozen or so topics to toast, don't you?"

"I'll say—let's drink to that!"

The two men laughed and drank as they stood at the bar, watching the antics on the crowded dance floor. Scott Troia soon joined them, and Jim found himself laughing uncontrollably as he observed the sophisticated Preston Wilshire swapping stories with his lovable, but less refined best friend. Within a half hour, the three men were like old pals.

Scott asked Preston, "Did Jim tell you what he did tonight? He gave me phony drink tickets! Told me to pass em' out to all of the employees and tell them to redeem them for mixed drinks. He said that beer and wine were free, but you were charging for everything else. I must'a spent twenty minutes passing out those stupid tickets before Charlie Ford found me and said we didn't need them and that drinks were on the house."

Preston laughed, "Perhaps we can devise some devilish scheme to get even." He pointed to the groomsmen, "I'll bet these young men could give you some ideas!"

"That's a great idea, Preston!"

Scott started for the dance floor, and then doubled back, "This is the best reception I've ever been to, Jim, the best!"

Jim spotted Shauna running toward him, looking afraid and shaken. When he saw the distressed look on her face, he ran a few steps to meet her and then bent down so he could hear what she was saying over the music.

"Dad—there's some guys outside that want to fight Tom."

"What?"

"Yeah—there's three of them, and they're pushing him around."

Jim said nothing, but darted around the dance floor at a trot. As he reached the hallway, he broke into a run. Anticipating trouble, he stripped off his tuxedo jacket, and dropped it on the floor just before the entrance of the reception hall. He hit the front door so hard, he thought it might shatter. He could feel the soreness on his palm where a bruise would undoubtedly appear.

14

JIM WAS TRYING TO SLOW DOWN FROM THE BREAK neck speed he had attained as he reached the three young boys surrounding Tom in the parking lot.

"Who's this guy?" one of them asked.

The pocket of Tom's tuxedo was ripped. His cheek showed pink finger marks contrasted against a face that was as white as a sheet. He had been slapped.

Jim was immediately on the offensive, "You've got bigger things to worry about than who I am—now, what do you want with my son?"

"Oh, I see—it's his daddyyy!"

Jim's head turned to the black teenager who made the comment. He noticed a hand signal intended for the other two boys. They spread out. Jim drew a deep breath. He could no longer see them all at once from his viewpoint. He swallowed hard and concentrated on the black kid, the leader. "I'm not going to ask you again—what do you want with my son?"

Jim waited for a response from the short, stocky teenager, who was too busy laughing to answer.

This dumb shit seems to think his "daddyyy" comment makes a mockery of Tom's manhood—idiot!

To Jim, he looked like a cagey sort who enjoyed fighting, or was it the drugs that made him seem that way? The boy wore baggy blue jeans with a crotch that hung down to his knees. His hair was capped with what looked like a woman's nylon stocking. Even under the lights of the parking lot, Jim could clearly see a deep gash in the boys left cheek. He was unshaven and his beard was patchy. Jim took a moment to size up the other two boys, who were dressed similarly, but wore backwards baseball caps. One of them was Hispanic; the other was a tall Caucasian boy with blond hair. All three were filthy, and high on something.

The black boy's teeth seemed to fluoresce in contrast to his dark face. He flashed them like a vacuum cleaner salesman as he answered Jim's question, "Look here, Mista O'Brien, your boy owes us money."

Jim's fists clenched at the belittling tone of voice, "What for?"

"Jus a little bissness' we been doing—right Tom?"

"WHAT FOR?" Jim persisted.

"Well, I don't wanna' be the one to give him up, know what I mean? Maybe you tell 'em, Tom?"

Tom noticed his fathers jaw tighten, "I don't know what they are talking about, Dad, I swear!"

The black boy frowned and shook his fist, "Oh, now you dissin' me, whitey. Spill the beans, or I do it."

This is getting us nowhere, Jim thought. "Enough screwing around—WHAT DOES HE OWE YOU MONEY FOR?"

The black teen's smile disappeared. He squinted his eyes, and his face took on a menacing quality. Jim knew he could take all three boys, especially in their current condition, but this boy still sent a shiver down his spine.

"Your boy been buying his *H* on credit. Time to pay what he owes."

Jim hesitated on his next question. He was praying that his guess was wrong, "What do you mean— *H*?"

"Man, you white mother fuckers are all the same—dumb shits!"

The boy was clearly enjoying giving up Tom's secret while antagonizing his father. He grinned again. His teeth appeared slowly, and then they took over his entire face, made him ugly as sin. He could see that Tom's father couldn't or wouldn't make a guess as to what he meant by *H*, so he threw the word out for him.

"His heroin, man—his heroin."

Jim went numb. His anger diminished, replaced by shock. He unclenched his fists, and stood up straight.

Now I know the drug.

Jim tried to sound tough, play to his audience, "We don't pay for drugs."

"Well, your boy's been payin' for it a long time," the black teen replied.

The other boys snickered; enjoying their leader's belittling banter with Tom's father.

"Deacon's lying, Dad, he's—"

Jim shot a glance at Tom, "SHUT UP! NOT ANOTHER WORD OUT OF YOU! Go back inside and stay there!"

"Hold up there old man," Deacon said, "you ain't runnin' this show. Tom leaves when I say he can."

Jim needed to get Tom to safety, "Let him go inside," he said calmly. "The four of us can talk about this alone."

Deacon assumed he had gained some kind of commitment. He was wrong. Jim nodded at Tom to go. Tom moved cautiously, as if he were still afraid they may do him physical harm. After taking a few steps backward, he turned and ran back inside the reception hall. Already Deacon Reynolds was regretting watching his prey run to safety.

"You plan on payin' Tom's bill, Mista O'Brien?"

"No, I don't," Jim said flatly.

"I see," Deacon said, more seriously now. "Ain't you afraid to be out here wif 'ta' three of us Mista' O'Brien?"

"The only thing that scares me about kids like you, is what you do to children. You sell them drugs."

The black boy nodded and pursed his lips, "And they buy 'em of they own free will—we ain't twistin' no arms. Now if your boy don't pay up—"

"You'll do nothing!" Jim snapped. "He's not going to pay up. Not now—not ever!"

"Now, now, Mista' O'Brien, I don't plan ta' lose money on this deal. You see, I stand ta' make some extra money on those gold coins a his."

Jim struggled to maintain his composure, "Well, that's too bad, son, because I took those coins from his room yesterday."

Deacon's eyes widened.

Jesus he's ugly, Jim thought.

"If you don't pay, we gonna hav'ta take action."

"Oh yeah," Jim asked smugly, "what kind of action?"

"The last person didn't pay up gotta' drive-by."

Jim wasn't sure he heard the boy right. "Are you threatening me with a drive-by shooting?"

"No, Mista O'Brien, we threatening your whole family with a drive-by. We done it before, an you got lots a kids don't you? Ought'a be easy to hit one of 'em—huh, boys?"

The teens began to laugh. The white boy said, "Shit, we could probably hit three or four of 'em!"

That was a mistake.

Jim could not control himself. He reached for the tall blond boy by his neck. It happened so quickly the other two boys were taken by surprise. With sheer strength Jim drew the boy in front of him, and then bent the boy over backwards, his thumb pushing in his Adams apple.

"How dare you threaten my children? I think it's time to call the police."

The black teen smiled his ugly smile once more. He reached around to the back of his pants; his hand returned wielding a knife. Jim recognized its shape from the reflection of the halogen lights along its wicked chrome edge. It was an immense Bowie knife.

"Well, well—now you got two things you gonna' regret Mista O'Brien. First, we gonna slice you up—next, we gonna get your kids. Maybe all of 'em! An we still gonna get our money. You can count on that."

Jim turned slightly, brandishing his captive in front of him. "You can count on going to jail, because that's where I'm going to put you before the evening is through!"

Deacon admired the Bowie's enormous chrome blade, "Is *whitey* here scaring you guys?"

Perhaps Deacon didn't notice, but the Hispanic teen was undeniably scared. *Maybe he isn't as high as the other two,* Jim thought. He kept his distance. Still smiling, the young black turned his attention to Jim's captive, "Oh, thas' right, Mikey can't talk wif'ta white man's thumb stuck in his throat. Guess I'll have to fix that."

Deacon began to wave the knife in small circles at first, then larger ones. Jim matched his movements, convinced he just wanted him to release the blond-haired boy, but he didn't. Instead, he repositioned him as a shield in front of him; certain he would not cut his accomplice. It was a miscalculation on his part. The assailant moved quickly, surprising Jim as he slashed both of them with a downward motion. Jim released the boy, realizing he was in much more danger than he thought.

"You son-of-a-bitch," the blond boy yelled. "You cut me!"

Deacon shrugged it off, "Hey, I got you free, didn't I?"

"He wasn't gonna hurt us dude, he was just bluffing."

The blond boy pressed his hand against his upper chest to form a compress against his cut. His white t-shirt was turning dark. Jim couldn't see the red color in the poor light, but he knew it was blood. If the boy had only zipped his coat before the skirmish, he probably would have escaped without a scratch.

Deacon's tone crackled with impatience, "Well, now he's gonna pay up. Gimme' the seven hundred dollars your kid owes me, or I'll cut you some more."

Jim felt something warm trickling down his wrist. He had no idea how bad he was cut, but he didn't want to take his eyes off the lunatic in front of him. "I told you, we don't pay for drugs. Go peddle them somewhere else."

"Your family—you want 'em killed?" Deacon taunted.

"No one's going to kill anybody. Don't you boys know I can have you arrested? Tom knows who you are."

The black teen looked over Jim's shoulder toward the building. His eyes became round. His two friends started to back away. Then Deacon's eyes briefly returned to slits as he looked at Jim and said, "This ain't finished, Mista O'Brien." He spun and ran to catch up with the other two boys, already darting across the parking lot.

Jim turned to see Scott and two of his brothers running toward him. He was shaking violently, and by the time Scott reached him, he had nearly fainted.

"It scared me when you left so fast," Scott explained, "so I coaxed Shauna into telling me what she told you."

Jim peered over Scott's shoulder. Tom was still watching from between the two sets of doors at the reception hall entrance. Jim scanned the parking lot. The three boys had disappeared.

"They're gone for now," Jim said, "but they'll be back."

Scott's eyes lit up, "When will they be back?"

"Probably not tonight, but they'll be back, I'm sure of it."

Noticing Jim's hand, his brother David spoke up, "Jesus, you're cut! What was this all about?"

"I'll tell you in a little while. Right now we have a wedding reception going on, and with any luck, it will come to a peaceful conclusion." He looked at his brothers. "David, Sean, I need you to watch the front door, take half hour shifts with your brothers until this thing is over. Keep all the children inside."

"You got it, Jim," Sean said assuringly.

"Scott, come with me, we need to talk to Tom."

Jim's wrist had been cut deeply. Fortunately, his wrist watch constrained the length of the cut, leaving it only about an inch long. He estimated five or six stitches would be necessary to mend the wound. Scott picked Jim's jacket up from the floor, and then hurried Tom to a small conference room just inside the facility. Jim was close behind. He pulled the door closed, leaving a bloody handprint on the knob. Noticing, he reached in his pocket for a handkerchief. Jim wiped the door handle and then dabbed his wrist, and rolled his blood stained sleeve to his elbow. Then he wrapped the cloth around his wrist and held it tight. Scott was quiet, waiting for Jim to take the lead. When Jim was satisfied that the bleeding stopped, he looked up at Tom with a solemn face.

"You could have been hurt badly, or even killed by those boys, Tom."

Tom shifted defensively. "Dad, I swear I don't know what they were talking about."

"STOP IT." No more lying. I found a syringe in your bedroom. I found a pipe and marijuana. I have seen you in a drug induced stupor several times. I know you've been using drugs; I just didn't know what kind—until tonight."

Tom became reticent. Jim wondered if he should go on, or shelve this discussion until tomorrow. He gave Scott a look that said he felt helpless and confused.

Scott stared at the floor, "Perhaps you both need a break, Jim. After all, this is your daughter's wedding reception. Everyone is still dancing—there's still time to enjoy the evening."

"I don't think I can enjoy the evening any more, Scott." After a short pause, he looked at his son. "But you're right, this will keep until tomorrow. Tom, I want you to rejoin the others at the reception. Do not mention what happened. Don't mention it to anyone at all! Do you understand me?"

Tom avoided his father's gaze, "Yes."

"And don't set one foot outdoors."

Tom slowly made his way to the door. When he reached it, he stared at the once bloody doorknob. He paused before turning to face his father. "I'm sorry, Dad."

Jim was angry, but he felt a touch of pity for Tom, "I know you are, son." With his head down, Tom made his exit.

Jim drew a deep breath. "I don't know about you, but I could use a drink—maybe three or four."

"What happened out there?" Scott asked.

"Those boys were trying to collect seven hundred dollars from Tom."

Scott was stunned, "SEVEN HUNDRED DOLLARS!"

"Yes," Jim said, "that's what he owes them for the heroin he's been using."

"Oh my God, I'm so sorry, Jim!"

"It gets worse," Jim continued, "they threatened us with a drive-by shooting if we didn't pay them."

Scott shook his head in disbelief. "Are you going to call the police?"

"You bet I am—just as soon as the guests have gone. We need to have a warrant issued for those three degenerates, and I'll want to have an officer watch our house tonight."

Scott glanced at Jim's wrist, "So how did you get cut?"

"That was my fault. They were joking about shooting my children—one of them said something about how many of my kids they could hit. For a moment, I pictured Danny or Molly getting shot. It was more than I could take—something inside me snapped and I went berserk. I grabbed the tall one and put him in a hold while I pressed my thumb in his throat. The black kid drew a knife. I positioned the kid I was holding in front of me, thinking he would NEVER attack me with his friend in the way, but I was wrong. He cut us both!"

Scott's jaw hung wide open, "That is the craziest thing I have ever heard. It just goes to show you, these kids have no respect for life."

"You can say that again. But here's the scary part. Those kids, especially that black kid, are ruthless! They are only about sixteen or seventeen years old. They aren't even mature enough to understand the consequences of what they are doing. And that makes them all the more dangerous."

"Jim, maybe you shouldn't wait to call the police, maybe you should call them now." Scott reached for his cell and held it out.

Jim considered it briefly, "No—I don't want to ruin Erin's reception! There are only a handful of people who even know about this. When the last few guests are leaving, I'll have a police officer meet me here. I'll file a report, and have him escort the family home while I go get a few stitches. What time is it?"

Scott glanced at his watch, "About twenty after nine, we haven't missed much of the reception."

"Good! Now, if we can just keep this quiet and get through the rest of the evening." Jim tucked the handkerchief around his wrist and underneath his watch to hold it in place. Carefully, he put on his jacket. "Thank God my tuxedo is black," Jim said gruffly.

Scott desperately wanted to lighten Jim's mood, "I'm taking you straight to the bar, Jim—I'm buying!"

Jim cracked a small smile. "You'll probably try to use those phony drink tickets—won't you, ya' big lug?"

Scott grinned, "Well, the thought did cross my mind."

"Well then, what are we waiting for?"

The two friends left the conference room. Just a few feet from where they appeared in the hallway, they saw Jim's brothers, David and Sean, keeping watch at the front door.

"Make sure you guys rotate shifts with Tim, Michael, and Mark, okay?"

David gave Jim a concerned look, "Aren't you even going to tell us what this was all about, Jim?"

"You bet I am," Jim said, "but first, give me a chance to see how our guests are doing. I'll check back with you guys in about a half hour and give you the whole story then, okay?"

"Can you have someone bring us a beer?"

Jim forced a smile, "Spoken like a true Irishman, Sean."

15

INSIDE THE RECEPTION HALL, THERE WAS NO INDICATION that anyone had noticed that Jim had been gone. He and Scott headed straight for the nearest of the three staffed bars. Scott ordered a gin and tonic. Jim ordered two bourbon and sevens. He downed the first one in a few gulps. Picking up the second glass, he studied his left wrist.

"Damn, it's bleeding right through the handkerchief. How can I dance with Erin if I'm bleeding like this?"

Scott spoke to the bartender, "Do you have a first aid kit back there?"

"No," he replied, "but there's one in the kitchen."

Jim looked grateful for the information, "Great, I'll be right back."

Jim started for the kitchen. He didn't notice Peg approaching them.

"Where's Jim going?"

"He has a cut on his wrist. There's a first aid kit in the kitchen, but he's going to need some stitches."

"Oh my God, how did he cut himself? Is he okay?"

"There was a fight in the parking lot, Peg, a brief skirmish."

"Who was fighting?" she asked. What was it all about?"

"Listen Peg, you guys are my best friends in the world, but it's not my place to discuss this with you. Let Jim tell you about it later—alone."

Peg looked puzzled and distraught. She wanted to pursue the issue, but Scott's tone of voice said the subject was closed. She changed the topic.

"Jim missed the father-daughter dance. He hasn't seen Erin all night."

"I know. That's why he's looking for the first aid kit. I think he's afraid he will bleed all over her dress."

"Is the cut that bad, Scott?"

"No, Peg. It's only about an inch long. A couple of stitches, and he'll be as good as new."

About ten minutes later Jim cornered the DJ, and requested a waltz so he could dance with Erin. With his wrist carefully wrapped in gauze and medical tape, he felt confident he could dance all night if he wished. At the moment, the groomsmen were going wild on the dance floor. Some of them were performing a mock break dance, spinning each other around and having a great time. Jim could tell they had already consumed plenty of alcohol. He walked up to Erin, who was in hysterics, laughing at the macho display, and grabbed her by the waist. "Do you think your old man should show them how to do it?"

"Dad! Where have you been?"

"Something urgent came up; I had to take care of it immediately."

"They called you to come up for the father-daughter dance, but you were gone."

The loud song that had been playing ended. The DJ kept his promise and a beautiful arrangement of *Moon River* began to play.

Jim smiled warmly, admiring Erin's beautiful glow.

"I'd like to make it up to you now."

He took her hand and led her to a clearing on the dance floor. With his right arm around her waist and his left hand holding her right, he began leading her in a graceful waltz. They immediately drew attention. Not only was it a dramatic departure from the loud number that just ended, few others knew how to waltz.

"Is your wedding turning out the way you hoped it would?"

"Even better, Dad, we're having so much fun. Can you believe what the guys did with the orchestra?"

"No, I can't," Jim grimaced, "I'm glad I didn't pay for it!"

"Me too," Erin said. "I know you spent a lot more than you had planned on our wedding."

"You can't put a price on happiness, kiddo. So tell me, are you happy?"

Erin's smile told the story, "The happiest."

"And Trent is he happy?"

"We're both happy, Dad. This is the best day of my life."

"Good," Jim said, "then it's one of the best days of mine."

A few older couples joined them on the floor. In the final seconds of the song, two of the groomsmen were dancing a polka together. Jim shook his head, "Trent's friends are a little weird, if you ask me."

Erin laughed, "They are so much fun, Dad. They've made the entire reception a blast."

Jim and Erin continued to dance until the song was over, and then Jim kissed her and gave her a long hug. "I love you, Erin."

"I love you too, Dad."

"Oh," Jim said, trying to sound absent minded, "here is my dollar. You know—for the dollar dance."

He handed Erin an envelope. "Now tell them to play a few more slow songs would you? I'd love to get your mother out there. I'll see you in a little while."

As Jim turned around to leave the dance floor, he could hear Erin exclaim, "Five thousand dollars! Dad gave us five thousand dollars!"

Peg met him half way across the dance floor, "Want to dance, big boy?"

"You read my mind, gorgeous."

A quick check of the wrist showed no blood, so Jim took Peg in his arms and began to slow dance even before the music started.

"We need to talk about that cut."

"I know," Jim replied, nestling his cheek against Peg's. Moments later, another blaring rock song began to play. Jim and Peg continued to hold each other. With her head on his shoulder, they swayed slowly back and forth. "This is the best part of the evening," Peg spoke loudly in his ear.

"Well, it gives us a benchmark to shoot for later tonight."

She lifted her head and looked into his eyes. "You always tell me that you exceed your benchmarks."

Raising his eyebrows, Jim smiled, "I'll sure as hell exceed this one."

The young kids were getting wild again. Jim and Peg were starting to get jostled, so they decided it was time to mingle with their guests.

For the remainder of the reception, Jim and Peg stayed together, greeting friends and family, watching their children dance, and posing for photographs. Before the wedding, Peg had gathered the children together for a new family portrait. It had been two years since the last one was taken. Jim took a brief break to carry a tray of beers to his brothers, Tom and Michael, who were taking their second shift watching the front door. When the guest attendance had thinned out, Jim sat Peg down and told her a few details about the incident in the parking lot. He withheld the part about the heroin, saying only that Tom owed the boys money. "When it's time to go," Jim said, "we need to leave quickly. I don't want anyone lingering outside for any reason." Peg assured him they would waste no time getting into the van.

It was twelve fifteen when Jim gave the go ahead to the older children to start loading gifts in the cars. The remaining guests were few, and mostly relatives. David and Sean's wives had stopped at the front door to take them home. They had just completed their third shift of guard duty. Jim thanked them. "You guys were life savers tonight. I don't think I would have been able to go back to the reception without you at the door."

"What happened tonight should scare the hell out of you, Jim. If I were you, I'd get on the phone and call the police."

Jim rolled his eyes, "Good lord, I almost forgot! He quickly found Peg and retrieved his phone from her purse. He dialed 911 and told the operator what had happened. The dispatcher said an officer would be dispatched to the reception hall, and should arrive within a few minutes. Megan, Eileen, and Morgan walked down the long corridor with their arms full of gifts. About thirty seconds later, Shauna and Katie followed. Jim grabbed a few packages and told Peg he was going outside to help load gifts until the police came.

As he opened the atrium's inner door he heard a muffled *crack*, then another. As he reached for the outer door, it shattered into a million pieces. Jim's reaction was pure reflex. He instantaneously hit the floor. Two more cracks, louder without the door glass to muffle the sound.

Gunshots?

He wasn't on the ground for two seconds before he pushed himself up and got to his feet. His hands were covered with blood from small shards of glass.

THOSE WERE GUNSHOTS, he thought. He ran outside, frantically scanning the area. *Is everybody alright? Where is the van? Oh God, is everybody alright?*

Jim never looked, but he could hear the loud exhaust system of a car speeding down the far end of the parking lot. Seeing their van, he ran to it. There was a bullet hole in the front windshield. His heart pounded. On the passenger side the cargo doors were wide open. There were gifts on the ground, and behind the gifts, there was someone laying there, someone small. Jim recognized his ten year old Katie, well before he could reach her. His other girls were just beginning to peek out of the van they had been loading with gifts.

Eileen saw Katie and screamed, "KATIE'S BEEN SHOT!"

Jim dropped to his knees in front of her. He was afraid to even touch her for fear that he might cause her further injury.

"CALL AN AMBULANCE—NOW!"

Jim saw her eyes. They looked at him briefly, before they became fixed in a permanent stare. He knew then she was gone. He slid his hands under her and lifted her frail body to his chest. He felt her warm blood mingle with his own. He stared at her in disbelief, hoping for the slightest movement, a flinch, a miracle.

She's too young, she can't be gone.

Jim's daughters wailed in the lamplight. Megan said, "Is she—is she—?"

She couldn't say the word. Jim saw figures running toward him. The tears in his eyes blurred them. He thought he recognized Peg's voice, but he wasn't sure. It was hard to hear over his own screaming. Although his mouth was closed, and his teeth were clenched, he could hear himself screaming.

Please God, he thought. *I can't think straight! Please, help me stop screaming!*

16

"THE FATHER AND MOTHER OF MISSING THIRTEEN YEAR old Cynthia Martin have not given up hope that they will find their daughter safe and sound. At day nine of the search, authorities are looking for this man, thirty-nine year old Jared Kane, for questioning in connection with the case. Anyone with information of his whereabouts is asked to contact the Polk County Sheriff's Department in Des Moines, Iowa. Here to talk to us about the case, is missing person's expert, Sharon Conan. Welcome, Sharon. What can you tell us about this man and his connection with the disappearance of—"

The television image of Jared Kane was forever engraved in Jim's mind. He was unaware that his seething stare disfigured him terribly. Jim hated CNN News, but as of late he spent most of his day and evening hours alternating between CNN, FOX, and the local the news channels. The doorbell momentarily distracted him from one of several stories he had been following for the last three weeks.

A casual glance at the door revealed a hulking silhouette behind the etched glass.

Peg approached the door and opened it. Jim could hear only whispers.

"Hi, Scott, thanks for coming over."

"Any time, Peg."

Jim had already returned his attention to the current news story.

"—and after this long without so much as a clue as to where she might be, the chances of her being alive are not very good."

As you know, Sharon, this disappearance follows closely on the heels of the Jonathan Michaels case. Do you see any similarities in how the authorities are handling the investiga—"

"Hello, Jim."

Scott Troia stood a few feet from where Jim was sitting on the sofa. He was in his bathrobe. His whiskers showed several days growth. His hair was uncombed and he looked as if he hadn't showered in days.

Absently, Jim said, "Hello, Scott, what are you doing here? Is there a problem at the office?"

"Yes, something is terribly wrong," Scott said. "Our president and CEO hasn't shown up for work in three weeks."

Jim's gaze remained on the television, his expression unchanged. "Did you know that Cynthia Martin is the second child missing from the Midwest in two weeks? There are dozens of kids currently missing across the country. Who are these sick bastards kidnapping children? Why haven't we deterred them from doing this? Did you know that there are over five hundred known sexual predators living in Omaha neighborhoods? These are just the ones we know of. There are probably twice as many we don't know about. Do you know how many women were raped or assaulted in our city last year?"

"Too many, Jim, even one is too many."

Jim looked despondent. "Why can't we stop them? There are shootings on the news every week— right here in Omaha. Kids killing each other, gangs fighting, selling drugs, stealing to support their drug habits. Violence! All around us."

Jim's gaze drifted from the television. His face took on a child-like quality, and his eyes began to roam around the room. Scott studied him intently.

Pursing his lips, Jim said, "I'm sorry. I'm not ready to come back yet."

"Don't get me wrong, Jim. Everything is running smoothly at the office, but we still need ya' there. You're our leader, the company's visionary, and your employees are worried sick about you. They need to know that you're all right. In addition, Vince Mitchell has been calling every other day for you; I don't know what to tell him."

"Tell him I'll call him when I return to work."

"When will that be?"

"I—I don't know. When I'm ready, I suppose."

"That's not an answer, Jim."

"It's the best I can do."

"Vince told me that you flew to Chicago on the night of Erin's prenuptial dinner to interview Tony Constantino—you never told me."

"I never had the chance, Scott. I was in a terrible rush on Erin's wedding day, and well—you know about the events that followed."

Scott grew solemn. "I know. How is everyone holding up?"

"We aren't coming apart at the seams, not visibly anyway. But every day I see the kids break down and cry. They congregate in the basement to watch TV and console each other. A few of them have been hiding out in their bedrooms. Peg has called the school counselors to get help. I don't know any other way to put it Scott. We're a family in crisis."

"What about you? How are you and Peg doing?"

Jim's eyes formed slits, his demeanor became cold. "I don't know—we haven't spoken much since the funeral. I guess it's just too difficult to talk about."

"Maybe you and Peg could use a little counseling as well."

"NO! It'll only make things worse. Peg blames me for Katie's death, for not calling the police sooner, and I blame her for ignoring Tom's *obvious* drug problem. No! No counseling!"

"I'm sorry, Jim. I've butted my nose where it doesn't belong. I apologize."

"Its okay, Scott. I know you mean well, but it's going to be a long time before this family gets better. We'll certainly never be whole again."

"Exactly, Jim—that's why I think you should come back to the office. You need to get your mind off what happened, focus on other things. It would be good for you."

"NO! Katie deserves a proper period of mourning. I don't want to think about anything else. I—I don't want to forget her."

Jim burst into tears, sobbing uncontrollably. He placed his head in his hands for several moments, and then raked his fingers through his hair.

"I can't go on, Scott, I can't go on."

Scott's vision blurred as he held back tears of his own. *His heart is broken,* he thought. *What can I possibly do?*

He placed his hand on Jim's shoulder. Feeling Scott's touch, Jim sobbed even harder.

After a few moments, Jim said, "She was so young, so innocent. I failed her. I've failed my whole family. I let those punks rob us of her precious life. I've hurt everyone."

At that moment Scott understood the magnitude of Jim's pain. He was not only feeling sorrow for the loss of the beautiful little girl he loved so much, it was also the guilt and shame he felt for depriving Peg and the children from the daughter and sister they loved as well. *How could a man live with so much pain without breaking in half? Jim is strong, but is he strong enough?* Scott had his doubts. He knew he had to keep Jim talking. It was apparent that Jim needed to get some things off his chest.

"Look, Jim, we need to get out of here for a little while. I want you to take a quick shower and get dressed. We'll go to Clancy's Pub for an hour or two."

Still sobbing, Jim managed a nod, and then disappeared down the hallway. When Scott heard his bedroom door close, he sat on the sofa. He noticed a picture frame protruding from under a sofa pillow and picked it up. He studied the beautiful portrait of the

O'Brien family taken at Erin's wedding. *Jesus,* he thought, *this must be hard for him to look at.* He put the portrait back under the pillow and headed for the kitchen. He found Peg sitting at the far end of their gigantic kitchen table watching FOX news.

When she saw him, she said, "Jim must be rubbing off on me. For two weeks, I've done nothing but nag at him to stop watching these depressing cable news stations, and here I am doing the same thing."

Peg stood up and turned the television off. "I'm worried about him, Scott, really worried."

"You mentioned that when you called, Peg. Tell me why you are so concerned."

"He's not himself. I don't know who he is, but he's not Jim O'Brien."

"What do you mean by that?"

"I told you he's been obsessing about the news, right?"

"Yes."

"Only the bad news."

Scott's inquisitive look prompted her to continue, "I've been observing him as he watches the news. He never flinches during a story involving a murder, robbery, or kidnapping, but he can hardly pay attention to a story relating to something positive. If it's not a report involving a rape, kidnapping, or murder, he searches for one. It's eerie. He's beginning to scare me—the kids, too."

"Maybe it helps him to know that he's not the only one with problems."

"I thought of that, but this is different. As he was watching the trial proceedings for a child molester, he began mumbling things like, 'Kill the bastard,' or 'He doesn't deserve to live.' His face gets contorted, his entire demeanor changes. I'm telling you, he becomes a different person. They were interviewing two gay men at a rally supporting same sex marriage. He said, 'We ought to wipe them all out, kill them all.' Yesterday, when Sergeant Jensen told him that they still haven't found the kids who sold Tom the drugs, he hung up the phone and said 'Maybe I'll have to take care of this on my own.' Do you see why I am so concerned?"

"I sure do, Peg. Please keep me informed on that kind of behavior. We've got to snap him out of the depression he's in. Right now, he's taking a shower. I'm going to take him down to the pub for a couple of beers and let him blow off some steam. He needs someone to talk to."

"Why won't he talk to me, Scott—why won't he talk to me?" Peg began to cry softly. Scott took Peg in his arms. He could see the terrible toll Katie's death was taking on the O'Brien family.

"I don't know, Peg. Maybe he will soon."

Scott was relieved to step out on to the O'Brien's front porch. The tension and sorrow emanating from the O'Brien household was almost too much for him to bear. *God, what they must be going through.* He had a positive thought as he and Jim walked to his car. *Maybe Jim will open up after a few beers.*

It was almost four in the afternoon on Wednesday, November twenty-third. Tomorrow was Thanksgiving Day, but Scott doubted the O'Brien's would even celebrate the holiday. At the moment, Scott was struggling to engage Jim in a fluid conversation. Even the waitress was subdued, as though she could sense the heartache at the table as they ordered their second pitcher of beer.

"Friday will be the three week anniversary of Katie's death, Scott. Three weeks! I keep expecting to see her run across the living room. Then reality sinks in and I realize I will never see her again—ever."

"Yeah, I don't suppose you feel like you have much to be thankful for tomorrow, that's for sure."

Jim craned his head, giving Scott a puzzled look.

"Thanksgiving—you do realize tomorrow is Thanksgiving Day, don't you?"

Jim didn't reply, shifting his gaze to the carbonated bubbles in his beer. Scott knew the answer as he watched him with pity. He swallowed hard.

"Listen, Jim, you said it yourself; your family is in crisis. We've got to figure out a way to begin a process of healing for all of you."

"Healing? How can we heal from this? How will my children ever heal from witnessing the murder of their little sister, gunned down at the hands of Tom's drug dealing friends? How do you heal from that?"

"I know it doesn't seem likely, Jim, but they will heal. Time heals all."

Scott knew he was approaching dangerous territory, but he had to ask the question. "Is it true they have no leads on the kids who did this?"

"Yes, those goddamned police have no idea what they are doing. I'm thinking about conducting my own investigation."

Scott raised his eyebrows, "Do you think that's a wise move?"

"Well, someone has to find them—someone has to make them pay for what they've done!"

"You're right, Jim, they need to pay the price for the crime they committed, but you need to let the police handle it. Those kids can't hide forever."

"They've eluded Omaha's finest for three weeks; they could be in Mexico by now."

Scott rocked back in his chair with a pondering expression on his face. Jim didn't notice. "Do you remember my offer to enlist the help of my uncle's family?"

Jim's voice grew sarcastic, "You mean your mafia connection?"

"Yes, my mafia connection."

"What exactly does your uncle do?"

"He owns a chain of dry cleaners. Most of them are run by his children, a few of them by his nephews."

"Sounds almost like the stereotypical mafia organization. I suppose it's a front for something else?"

"He's a bookie."

"Why didn't I guess that?"

Although there was no smile on Jim's face, the comment was made with a small amount of playfulness. For an instant, he almost sounded like the old Jim.

"He's not into drugs, Jim, but many gamblers are. I have no doubt he can locate these boys."

"Then let's do it!"

"There is just one condition, Jim. Once we find them, the police take over, okay?"

Not in a million years! Jim thought, and then he struggled for the answer Scott was looking for. "Okay."

"Do you have the names of the boys?"

Jim grabbed a napkin and began writing. "I have the first names of two of the boys, Carlos and Mike. They referred to him as Mikey. The black kid's name is Deacon Reynolds. He is the one Tom conducted all his business with. He's the one that made the threat: he's the one we've got to get!"

Jim shoved the napkin across the table. Scott glanced at the names, and then studied Jim carefully. He was trying to come up with the word that best described the look on his face. There was an evil glint in Jim's eyes—a frightening look.

What is the word I am looking for? Sinister, that's it—sinister.

Scott went on, "Speaking of Tom, how is he doing?"

"I'm not sure you want to know."

"Is it that bad?"

"Worse. You already know that Tom was buying heroin from this Deacon character. What you don't know, is that he had a four hundred dollar a day habit."

Scott's silence was louder than words. He could only look in Jim's eyes.

"That's right, while Peg and I ignored all the signs that he was using drugs, he was busy stealing car stereos, power tools, jewelry, and anything of value from all over town. He even stole from me."

"I can't believe it—why would he steal from his own father?"

"It makes him sound worse than a common thief, doesn't it? That's what I thought, but the police counselors tell me not to take it personally. Once a person develops an addiction to drugs, nothing in the world matters to them except getting their next fix. Addicts don't think clearly enough to reason who they should or shouldn't steal from—they just steal. I discovered that he has taken almost every power tool I own. In addition, he stole a video camera from his sister, Morgan. She saved her babysitting money for six months to buy it. If you add up the jewelry, power tools, and all of the other things we know of so far, he has taken over six thousand dollars worth of goods from his family alone."

"I don't know what to say, Jim, this is absolutely unbelievable. I had no idea you were dealing with this on top of everything else. What are you going to do with him?"

"It's already done. I placed Tom in a ninety-day drug rehabilitation program. We enrolled him a few days after Katie's funeral. I had to do it quickly before the police could file charges against him. They discovered most of my missing tools at Sam's Jewelry and Loan. I loathe that place. Like most pawn shops, they look the other way while kids like Tom pawn or sell stolen goods for pennies on the dollar. You won't believe this, Scott; I had to buy back my own tools."

"You What?"

"That's right. Nebraska law is absurd. They make you pay to get your recovered property back. The pawn shop isn't responsible for their bad judgment. What's worse is that they knew these items were stolen when they purchased them."

"What makes you think they knew the goods were stolen?"

"Well, for starters, Tom pawned sixteen cordless drills. Show me a seventeen year old boy who owns a single cordless drill, let alone sixteen of them. You can't tell me they didn't suspect these items were stolen. I just don't buy it. These goddamned pawn shops look the other way and allow thousands of kids to sell stolen goods to buy drugs. They're enablers, and Sam's is one of the worst in the country. I asked the police how this could be permitted. Do you know what they told me? Sam's has a lobbyist in Lincoln. Apparently they have friends in high places."

"So they have a lot of influence in the capital, eh? Can you do anything to expose them?"

"I don't know yet, but I'm going to find a way, I swear to God I will! The police also discovered that Tom pawned about seventeen thousand dollars in goods from other people. Unfortunately for him, a lot of it was reported stolen. When he gets out of the drug rehabilitation program, he'll be facing numerous theft charges."

Scott was overcome with emotion. "I need another beer. Oh hell, let's order another pitcher." He signaled the waitress who knew both men quite well. "Sandy, bring us a pitcher, and keep 'em coming." Scott thought about Tom's predicament, "When will you be able to visit him?"

"We can't. He's in confinement without visitation for the entire ninety days. We'll be allowed to speak to him by telephone on weekends, starting in two weeks."

"How are the kids handling this?"

"Not well. Most of them are in counseling. It was bad enough losing their sister, but now their brother is gone as well."

Scott thought again about Tom. In the past two years, he had spent quite a few hours with him, prepping him for the business Jim hoped he would someday take over. "I feel sorry for him, Jim. He's just too damn young to be away from home."

"I feel bad for him too, Scott, but he needs to go through this program. He needs to see the other side of drug addiction. He needs to see the damage he's done to himself and to his family. If it wasn't for his drug habit, Katie would be alive today."

"That's going to be a heavy cross for a young boy to bear."

"Maybe so, but it's a cross he fashioned with his own two hands."

Scott was a little surprised at Jim's comment. It seemed a little harsh, even considering the circumstances.

"Let me be frank with you, Jim. Earlier this afternoon, when I first arrived at your house, you seemed to be a totally different person from the guy I've known for so long."

"What do you mean?"

"I can't explain it, but if I were meeting you for the first time, I would describe you as a cold, bitter man—maybe even heartless. There's a viciousness inside you and it scares me. It scares Peg, too."

"Oh, I see, so the two of you have been comparing notes, have you?"

"Don't be upset, Jim."

"No, no—I'm not upset. Just because my wife and my best friend have decided that I should still be my jovial self after losing my daughter, and seeing my drug-ridden son placed in rehab, that's no reason to be upset."

"We're just concerned about you, that's all."

"Why—because I'm pissed off that the world we live in stinks, that it's full of corrupt people? You're damned right I'm upset. I'm goddamn raving mad!"

Jim picked up his glass mug and peered into its center. He rambled on, "Go back twenty years, Scott—hell, go back ten. The majority of the liberal assholes that existed ten years ago would be disgusted to see our world today. They would be shocked, even repulsed by what they saw. Day by day we are destroying our families. Our children have been subjected to too much sex and violence on TV. Have you seen the latest Victoria's Secret commercials? Hell, the kids can't even watch a commercial without some model's boobies busting out of her blouse. Condoms, lubricants, contraceptives, they are all advertised as must-have products for today's savvy young people. Today's movies—way too graphic! When a movie actor gets shot, they don't just clutch their chest and fall to the ground like they did when we were kids. First, we've got to splatter their blood and guts all over, so our children can enjoy some demented director's sense of art. Little by little we push the envelope, desensitize them for the next bloody scene, and the next. The word gay used to mean happy or carefree. Now it means that two men or women have sex with each other. I don't want to get used to a society that allows this crap. It's wrong—it's just plain wrong!"

Jim gritted his teeth, "Drugs, sex, violence, corruption. We need to wipe them out. We need to take a step back, rediscover the difference between right and wrong. No one knows anymore." Jim took a deep breath. "I thought you'd understand, Scott, bad things are happening to good people. We have a wrong to right here, even if it means taking up arms to do it."

"What are you saying, Jim? Are you going to shoot someone?"

"Don't put words in my mouth. I never said what I meant by taking up arms. But I will tell you this. If Americans don't start fighting immorality and corruption, you won't be able to tell the average Joe from one of your mafia friends. I still have ten children.

I owe it to them to make their world safer and better than I did for Katie. I failed her, but I won't fail the rest of them. Maybe Tony Constantino had it right. He created a protected environment for his family. He took care of them, kept them safe while he dealt with the outside world on his own terms."

Scott looked puzzled, "Look, Jim, Constantino was a killer."

"He was first, and foremost, a family man!"

There was silence. The long time friends looked at each other like they were strangers. Jim took several gulps of his beer. Scott felt like there was a great fire burning within him. And suddenly through the dense fog of tragic news stories he had focused on over the last three weeks, Jim began to think deep thoughts until he experienced what he felt was an epiphany.

I can't fight anyone in my bathrobe, Jim thought. *I need to find Katie's killers. I need to wage some kind of campaign against the number one threat in America—tolerance!* He pictured Constantino's face once more. *I know just how to do it too.*

"I'll be at work on Monday morning."

Scott wasn't sure he heard him correctly, "Really?"

"I'll start working half days until I'm ready to come back full time."

"That's a great start, Jim."

Scott held his glass high to coax Jim into a toast. As Jim's glass met his, he smiled for the first time since that awful night.

Constantino had it right, Jim thought, *I've got to protect my family at any cost—even if it means taking the law into my own hands.*

17

THE LONG DRIVE INTO IOWA PROVED TO LIFT JIM'S spirits. It was twenty-three degrees outside, but from within the car it seemed like a warm, sunny day. He had passed through Des Moines almost two and a half hours ago and was approaching Iowa City. It wouldn't be too long before he would reach Davenport, where he would spend the night. The premise of his trip was to visit a prospective customer in Davenport. The company, Cornell-Madison Publishing, had actually contacted Jim for help a month ago, but Jim told them he couldn't take on any new accounts because he had an enormous backlog of business. After Jim's meeting with Scott he called the company back and told them he had hired additional help, and said he could be in town on Monday.

Jim could have flown to Davenport, but then he would have to rent a car, something that didn't fit into his plans. By driving his own vehicle, no one could track his mileage from Davenport to Chicago. After all, the real purpose of the trip was to retrieve the items Constantino had stored in a second floor locker in an old

Chicago building on 42nd Street. The trip to Davenport would get him within two hours of the Windy City, and give him a hotel receipt for the business portion of the trip.

Jim planned his itinerary carefully. Although no one would ever suspect the real motive for his trip, he took no chances. His years in computer forensics taught him that even the slightest details can come back to haunt you. He would leave no trail, no trace of his side trip to Chicago. He even used a demonstrator computer at Comp USA to print a map and turn-by-turn instructions to the Farm Credit Building on 42nd Street.

Jim still had about an hour before he reached his hotel in Davenport. He was nervous about obtaining the items from Constantino's locker. He knew most of the contents were legal documents, including his will. He was supposed to walk the documents across the hall to the office of Constantino's attorney, Michael Lanza. There was also an address book containing important contact information for Constantino's successor, Jimmy Bonaiuto. He was supposed to deliver it to him in person. Constantino had given Jim his diamond ring as a means of protection, but Jim left it in his safety deposit box in Omaha. He had no intention of making either delivery in person. His identity and the safety of his family were much too important to risk on such an endeavor. Besides, the address book also contained the string of ASCII code characters Jim needed to test the Ethernet card he confiscated from Constantino's computer. He wanted time to scour the book for other relevant information before sending it to Constantino's successor. He wondered what else he might find there. Tomorrow couldn't come and go quickly enough for Jim.

Jim began to run through tomorrow's schedule in his head. *Get up at three o'clock in the morning. Shower and leave by three thirty. Place a DO NOT DISTURB sign on the room door. Two and a half hours to the Farm Credit Building. Take duffel bag to second floor rest room; locate the locker on the far right. Combination, seven, four, six. Place everything in the duffel bag. Leave no later than six thirty. Drive back to the hotel, arrive between nine and ten o'clock. Change clothes and check out of the hotel at ten forty-five. Take customer to lunch at eleven o'clock and get a receipt. Leave for Omaha by one o'clock. Arrive home between six forty-five, and seven o'clock.*

It was about the tenth time he reviewed his plan. In his estimation, the schedule appeared to be realistic. He even allowed an additional hour and forty-five minutes to accommodate rush hour traffic, a distinct possibility in Chicago. The long drive to Davenport was making Jim tired. He was glad. He should have no trouble falling asleep at his intended bed time of eight o'clock. Seven hours of sleep would be plenty to get him through tomorrow's events.

Jim pulled into the parking lot of the Citadel Hotel, a clean, reasonably priced facility where he had stayed before. It was right off I-80 and would allow him a quick start in the morning. He left a wakeup call for eight o'clock, even though he knew he wouldn't be there to receive it. Most wakeup calls were programmed into an automated calling system anyway, and Jim recalled this hotel used such a system. Even if he never answered the call, he could say he was in the shower. He requested and received a room on the first floor. It was about six o'clock when he reached his room. He picked up the hotel phone and ordered a sandwich from room service. From his travel bag, he fetched a clean shirt, slacks, and a sport coat, and hung them in the closet. He found his travel alarm and set the wakeup time for three o'clock. He set the hotel's wakeup alarm for eight o'clock and switched it to the *off* position.

For a moment, Jim wondered if he was crazy to go through such painstaking details to leave false clues behind. *I'd better get used to it,* he thought. *With the things I am about to do, I will never be able to take anything for granted again. My life is about to become forever complex.* He then opened his briefcase and retrieved a compact folding keyboard and another small item, about the size of a postage stamp. He set the items on a round table along with his Smart Phone and went to the television. He picked up the remote control and sat down in a chair behind the table. Turning on the TV, he immediately sought a major cable news channel. When the call letters at the bottom of the screen displayed FOX NEWS, he stopped searching.

He unfolded the keyboard and clicked its power switch to *on*. His Smart Phone recognized the Bluetooth signal, and the two devices connected. He picked up the postage stamp sized memory card and inserted it into the phone. From the two commands that popped up on the display of the device, Jim chose the Restore command, and then proceeded to open the Notes program. A list of eight notes was displayed. Jim opened the fifth note. It was inconspicuously labeled "Birthday Gifts." Upon opening the note, it was clear that this was not a gift list at all. It was in fact, multiple pages of a journal Jim began to keep immediately following his meeting with Scott Troia at Clancy's Pub.

The first few sentences read—*In my interview with Tony Constantino, I realized that in several respects, he was a good man. His entire being was divided into two entities, the loving, protective family man, and the ruthless, mafia leader. While he sometimes killed for selfish reasons and profit, I will kill for the betterment of mankind. I will put the fear of God in every man who will not repent and change his ways. I will sacrifice a handful of human lives to save countless others. It is not unlike a war. Our country is threatened by an enemy, who must be destroyed. The enemy is sex, violence, greed, and deceit. I will –*

Jim used the page down key to find the point where he made his last entry. He read the last sentence. *Tomorrow I leave for Chicago to retrieve the ASCII code required to activate Constantino's Ethernet card.* He added more content:

December 1, 2009 – I am spending the night in Davenport, Iowa. By six thirty tomorrow morning, I will have emptied the contents of Constantino's locker. I will comply with his wishes and deliver all of the items as agreed, but I will delay the delivery for about six months. I will notify Jimmy Bonaiuto that I have Constantino's possessions, and hold them ransom until they agree to help me with my plan. When I have achieved my goals, I will return everything by courier. Tomorrow, I will begin scouring the address book to extract the information I need to reverse society's departure from morality, even though it means that I, myself, must become immoral. Living a life of hypocrisy will be my sacrifice, the price I must pay to save my family and my country.

Jim was aware that his writing style was a little flamboyant and self righteous, but it had to be that way. How else could a sane man read or write these things, unless he felt some notion of nobility toward his cause? For the last four days a major battle had raged in the far reaches of his mind. The pain and guilt he felt over the loss of Katie easily defeated the moral limits his conscience tried to impose on him. With each passing day, he was able to suppress many of the moral convictions in which he so strongly believed, until deep in his soul he knew he could kill a man. Then he provided himself with the ultimate justification for his actions. It was not just vengeance. Although he had vowed he would find Katie's murderers and make them pay, Jim knew he had to restore morality and justice to a country who had completely lost its way.

Jim was a staunch Right-to-Life advocate and frowned upon capital punishment. But in the last few days he had completely reversed his stance on the issue. *If our country had properly utilized capital punishment,* he thought, *and could have expedited executions in a timely fashion, we could have wiped out the majority of violent crime. Our society is filthy, immoral, and corrupt.* Jim's Catholic upbringing rebuked many of those thoughts, but still, his subconscious kept forging ahead for a way to justify what he felt he needed to do. *Those that will die in this moral war, don't deserve to live anyway. The death of a handful of men could reverse our country's terrible fate, and restore the Christian lifestyle that has nearly disappeared in the last several decades.*

He continued to write: *I have decided on a name for the organization I will create in order to wage this battle. Communicating through America's newspapers, I will call this organization the Moral Mafia. With Constantino's Ethernet board, I will control a large sum of money, and direct a network of hit men to force moral decision-making where it no longer exists. Over time, no one will dare commit a crime against humanity for fear of retaliation by the Moral Mafia. Although I do this for the good of my family, and the good of mankind,*

I ask God's forgiveness every day, for the horrible acts I am about to commit.

Jim had a stern look on his face as he reviewed his notes. *Am I crazy? Who else but a mad man would even consider doing these insane acts? Who else but a madman would assume he could change the lifestyles of millions of Americans.* He felt perfectly sane, but then again, how many people could recognize their own madness? He backed up the notes on the tiny memory card, and deleted them from his Smart Phone.

After dinner, Jim called home to check-in with Peg. Like all of their conversations of late, it was factual, and devoid of any sentiment or emotion. The kids were fine, and there were no new problems to deal with this evening. Peg said that Tom was allowed to call home almost ten days earlier than scheduled. He was very sick during the first two weeks of his treatment. He told his mother that the withdrawal symptoms were almost unbearable. She said he spoke so fast and so much during the five minute call, she was unable to say a word in response. His hyper behavior was typical of someone recovering from a serious drug addiction. Soon, he would be allowed to have weekly scheduled telephone visits on Sundays. It was seven thirty, and Jim was ready for bed. He closed the drapes and climbed into bed with the remote control. He wanted to catch a few more headlines before going to sleep. He changed the channel to Headline News and fluffed his pillow. Before the third story, he was sound asleep.

When Jim's travel alarm sounded at three o'clock, he pressed the snooze button. Five minutes later, it went off again. He got up slowly and draped his legs off the side of the bed. It took him another two minutes to stand up and head for the shower. As he passed the mirror, he paused and looked himself squarely in the eyes. *Let's get this done, quickly, and without mishap.* Jim was ready in twenty minutes. As he hung the *DO NOT DISTURB* sign on the door knob, he checked his watch. He was five minutes ahead of schedule. He left everything in the room, including his dress clothes. Instead, he wore unassuming attire, blue jeans and a heavy navy coat.

18

THE DRIVE TO CHICAGO WAS QUICK AND UNEVENTFUL. As he neared his destination, traffic began to pick up. By the time he reached the Farm Credit Building on 42nd Street, traffic congestion was thick with highway commuters. He was unable to park on the street, but staffed parking lots were plentiful. He selected a parking lot across the street, and a half block away from his destination. As he pulled into the lot, he placed a navy blue stocking cap on his head. The attendant gave him a parking stub.

It was still dark as he walked to the entrance of the stately, old building, and entered through a revolving door on the east side. The lobby was smaller than Jim expected. Its center was surrounded by first floor offices elegantly adorned in marble and carved oak trim. He saw the elevator, but decided to use the stairs. As he ascended the stairs, he had a frightening thought.

What if the building had been locked?

At this hour of the morning it was certainly plausible. Although the oversight wasn't costly, it could have been.

When he reached the second floor, he walked down the hallway in search of the men's rest room. He paused at the door of a law office. The sign on the door read, *Michael P. Lanza – Attorney at Law.* The interior behind the glass was dark, but it is not uncommon for employees to begin work at an early hour.

I'd better get going, Jim thought nervously. Just a few more steps down the hall, he discovered the men's restroom. As he entered, he turned on the lights, revealing an enormous room. Its size more closely resembled an athlete's locker room. Like the lobby, it was lavishly appointed in marble and carved oak trim. There were four sinks, each with elegant gold faucets. Off to one side, there was a chair bolted to the floor. Jim wondered if it was used by a barber, or perhaps as a shoe-shine station. The entire restroom was spotless, every nook and cranny polished to a mirror-like finish. Jim noticed a doorless opening. It led to a dressing area. Through another opening, he could see a small portion of what he assumed was the shower area. A row of lockers divided the two spaces. Jim immediately went to the last locker on the right. An unusual looking padlock protected its contents.

Jim frowned. The padlock had a combination dial, but it also had a cylinder for a key. Jim didn't have a key. Remembering that Constantino used Independence Day's date as the basis for the combination, he began to work. He grasped the lock in his left hand and spun the dial with his right. After several spins of the dial in the left direction, he countered to the right, and came to a stop at the number seven. *That's the month,* he thought. Turning the dial a full turn the opposite direction, he lined up the next number, four. *That's the day.* On the final turn of the dial, he brought the number six to rest at the locks pointer. *That's the last digit of the year 1776.* He gave a slight tug on the base of the lock and the shackle disengaged with a welcome click. Jim sighed and removed the padlock. Then he opened the locker door.

Jim withdrew a pen flashlight from his pocket and peered inside the locker. There were two items, a leather pouch containing multiple items, and an accordion style file folder. The file folder was heavy, and about two inches thick. Jim spent no time analyzing the contents, but placed them directly in the duffle bag. He took a final look to make sure he didn't miss anything, before he repositioned the padlock and snapped it shut. Jim knew there was no one in the building, but he felt uneasy. He picked up the bag, and left the building as quickly as he could. He estimated he was only inside for about eight minutes. As he exited the building, he noticed a tall, lanky young man walking in his direction. He was about twenty-two years old, with dark, neatly combed hair. The young man had a cell phone in his hand. He dialed a number and placed the receiver to his ear. Jim didn't think it was possible that he had met the young man before, but somehow he seemed awkwardly familiar.

He immediately put it out of his mind as he crossed the street and headed for the parking lot about a half block away. The young man continued walking his direction, but he didn't cross the street. That put Jim at ease. When he reached the parking lot he noticed something peculiar. The parking lot attendant had been in the lot. He was returning to the ticket booth while talking to someone on his cell. *Who could he be talking to at six-twenty in the morning?* Jim glanced over his shoulder, across the street. The tall, lanky boy still had his phone to his ear.

Were they talking to each other?

Jim nervously made his way to the far end of the lot. He got in his car, slammed the door, and began looking for a place to stow the contents of the bag. He decided against it. He was wasting precious time. *One way or another,* Jim thought, *I'm driving out of here right now.* Then he reached in his wallet and withdrew six dollars, the first hour's parking fee, and started his car. Carefully backing out of his space he started in the direction of the attendant's booth.

"Good morning sir."

"Good morning," Jim said as he reached his arm out the window, "Six dollars—is that correct?"

"Yes it is, but I'll need to see your driver's license and registration."

Jim frowned, "Why?"

"We've had a lot of problems with vehicle theft recently. I just want to make sure you are the owner of the vehicle."

The attendant was a heavy set, middle aged man who looked as if he were of Italian ancestry. He was obviously uneducated, but polite. Although Jim didn't know this man, he could sense that he was uncomfortable about something.

"You know I'm the owner, you just saw me not more than ten minutes ago when I dropped my car off. You gave me this ticket stub," Jim held it up. "It matches the one you put under my wiper." He pointed to it and handed the stub to the attendant with the money. The attendant pretended to study the matching numbers. The tall, lanky boy was still watching from across the street. He was no longer on the phone.

"Yeah, you look like the same guy, all right, but I still need to see some ID—" Jim looked ahead of the car. There was no barricade keeping him there. "—its company policy, and—"

Jim stepped on the gas, and in three seconds, the parking lot was just a reflection in his rearview mirror. Feeling relieved, Jim was about to smile, but he frowned instead. The tall, lanky young man was crossing the street.

Where have I seen that young man before? Where?

Rush hour traffic did add eighty-five minutes to his return trip, but Jim was back in his hotel room by ten fifteen. He changed into his dress clothes and kept his appointment with the Director of IT at a large publishing company in Davenport. Throughout lunch, Jim was troubled by his inability to place where or if he had met the tall, lanky young man. The more he thought of it, the more he was certain that he had seen him before.

The drive home was tense and exhausting. Jim kept thinking about the two men who wanted to know his identity. But why? Did they know he was in the second floor restroom? Did they suspect what he was doing?

There was no way they could know, Jim concluded, *not unless there was surveillance equipment in the room. Surveillance—that's it! The tall, lanky young man, he was Constantino's nephew, the surveillance expert.*

There was a lump in Jim's throat. He almost choked on a mouthful of coffee. *I've been seen. Did Constantino have an opportunity to talk to him before he died?* With the FBI outside his door, he doubted it. *But the locker, did they know what he kept in there? Were all the painstaking precautions I took to leave no trail and the perfect alibi for nothing? Did they get my license plate number? Will they be able to find me?*

Jim's mind was racing during the remainder of his long journey home. He evaluated several possible scenarios as to what might happen next. He did not like some of them.

About thirty miles from Omaha, Jim stopped for gas. While the tank was filling, he opened the trunk to stow the pouch and accordion style folder. The first thing he looked for was the address book, the one containing Constantino's contacts. He found it. It was a black leatherette book with neatly printed pages containing a hundred or more names. *This is the answer,* Jim thought. *Combined with the circuit boards from Constantino's computer, the content of this address book makes me one of the most powerful men on earth.* He recalled the image of Katie's blank stare, her lifeless eyes reflecting the lights of that God forsaken parking lot. *Now I will have my revenge, and then I will do whatever it takes to make the world a better place. So help me God!*

19

ON THIS FRIDAY MORNING, AN ATTRACTIVE YOUTH counselor had far exceeded her threshold for frustration. She loathed seeing this particular patient. *Who is this animal? This boy is evil; he certainly couldn't be a product of the O'Brien family.* She hadn't met Mr. O'Brien, but she had met with Tom's mother twice. Mrs. O'Brien was as close to a saint as Susan Jensen thought she was ever destined to meet. But she certainly didn't know her son; she didn't know him at all.

With the comment this boy had just made, Susan decided it was time to trade this patient for another. Perhaps one of the male counselors would make a swap. But she wasn't letting him go yet, not until she spoke her piece.

"I'm tired of the sexual innuendos, Tom. No, I don't want to hook up with you when you get out of here. No, I don't find you attractive in any way, and my sexual preferences are NONE OF YOUR BUSINESS!"

"Hey, I'm just responding to your body language, that's all."

Susan's cheeks reddened, "What do you mean by that?"

"You know—the way you look at me. I know you find me interesting. I'm pretty sure you'd like to get me in bed."

A glint of rage shone in her hazel eyes, "The way I look at you is with pure disgust. You're lazy, dishonest, disrespectful, and for some reason you feel the world owes you something. Well, let me tell you something, Mr. O'Brien, the world doesn't owe anybody anything—least of all, YOU! You have to make your own way in the world, but not by taking what doesn't belong to you. Your father is a very successful man, and highly respected too, but he earned that respect with honesty and hard work."

"My dad's a fool. His company makes so much money, it's incredible. But he throws it away on his employees, gives them top pay, the best benefits, and big bonuses. Tell me that's not stupid."

"I'll tell you what is stupid, Tom. Your inability to tell the difference between good business and squandering money."

Tom didn't like the comment, "You're kind of a bitch sometimes, aren't you?"

Susan took a deep breath. "Tom, this is my last session with you."

"Really, are you letting me go home?"

"Not hardly, and if I had my way, they would lock you up for a lot of years. Do you hear me—a lot of years!"

"I'm going to have you transferred to a male counselor. I don't think any of the female counselors could put up with your sexual innuendos."

Tom grinned and then purposely stared at her breasts. Susan was clearly uncomfortable. She leaned over to a nearby chair and grabbed her cardigan sweater. "I have never seen a young man treat women so poorly."

"I can treat a woman nice—I'll bet I could treat you really nice." He raised his eyebrows and smiled.

"I mean treat a woman with respect! Anyway, I do not know your father, but your mother is one of the sweetest people I have ever met. I find it hard to believe that you are the product of these fine people. Surely you don't act this way at home?"

With her breasts covered by the sweater, Tom now looked her in the eyes, "I act the way I want to act—period!"

"You don't seem to have any remorse for the things you have done."

"Why should I?"

"You've hurt a lot of people. What about all the personal property you have stolen? Do you plan to make restitution?"

"Not unless I have to."

"You don't feel bad about taking things that don't belong to you?"

"Look, nobody got hurt. I took a few things, that's all."

"Most people work hard to make enough money to buy nice things. How do you think they felt when they found their property was stolen?"

"Pretty stupid, I guess."

Susan looked puzzled, "What do you mean?"

"I imagine they felt pretty stupid for parking their cars in the street, or leaving their garage doors open. If they closed them, they'd still have their stuff."

Susan couldn't believe her ears. The boy didn't even have the decency to lie to her, to tell her what she wanted to hear.

"What about drugs? Do you plan to stay clean once you are released?"

"Sure, probably." The answer was anything but convincing.

"You have been clean for several weeks, Tom. Isn't it good to be able to think clearly?" Susan knew it would take months for the boy to regain the clarity of thought he once had. He probably wouldn't be out a week before he was high again.

"I don't know. I kind of liked being high. It makes you forget your problems—makes you feel like you can do anything."

"What kind of problems did you want to forget, Tom?"

"I dunno, just stuff."

"Do you still have problems you would like to forget?"

"Sure, doesn't everybody?"

"What about the death of your sister? Do you feel any guilt about that?"

Tom's eyes rounded, Susan knew she hit a nerve.

"My sister's death was my dad's fault! He should have called the police earlier, even my mom says so!"

"It was your drug dealer that killed her, Tom. You can't blame this on your father."

Tom jumped to his feet, his fists clenched.

"What do you know, bitch—just what the fuck do you know?"

Susan saw the rage in his eyes. She became afraid for her safety. She pressed the buzzer on her desk.

"It sounds to me like you DO have some remorse, Tom. If you had treated me better, I might have been around long enough to help you deal with it."

Tom smiled again, "When I get out of here you can help me deal with it. I know a great way you can help make all my troubles go away." Susan shuddered as a correctional officer entered the room.

20

IT WAS EIGHT THIRTY IN THE MORNING ON THE FIRST Friday in December. Chatter around the office was unusually high, because at ten o'clock, Jim was going to conduct a brief company meeting. Scott Troia recommended it as a way to lift employee spirits, which had eroded substantially during Jim's three-week absence from work. Jim embraced the idea, and it was an opportunity to announce his new hire, Meg Andrews, who attended college with Miranda Peters. Although Jim reviewed her resume and conducted a short interview, it was Miranda's recommendation that solidified his decision to hire her.

Jim was carefully studying some documents at his desk when Scott walked in.

"Good morning, boss man. How was your trip yesterday?" Jim picked up the short stack of papers he was reading and placed them behind him, on top of an accordion style folder on the credenza.

"Terrible, Scott."

"I'm sorry to hear that Jim, what happened?"

"We picked up another account—more business we don't have enough staff to handle."

Smiling, Scott said, "I should have known. I can't remember the last time you came back empty-handed."

"Well, it's a problem, Scott, a real problem. I can't continue to pick up new accounts without the personnel to staff the projects. We need more people."

"Well, Meg Andrews looks like she'll work out fine."

"I agree, but for the workload we have, we could still use two more people."

"It's only a matter of time before we find them, Jim, at least we have plenty of work."

Jim sighed, "You're right, Scott, I suppose we could have too many employees and not enough work. I should be grateful."

"I don't mean to change the subject, but Linda told me Vince is coming in to pick up Constantino's computer. Is it true?"

"Yes, there is nothing more we can do with it."

"I hope they haven't lost faith in us."

"No, no, of course not!" Jim said sternly. "Actually, Saunders tried to point out to Vince, that this was our first unsuccessful project in fourteen attempts, but I corrected him. I told them both that this was our fourteenth successful project for the FBI. It was simply the first *clean* PC they have given us. We're having lunch, you're welcome to join us if you'd like."

"I'm sorry, Jim. Vince Mitchell is a great guy, but that Frank Saunders freaks me out. I can't be in the same room with that spook for more than five minutes. There's only one thing worse than trying to figure out what he is thinking behind those dark sunglasses."

"What's that?"

"Looking at his eyes when he's not wearing them. He always has this maniacal look in his eyes."

"I've seen that look first hand, Scott, but there's nothing to worry about. Vince is the man in charge, and fortunately, Vince does all of the talking. In fact, he claims to have two new cases for us."

"That's good to hear. Having the FBI top our client list doesn't hurt our image at all."

"You won't get any argument from me."

"Look, Scott, I am a little pressed for time this morning. Are there any issues you need help with today?"

"Not really, I just wanted to tell you how good it is to have you back at the helm."

Jim gave Scott a grateful look. "You were right about keeping busy. Coming back to work was the right thing to do. But you should know I still plan to take several afternoons off over the next few weeks."

Scott nodded, "The important thing is that the employees see you back in the driver's seat, Jim. This company is worthless without you."

"Thanks for the kind words, Scott. Now I have a few things I need to finish. Can I catch up with you in a little while?"

"Sure, I'll see you at the meeting."

As Scott left the room, Jim returned his attention to the stack of papers on the credenza. It was just a small portion of the documentation from Constantino's two inch thick accordion file. Jim spent two hours separating the entire contents last night. He separated Constantino's will and personal documents, which he planned to send to Michael Lanza immediately. He also found a financial ledger and several bank account statements, which he would forward to Lanza as well, as soon as he had time to review them. The documents in front of him were particularly interesting. He was studying an intricate organizational structure of the Constantino family. It not only included family tree information, but the names of bosses, superintendents, and the legitimate and illegitimate businesses they managed.

There was a descriptive paragraph for each family member. The detail was astounding. At the end of some of the male member's descriptions, were codes. Jim was certain he had deciphered the meaning of these codes, but he was looking for confirmation because he knew they were vital to his plan. He was a little nervous about bringing these documents into the office, especially with Vince Mitchell visiting him at noon. But his curiosity and fascination were

overpowering traits of his personality. He could hardly put them down. Jim was searching for a key, something that would confirm the five codes that he had identified so far. After thirty minutes of scrutiny, he was barely closer than when he began. Since he was leaving the office after meeting with the FBI, he decided to conclude his research from home.

At ten o'clock, Jim's eleven employees gathered in the break room. There were lots of smiles. Everyone seemed to be in good spirits after hearing that Jim had gone on a business trip on Monday. Jim poured himself a cup of coffee as his staff located empty seats at three round break tables. Taking a few steps toward a spot he gauged provided the best vantage point to address the group, Jim said, "Good morning, everyone."

There were enthusiastic responses of "good morning" to Jim's salutation. He began on a serious note. "Let me begin by apologizing for my absence during the last three weeks. My family and I remain in somewhat of a crisis after the death of our daughter, Katie. It will probably take years for us to fully recover from our loss, but as my good friend, Scott Troia, pointed out, work can be good medicine. Let me say it's good to be back with my extended family."

There was a brief round of applause from the tables. Jim was touched with emotion. "Yesterday, I had lunch with Henry Stoker, of Cornell-Madison Publishing, in Davenport, Iowa. We worked out the basic infrastructure for a security contract to include all fourteen of their publishing companies. In addition, I have decided it is time for us to offer some of our proprietary software tools to the business community. By doing so, we can more than triple our revenues from this point forward."

Steve Wakeman asked, "Won't selling our software jeopardize our value in these accounts?"

"Not at all, Steve. We are still the experts. Even though we can teach someone how to run the software, and identify the existence of a problem, only we can truly analyze and interpret the results."

"This brings me to a related topic. Finding more experts." Jim opened a plain manila folder and withdrew an envelope. "We are starting an aggressive recruiting program. We need more staff, but as you know, I'm pretty selective. Not just anyone can work for us.

I need to find tremendously intelligent people with your passion and determination for troubleshooting. All of you interface with industry peers on a daily basis, and this is where we need to identify future employees. Miranda Peters recommended that we hire Meg Andrews, one of her classmates from Harvard. Meg begins work here on Monday, and Scott and I believe that she possesses the same high level of skills and professional attributes as the rest of you."

"For her recommendation, I'd like to present Miranda with a check for five thousand dollars." There were gasps among the employees as Jim approached Miranda and handed her the envelope. The stunned look on Miranda's face pleased him. "If Meg is still with us three years from now, Miranda will receive another check for the same amount." The room was charged with excitement. "I hope this incentive will help us build a better company. I am counting on all of you participating in the program. There is nothing I would rather do than write more checks." As his eyes surveyed the room, Jim could tell he hit a home run with the announcement of the new recruiting program. "Now, let's review what we have accomplished during my absence."

For the next twenty minutes, Jim was brought current on most of the projects that had been completed while he was gone. Scott was upbeat as he watched him interface with his employees. *The way he commands loyalty and respect from his employees is effortless,* Scott thought. *He's a natural leader. Everything comes so easy to him. I wonder if there is anything he can't do.* The images of the depressed man he had seen only a week ago were fading into obscurity. The man he was gazing at now appeared to be the same man he had admired for so many years.

By eleven fifteen, the meeting had ended and everyone returned to their desks. Jim was tired and anxious to go home to review Constantino's documents, but he couldn't. Vince Mitchell and agent Frank Saunders were scheduled to arrive at the office in about fifteen minutes. Jim liked Vince. The two men shared a mutual respect for one another. Vince was a former Information Technology Director for a large Midwest manufacturing company. He rose through the corporate ranks at a very young age, but his sense of adventure eventually led him to join the FBI. Within sixteen months of joining the Bureau, Vince was promoted to Director of Computer Forensics for the Midwest region. He had followed Jim's career for years, and the two finally met at a technology symposium in Kansas City six months ago. It followed a keynote speech Jim delivered to a national computer forensics organization. Vince asked Jim to meet with him later that same day and, within two weeks, he had bypassed the usual government red tape to offer Jim a lucrative contract to assist the FBI's Midwest Regional office. In the last five months, Vince had come to depend on Jim's company, CFC, to help him solve some very important cases. Of course, Jim's acutely curious nature was one of the things Vince liked most about him.

21

AT ELEVEN THIRTY SHARP, VINCE MITCHELL AND FRANK Saunders entered the reception area of Computer Forensic Consultants. Linda picked up the phone and announced their arrival. Jim told her to escort them to the storage room. He was waiting for them when they walked into the room.

"Hello, Vince." Jim shook his hand vigorously.

"How are you, Jim?" Vince brandished a warm, genuine smile that Jim found contagious, most of the time.

"I'm fine, thank you."

Vince was not a tall man. Jim estimated his height at about five feet seven inches. He had a young, almost feminine face, which provided a sharp contrast to his pure white hair.

"I am so sorry about your daughter, Katie." Jim was surprised he remembered her name. "Is there anything I can do to help you?"

"Yes, you can find the boys who murdered her and put them behind bars."

"Unfortunately, I do not get involved in this type of case, but I spoke to a good friend of mine in the Bureau, Tom Mackie, and he has agreed to help you as much as he can." Vince handed Jim a business card. "I'd call him as soon as possible."

Jim's face showed a sincere look of gratitude.

"Thanks, Vince. I really do need all the help I can get. The Omaha Police still have no clue as to where—"

"Is this Constantino's computer?"

"Frank, you're interrupting Jim."

"Oh, I'm sorry. I thought we were here on business, not to discuss O'Brien's personal problems."

"Well, I'll tell you what, Frank, I'll stay here and discuss Jim's personal problems while you load Constantino's computer in the car. And please do it quickly. We have lunch reservations at noon, and I don't want to be late."

The sunglasses hid his eyes, but every bit of his rigid body language said Frank was steaming mad. He picked up the CPU chassis, and made it a point to reach directly in front of Jim to pick up the keyboard, mouse, and cables.

"I'll be right back," he said in his usual cold tone of voice as he left the room.

"I've been anxious to ask you something, Jim. Frank's attitude toward you seems to have changed dramatically since you met him in Chicago the night Constantino died. Is there something I should know about?"

"I'll fill you in later, Vince, but not here, not now."

"So there is something between you—bad feelings perhaps?"

"Yes, but I'd like to discuss it privately."

"I understand. Can I call you later today?"

"Call my cell. I'm headed home right after lunch."

"Good enough, Jim. Now let me give you these, before I forget." Vince opened his brief case and removed two thick envelopes.

"There are background summaries for each of the hard disks in these envelopes. The reports will provide you with the basic information for each case and the nature of the information we are looking for. Are you sure you don't need the entire computer?"

"Yes, Vince, space is getting very tight here, and it is actually easier to manage a small hard disk than an entire computer."

"Great, just sign these release forms and we can go get some food. I'm starving."

Frank returned from loading the CPU in the car. Jim and Vince walked right past him. Vince turned around and said, "Don't forget the computer monitor, Frank." He looked at Jim and winked.

On the way home from lunch, Jim contemplated just how much his relationship with Frank Saunders had soured. Neither man liked the other from the onset of their first meeting, but now there was contempt between them. Saunders continued to interrupt Vince and Jim's conversation throughout lunch until Vince finally asked him to leave. This gave Jim an opening to offer more detail as to what transpired in Chicago the night he interviewed Constantino.

He explained that Constantino kept his interest in a complex story about a seemingly far-fetched technology that allowed him to retain complete anonymity when web surfing, using e-mail, or FTP sites. He said Constantino's physical state deteriorated so rapidly, that by the time Jim began to suspect his story may be fictional, it was too late. Constantino confirmed his suspicions when he called Frank into the room and told him how he manufactured the entire story. He made fun of Frank and taunted him ruthlessly. When Frank left the room he was infuriated. He lashed out at Jim for failing to unravel the secret to how Constantino had evaded detection of any kind on his computer. Frank had already told Vince the story, albeit a bit more exaggerated, but there was one thing he wasn't told.

Jim wanted to remain anonymous and asked to leave the hospital from a rear exit rather than through the front doors. Constantino told Jim that his men would be posted all over the building. Frank not only forced Jim to leave from the front door, but made no effort to give him any sort of concealment or protection. Vince was clearly upset to hear this.

"You have my sincerest apologies, Jim. You can be assured that Frank will be reprimanded. It's the FBI's responsibility to protect our associates at all times."

Jim said, "It's water under the bridge, Vince. I made it home safe and sound."

"But things may have turned out differently. Frank acted out of anger. He needs to learn to keep his personal feelings separate from his professional duties. Just so you know, Jim, I didn't hand-pick Saunders. I inherited him. This isn't the first time he's acted irresponsibly." Vince stopped short. "Well, let's just say he'll be reprimanded, and leave it at that."

Jim and Vince finished lunch while discussing some of the other cases they were working on, and then Jim left for home. As he pulled into his driveway he had one last thought regarding Saunders. *Oh well, our relationship really can't get much worse—I hope.*

22

AS JIM ENTERED THE FOYER, HE WAS GREETED BY HIS youngest daughter Molly.

"Hi Daddy!"

"Hi baby, how are you?"

"Daddy—don't call me a baby!"

"I'm sorry Molly. You're a big girl aren't you?"

"Yeah, and I'm gonna be a mom when I grow up."

"I'll bet you'll be the best mom in the world."

"Me too."

"Where's your mother?"

"She's in the bedroom."

"Let's go see her, okay?"

Jim took Molly's hand and led her into the master bedroom. Peg was smoothing the wrinkles from the bedspread when she saw him.

"Hi Jim, I wasn't sure I'd see you before six."

"I'm only working half days, remember?"

"Oh, that's right. I guess it just doesn't seem normal to see you leave work early. How did everything go at the office?"

"Everything was fine. I'm just not ready to put in full days yet. I have a lot of personal things to take care of."

"What kind of things?"

"I still need to see if I can identify the stolen jewelry and coins I found in Tom's room as well as a handful of other things I haven't followed-up on."

Peg didn't look at Jim directly when she spoke, "I was thinking maybe we could have some time to talk. We really don't talk much any more."

"That's a great idea, Peg. We should set some time aside later this week to do that."

Jim gave Peg an emotionless kiss on the cheek and then rushed to his study. Peg fluffed one of the decorative pillows on their bed as Molly watched. She began to knead the pillow like bread dough. Molly studied the look on her mother's face. "Are you sad Mommy?"

"Yes dear, mommy is a little sad, but I'll be okay."

"Is it because Katie died?"

Peg took Molly into her arms and squeezed her tightly, *It's because two people died sweetheart,* she thought to herself.

In his office, Jim spread several papers across his long credenza. He opened Constantino's ledger and began to study payments made for services rendered. The amounts of many of the transactions were substantial, some exceeding fifty-thousand dollars. The name of the individual or business was clearly marked in the *Payee* column. There were codes in the comments column. Each code followed a specific order. Jim recognized *EFT* as electronic funds transfer, and *CHK* as check. Then Jim saw the familiar codes he was looking for, the same codes he saw in the description paragraphs for some family members.

The codes had no more than three letters and examples included HIT, SGD, DRG, FNC, PRT, BUY, SEL, GFT, and several others. Jim had already concluded that the codes were not meant to be cryptic, but were simply shorthand abbreviations. The comment column was small and this was Constantino's method of cramming a lot of information into a small area. HIT stood for a killing, a mafia hit. His eyes were drawn to a specific comment line. The transaction was an electronic funds transfer for twenty-five thousand dollars, deposited into the account of someone named Mario Manetti. In the comment section he read the codes HIT, LANG, 081609, EFT, :104000970: 648959, A01.

Using the internet and the Google search engine, Jim had deciphered the entire scenario in about twenty minutes. A man named William Lang was murdered shot in the back in mid-August. Lang was the CEO of LSI Industries, the company, Jim recalled, that offered Constantino a royalty in exchange for Dr. Andrew Simmons stolen virtual memory chip design. Oddly though, the body of the Chicago based CEO was found off a pier in Miami.

Apparently, Manetti was paid twenty five thousand dollars for the hit. He was paid by electronic funds transfer to routing number 104000970, and account number 648959. The hit on Lang was made on August 16, 2009. All of the data corresponded to the simple abbreviations in the comment line. Jim examined smaller transactions and found that GFT stood for gift. He found such an example in a one thousand dollar check to Christine Vecchio for graduation. Locating her name in the address book, Jim discovered that she was Constantino's niece. Jim thought about Constantino once more. How was it that a single ledger could contain such thoughtful, heart felt gifts, mingled with transactions for murders, drug deals, and thefts?

Jim now felt that he could unravel the rest of the codes in a day or two, as well as how to control the organization's finances. Every family member had a bank account at the same Chicago bank. Jim knew there had to be a family insider at the bank, because all deposits over ten thousand dollars are required to be reported to the Federal Government. He was certain that this was not occurring. Scanning the descriptive family member paragraphs for about forty minutes yielded the answer Jim was looking for. Jim had located the name of the family banker, Max Walker, who had married Tony

Constantino's sister, Isabelle. Soon, Jim would contact Walker and open at least two accounts under an alias.

At about seven thirty that evening, Jim went for a walk around the lake in his neighborhood. It was freezing cold, but he didn't seem to notice. His head was spinning from all that he had learned about Constantino's organization in the last several hours. Jim had already put most of the final pieces of the puzzle together. He found four bank books, one from a Swiss Bank. When Jim learned that the balance of this account contained well over two billion dollars, he could no longer concentrate. This was the account used for the *Great Cyber Robbery*, and for the moment, he controlled it all. He now had the ability to communicate with and compensate any member of Constantino's family. He could, in fact, take control of the very position that Tony intended Jimmy Bonaiuto to assume.

Could he do it? Would Constantino's family cooperate? Jim wasn't certain, but he controlled the money. Without it, he was pretty certain the family would stagnate and wither away. He was trying to fathom just how powerful Constantino was, and in turn, estimate the degree of power he would wield. Jim swore to himself he would make the world a better place, but again, he was struggling with his own corruption. He knew he couldn't simply force his views of morality on America, but perhaps he could control the factors that influenced morality—Lawmakers.

He planned to have them impose stiff censorship on all forms of media, cut off the sources of sex and violence on TV. He would have inappropriate video games, books, and magazines stripped from store shelves, and change the laws that allowed corruption to gestate. Perhaps most important of all, he would control news headlines that would force everyday people to consider joining his cause in this righteous battle. Jim was a conservative. He had nothing against liberals, but he felt that the extreme liberal movement had promoted the moral decay of America in tiny doses of what they call *tolerance*. Therefore, they would be the main focus of his attack. Those who refused to conform to his wishes would be killed, and the Moral Mafia would claim the credit for each killing as a form of intimidation to other liberals.

Unless he used the analogy of fighting a war against evil, Jim knew he would be unable to continue his mission. His conscience was already mounting another battle within him. He kept thinking about Katie and Tom. What happened to them was indeed a direct result of a society that was failing. If he could use Constantino's wealth and organization to force a change, regardless of the means, he could keep other families from having to suffer the same fate. This was the best justification he had come up with to-date. Jim's hands were getting cold. He put them in his coat pockets and picked up the pace of his walk. In his mind he repeated a phrase over and over, *This is for the greater good of mankind.*

23

THERE WAS AN AUDIBLE TWANG EMANATING FROM the vibrating handle of the rosewood letter opener. Jimmy Bonaiuto had just jammed it into the top of a mahogany conference table. Its ornate carvings were just a blur.

"I want this son-of-a-bitch found by the end of the week, do you hear me? The end of the week!" All eyes focused on the sharp gold blade as the twang of the vibrations dulled to a hum. Bonaiuto had lost his temper again, and appeared likely to explode into flames.

Yesterday he had thrown a marble cigarette lighter at the wall, breaking the glass in a picture frame. Bonaiuto didn't possess the even temper of his predecessor, yet Tony Constantino had been much more feared by the family. He was also deeply admired. But Tony was dead, and circumstances were not good for his successor.

No one responded. No one knew where to look for the man Bonaiuto could only describe as the head of the Moral Mafia. The conference room was built to accommodate eighteen people. Forty-two were present for this meeting. David Manetti, the family's young surveillance expert, stood in the corner of the room and listened with the others as Bonaiuto continued.

"He's got our bank accounts, our real estate holdings, and the families' wills and trusts! He's got Tony's fuckin' address book, for God's sake! Do you guys know what that means? He can make any one of us! He's got enough information to send us all away for the rest of our lives."

Angelo Manetti spoke. He was now number two and the only family member close enough to Bonaiuto to get away with stating the obvious.

"Jimmy, we got nuthin' to go on, except for the name of his organization. Who the hell is this *Moral Mafia* anyway? Is this a new Chicago family, or what?"

Bonaiuto was clueless, but he did his best to keep his composure and play the role of a commanding don, a figure worthy enough to succeed Constantino.

"No, I don't think so. I think the Corsetto's or the Scarpello's got to Tony's files. I think they are fucking with us. The question is—how the hell did they get them?"

David watched his father with pride. He was one of two Manetti's who were included in the organization's trusted inner circle. Angelo Manetti ran the family's most profitable business unit. His drug connections to Colombia, Russia, and most recently China were legendary. David's uncle, Mario, was the family's most trusted hit man. Angelo wanted his son to participate in the family business too, but he insisted in providing a safe role for him. David had graduated from the University of Chicago seven months ago, with a degree in computer science. During that period he devoted all of his spare time learning about the multitude of electronic devices used for surveillance. The family was beginning to rely heavily on his expertise. Angelo knew his son could work safely behind the scenes, while his function would gradually increase in importance to the family. David worked long hours to satisfy the family's needs. He wanted nothing more than to be inducted into the inner circle.

He thought of little else.

"How do we know anybody got to Tony's files?" Angelo asked. Can we prove it?" Bonaiuto removed a small box from his pocket, "I think this is proof enough!" He removed a large ring with a massive diamond and placed it on the little finger of his right hand and raised it in the air. "It's Tony's alright," Angelo said.

Bonaiuto fumed, "He was supposed to leave it to me as head of the family. I received it along with Tony's will in the mail with a note from the Moral Mafia." Bonaiuto's face got ugly. "The fucking mail!"

David Manetti almost spoke, but decided to hold his tongue. He had seen the ring on Tony's finger in the hospital the night he died. But if he said even a single word about it, the pressure would be on him to deliver up the wise guy who took it. *I'd better wait until I have some concrete evidence,* he thought.

"You said you spoke to this guy on the phone yesterday, Jimmy. What did he say?"

"He said he's going to keep everything for a while. He said if we cooperate with him, he'll return all the goods within six months. Well I got news for you guys; the Moral Mafia has our operating capital. We can't get by for six months without those bank accounts. I want all unnecessary spending to stop as of right now!"

Angelo stroked his chin, "What'd he mean—cooperate?"

The veins on Bonaiuto's temples bulged. Shadows exaggerated them greatly. "I don't know yet. He wants to set up another call with me and Michael Lanza."

Angelo lowered his voice, "Maybe you can trace the call."

"Yeah maybe, but I'm guessin' this guy's too smart for that. But just to be safe, I'll want your boy, David, to set things up. Is he here?"

David raised his hand from the corner of the room.

"I wanna' talk to you after the meeting." David nodded. *Who could have gotten that ring from Tony?* he thought. *I was there the whole night.*

24

A PEACEFUL SNOW WAS FALLING THIS MONDAY EVENING, just six days before Christmas. The snowflakes were enormous and blanketed tree limbs and rooftops with several inches of fresh powder. Miranda Peters and CFC's newest recruit, Meg Andrews, admired the sight from the bay window of the O'Brien's living room.

"I've never seen snowflakes so big have you, Miranda?"

"No, it's not like a typical New York snowfall is it?"

"Oh, I wouldn't say that. I can remember a lot of snowfalls like this one as a child, but ours were much more scenic. The countryside in upstate New York is quite a bit more interesting than Omaha's."

"I'll bet I can show you a couple of views that would compare with upstate New York."

"Oh Jim, I hope you don't think I'm making fun of your quaint little town."

"Not at all, Meg, but this quaint little town of ours has twenty times the population of any town close to where you grew up. I'd have to say Omaha is a booming metropolis compared to your old neck of the woods."

"That's true, but I did spend the last four years in New York City."

I'm sorry to hear that, Jim thought.

"Then you should have a deep appreciation of what Omaha has to offer. It's a good sized city with a variety of cultures and economies. It's not overly crowded, and it's probably one of the best places in the country to raise a family."

"The mayor of Omaha must require all of its residents to say that Jim, because I hear it a lot here."

"Just give it another six months, Meg; you'll be saying it yourself."

Miranda gave Jim an adoring glance. "We were just admiring the beautiful snow. It makes everything look so clean, doesn't it?"

Jim was captivated by her eyes; they were so innocent, yet provocative.

"Yes, there is nothing like a fresh snowfall." A few seconds passed, and his eyes were still locked with hers. "I—I hope it doesn't get too deep, it's coming down heavy and it's only seven o'clock."

Meg hadn't seen the way they looked at each other, although she suspected that Miranda was developing a crush on Jim. "Don't worry, Jim. We won't abandon your Christmas party because of a little snow—that is, if the liquor supply holds up."

"Thanks Meg, I don't think that will be a problem."

"Of course, if you would hire a few eligible bachelors, I could be convinced to stay even later."

Jim grinned, "Now Meg, there are several fine bachelors here this evening. In fact, why don't I call Howard Beekler over?"

Meg stepped in Jim's path and looked him squarely in the eyes. With an animated grin and a facetious tone, she said, "Don't you dare! That would require me to drink a lot more liquor than you likely have in your cabinet." She looked at Miranda's wine glass. "You need a refill, sweetie, let me get it for you."

As Meg walked in the direction of Jim's wet bar, Miranda stood up and took a step closer to Jim. "You have a lovely home. How do you keep it so organized with eleven—ah—so many children?" Miranda's cheeks reddened. Jim and Peg no longer had eleven children. She wished she could rephrase her question.

"Its okay, Miranda; it's a little clumsy for all of us at times. To answer your question, it's a full-time job, I can assure you. Peg has learned to deal with the chaos over the years. That includes hauling the kids in a million different directions. I'm not certain I understand how she does it either."

"Well, you're a lucky man, Jim, and Peg's a lucky woman."

Jim began to blush. He felt a little warm. "Your time is coming, Miranda. You are going to be one hell of a catch for the right man."

Miranda smiled warmly, "Do you really think so, Jim?"

"I do. You're attractive, intelligent, and I might add, you have a very sweet disposition."

Miranda looked deeper into Jim's eyes as if she wanted to read his every thought. Jim turned and faced the window. "My two oldest daughters found perfect companions. It always happens when you least expect it."

Miranda's voice was soft, "I don't know if my Mr. Right is out there."

"That's nonsense, Miranda. The guys must be lined up to go out with you."

"Oh, I don't have a problem finding dates. I just can't find someone I want to go out with a second time. Most men are selfish and immature. And they only want one thing—."

Jim nodded, "I know what you mean. With nine—I mean eight girls; I lose a fair amount of sleep thinking about the creeps they might get involved with. It's unsettling."

"I knew you understood, Jim. You are very insightful."

"You know I want the best for you, Miranda, and for all my extended family. Let me know if there is ever anything I can do to help."

Miranda's smile made her glow, "You are the kindest man I've ever met, Jim. That's one of the things I love most about you."

154   She could hardly move any closer to Jim than she already was, so

when she started to lean toward him, he disconnected from the conversation.

"It's almost time to eat. I'd better see if Peg needs any help with the food."

25

MARIO MANETTI SAT BEHIND A WORN CONFERENCE table in an abandoned Omaha coffee warehouse. He had a fondness for abandoned buildings. They were dark, desolate, and set a mood of fear, an important tool of his trade. The two boys sitting across from him were indeed afraid. They followed his orders and stared only at the floor. A mammoth looking figure opened the door and flung a black boy toward them. The boy's thigh hit the table hard. He planted his palms on the table and grimaced in pain. With clenched teeth, he looked at the other two boys, whose facial expressions were now filled with horror. Seeing the fear in their faces didn't help Deacon Reynolds retain his composure.

"Carlos, Mikey, wass going on man—wass this all about?" Neither boy answered. They returned their gazes to the floor.

Manetti studied Deacon. He was short, and in his mid- teens, but he had a stocky build. A deep gash marred the left cheek of his face. With a comment to his gargantuan partner, Manetti professed his initial impression of the crude looking young man.

"This one has no manners either, John Henry. Perhaps he needs a lesson like the other boys received." Without looking up, the blond boy started crying, almost gasping for air between sobs. Manetti ignored him.

"What's your name, boy?"

"Who wants to know?" Deacon answered. His tone implied an attempt to maintain his stature and dignity in front of his two friends. That was a mistake. John Henry took three steps and backhanded Deacon so hard he skidded sideways across the table and onto the floor on the other side.

Manetti directed his eyes down to the floor where the boy rubbed his jaw. "Do you know why we call him John Henry? It's not just because he is a giant. He's as strong as any three men combined. And every time you speak without being spoken to, or answer my questions unsatisfactorily, he's going to inflict a great deal of pain on you—do you understand?"

The boy did not get up, but rolled to one side and softly said, "Yes."

"Good, so you aren't as dumb as you look. Now, what is your name?"

"D-Deacon, Deacon Reynolds."

"That's much better. Now, have a seat next to your friends."

Deacon got to his knees, then used the edge of the table to hoist himself up. He walked around the table and sat next to Carlos. Manetti reached for a plastic bag on the chair next to him. There was a heavy clunk when he set the bag on the table.

"John Henry, pour these boys a drink."

John Henry grasped two bottles, each wrapped in their own brown bag, and slid the bag off the ornate bottle. It was an Italian wine. He slid the bottle toward Manetti. Next, he filled three paper cups to the brim with a clear drink from the bottle still sheathed in brown paper. The three boys exchanged puzzled glances as John Henry set a paper cup in front of each of them. Manetti opened the decorative bottle and poured into two cups until they were one quarter full.

"Shall we have a drink with our friends?" The cup Manetti handed to John Henry seemed to completely disappear in his massive hand. Manetti said, "Let's drink to their resourcefulness and ingenuity. Here's to you, gentlemen." He raised his glass in a toast. The boys raised their glasses slightly, and followed his lead by taking a drink of the colorless liquor. They all swallowed hard. Mikey began coughing.

"Oh come now boys, I would hardly call that a drink. A real man can down an entire glass without blinking an eye." Two of the boys were still struggling to breathe. Manetti paused long enough to let them gain their composure. When he had their complete attention, he reached in his shoulder holster producing a 9mm pistol. He set it on the table's edge.

"Let's try it again."

Once more, Manetti raised his glass, and then put it to his lips. They hesitantly joined him. He drank slowly and continuously, watching the boys to make sure they finished the entire glass. When they were finished, he smiled and watched all three boys hack and cough while attempting to catch their breath.

"Do you boys know why you are here?"

No one heard his question, or if they had, they were unable to answer. Each of them sat wriggling in their chairs. Unable to breathe, Mikey fell to the floor, as if sprawling out would help. A few moments passed, and Manetti heard a wheezing sound as Mikey finally inhaled. Manetti repeated the question. Carlos and Mikey answered by shaking their heads from side to side. Although Deacon's throat was still burning from the liquor, he tried to respond. He couldn't.

Manetti watched them writhe in agony for another minute.

"Someone wants you boys dead. Now, what could you have possibly done to make someone want to kill you?"

"Nothin' sir," Deacon said in a raspy voice, "we ain't done nuthin to nobody."

"I believe you boys, but I have a contract with your names on it. What am I supposed to do?"

The boys looked at each other with wide eyes. Deacon spoke quickly, "Just let us go! We won't tell nobody, we'll just disappear—no one will ever know!"

"I'll tell you what, let's have another drink and we'll discuss your options. Refills, John Henry!"

Manetti poured another drink for himself and his associate. The boys braced themselves as they watched John Henry fill their cups to the edge of the rim.

"Let's drink to second chances."

This time, the boys raised their glasses a little higher in the air. There was no question as to why they were cooperating. They undoubtedly understood the words, *second chances,* and were hopeful they would live to see another day. The boys didn't take their eyes off Manetti, as he slowly emptied his cup. They finished theirs just like the first drink. It took two minutes for them to catch their breath and compose themselves. Mikey was turning pale. All three boys looked sick and were still thrashing about their chairs when Manetti continued.

"Now, let's discuss second chances. Which of you is the best driver?"

Quickly, Deacon gurgled, but no words came out, so he raised his hand.

"And you boys know this neighborhood pretty well, don't you?"

With tears streaming down his cheeks, Deacon forced an answer. "Yes sir, we grew up here."

"Do you know the location of the Alliant Tire Company?"

"It's just down the hill by the river, 'bout three blocks from here."

"That's correct. And that's where the contest will end."

Deacon's eyes narrowed. "Contest?"

"That's right boys, John Henry would be content to finish off the three of you right here and now, but I think you should have a sporting chance, don't you agree?" A sporting chance was better than no chance at all. All three nodded.

Mikey said, "Thank you sir."

"Now, here are the rules. I have two cars waiting for us. The three of you will take one car, John Henry and I will take the other. We will all drive to Alliant Tire. There, you will find an orange flag planted in the ground at the far end of the parking lot. If you can reach that flag before I put a bullet in the driver's head, I'll let all three of you go. Is that clear?"

Deacon frowned, his face became ugly. He was sweating and he removed the nylon stocking from his head.

"That doesn't sound like much of a chance to me."

"John Henry, show Mr. Deacon the alternative."

John Henry reached for the pistol on the table in front of Manetti. It looked like a toy in his hand. He pointed it at Deacon's head and cocked the trigger. Deacon's eyes immediately lost their ugliness, and began to well with tears. He looked exactly like the frightened little boy he was.

"Okay, we'll do it!"

"Good, let's drink on it. John Henry—fill their glasses."

This time the tasteless liquor didn't quite reach the half full level in their cups. The bottle was empty. Manetti handed John Henry a cup he exchanged for his gun. He reached into his left pocket and produced a long, thick barrel. Screwing it to his pistol, he continued to speak.

"All right boys, this final toast is very special. Do you know why?"

The boys shook their heads, no.

"Because it may well be the last toast you ever make. We are going to do our best to kill the three of you before you reach the flag. In order to save yourselves, you are going to have to drive very fast to stay ahead of us. The more distance you put between us, the more difficult it will be for me to shoot and hit the driver. Does everyone understand?"

All three boys nodded.

"Good, then let's drink a toast to your success. May you boys reach the flag quickly and safely."

Mario Manetti and John Henry finished the equivalent of a shot glass from their cups with a quick flick of their wrists. Manetti leaned back in his chair. There was a satisfied look on his face as he watched the boys struggle to devour the last drink. Deacon finished first, followed by Carlos, and then Mikey. Mikey returned his cup to chin height and began to gag.

"If you vomit, I'll shoot you here kid!" Those were the first words John Henry spoke since they entered the room. Mikey lowered his head and clasped the edges of the table with both hands. He was concentrating, swallowing repeatedly to prevent himself from gagging. The liquor he just drank had already reached the back of his throat. Finally, Mikey took a deep breath and relaxed a little.

"Give them each a glass of soda, and a few minutes to compose themselves. Is everything else in order, John Henry?"

"Yes, everything."

Manetti headed toward the door, carrying an unnaturally long gun. He said; "I'll be in the garage when you're ready," and then he disappeared. John Henry reached into the plastic bag and retrieved a can of soda pop. He split it evenly into the three glasses.

"Drink up, boys."

All three welcomed the non-alcoholic beverage, and consumed it quickly. What the boys didn't know is that the soda would act as a catalyst, speeding up the process of alcohol absorption.

John Henry collected their paper cups, the soda can, and the liquor bottles. He wiped them clean and inserted them back into the plastic grocery bag. When he removed the wrapping from the clear liquor bottle, Mikey could make out the brand name on the label, *EVERCLEAR*.

John Henry went to the door, opened it, and peeked around the corner. Mikey whispered to the others, "Jesus, no wonder I feel so woozy. That stuff's a hundred and ninety proof!" John Henry stood in the doorway for ten minutes, and then he followed the boys to the garage, and to Mario Manetti, who was on the phone. The unsteady boys were already clearly drunk. Only fear kept their behavior in check.

Manetti concluded his conversation, "Give us three minutes, Mike. We'll pick you up shortly."

They stood before two vehicles in the dimly lit maintenance garage. One was a black, late model Mustang, and the other, a black Lincoln Town Car. John Henry opened the passenger door of the Mustang, and threw the bag containing the bottles and cups into the back seat. He looked at Mikey and said, "Get in!" Mikey crawled into the back seat and nearly collapsed. Then John Henry barked the same order at Deacon and Carlos who climbed into the front driver and passenger seats. Once in the Town Car, John Henry started the engine and pulled forward into position, just outside the warehouse garage. He turned on his headlights and waited. Enormous snowflakes seemed to fluoresce in the path of the headlight beams. Manetti approached the driver's door of the Mustang. Handing Deacon the keys, he said, "Remember, kid, speed is the key. Good luck!" He lingered a moment to make certain Deacon saw him chamber a round in his 9mm. As Manetti walked in the direction of the Town Car, Deacon started the engine.

Alone and able to speak freely, Carlos said, "Shit man, I can't see straight—there's no way we're gonna beat those guys to the flag."

Deacon was intense, "Shut the fuck up dude! I need to concentrate!" Before Manetti could open his car door, Deacon had floored the gas pedal, squealing the tires. Just outside the garage the Mustang made contact with the fresh snow. As Deacon reached the driveway's end, he tried to turn right onto Pierce Street. He was moving too fast, and the car slid straight hitting the curb hard. Shaken and gripped with fear, he quickly regained control and pointed the car's nose downhill, east, toward the Missouri River. He drove over the curb and sidewalk and accelerated slowly at first, but the car quickly gained speed. Carlos turned around in his seat to see the Town Car pull out into the street.

"They're coming!"

"I can see them in my mirror, you dumb shit. We've got a half a block lead on em." Deacon passed the first intersection and almost as quickly passed the second. As he approached the final intersection just ahead of Alliant Tire's parking lot, he was struck by a frightening thought. He screamed it to the others, "No matter how the contest ends, those guys ain't lettin' us go, so I'm gonna' grab that flag—then we're takin' off! Gonna' just keep going".

They flew by Alliant Tire's sign and onto the parking lot. They didn't even notice Sloan standing by the chain link gates. The Mustang's headlights lit up the target they sought. "There's the orange flag," Carlos screamed triumphantly. It's at the far end!" The far end soon became the near end, and Deacon slammed on the brakes. Nothing. When the brakes didn't respond he stood on the brake pedal and arched his back frozen in a rigid position. Carlos watched Deacon's every move. When the brakes didn't bite, he stretched both arms across the dash attempting to brace for the impending crash. Both boys screamed. The Mustang had reached about sixty miles-per-hour and was still picking up speed by the time they passed the orange flag. A second later they were airborne. The sensation must have been frightening in the darkness, wondering at which moment they would plunge into the river. The impact was violent, throwing Deacon and Carlos into the windshield. The glass cracked where Carlos's head made contact.

Mikey groaned from the back seat floor. Having been in a prone position his body had slammed against the front seats upon impact. "What's going on, man?" There was no answer. He fidgeted trying to right himself. He didn't know where he was. He had no concept of which way was up, but he knew what ice cold water felt like. It was engulfing him. He screamed in discomfort. He screamed in fear, but he couldn't seem to sit upright.

The Town Car had slowed down and stopped at Alliant Tire's entrance. Mike Sloan was already rolling the second section of the front gate across the entrance.

"Stupid punks, huh?" said John Henry.

"Yes, they never question the contest, do they?" said Manetti. All they can see is a way out—a second chance. It works every time."

Mike Sloan joined them in the car, "Can you turn up the heat, John Henry? It's fucking cold out there." Manetti took a last look at the tire tracks leading across the parking lot to the river.

"I don't know what those boys did, but I have a feeling Omaha's streets are going to be a little cleaner tonight. Let's go home boys. Chicago's a long way from here."

26

AT TIMES THROUGHOUT THE EVENING, THE LAUGHTER was deafening, especially during the gag gift exchange, an employee tradition Jim started three years ago. With all the employees still gathered in the living room, Jim looked at the clock on the mantel. It read nine forty-five. He rushed into the adjoining study and snatched a bundle of envelopes on his desk.

As he re-entered the living room, he said, "Okay everyone, it's time for your real Christmas gift!" Peg took a seat next to the fireplace. Everyone else found the chairs they had just vacated.

Jim passed out two envelopes to each employee. He asked everyone to open the large envelope first. As they did, he explained its purpose.

"This is a rewards catalog. In the future, I plan to use it for small bonuses to say thanks for a job well done. As part of your Christmas gift, you have all been given enough points to redeem for the most expensive item in the catalog. Of course, you can order multiple smaller gifts. I hope you like it."

"These gifts are wonderful," Linda Simmons said. "It's going to be difficult to make a selection."

"I'm glad you feel that way, I was looking for something to satisfy everyone, married or single, and this looked like it fit the bill."

Miranda hadn't opened her envelope; she was enjoying watching the reaction of the others.

Mike Smart grinned, "Hey, Howard, here's your chance to get that new Smart Phone you were talking about."

Howard could barely contain himself, "Where do you see it?"

"Try page forty-two, lower left corner." Howard quickly thumbed his way to page forty-two. The smile that appeared on his face told Jim the idea of using a catalog was a good choice. Everyone had forgotten about the second envelope.

"There is one more gift," Jim said as he stood up. "But before you open it, I need to explain the way it works. This envelope contains a Christmas bonus. Although I hope to make this an annual gift, bonuses come from profits, so there is no guarantee you will receive one every year. There is a base bonus; each of you receives this amount. There is also a multiplier based on our profits, and the number of years you have been with the company. The longer you stay with us, the larger your bonus will become. I hope this will help with your holiday expenses."

Envelopes were quickly opened. Scott Troia looked like a child as he opened his. Heads were bobbing, eyebrows were raised, and the group became almost solemn. Scott lowered his envelope, "This is a generous bonus, Jim."

"We had a good year. I'll repeat what I said a moment ago, there is no guarantee we will ever do this again. If we continue to work hard, I'll make certain the tradition continues." Miranda had not opened hers, Meg noticed. "Aren't you curious, Miranda?"

"Not at all, Meg, I know it will be more than I deserve." She stood up and looked at her co-workers, "Am I the only one who feels like I have the best employer in the world? When I tell my friends about CFC, they can't believe it. They can't believe how much I look forward to going to work each day. The bonuses, the gifts, the perks, they are all fine, but I am just grateful to work for such a wonderful company, a place that appreciates me and makes me feel important." Her eyes were welling up with tears. "Thank you, Jim, thanks so much for caring about us."

Scott Troia was stunned by Miranda's emotional outburst. *This is a Christmas party,* he thought, *why is she so emotional?* He acted quickly and picked up his glass.

"Miranda is right; I think we should have a toast to Jim and Peg. They've worked hard to build the company we work for."

Randy Burks was usually pretty quiet, but he had consumed his fair share of libations for the evening.

"Here here!" he said in a boisterous voice. Everyone reached for a glass, and all were raised to acknowledge their hosts.

Jim walked over to Peg and handed her a glass. She, too, was caught up in the emotion of the moment. As everyone drank in their honor, Jim wondered how Manetti had fared this evening.

27

JIM HEADED TO THE BREAK ROOM COFFEE POT FOR A much needed second cup of coffee. He filled the new stainless steel mug he received from Tom for Christmas to the brim. Actually, it was a gift from Peg, but she labeled it from Tom, as she had done with several other gifts for the children. Although Tom was allowed to call home on Christmas day, he kept the call short. He sounded much like his old self, and Jim thought he sensed a little remorse in his voice.

As he placed the lid on the cup, Randy Burks and Charlie Ford were entering the break room from the front entrance. The two employees were good friends inside the office, but their political views were polarized in opposite directions.

With newspaper in hand, Charlie said, "Have any of you seen this?" He plopped the *Omaha World-Herald* newspaper on the table occupied by Linda Simmons. Jim approached the table and read the headline:

MORAL MAFIA PUTS AMERICA ON NOTICE

"What is the Moral Mafia?" Jim asked.

"You have to read it for yourself. There is no way I could possibly explain it."

Jim sat in a chair he had moved close to Linda. He noted that the entire front page of the January seventeenth newspaper was in bold typeset. They both began to read the front page together.

Read this carefully America! You have been put on notice by the Moral Mafia. Who is the Moral Mafia? As you read ahead and understand our mission, you will be inclined to assume that this is a hoax, or that this was written by a madman. I assure you that this is not the case. To make any assumptions with regard to this organization could be deadly for those who choose to ignore our demands.

Our country is in a state of moral decline. Our society has grown tolerant of sex, violence, and corruption. Our feeble government has become ineffective at protecting its citizens from the extreme liberal movement, which has long poisoned us, and now poisons the minds of our children.

Our forefathers fought for our freedom, but never intended these freedoms to harm others. We established laws to protect our citizens from violence and acts of immoral behavior. The constitution was mingled with Christian beliefs which have long since disappeared from our classrooms and public institutions. The removal of God and his commandments from our society has left us corrupt and confused. There has been no leadership to correct the immoral path we have traveled for several decades. So, from this day forward, the Moral Mafia will provide a new direction for America. Our mission is to protect the family and nurture it by restoring law and order. We will establish moral guidelines, a code of ethics our citizens will live by. America will again become a just nation of righteous people. Politicians and those who wield power will be asked to use these guidelines for the good of our people. Those who do not comply will be assassinated by our organization. We will communicate to our citizens through the use of America's newspapers, and on February 1st, the Moral Mafia will publish our initial list of demands. This will entail a code of ethics and behaviors we expect our citizens to adhere to. Those who do not comply, will also be killed. Immoral behavior of any kind will not be tolerated. Those who wish to abide by the old ways should hide, or be destroyed.

Those who would claim that the Moral Mafia itself is immoral, should consider this: we are waging a war against immorality. It is not unlike any other war documented in our history books. There will be casualties. A few will be sacrificed for the many. In the long term, America will become a better place to live. Our children will grow up in an environment with minimal influences from gratuitous sex, violence, and corruption. We urge the public to support our mission, and we ask this in God's name!

—THE MORAL MAFIA

Jim rocked back in his chair, *I did it!* he thought. *I really did it!*
"Has this hit the radio and television?"

"Yes," Charlie said, "we heard it on the radio on the way to work. We had to stop at three drug stores to find a newspaper."

The television in the break room was rarely used, but Jim went directly to it, and turned it on. The ABC affiliate was reporting on the story, and an interview with a spokesperson from the Associated Press was well under way with Simon Page, an AP spokesman.

"Mr. Page, what do you make of the Moral Mafia? Is this claimed organization for real, or is this the work of a lone madman?"

"Our CEO, Miguel Rodriguez believes the organization is real, or he would not have distributed the story for national publication."

"Does he have some proof of the organization's existence?"

"He says he has proof, but for his safety and the safety of his family, he was unwilling to share any details. You must understand that both he and his family were threatened by the Moral Mafia. I have never seen him so terrified."

"Did Miguel Rodriguez speak to the leader, or anyone in the organization?"

"Not in person. He received a letter which he read several times before he burned it."

"You say he burned the letter? Why wouldn't he have handed it over to the FBI?"

"Those were his instructions, and he followed them exactly as they were laid out."

"Do you have any idea what the letter said?"

"It contained the proof of the organizations intentions. It also described how they wanted today's front page to appear and instructions as to how to convince the major papers to print it."

"What advice did he give?"

"I cannot say at this time, but I believe that information will surely be forthcoming."

"Can you tell us anything at all about the leader of this organization?"

"I was told that he or she is highly intelligent. The letter, while threatening in nature, was written eloquently. There is no question that this person is highly educated and passionate about their cause."

"Do you believe the Moral Mafia would have followed through on their threat if the story had not been released?"

"I don't really know, but would you be willing to gamble your family's lives on the chance that this was a hoax?"

"I—I suppose not, but it is still unclear what proof Mr. Rodriguez has with regard to the authenticity of this organization."

"I don't have that information, but I believe something terrible happened to Mr. Rodriguez, something so convincing that he literally pleaded with the national papers to print the story exactly as he laid it out."

"So what is his next step?"

"We will forward the Moral Mafia's demands to the papers next week. They will be printed across the nation on February first."

"What kinds of demands do you—"

"Amazing," Jim said softly as he turned off the television, "what do you think about all of this?" He looked at Linda, so she answered first.

"There is no doubt this guy is a madman. He can't possibly control the entire country."

"I don't think he intends to," Jim replied. "It appears to me that he wants to change some laws to hold us more accountable for our actions."

"Sounds like a kook to me," said Randy.

Charlie shot his friend a sideways glance, "I don't know America can use a little cleaning up. If he is successful in doing so, he'd be a hero—wouldn't he?"

"Maybe so," Randy retorted, "but America can police itself. We don't need some quack threatening to kill anyone who doesn't see his point of view."

Jim carefully listened as his employees continued to banter about the topic. This was the kind of response he had hoped for. If the country is split into similar camps, it could result in as much as twenty-five percent of the population supporting the Moral Mafia. Charlie was beginning to raise his voice.

"Well, I say this guy is trying to make a point! It's high time someone stands up to the crap we're subjecting our children to."

Randy chuckled, "You don't even have any children, Charlie."

"Yeah, but when I do, I'm not so sure I want to raise them in this cesspool of a country we live in!"

Randy was getting combative, "THIS CESSPOOL, AS YOU REFER TO IT, IS THE GREATEST COUNTRY IN THE WORLD!"

"I agree. All I am saying is that we have gotten off-track in terms of our value system. What we accept as normal advertising today would have been banned from the air waves as pornographic twenty years ago."

"I suppose if it were up to you, we'd still be watching TV shows like *Father Knows Best,* and *Leave it to Beaver.*"

"What's wrong with those? At least they were family programs. How many family programs can you name today?"

Randy paused for a moment. He looked a little flustered as he tried to recall a current family TV program. "Well, I don't watch that much television."

"What about radio, Randy? Do you support all the rap singers who refer to their girl friends as bitches, and talk about killing cops? Is this what you think children should be listening to?"

"Kids don't listen to the words of those songs; they just like the music."

"The hell they do," Charlie snapped, "my nephew can recite the words to every song, and he's eleven. These kids know the words all right, they know EVERY damn word."

Linda tried to inject some levity into the conversation. "That's not singing, at all. Rap is just a bunch of guys rhyming bad lyrics to a thumping beat."

Charlie capitalized on the opportunity to make a final comment, "You're right, Linda, there's not much talent involved in making rap music. If you speak bad English, have no respect for anything, like to swear, and have no talent, you can be a rapper too."

Randy's eyes narrowed, "So you think this Moral Mafia guy is a hero, Charlie?"

"I can't say I approve of his methods, but I think his cause is honorable."

"Does the end justify the means?"

"Only time will tell. We don't even know what their plans are yet. Ask me in a few weeks."

Jim had a satisfied look on his face. "Morality," he said, "is an emotional subject. Let's not let it get the best of us, especially in the workplace. As always, we've got a lot of work to do." He took a few steps in the direction of the coffee pot, and topped off his tall mug. When he turned around, Charlie was smiling and patting Randy on the back.

28

ABOUT SEVEN O'CLOCK THAT EVENING, JIM LEFT THE house for a walk around the lake. The forty-five minute walk had now become an evening ritual. Peg was not pleased, because Jim used to spend this time with the youngest children. He didn't seem to have much time for family these days. Lately, he would arrive home just in time to kiss the youngest children good night.

The temperature was about eight degrees, but the wind made it seem much colder. Even a scarf and stocking cap seemed to make little difference. The cold cut right through his outer garb, and he was beginning to regret leaving the house. It was difficult to concentrate on the day's events, which had gone exactly as planned. Jim had introduced the nation to the Moral Mafia. Commentaries engulfed every program on radio and television. Before the day was through, protests against and in support of the organization had sprouted in many major cities. Politicians quickly denounced the organization, saying they would never succumb to their demands. "America is already a nation of 'unshakable' moral character," said the Democratic Minority Leader. The biggest question posed by commentators was pointed directly at the AP's CEO, Miguel Rodriguez. What did the Moral Mafia do to convince him to send this unbelievable story to every paper in the country?

Candlewood Lake was mostly surrounded by homes, but fifteen minutes into the walk, Jim was approaching a small playground where he and Peg often took their children to swing and climb on the jungle gym. At the far end of the park was a small sand beach and fishing dock, and the entire area was secluded by mature trees. The wind had picked up since he first left the house. The exposed portions of Jim's face were numb. He decided to take advantage of the wind break provided by the first grouping of blue spruce trees and he stepped between them for a moment. The lack of wind made him feel warmer almost immediately.

He stood there quietly, still reflecting on the day's news reports of the mysterious organization he had created. *The Moral Mafia*, he thought. *Even the name generates controversy.* One thing was for certain, there was unmistakable fear in the voices of many of those interviewed throughout the day. Some feared oppression by the Moral Mafia, some feared for their personal safety. But as the lines were drawn dividing the country into their supported camps, there was an underlying fear that generated the greatest controversy of all—the possibility of a civil war. Someone on TV mentioned it casually, and then it spread like wildfire.

Jim immediately dismissed the thought as ridiculous. Yes, Americans were sharply divided in their responses to the claims that the nation has become poisoned and wicked. That was expected. After all, the Moral Mafia's allegations came right out of the blue. The country was simply taken by surprise and needed time for the charges to sink in. After a few sharp debates, American's would realize it was true, and force lawmakers to steer a new course for them, a return to Christian values and good behavior. But change, even if fueled by fear, would have to come from the people. Extremist liberals took every opportunity to create media sound bites to make the case that there was little if any deterioration in the morals of America's countrymen, while right wing conservatives took the opposing view. Both sides agreed that consenting to censorship could not be allowed at any cost. *They will consent,* Jim thought.

"Mr. O'Brien?"

Jim was so startled when he heard his name, he stepped back and clenched his fists. He could see no one. He took his stocking cap off to improve his hearing. He tried to sound unafraid and assertive as he answered, "Who's there?"

"Don't be afraid, Mr. O'Brien, I just want to talk to you for a moment."

The youthful voice was definitely male. "Come out where I can see you."

From between two trees a tall, lanky figure appeared. "I'm glad you decided to take shelter, Mr. O'Brien. I don't have a hat, and this wind is grueling."

"Who are you?"

"My name is David Manetti. I am related to Tony Constantino." Jim's heart sank, he had nearly forgotten about the young surveillance expert from Chicago.

"What do you want, son?"

"I think you already know what I want, Mr. O'Brien. Are you going to make me spell it out?"

Jim could hear the snow crunch as he took another step back, "I have no idea who you are, or what you are talking about."

"Come now, Mr. O'Brien, it took me two months to put all the pieces together. You were with the FBI the night Tony died. I'm not sure why you were there, but I know one thing, my uncle was wearing a diamond ring when you went into his room, and when I saw him later that night, it was gone."

This boy is bluffing, Jim thought. *He was not allowed to see Constantino later that night. He has no evidence as to who sent the ring to Bonaiuto. All he has is a hunch, a darn good hunch.*

"That ring belongs to Jimmy Bonaiuto, the head of the family, but then again, you already know that. After all, you mailed it to him with Tony's will. What you neglected to send is Tony's personal ledger, phone book, and bank accounts. Uncle Tony was worth millions of dollars." *Wrong,* Jim thought, *he was worth billions.*

"The family wants the money, and Jimmy wants the ledgers and phone book. He has announced a reward of two hundred thousand dollars for the return of Tony's possessions. I believe I am the only one who knows where they are."

"That is an incredible story, David, but I can't help you."

"Oh, you can help me, Mr. O'Brien, and you will!"

The young man removed his right hand from his pocket. Moonlight glistened along the edge of what appeared to be a 9mm hand gun. He held it confidently at his waistline. Jim fell silent, he was struggling for a response, but nothing came to mind.

"You see, Mr. O'Brien, we also saw each other early one November morning in Chicago. I had worked all night in my shop in the basement of the Farm Credit Building. I was just getting ready to go home and get some sleep when a sensor in the locker room was tripped. The family owns the building and every inch of it is wired with cameras and microphones. I watched the video monitor and saw you open Tony's locker and empty the contents into a duffel bag. I never suspected he kept anything but gym clothes in there. The video wasn't very clear but it was good enough to see that it was file folders and not clothes that were taken. I would never have guessed it was you, but the parking attendant got the license plate number of the man who was there. I traced the plates, Mr. O'Brien, they're yours. You did get his possessions, didn't you?"

Jim was impressed by the well spoken young man. He was clearly well educated and articulate. Perhaps he could reason with him.

"Listen, David, Tony and I made a deal. I did promise to deliver those items to Jimmy Bonaiuto, and his attorney Michael Lanza, but I never said when. I will keep my promise, but not yet, not right now."

"Why, Mr. O'Brien? Why do you need any of Tony's things? What are you doing with my family's money?"

"I cannot say."

"There is talk about an outsider who has been giving orders to the family. From what I hear, Jimmy is cooperating, but he is anxious to take his rightful position as the head of the family. It's a little hard to do when someone else controls your finances. When I heard that

Mario Manetti made a trip to Omaha last month, I figured it was for you. Uncle Mario is a hit man, Mr. O'Brien. Did you have someone killed?"

Uncle Mario, shit! Jim struggled to keep his composure, "None of this is any of your affair, David."

"I think it is. Jimmy would reward me handsomely for revealing your identity. I would gain favor with him and be promoted to a trusted position. I have always wanted to be in the inner circle."

"Your position in the family—it's more important to you than money, isn't it?"

"Everyone in the family has money, but position is respect. Unfortunately, that's not the issue right now. I want everything you took from Tony's locker—tonight."

"You can pull that trigger David; it won't help you at all. I am the only one who knows the whereabouts of the files and bank accounts. No one else has a clue."

"I didn't want to do this, Mr. O'Brien, but you're about to lose a kneecap." David lowered the pistol to Jim's knees, "Do you have any idea how much that's gonna hurt?"

Jim called his bluff, "Then you'd better kill me, because I can have you suffer the same fate with a single phone call."

"My family would never touch me!"

"What makes you think yours is the only family I am working with?"

The moon cast a sliver of light through the trees to illuminate David's face. His eyes were stern, he looked uncertain, maybe even beaten. He took a step back and lowered the gun.

"Then I'll simply expose your identity, and collect the reward. Like I said, Jimmy will be more than grateful, Mr. O'Brien. And he wouldn't hesitate to use your family to get what he wants."

Jim's eyes turned into slits. Taking his next breath was difficult. He felt like a caged animal. He was caught dead to rights, and there was nothing he could do about it.

Maybe if I told the truth, he thought in desperation, *if this doesn't*
work, I'll have to kill him.

"I spoke with Bonaiuto and Lanza by telephone about three weeks after my trip to Chicago. I told them I would return everything if they helped me for six months. I promised to take care of the family in the interim. They agreed to my terms, and I have kept my promise of tending to family business. I don't think you want to get involved in this David. If anything, you will ruin our plans."

"Then why did Jimmy offer a reward for the return of Tony's belongings?"

Jim had no prior knowledge of this and was legitimately concerned, "I don't know. Maybe Jimmy is hedging his bets, or just going through the motions to save face. Either way, I think you're way over your head in this matter."

"When your children begin to disappear, Mr. O'Brien, just remember—you could have avoided this."

David put his hands in his pockets and smugly walked past Jim and into the clearing.

I can't let him go—I can't!

"Come back, David, let's talk some more."

"Will you give me what I want?"

"Yes, if you are willing to compromise."

David walked back into the shelter of the trees. "What kind of compromise?"

"Does anyone else know about this?"

"No, just me."

"What about the parking lot attendant?"

"I never told him why I wanted your license plate number. He just wrote it down and gave it to me."

"Assuming you are the only one in the family who knows I was with Tony the night he died, it's a safe bet that, except for you, my identity is a secret, correct?"

"Correct."

"Then I'll agree to turn everything over to you in ninety days. That will give me time to accelerate my plans and still accomplish my goals. You'll be a hero in the eyes of the family, entitled to a reward and the recognition you seek. In three months' time, Jimmy will undoubtedly be even more desperate and therefore, more grateful."

David was quiet while he pondered the benefits of Jim's proposal. It was clear to Jim that the boy didn't want to kill anyone.

"How do I know you won't spend all of our family's money?"

"You don't, David, but from the improvements I'm making to your family's finances, you may just be better off when I'm done."

David was quiet for half a minute or so, and then he spoke. "Alright Mr. O'Brien, not one minute past ninety days!"

"Agreed, but there is one more thing; my identity must remain a secret—forever. I'll come up with a credible story you can tell Jimmy and Michael, but my family's name must remain anonymous."

"That's a reasonable request. I'll honor it."

"Shall we shake on it?"

"In my family, our word is good enough. I'll see you in ninety days." David started for the street where his car was parked. About half way, he turned around and said, "By the way, Mr. O'Brien, the Moral Mafia has a nice ring to it."

He's bluffing, Jim thought, *there is no way he could know anything about the Moral Mafia. He's making assumptions based on the timing of the newspaper article* Then he remembered the ring he mailed to Bonaiuto with a note from the Moral Mafia. If Jimmy shared this information with David, it wouldn't be too difficult for him to piece everything together. Jim watched him drive off. His legs began shaking violently. Making his way back home was a nightmare. He thought about his children. He saw Katie's dying face in the dimly lit parking lot. Unwelcome thoughts of his other children being kidnapped or hurt crept into his mind.

What have I done? How can I trust him? I've endangered Peg and the children. The lives of my entire family are in this kid's hands.

29

AT THE OFFICE A FEW DAYS LATER, JIM SAT AT A BREAK room table rubbing his eyes. He wasn't sleeping well since his encounter with David Manetti. Even with his hair neatly combed, Jim looked as if he had just rolled out of bed. About five minutes earlier, Linda concluded some colorful remarks regarding the Moral Mafia's published list of demands from the morning paper. She was so angry that Jim intentionally kept the conversation short.

Even days before the demands were published, Jim was becoming concerned that Americans were sitting on an emotional powder kcg with a very short fuse and a book of matches. It seemed as though Americans welcomed every opportunity to argue about the state of morality. Other than sharply dividing the country, Jim wondered if he had really accomplished anything. Abortion had now surfaced as the greatest of all immoral acts, and Jim addressed it in today's front page message from the Moral Mafia. What worried Jim most was that there always seemed to be a maverick looking for trouble at every rally or demonstration.

There are too many lunatics in the world, Jim thought. *and unfortunately, I may be one of them.*

Almost like clockwork, Charlie Ford entered the break room with a smile on his face. He was followed closely by fellow employees Randy Burks, and Wayne Turley. He waved the morning paper in the air.

"Did you see this, Jim?"

"Yes, I did. In fact, Linda and I—correction, Linda just finished talking about it."

Charlie's smile broadened. He placed his hands on his hips and in a mock impersonation, rocked them back and forth.

"I can just hear Linda saying, 'If this guy thinks he can waltz into our lives and tell us how to live, he's just plain nuts.'"

With a smile, Jim said, "I believe that's a pretty close assessment, Charlie."

"Well, I think it's great! For a week now, the Moral Mafia has dominated every headline and talk show in the country. Our morality, or lack of it, is now the most hotly debated topic in history. I believe that people are actually beginning to evaluate their lifestyles."

Wayne spoke up, "Yeah, but can the Moral Mafia really succeed in reversing the trend of SVC?"

Mike Smart appeared at the doorway, "What's SVC?"

"Haven't you seen all the 'STOP SVC' buttons and T-shirts? It's an acronym for sex, violence, and corruption."

Mike rolled his eyes. "Right, right, I forgot. What about drugs?"

"What do you mean?" Wayne asked.

"The saying should read, 'STOP SDVC.' The company making the T-shirts forgot to include drugs. Kind of a big omission, don't you think? Idiots."

Charlie wasn't listening, or he was just uncontrollably excited, "If the entire country is thinking about morality, then the Moral Mafia has already begun to reverse the trend!"

Mike Smart looked like he was guarding a secret, "They've made an impact alright. Did you hear about Senator Hill and Senator McMillan coming to blows after yesterday's session?"

Jim looked concerned. "No, what happened?"

"Apparently, the Republicans want to re-write the Constitution to include a strict moral code. The Democrats will have nothing to do with it. McMillan and Hill got into a heated debate. The next thing you know they were punching each other. If you ask me, there is a political war brewing."

"Or maybe a civil war," Wayne added.

"Politicians aren't the only ones fighting," a feminine voice interrupted.

Jim looked up noting Miranda Peters' troubled expression.

"If you watch the national news, you'll see that this is affecting everyone. I have never witnessed such hatred among Americans. We seem to have lost respect for each other's opinions. It's causing a sharp division among friends, neighbors, and families. It's even happening in my own family."

Jim looked disappointed. *This is not what I intended,* he thought. *I want to make the world better, not tear it apart.*

Jim took the helm, "I can sense the same thing happening in this office, Miranda. Some of us have mistaken exuberance for disrespect. If we are going to remain a cohesive team, we need to show respect for each other's opinions. While some of you feel that the Moral Mafia is doing the country a great service, others believe that this is an evil organization. It shouldn't really matter which opinion you share, as long as we can be respectful about it." As hard as it was to say, Jim forced his next comment, "After all, we are supposed to be a nation of tolerance."

Scott Troia was leaning against the rear doorway to the break room.

"'That's the problem, Jim. Since the sixties, we've become tolerant of every opposing view and lifestyle, but it's gone too far. Now the Moral Mafia is forcing people to take a stand, to choose sides. I agree with Miranda. I am open to debate these topics, but not at the cost of losing my friends and family."

Jim stood up, "We cannot let this happen to us. We've got to support each other as friends and co-workers. Do you all agree?"

Everyone answered Jim with a firm yes, except for Charlie, who murmured an acknowledgment under his breath. "Maybe we should talk about this at lunch. I can have Linda order pizza."

Miranda still appeared to be distraught, "That sounds fine, but I worry about things getting out of hand. Some of these topics are just too explosive to discuss."

"You're right, Miranda. We must keep in mind that this is not about red states against the blue states. It is simply a chance for us to voice our feelings about what is going on. Political affiliations have no business rearing their ugly heads."

Jim had no way of knowing, but neither he nor Miranda would be present for lunch.

"Meanwhile, let's get our coffee and catch some bad guys. We have five open FBI cases we need to crack. Miranda, when you have finished here, can I see you in my office?"

"Sure, Jim, I'll be right there."

Miranda filled her cup from the water cooler, and trailed Jim by half a minute. As he approached his desk, Jim noticed an old December copy of the Chicago Tribune on his credenza. He quickly glanced at the ad He had circled—the one Manetti had placed under Home Furnishings. It read:

Old refrigerator needs new compressor.

Free to anyone with a pick-up truck.

See at 1425 Old Post Road

Job 001 Complete

Jim had a daily subscription to the Chicago Tribune. The ad was completely fictitious. Job 001 referred to the first hit Jim had hired Manetti to perform. It notified him that the three boys, who had killed his daughter Katie, had been taken care of. Of course, Jim had read the article in the local paper, but it was comforting to see that their subtle form of communication worked. Each successive hit was accompanied by the same ad, but the job number told him which hit was complete. Jim had saved the paper as a souvenir, relishing the fact that he had avenged his daughter's death, but saw no need to keep it any longer. He threw it in the trash.

When Miranda entered his office, he asked her to close the door.

"Miranda, I don't want to pry, but you look very troubled. Is there anything I can do for you?"

She forced a smile. "No, I'm fine. It's just that the world seems like such a dangerous place right now. With all this talk about morality, it's as though we are scrutinizing each other, analyzing our friends and families under a microscope. Some of my friends seem to be passing judgment on each other. It makes me uncomfortable."

"I get the same uneasy feeling," Jim confessed. "You mentioned your family. Is everything okay with your folks?"

"My father and brother had a terrible fight yesterday. While Dad was denouncing gay marriage at the dinner table, Zach interrupted him and said he didn't see anything wrong with it. The conversation exploded, and now Mom says they aren't speaking at all."

"How old is your brother?"

"Seventeen, he's a senior in high school."

"Consider this, Miranda; your brother has never lived in a historical era when gays were really looked down upon."

"Mom told me his home room teacher is gay."

Jim smiled and nodded. "That explains a lot. Once you get to know a gay person and can identify with him or her, it tends to skew any views you have about homosexuality. It is no longer an issue of right or wrong, but becomes an issue of whether an acquaintance is being cheated of the right to have a relationship of his or her choosing."

"You have such a keen perspective, Jim. How do you feel about gay marriage?"

"I don't hate gays. I don't hate anyone. Nor do I think gays can help being who they are, but I do believe that acting upon their sexual desires is wrong. I think homosexuality goes against God's laws, and quite frankly, I have a hard time understanding how our society ever became so accepting of it."

"Me too; it's just unnatural."

"There are a lot of people who would disagree with us."

"According to the Moral Mafia's list of demands, public displays of gay behavior will not be tolerated." How can the Moral Mafia possibly enforce such a thing?"

With pure fear, Jim thought. "I don't know. I guess we'll have to wait and see."

The telephone rang. Jim pressed the speaker button. Linda said, "Jim, its Vince Mitchell. He says it's really important."

"Put him through Linda."

"Hello, Jim?"

"Hi Vince, how are you?"

"Up to my neck in alligators, I'm afraid. I really need your help, Jim; can you meet with me this morning?"

"Sure. Where and when?"

"Downtown at City Hall, ten o'clock, room 300. Can you make it?"

"You sound a little frazzled, Vince. Is everything okay?"

"My department has just been assigned to a Federal Task Force. We are charged with tracking down all of the members of the Moral Mafia. I would like to consider your company as an integral part of my team. Will you help us?"

Jim couldn't believe what he was hearing. What were the odds of being asked to help capture your own organization? "Of course, Vince, I'll be there. Can I bring Miranda Peters with me?"

"Bring anyone you want, as long as you trust them."

"Fine, I'll see you at ten."

Miranda was pleasantly surprised. As Jim pressed the speaker button to hang up, she asked, "Do you really want me to go with you?"

"Yes, is that okay?"

"Yes, it's very exciting; it's just that I thought you would take Scott instead."

"Scott has a lot of projects in the works. We'll keep him informed about what we're doing and get him involved if necessary."

Jim expected an improvement in Miranda's spirits and he was rewarded with a heart-warming smile that made him feel better as well.

She really is beautiful when she smiles, he thought.

30

OMAHA'S CITY HALL FACED FARNAM STREET AND WAS adjacent to the Douglas County Court House. The front steps of the court house were often littered with smokers waiting to make a court appearance. Jim recalled images of some of the unsavory types he saw in the courtroom a few months ago when he accompanied Tom to his probation sentencing. As he and Miranda turned the corner from Seventeenth Street to Farnam, he noticed a familiar crowd on the Court House steps, but something was different. There was a lot of foot traffic between the Court House and City Hall. Jim spotted a car pulling out of a metered parking space ahead, and quickly claimed it.

"Luck is on your side, Jim, you couldn't have found a better parking spot if you tried!"

"It doesn't happen often, that's for sure."

As Jim plunked several quarters into the parking meter, he glanced down the street and recognized picket signs.

Oh great, he thought. *I wonder who's staging the protest?*

As they approached City Hall, Jim said, "This is one time I wish there was a side door."

"Me too, Jim. But at least it looks peaceful."

"It's probably just a union group picketing for higher wages, but I always feel uneasy crossing a picket line."

Miranda joked, "You might want to make sure that none of your employees are in that group, Jim."

They found room 300. It was the Mayor's office. Jim introduced himself to the mayor's receptionist, who escorted them to a conference room down the hall. Vince spotted Jim and Miranda and was quick to welcome them.

"Thanks for coming on such short notice, Jim."

"You know you can always count on us, Vince. I'd like to introduce you to Miranda Peters; she's one of my best associates." Jim noticed Vince's body language as he gently took Miranda's hand. He was no doubt taken with her beauty.

"It's a pleasure to meet you, Miranda; Jim speaks very highly of you."

Miranda blushed, "I have also heard good things about you, Vince. We enjoy working with you and the Bureau."

"Believe me, the pleasure is ours. I hope you don't think I'm unsociable, but we only have about five minutes before the meeting begins. Let's step out in the hall and I'll give you both a briefing."

Just outside the conference room, Vince explained, "The President of the United States has directed us to stop the Moral Mafia before it sends the country into an irreversible panic. We believe the organization is real and that they will follow through with their threats to kill public figures that refuse to cooperate with them."

Jim prodded, "How do you know this *Moral Mafia* is real?"

"I'll let Janet Stratman answer that question."

"Who is she?"

"Stratman is heading up the Federal Task Force. She's a tough old broad, and she is tapping every resource possible from the FBI, CIA, Homeland Security, Armed Forces, and the business sector as well. The President told her to spare no expense to resolve this problem. She has *carte blanche,* and she'll use it too. This is her second meeting this morning. By the end of the day she will have traveled to, and met with, all six regional teams. How's that for a go-getter?"

"I'm impressed, but I have yet to see any proof that this isn't just a well orchestrated hoax."

Vince looked at his watch. "We only have a minute, but I'll tell you what I know. We have been questioning the president of the Associated Press, Miguel Rodriguez ever since he distributed the Moral Mafia's first story. He was reluctant to cooperate with us until we placed his family under special protection, but a few days ago he gave us the proof we needed."

"What proof?"

"Everything I tell you from now on is privileged information; you cannot share it with anyone."

"Agreed," Jim said.

"In a letter the Moral Mafia sent to Rodriguez, he was given the locations of three remote controlled bombs. One was placed in his home, one in his wife's car, and one in his daughter's college dorm room. He was given instructions to retrieve them and take them to a junk yard. There, the Moral Mafia detonated one of them to prove they were real. He told Rodriguez if he didn't cooperate, the next bombs would find their targets."

Jim shook his head, "I'm surprised he is cooperating with the FBI. I'm not certain I would risk it."

"As long as the Moral Mafia is unaware of our conversations, his family will be safe."

"This is incredible," Jim said convincingly. "Let's just hope that the Moral Mafia's intelligence capabilities are not as good as the FBI's."

The Task Force meeting lasted a meager thirty-five minutes. Janet Stratman was an imposing figure. Jim surmised that she was in her mid-fifties, and stood about five-feet-ten inches tall. There was no attempt on her part to conceal her age. Her hair was mostly gray, but showed a few large streaks of brown. Her face was stern, and she was all business as she directed the meeting and introduced her staff of specialists, one by one.

Everyone attending the meeting received a briefing packet containing contact information for members of all six regional task force teams, and a synopsis of what they currently knew of the Moral Mafia. Jim wasn't at all surprised to see his name on the list, even though Vince had only asked him to participate two hours ago. Vince introduced Jim as the country's foremost authority on computer forensics. He was immediately introduced to Janie Meehan, a nationally known psychologist, who provided the team with a profile of the Moral Mafia's leader, whom she aptly nicknamed Mr. M. Jim was impressed by the fact that much of her evaluation actually matched his personality profile, but he was a bit troubled by a few of her assessments.

The Moral Mafia leader, Mr. M, was described as a righteous and highly intelligent man, a careful planner who would be extremely difficult to track down. The report also assumed he had vast wealth, and a reasonably good grasp of technology. Jim scowled when he read a comment that described him as delusional and power hungry.

They have no idea what drives me. A corrupt society took my daughter from me, and turned my son into a drug addict. My actions are not selfish, if anything, they are selfless. I'm restoring my country to a better way of life. Reading the comments soured Jim's mood.

Stratman said it was Vince's job to focus on Mr. M's communications. Thus far, the FBI had little to go on. They had possession of two e-mails. Since both of them were in an electronic format, there was no physical evidence to examine. The first e-mail was the Moral Mafia's original front page address to America, accompanied by some content for the second page story published last week. The second e-mail was sent to the Associated Press only yesterday; its content appeared as this morning's list of demands. Both e-mails were forwarded to the FBI's forensic laboratory for analysis. A courier had delivered a third document to Rodriguez, but heeding the Moral Mafia's warning, he burned it. It contained the threatening comments and bomb locations Vince Mitchell had mentioned earlier. The FBI attempted to reconstruct its verbiage for the sole purpose of helping Janie Meehan to profile Mr. M.

Two of the three bombs were recovered as well. They were described as very expensive, and highly sophisticated. Jim had the timers designed by Keith Napierilla, the electronics engineer who originally worked for the late William Lang at LSI Industries. Modified Smart Phone devices would detonate the bombs based on a specific date and time. The FBI feared that these compact devices could be planted in strategic locations months in advance of a planned assassination. It was assumed that the Moral Mafia wanted these sophisticated detonators to be discovered as further proof of their intentions, as well as their technical and financial might.

When the meeting concluded, Jim remained at the conference table scrutinizing a printout of the Moral Mafia's e-mailed list of demands. The text matched the front page of this morning's newspaper word for word. It was a plain looking e-mail addressed to Miguel Rodriguez, but sent to the AP's customer service department. In the destroyed letter, Mr. M indicated that he would continue to use this e-mail address to communicate with Rodriguez in the future. The AP created a new e-mail address for customer service use, leaving the original strictly available for future Moral Mafia correspondence.

Jim noticed a random string of ASCII characters in the e-mail's *FROM:* field and directed Vince's attention to it.

"Vince, look at this character string in the *FROM:* field. Do you think it was manually typed, or was it generated randomly?"

"I knew you'd catch that right away, Jim. I don't know. We'll have to wait until we receive the next e-mail from Mr. M to know if there is a pattern of any kind."

"We don't have to wait at all, Vince. We have two e-mails sent to the AP's customer service department. Look at the character strings, they are completely different. I have never seen anything like it. Miranda, what do you think?"

Some of her beauty ebbed away as she scrutinized the documents. "It's hard to say, Jim. I really can't make any sense of it. There is no @ symbol, nor is there any .com or .net suffix. It really does appear to be characters."

Mitchell stared at the random gibberish, "Well, Jim, unless you can decipher it, Mr. M is untraceable, just like the late Tony Constantino."

Jim baited Vince cautiously, carefully. "Do you think there is a connection?"

"Nothing points that way, but right now, I'd say that just about anything is possible. I need you to put your entire team on this. Just keep track of your hours, and we will make it financially worth your while. And please, Jim, give it all your resources."

"Alright, Vince, we will start researching possible scenarios as to how this e-mail was sent later today. Meanwhile, we'll need to visit the Associated Press, and take a look at the server that received the e-mail. In addition, we'll probably want them to forward the files to our office for additional analysis."

Jim's expression became slightly tense, and somewhat contorted. Mitchell noticed, "Is everything alright, Jim?"

"I have a feeling you've just given me the most difficult case of my career—yes, Vince, everything is just fine."

In the back of his mind, Jim was experiencing a completely different train of thought; *Incredible. The whole country is looking for me now—even me!*

Vince stayed behind to spend a few valuable moments with Janet Stratman, before she left for Los Angeles. Jim and Miranda found the elevator and began their descent to the first floor. Miranda stared at Jim, who still appeared somewhat tense.

"It's a lot of pressure isn't it, Jim?"

"I suppose so, but you know me, I always welcome a challenge."

"Just think, of all the people that could have been chosen to help the FBI, you alone were selected."

"No—we were selected, Miranda, our team, our company. That is why we must stay close. We can't let the current situation divide us. We need to be sharp if we are to expose this—Mr. M."

The elevator door opened. As Jim and Miranda rounded the corner, they were stunned at what they saw. Through the east windows they could see half a dozen men fighting among a gathering of spectators. It looked like the start of a riot.

31

JIM GRABBED MIRANDA'S HAND AND DARTED TOWARD the front door of City Hall. When they reached the entrance, he placed his hands against the glass windows and peered outside to study the crowd, which had spilled from the steps to the street. They were not union picketers as Jim had first thought. They were gay rights activists. There was no fighting taking place, but the original picketers had been engulfed by a horde of agitated protesters. There were plenty of picket signs, one read, "Gays Are God's Children." Another read, "Gay Rights." Still another said, "Go Moral Mafia!" In other circumstances Jim may have laughed out loud when he read the sign that read," Make Love Not War." It was held by a long-haired man wearing a green Army jacket. But Jim was too tense to laugh. At this very moment, he was especially concerned for Miranda's safety.

A solitary police officer had just made his way through the crowd to the front entrance just outside the revolving door. Besides Jim and Miranda, there were about twenty onlookers watching the event from the safety of the lobby. Jim turned to Miranda, "I don't see any fighting out there, but I don't think it's safe for us to leave. That mob looks like a powder keg waiting for a spark. I think we should wait in here until things calm down."

"Thank God, Jim, I just know we would run into trouble out there."

"Look at them," Jim said. "Why are they so angry?"

"Did you read the Omaha World-Herald this morning? There's no doubt—this is the result of the Moral Mafia's list of demands."

Jim looked grim. In his mind, he knew it was true. His language was particularly harsh on gays. The fourth demand made it clear that the Moral Mafia would tolerate no public displays of gay affection. The fifth demand called for legislation outlawing gay marriages in all fifty states. He knew his insensitivity to their lifestyle would anger them. He was about to find out how much.

Jim stepped in front of Miranda to block her view of the image outside. He tried to inject a little levity to ease the tension. "Who knew there were this many gays in Omaha, for God's sake. Maybe they bused some in from California."

Miranda did her best to smile, but it was a nervous smile. She peered around Jim's shoulder, intent on watching the crowd. "I can't wait to get back to the office." Jim was jolted when he saw her eyes widen, and then she gasped, "OH MY GOD!"

Jim spun around to see what Miranda was gawking at.

The police officer, he's down!

Standing over him waiving the officer's billy club was a tall, muscular blond man. Jim couldn't hear through the glass, but a portion of the crowd seemed to be cheering. Another glance downward and Jim could see a trickle of blood had left a trail from the officer's forehead over his right ear. Jim reacted without taking time to think. He pushed against the revolving door and was outside, face-to-face with the burly blond protester.

Over the noise of the crowd, Jim screamed, "This man needs medical attention, NOW!"

"Well now, that's too bad. I guess the ass-hole shouldn't have pushed me. Now, leave him alone!"

Jim dropped to his knees, "Can you hear me? Officer, can you hear me?"

There was no response. Jim noticed his eyelids fluttering. He placed his hands under the officer's arms, and began to lift him up when he felt a sharp blow to his right shoulder. Reeling in pain, Jim dropped the officer, whose head thumped hard on the pavement. He realized he had been hit with the officer's baton. He tried to stand up, but was on the verge of blacking out. Jim stayed on his knees for a moment, struggling to remain conscious. He didn't take his eyes off the officer. As his head cleared and his vision improved, Jim became angry. He could hear his assailant still talking to the crowd.

"WE ARE FREE PEOPLE. WE CAN LIVE ANY LIFESTYLE WE CHOOSE. IT'S TIME AMERICA RECOGNIZED GAY RIGHTS, AND OUR RIGHT TO SAME SEX MARRIAGE!"

Jim knew the blond-haired man was bigger and stronger than him. If there was a chance to get the officer inside the building, he had only seconds to act. While the man continued to speak, he got to his feet slowly, unnoticed.

"IF WE REMAIN UNITED, WE CAN BATTLE THE LIKES OF THE MORAL MAFIA AND ALL BACKWARD THINKING PEOPLE! WE HAVE THE SUPPORT OF THE DEMOCRAT—."

The man turned around when Jim interrupted him with a tap on his shoulder. Jim grabbed his coat by both lapels, lowered his head and pulled the man toward him with all his might. He planted a smashing head butt against the man's forehead. Jim quickly pushed him backward and the man flailed his arms, tumbling down the concrete steps. Jim was certain he hurt the blond protester, but he didn't linger long enough to find out the extent of the damage. He was frightened and shaking, but easily found the strength to scoop up the officer and drag him through the revolving doors.

Miranda was nearly hysterical as Jim gently laid the officer down.

"Jim, are you all right? That man hurt you badly, didn't he?"

Jim wasn't listening. He asked a bystander to call an ambulance while he knelt down to check the officer's breathing, and then removed his cashmere coat and placed it over him.

"I think he's in shock, we really need that ambulance."

Miranda knelt down beside him and placed her hands on his cheeks. Pulling him near, she kissed him with such tenderness that Jim felt calmed and comforted. A second later his mind began to regain the level of clarity he had before the incident. He had a terrible thought, and turned his head toward the front entrance. A mass of protesters was peering in the windows. They were observing the burly gay activist and an accomplice who had stepped inside the building. *They snuck in,* Jim thought. *The revolving door prevented the outside noise from intruding into the building.*

The muscular blond-haired man didn't look too happy. He had already removed his coat, and was laying it on the floor. His physique was far from the image Jim had conjured for a gay stereotype. Not that his notion painted them all as feminine, but this man had the macho appearance of a professional body builder. The second man was also blond, but fit Jim's gay mold perfectly. He had frail, soft features, and one of his eyes was slightly offset. It gave him the eerie look of a crazed man. He smiled in a repulsive way as he repeatedly slapped a police baton against the palm of his hand.

He looks overly confident, Jim thought. *I guess I would be too if I was standing next to Hercules there.*

Jim stood and looked the larger man squarely in the eyes "Haven't you done enough damage?"

"Not yet. Not until you've joined your friend there on the floor." The big man glanced down at the officer and smiled. "I plan to put you there with my bare hands."

Jim desperately wanted to avoid a fight, but didn't want to appear frightened either.

"We outnumber you, blondie; you can't possibly fight us all."

"Yes, I can see how all of these brave men have come to your assistance."

Jim looked around. Some of the bystanders had backed away to the outer edges of the lobby; most had disappeared elsewhere in the building. Talking suddenly seemed like a better alternative than angering his opponent any further.

Jim set his jaw and cocked his head. "Why do you want to fight me?"

He gestured toward the door. "You hit me out there."

Jim rolled his eyes. "I don't suppose you remember why, do you?" He pointed to the floor. "You may have critically injured this police officer, and when I tried to help him, you crushed my shoulder with his baton."

The blond man's square jaw cradled a snide grin, "Yes I did, and maybe your GIRLFRIEND would like to have some fun with it when we're finished with you, eh Derek?"

Both men laughed.

Sneering at them, Jim said, "You are sick people; gay, sick, queer people."

"You don't approve of the gay community?"

"I think my last comment covered my feelings perfectly."

The big man began walking toward Jim. "How fortunate for me, now I'll enjoy this even more."

Jim pushed Miranda aside, "Go get Vince, hurry!"

The man named Derek ran after Miranda and tackled her before she could travel ten feet. Jim was on top of him in an instant. His eyes darted at Miranda.

"GO!—NOW!"

He wrenched the baton away from him, and pushed it hard against his throat, choking him. He looked over his shoulder only to see a large figure approaching.

I've got to put this guy out of commission.

With a sense of urgency, he shifted his left hand over the man's throat and with his right hand grasped the baton. With a powerful swing of the club, Jim cracked the man across his cheek. *For God's sake,* he thought, *I hope I didn't kill him!*

Before Jim could stand, he was grabbed from behind and thrown several feet. He landed hard on his right side. The baton skidded across the floor. Jim got up slowly, but just in time to avoid a backhand. He kept backing away, but the blond-haired man approached relentlessly. Jim tried to block a punch with his forearm, but it was planted with such force that his own fist was driven into his right cheek. The jarring blow shocked and frightened him. Jim felt a throbbing sensation.

Jesus, he's strong. I've got to stay out of reach.

Jim sidestepped another fist, and then began to back away.

He's clumsy, Jim thought. "What's your name, Blondie? I'd like to know who I'm fighting."

The blond-haired man laughed, "You call this fighting? It looks to me like you're trying to keep your distance."

"I'm just waiting for the right opportunity to kick your teeth in, Blondie."

Jim had an idea. He slowly began backing up toward the entrance.

"THE NAME IS AARON," the blond-haired man grunted as he took another wild swing. He kept stepping forward, trying to close the distance between them.

"Tell me, Aaron, which role do you play in your gay relationships, the boy or the girl?"

Jim's taunting was working, Aaron pursued him recklessly. As Jim neared the revolving door, Aaron sensed he was being coaxed outside, and picked up his pace. Jim darted into a quadrant of the door's four sections and began pushing. Aaron tried to enter the same section, but the door was closing too fast. The heavy door slammed against his arm, pinning him on the other side. Aaron let out a blood curdling scream. Jim was amazed.

That impact would have broken an average man's arm. I've got to keep him pinned here until Miranda gets back with Vince.

Jim was relieved to have a safe layer of glass between him and the madness that waited at either end of the door. On one side of him was an angry mob, on the other, a muscle-bound protester who wanted to hurt him badly. With only seconds passing, Jim's feet were firmly planted on the ground, his arms outstretched, and his hands pushing against the glass.

Jesus, I'm trapped. I wonder how long I can keep Blondie's arm pinned in the door. He began to observe the crowd outside. His face reddened as he pushed with all his might. More police had arrived. About fifty percent of the crowd had dispersed, but the remaining protesters were now engaged in fighting with each other and the police.

Two spectators, who had been watching Jim and Aaron through the windows, were signaling a third man to join them. When he reached them, one of the men began talking and motioning with his arms. Jim's heart sank. He could not hear the conversation, but he clearly understood what they were going to do. He braced himself and began to push even harder as the three men countered and drove the revolving door against him. Jim held his ground for about thirty seconds, but gradually began to lose his footing. He was nearing exhaustion.

The door reversed its direction, and Aaron freed his arm. After rubbing it briefly, he grabbed the edge of the door and started helping the others. Jim was quickly overpowered and flung to the lobby side of the entrance. Once again he found himself face-to-face with Aaron. He rushed him, hoping the element of surprise would be to his advantage. He was right. Aaron fell backward onto the floor. Jim pushed the revolving door and quickly made his way outside. He punched one of the men who had called the third man over. The other two ran into the crowd.

Jim scanned the crowd looking for a blue uniform. It made no difference; the police were scuffling with picketers. He sensed the revolving door begin to turn, and darted back into one of its quadrants. Aaron scowled when he saw Jim safely insulated by a pane of glass. The two men pushed the door until it traveled in a full circle. It seemed like slow motion to Jim as their eyes locked in hatred and disgust. Aaron must have determined that it was fruitless to pursue him any further. More police were arriving by the minute. Jim assumed that Aaron had weighed the advantages of throwing a few more punches versus getting arrested. He pushed the door a few more inches and stepped outside leaving Jim in the shelter of the revolving door. Jim noticed Aaron's gaze suddenly shift away. The brawny blond shook his head, communicating the answer, "no," to someone behind him. Jim looked over his shoulder and saw that

Derek had picked up the baton, and was standing at the opposite end of the door's entrance. Aaron motioned for Derek to come outside. The door began to revolve, and the two men exchanged brief glances through the single pane of glass. Derek's crazed look had turned into one of loathing. When Jim's quadrant reached the lobby, he stepped out.

Realizing Jim couldn't hear them, the two men took a few steps back. Aaron outstretched his arm and fashioned a gun with his hand. Pointing it at Jim, he pretended to pull the trigger. Jim understood the message. Aaron smiled, and Derek's mouth opened wide in laughter, but only briefly, as doing so made him wince in pain.

I hope I broke his jaw, Jim thought.

The two men surveyed the crowd and slowly walked to safety. As Jim stared, he saw Derek swing the baton and buckle a man's legs beneath him. He continued strolling as if he were out for a walk on a beautiful day. Jim watched them until they were out of sight. In his relief that their encounter was over, Jim suddenly realized that his head was pounding. In the commotion, he hadn't even noticed just how badly his shoulder ached. As he scanned the room for a place to sit, he remembered the injured police officer. He went to him and knelt down beside him. The officer was still breathing, but it had become shallow. *Where the hell is that ambulance? Where are Vince and Miranda?* Becoming impatient, Jim dialed 911 on his cell phone, and requested an ambulance again. He stressed that an officer was down in the lobby of the City Hall building. Trembling, Jim moved into a sitting position next to the officer and closed his eyes for a moment. That was the last thing he remembered.

32

IT WAS SEVEN IN THE MORNING. PEG STOOD MOTIONLESS beside the bed, watching Jim sleep. He looked so peaceful; she didn't want to wake him. For now, the sorrow was gone from his face. It brought back memories of him as he was before Katie's death. He was so kind, so considerate. Jim and Peg spent every spare moment together, and with the children. Now, she rarely saw him. He spent long evenings behind the computer in his den. He rarely spoke of work anymore. In fact, they hardly spoke of anything. Peg knew he was working with the FBI on the Moral Mafia case, but she had doubts that he was devoting all those long hours to research. *What does he do until three o'clock every morning?*

Jim was typically up by six, but today, he slept right through the alarm. Peg considered waking him, but decided he could use the extra rest. Since the riot last week, Jim was moving slowly. He had a large knot on his shoulder where he had been hit with a police baton and a few other bruises from his altercation with a gay activist. A newspaper article in the Omaha World Herald outlined the story of two gay activists who attacked a police officer, nearly killing him. Jim's intervention saved his life. Peg was worried sick about him.

What has happened to our life, our wonderful life?

Even the children were concerned. They couldn't put their finger on it, but they knew something was wrong. When they spoke with their father, he still sounded the same, answered their questions, and offered advice when they had problems. But these days he seemed preoccupied. His role as a husband and father lacked the heart it once had. The older girls wanted to confront him, find out what they could do to help him, but Peg said the time wasn't right. She said that Jim still needed to recover from Katie's death. She insisted that work was the best medicine to heal his wounds, but she too, was growing impatient. Peg was afraid something had fundamentally changed in Jim's character, and that the changes might be permanent. She didn't want to admit it, but she wasn't certain if he would ever be the same man she married.

"Jim? Honey? It's time to get up; I let you sleep in a little today."

Jim didn't open his eyes, but managed to frown. "What time is it?"

"It's seven."

"Seven o'clock? You shouldn't let me sleep in like this; I have too much work to do!"

"Nonsense, you have been getting by on a few hours of sleep every night for a month. You need to take better care of yourself."

Jim threw his legs over the side of the bed and rubbed his eyes. "I know you are just trying to help, Peg, but there are only so many hours in a day, and today, I need all of them."

"You only slept an extra hour. What's so pressing that you can't sleep an extra hour? And what do you do in your office until three in the morning?"

"Research—for the FBI!"

Peg could tell his answer lacked sincerity. "Is research more important than your family? We don't see you anymore. You haven't spent any time with us in months. Do you really care more about this case than your children—than me?"

The pain in Peg's face was more than Jim could bear. His eyes began to moisten. He looked away.

"I'll make it up to you, Peg. I'll make it up to all of you, just as soon as this is over."

"You don't have much time to make things better. Each day you ignore us, the damage becomes worse. Danny and the little girls are starved for your attention, and you haven't spoken to Tom in a month. He thinks you have abandoned him. He's coming home on Saturday. What will you tell him?"

Saturday? I'm nowhere near ready for this, Jim thought.

"I'll cross that bridge when I come to it."

"That's the problem! You have had lots of chances, but you haven't crossed any bridges."

Jim stood up and headed for the bathroom. "I have to shower."

"This is exactly what I am talking about. You need to face your problems, not walk away from them."

"I would, but someone let me sleep in. I'm late."

Jim closed the bathroom door behind him. As he stepped into the shower, hundreds of images flashed across his mind. He saw Katie's lifeless stare. He saw Constantino's pasty gray face. He saw the three boys that attacked Tom in the parking lot. He leaned against the shower wall and let the water jets drench his hair. He saw David Manetti, Aaron, and that crazed man. The images kept flashing faster and faster. Suddenly, he saw Miranda, and felt her soft lips against his, and his fears melted into calmness. He was ashamed for having such thoughts, but lately, it was becoming increasingly difficult to avoid them. Suddenly, Jim realized what day it was. *I've got to get to the office; the first bombs will be detonated any minute now.*

Jim pulled into the Computer Forensic Consultants parking lot at seven thirty. Thus far, there was no word of any bombings on the car radio. This puzzled him, as it was already eight thirty on the East Coast. *Did the bombs not work?* As he entered the office and walked down the main corridor, he noticed that Howard Beekler was already hard at work. Through his thick glasses, Howard offered his usual enthusiastic salutation, "Good morning Jim!" Jim returned the greeting and continued walking toward Miranda's cubicle. She too, was working early. She looked up with hopeful eyes, her gaze almost pleaded with him for attention. Jim kept walking. He didn't know what to do about her. He never meant for anything to happen between them, but after being clubbed by a gay demonstrator at City hall, Miranda had kissed Jim on the lips. At first, he didn't give it much thought, but the memory lingered, and now it was becoming a distraction. Jim knew that such distractions could be dangerous, even fatal. He really needed to concentrate on directing the Moral Mafia's next moves to avoid getting caught.

Jim had always idolized Peg, and although many opportunities to stray presented themselves, he remained steadfast in his faithfulness to her. Even in his thoughts, he had never been unfaithful to her, or desired another woman, but now he found himself thinking of Miranda at odd times of the day.

Focus, Jim thought.

He had only a few months to finish the Moral Mafia's business, and then he would have to turn Constantino's belongings over to David Manetti. He wanted it to be over. With each passing day, he became more apprehensive about the terrible things he was doing. To-date, he had contracted with Bonaiuto's hit men to kill nine people. Although three of them were the boys who had murdered Katie, the others were simply headstrong people Jim wanted out of the way before making a plea with Congress to enact new morality laws. Even in the name of a worthy cause, Jim's actions were grinding against the very principals in which he believed. With a few keystrokes he could craft an e-mail and send a man to his death. The power he wielded was unsettling, and living with his actions was becoming almost unbearable. Jim expelled those thoughts.

Soon, the war will be over, he thought. *Those who have spoken out against the Moral Mafia will serve as reminders to the rest of the country—cooperate or perish.*

Jim stopped in the break room to get a cup of coffee. When he reached his office, he set down his brief case and turned on the radio. The regular talk radio program was conceding their air time to their national affiliate. *This is it!* Jim gripped the edges of his desk as he listened. The host was almost frantic as he delivered the breaking news.

—Good morning, this is John Dunning reporting from ABC news in Washington. Thursday, February eighth, will undoubtedly go down as one of the most tragic days in history. There has been a series of car bombings all across the nation's capital. While the FBI has confirmed at least six explosions, multiple sources indicate there have been as many as fourteen bombings within the last hour.

At this time, the FBI has not commented on the identities of the bombing victims, but one of our correspondents was told by a White House insider that the targets were high ranking politicians. Joining me now is political analyst, Brian Manning. Brian, what can you tell us about these bombings?

Well, for starters, John, let me tell you there is pandemonium in the nation's capital. The streets are flooded with cars trying to get out of the city, as reports of the bombings begin to reach the public. I have been on the phone with some of my contacts in the White House, and indeed rumor has it that many, if not all of the bombings, were targeted at government officials.

Although they have yet to claim any responsibility, Moral Mafia has already been credited with these insidious acts of terrorism. Six House members were killed last month, simply because the Moral Mafia said they were in the way, and now it looks like it's starting all over again. Just days ago, threats were made to lawmakers in an attempt to coerce them to pass new legislation to censor all forms of media containing violence and sexually explicit content. Many of our lawmakers went on record to say they would not comply with the Moral Mafia's guidelines. Now we wonder whether they are the targets of this nightmarish act.

The President of the United States has dismissed the house and senate, and ordered all Federal Government offices closed until further notice. He is asking that all government employees use public transportation. I repeat, if you work for the government you should not drive your personal vehicle—your safety may be greatly compromised.

Is the order to close Federal offices confined to Washington, or is this a nationwide directive?

This is a nation-wide directive from the president. All Federal Government Offices have been ordered to close.

Brian, I understand that the first bombing occurred at about six forty-five this morning. Yet, we did not receive any reports until well after eight. Can you tell us why?

I am told the mayor was concerned about starting a panic. The governor advised him to delay any announcements until after the rush hour. Meanwhile, the White House set up a task force to contact Senators and Congressmen. Most Federal employees were met at the door and told to return to their homes. By eight fifteen reports were beginning to leak to the press and the mayor made a public statement.

The freeways are currently bumper-to-bumper, and drivers are beginning to panic. There are reports of drivers abandoning cars, and authorities have begun to orchestrate the city's evacuation, but it's too late. The congestion will probably take hours to clear. City officials tell me there is no imminent danger of explosions to the general public. We are asking all commuters to evacuate the city in an orderly fashion. If you can delay your departure for a few hours, please do so.

When will we learn the identities of the victims?

I think it may be several hours before we know anything, John, maybe even days. There has been very little information coming to us from the authorities.

Just a moment, Brian, I have just received a report from our Minneapolis affiliate. At seven thirty central time, there was an explosion at Governor Glenn Christensen's mansion. We do not know whether anyone was hurt in the explosion, but we will follow-up with more details as soon as we have them.

This is terrible news, John. If these bombings are connected, there may be several more yet to come. It is still only five-forty in California.

That brings up a good point Brian; there is a window of opportunity to warn west coast officials and politicians before any more lives are lost. I hope the President's task force has an effective plan for contacting them.

Once again, we have received reports that several high ranking government officials may have been the targets of bombings. The FBI is asking all Senators and Congressmen to stay away from their vehicles until they can be examined by local bomb squads.

Jim looked at his watch and clicked the radio off. It was seven forty-three Central Standard Time. He wondered how many of the approximately seventy bombs would find their targets before the day was over. He had been instructing Bonaiuto's men where to plant them for over three weeks. Most were hidden in automobiles, but a few were strategically placed in homes and offices. The bombs contained intricate calendar timers that were set to arm themselves automatically on February eighth at five o'clock in the morning. Each device could then be detonated at a turn of an automobile ignition switch, the opening of a door, or in a few instances, by remote control. He now had confirmation that Napierilla's unique bombs were being detonated successfully. It would be several hours, maybe even days before he knew the identities of those killed today.

He closed his eyes. He was exhausted. The long hours he spent orchestrating the Moral Mafia's next moves and tending to the family business left him little time to sleep. He knew he must stay sharp to avoid making costly mistakes, mistakes that would lead the FBI right to him. After all, David Manetti found him. But that was pure coincidence. If David had not been working all night in the basement shop of the Farm Credit Building, he wouldn't have gotten Jim's license plates.

I should have rented a car, Jim thought as his throat tightened. *How many other coincidences are destined to happen? I need a nap. Maybe I'll take the afternoon off. With the barrage of news reports coming in, I don't think I can concentrate on anything else.*

Jim was grateful that Troia had picked up some of the slack at CFC. Scott was doing an admirable job of managing the day-to-day operations of the company. Jim meanwhile, concentrated most of his time on trying to solve the Moral Mafia case. Of course, he had to lead his team in the case. If not for appearances sake, then to be the first to know if and when a clue was found that could explain how to track the Moral Mafia's e-mail correspondence. Jim didn't attempt to impede their progress. He was confident their efforts would fall flat. And so far, they did.

The members of his team were bewildered. They had never faced a case like this before. They spent long hours studying the Moral Mafia's e-mails. The ASCII characters in the *FROM:* field made no sense at all. With the permission of the FBI, Jim had enlisted the help of a handful of mathematicians and cryptologists to attempt to characterize the ASCII data. They were as dumbfounded as the FBI.

Miranda was brilliant in the way she approached the case. She organized CFC's team efforts, and category by category began to define and eliminate various scenarios and technologies. Her approach was simple. By defining how the software didn't work, she had hoped to shed light on ways it might work. The word "random" was now commonly used by everyone involved in the case, to describe how e-mails reached their destination. *They are right on the money,* Jim thought. But other than that profound discovery, they had no way to know how to track down something that was random. How could they? How could anyone?

33

FOR LUNCH, JIM GRABBED A BIG BRONCO AT HIS FAVORITE hamburger restaurant, and devoured it on the way home. He had recently realized he was forgetting to eat. This was not by choice. Jim was so consumed by each day's activities, he sometimes forgot to take care of himself. This concerned him.

He continued to ask himself, *What else am I forgetting?*

He walked in the house at about one thirty. Peg greeted him with a note of alarm in her voice.

"Have you heard the news? Twenty-two car bombings so far today, and they just announced three bomb threats."

"I've been catching some of it on the radio, Peg, but that was hours ago. Who received bomb threats?"

"Playboy Magazine, Victoria's Secret, and the WB are evacuating their headquarters buildings right now. The FBI received an anonymous call warning them to evacuate all three corporate headquarters buildings immediately."

"This is absolutely crazy," Jim said, trying to feign concern. "The day's events are just plain hard to believe."

"I can understand why the Moral Mafia targeted Playboy and Victoria's Secret," Peg said, "but why the WB?"

"Are you kidding?" Jim asked. "The WB has introduced more teenagers to sex, than ABC, NBC, and CBS combined. For years, the WB has painted an unrealistic picture of teenage life. They've made kids believe it is normal to jump from one bed to the next, and now that's exactly what they are doing."

Peg went on, "Some analysts are predicting a widespread panic across the country. People are already hoarding water, groceries, and gasoline—it's madness!"

"Looks to be a good time to sell bomb shelters too," Jim said with a sarcastic edge. "The crazy people are going to be coming out of the woodwork."

"They are just reacting to the situation," Peg said. "We could use a few things from the store too, Jim. I didn't make it to the market on Saturday."

"Why don't you do that now, Peg? I need to take a nap. Can you wake me around four o'clock?"

Peg's eyes rounded and her jaw fell. "You're taking a nap?"

"You were right earlier. I can hardly keep my eyes open. If you wake me by four, we can catch up on the news together."

It wasn't exactly a date, but Peg would gladly take the opportunity to spend some time with Jim.

Even a brief nap can have dramatic effects on a person's state of mind. That was the case with Jim. By four thirty in the afternoon, Jim and Peg sat with the remote control, flipping between news channels, and commenting on the unbelievable events of the day. It appeared that some events were still unfolding on both coasts.

The evacuations at Playboy, Victoria's Secret, and the WB were completed just in time. All three buildings received powerful blasts, knocking out their data centers. Two other organizations were the targets of bigger explosions, but there was no warning, no call for evacuation. The American Civil Liberties Union in New York City, and the National Center for Lesbian Rights in San Francisco, received multiple blasts at one o'clock Pacific Standard Time. Initial reports claimed that both buildings were leveled, and 52 people were killed in the combined blasts.

When Jim heard the news, he was content that his plan succeeded, yet he took no satisfaction in the deaths. It wasn't gays and lesbians he deplored, but rather their lifestyles. He realized that gay or not, these people have families, loved ones, and friends that will miss them. Jim never thought he would feel so remorseful, but after watching a video of the aftermath, he was feeling differently. Loved ones were crying and wailing during their search through the rubble. It was becoming difficult for him to keep this war faceless. It was far too late for that. The country was in shock, paralyzed after a long string of savage events. Even the syndicated reporters were walking on eggshells. They reported facts, snippets of information, but withheld their usual pointed commentaries. The CNN anchorman just announced that the President of the United States would address the nation at nine o'clock Eastern Standard Time.

Jim and Peg sat close together on the sofa. The three youngest children played at their feet.

Peg wondered out loud, "What can the President possibly say to ease the fears of the people?"

"I don't know, Peg. I don't suppose the right words exist. But there is no question that he has got to do something. It's almost six. Nine o'clock Eastern—that's eight o'clock our time. What do you say we get dinner started so we don't miss his speech?"

"I don't know if I want to move a muscle," Peg said softly. "We haven't sat together in months."

Jim felt ashamed. "I'm trying Peg. I think about the way things used to be."

A single tear ran down Peg's cheek. "I miss you Jim."

He gave her a long hug and asked her for just a little more patience.

"I'm coping with some issues, working them out as best I can. Maybe soon we can see a counselor."

Composing herself and wiping her cheeks, she said, "Okay then, it's time to get dinner."

Peg stood up and made her way to the kitchen. Jim sat on the floor with the kids and played their favorite game, UNO. Peg held her breath for a moment and savored the familiar sounds of laughter.

34

SENATOR GRANT ROBINSON OPENED THE STYROFOAM cooler to peek at his catch one last time. He was giddy with excitement. From dawn to dusk, he and tobacco lobbyist, Larry Werthing, caught sixteen trout. Robinson had never caught more than three in a good day at Lake Needwood in the spring and summer months. The popular seventy-five acre freshwater lake in Rock Creek Regional Park was technically closed for the winter months, but status had its privileges, and Werthing was adept at providing unbelievable perks for his special business associate.

When they had arrived in the park just before five this morning, they loaded their fishing tackle onto a golf cart. They then drove to a hand picked spot where a fifteen foot tent had been erected over the frozen lake. Inside, two holes had been drilled though the ice. Canvas folding chairs flanked the spot and an eight foot table was crammed with expensive delicacies, including caviar and fine scotch. The senator wondered what this lavish setup cost his friend, but the thought quickly passed. He rarely gave such things consideration anymore. He deserved every bit of the royal treatment he was given. After all, he had saved Werthing's cigarette manufacturing company millions of dollars by slowly converting the devastating fines they suffered in tobacco lawsuits, to less costly penalties, such as public service announcements warning consumers of the dangers of tobacco. Werthing had an enviable job and an unlimited expense account. The sixty-two year old senator didn't hesitate to take advantage of it whenever he could.

As Werthing drove the senator to their hotel, they heard a radio broadcast depicting the day's events. The commentator read a list of Senators names thought dead in the bombings, and Senator Barry Christensen, a good friend and golfing partner of Senator Robinson's, was one of them.

"Jesus, Grant, if you hadn't taken vacation you could have easily been in one of those explosions. You've been pretty outspoken in your refusal to cooperate with the Moral Mafia."

Senator Robinson looked shaken, "You're right, Larry. I'm as much a target as any of those killed today, maybe more so." A tear streamed down his cheek, "Those goddamned religious freaks. They took away my golfing buddy of twenty years. If it kills me, I'm going after those lunatics with everything I've got."

"Be careful, old friend. I don't think anyone really knows what we're dealing with yet."

Robinson pondered a moment. "I need to get to my cell phone, Larry. I know I said I'd spend the night, but I think I'd better get back this evening."

Fifteen minutes later, Werthing loaded the senator's Mercedes station wagon, while Senator Robinson went to his hotel room to make some calls. The trout were already on dry ice.

Man, its cold, Werthing thought as he got in his car. He clicked the heating system to the warmest setting. Then he backed his car out and parked four spaces away from the Mercedes.

I still think Grant should have his car checked out, he thought.

When Senator Robinson appeared, he had a serious look on his face. He was on his cell phone, no doubt talking with one of his peers. He tossed his bag in the back and closed the hatch. Werthing ran to him as he approached his door.

"Grant, maybe you should have your car checked before starting it—just in case."

Robinson laughed, "You don't need to worry, Larry, there's no bomb. I drove it here, didn't I? And I never told anyone where I was going. Call me next week, we'll fry some trout."

The senator slid behind the wheel. Werthing ran to his car, got in, and pulled the door closed just before the blast. He felt his car rock as it was slammed by an adjoining vehicle. For seconds, all he could see were flames everywhere. When they subsided, he opened his door and ran to the senator's car. He backed away from the intense heat and was startled when he seared his hand on the door of the neighboring car. When he focused on the charred body behind the steering wheel of Senator Robinson's car, he began to cry.

35

LADIES AND GENTLEMEN, THE PRESIDENT OF THE UNITED States.

The CNN commentator broke into regular programming without warning. The President's popularity had risen and fallen like the stock market in recent months. He was currently halfway through his second term and faced with a catastrophe of unbelievable proportions. The President began his speech.

Good evening, my fellow Americans.

By now, you have undoubtedly heard about the tragic events that took place today across our great nation. All of America grieves over these senseless killings. I wish to express my heart felt condolences to the spouses, families, and friends of all those who were killed today. Please know our thoughts and prayers are with you now and always. This is indeed a day of great mourning and sorrow for all Americans whose freedoms are under attack. It is a day that beckons to each of us to reach deep within our souls to summon courage at a time when many of us are frightened.

Today's bombings were sheer acts of terrorism from a merciless organization known as the Moral Mafia. The leader of this organization is attempting to advance a personal agenda under the guise of morality. Yet his actions are as immoral as any this country has ever seen. He has referred to this as a war, but the only casualties we have seen so far are those of innocent men and women. I am asking the American people to stay strong and to remain steadfast in their resolve to win this war.

Last week, I created a special task force using the combined resources of the FBI, the CIA, Homeland Security, the Armed Forces, and several corporations from our country's business sector. Together, we will track down the Moral Mafia and bring these cowards to justice. The FBI has several leads in the case, and it is simply a matter of time until we capture them.

Jim was jolted by the last comment. *The FBI has several leads? It is simply a matter of time until we capture them? It can't be. The President is lying to calm the public,* Jim thought. *Just in case, I'd better call Vince first thing in the morning.* Jim continued listening.

I knew many of the men and women who were killed. They were democrats and republicans, liberals and conservatives. They served their country with a passion for what they believed. To snuff these lives out for personal gain is incomprehensible. For the Moral Mafia, there will be a stiff price to pay and they need to know this: I will catch them, and I will punish them.

I have dismissed Congress, the House, and Senate through next week, while we implement new safety measures in our nation's capital.

As for you, the American people, there is little impending danger of loss of life. The biggest risk we face is that of intolerance. We are a great nation. We have always stood united in the cause of freedom. I ask that you continue to stand united and support every American's right to live the lifestyle they choose. Whether the issue is sexual preference, abortion, religion, or politics, we have created our own government and our own system of law making. You—the people—cast your votes to elect congressmen and senators to do your bidding in Washington. Ours is the most successful form of government in the world, and we need to allow it to continue to work for us. I ask that Americans continue to embrace their work and recreation just as they have always done. We cannot allow these madmen to beat us. We must be vigilant, and courageous.

The Moral Mafia has forced us all to take a look at our lifestyles, and indeed, there has been much debate about morality in the past weeks. One of the charges the Moral Mafia has leveled against our citizens is that we allow our children to watch too much sex and violence on television, and in videos. I have met with a group of researchers to address the issue, and I am happy to announce we have a solution to the problem. The technology already exists to add special coding to DVDs and videos, and to withhold marked scenes with the press of a button. In other words, we can make videos age appropriate for any audience. We will be taking a look at more technologies to protect our children from age inappropriate content.

I am asking the leader of the Moral Mafia to contact me directly at the e-mail address shown on the television screen. We want to open a dialog and work with him to prevent any further loss of life. I ask that no one else use this e-mail address. The FBI assures me that there is an identifying mark on the Moral Mafia's correspondence that will allow us to authenticate it, if it is indeed from them.

Meanwhile, I ask that you, our citizen's, be patient for a short time, and to support each other in this hour of crisis. We are the strongest nation on earth. We have weathered many storms, and we will emerge from this crisis a nation stronger and greater than ever before. May our people find abundant strength and courage to rally and support each other. May God bless us and keep us safe, and may God Bless America. Good night."

Jim muted the television and the CNN commentator reappeared on the screen, "What do you think, Peg?"

"It was a pretty short speech, but probably about as good as anything you could hope for, given the circumstances. What about you?"

"I think it was brilliant. The president expressed his condolences; called the leader of the Moral Mafia a madman and a coward, supported every American's right to freedom, and baited the leader of the Moral Mafia with that awful proposal."

"What do you mean?"

"The President proposes to add special encoding to DVDs so that a single disc is age appropriate for any viewer. It's a good idea, and quite frankly, I don't know why it wasn't done years ago. The user might have to enter a special code to allow harsh language or sexually explicit scenes to play; otherwise they would be automatically omitted. It's a great scheme except for one thing—"

"What's that?"

"This would require responsible parents. Are you aware of how many parents allow their children to drink alcohol at home or have unsupervised parties? I know plenty. Most of these parents would just give their children the codes. It's a great idea, but it won't work. The President is baiting the leader of the Moral Mafia to contact him with the promise of solutions to morality issues. No doubt, he wants to keep his friends close and his enemies closer."

"Do you think it will work?"

"No, the leader of the Moral Mafia is probably too intelligent to fall for such an empty scheme, but then again, only time will tell."

36

THE TWO MEN ARGUED FOR MORE THAN AN HOUR. Gary Brennan played the perfect devil's advocate, trying his best to shoot down each of Frank Saunders's scenarios with regard to Tony Constantino's computer. He finally grew tired of the game.

"Even if you did figure out a scenario that made sense, you still couldn't prove it. Besides, you're no longer on the case."

"Yeah, thanks to that son-of-a-bitch, O'BRIEN!"

"You did break protocol, Frank."

"I got O'Brien to his plane safe and sound. I don't know what he was complaining about."

"You knew Constantino's men were all over the hospital the night he died. You should have escorted him through a secure exit—not parade him through the front door."

"Like I said, he made it home okay—no one knows he was even there."

"You'd better hope so, Frank, or you'll be doing more than sixty days of desk duty."

"Don't remind me. First I'm off the Constantino case, and now I'm missing my chance to nail the Moral Mafia. The case will probably be solved before I'm off desk duty."

"I don't think so. From what I hear, Vince doesn't have a solitary lead in the case."

"You've gotta' be kidding! They should have a few leads by now."

"Nope—all I heard is that no one can trace the e-mails sent by the Moral Mafia, not even your friend, O'Brien."

Saunders almost choked on his soda. "What do you mean?"

"You haven't been reading your bulletins, have you?"

"I don't need a lecture, Gary; just tell me what you know."

Gary reveled in the opportunity to make Saunders feel foolish, "The e-mails the Moral Mafia has sent are untraceable. The entire bureau was alerted to report any e-mail correspondence that has an unusual string of characters in the *FROM:* field. Apparently, the e-mails we have confiscated so far have no @ *symbol* or extension suffix like *dot com or dot net.*"

Saunders looked most serious as he pondered some very interesting thoughts.

Constantino's scam was untraceable too. Is there a connection?

The FBI was certain Constantino's computer had been used to siphon "point of sale" funds from American Express card holders into a personal bank account. An informant from within America Express identified the individual responsible for giving Constantino the data he needed to complete the task. Only after days of questioning did the suspect confess to his part of the crime, but he had no knowledge how Constantino did it. Both the FBI and O'Brien's company failed to find even the slightest clue. In fact, it appeared as though Constantino's browser and e-mail software had been untouched since June of this year. Except for the spreadsheet and word processing programs, it was like he had stopped using his computer altogether. The FBI had recovered some innocent looking e-mails that were written prior to June. They were from Constantino's personal AOL account. But why was there no correspondence since then?

Like a lightning bolt, it hit him. "Constantino may have been using the same technology as the Moral Mafia!" Saunders exclaimed proudly. "Maybe they're the same organization!"

"Sorry Frank, I'm finished playing that game."

"No—I mean it! Consider this; Constantino was the head of the Chicago mafia."

"So?"

"The Moral Mafia surfaced shortly after Constantino's death!"

"Again—so?"

"In both cases, there are no computer clues. We couldn't track how Constantino ripped off American Express customers, and we can't track the Moral Mafia's e-mail correspondence."

"Those are two completely different things Frank."

"Yes they are, but there is no trace of any e-mail correspondence on Constantino's computer after June of this year. What if he had begun using this technology in June?"

"We have no proof that the technology leaves no trace of anything on the computer, Frank—we only know that their e-mails can't be tracked to the source. I think you are reaching here."

What a puny mind, Saunders thought. *This is why I am vastly superior to the twits and morons in the bureau.*

"I can prove it, Gary. All I need to do is find someone Constantino e-mailed just before he died. If the characteristics of the e-mail are the same as you described, we'll know the technology is the same. Maybe the story Constantino told O'Brien wasn't so far fetched after all—maybe O'Brien knows something he ain't sharing! Maybe we can solve both cases at once."

Brennan considered the scenario again. "The idea does have some merit, Frank, but you're off the case, and Vince is probably too pissed off to listen to any of your ideas." Brennan smirked, "You really do come up with some crazy ideas, Frank."

"Yeah, crazy like a fox," Saunders boasted. "We need to get to Chicago."

Brennan didn't respond. *It'll be a cold day in hell,* he thought.

He almost shook his head in disgust, but didn't want to upset Saunders. The tightly wound FBI agent had quite a reputation for

222

flying off the handle, and his crazed look sent a chill down Brennan's spine.

"Whaddaya mean, we?" Brennan asked. "No one's going to approve a trip to Chicago."

"We don't need an approval, Gary." Saunders was busy opening and slamming drawers. "I don't know where anything is in this goddamn office. Help me find the vacation request forms, would you?"

37

FOLLOWING THE PRESIDENT'S SPEECH, JIM TYPED THE long string of ASCII characters required to invoke the stealth software that made him so powerful. A window appeared on the screen the instant he pressed the Enter key. The program looked ancient. It did not use a graphical interface, as did most software programs of the day. Instead, the screen was divided into sections using simple ASCII characters to form borders around them.

In the *TO:* field, Jim typed the e-mail address he saw during the president's speech. He checked his spelling: u_s_a_1_@_m_o_r_ a_l_a_m_e_r_i_c_a_._g_o_v. In the *SUBJECT:* section, he typed, *Response to your speech.* And then he pressed the Tab key and began crafting a response to the President of the United States.

Dear Mr. President,

Thank you for giving me an opportunity to communicate with you, however, this shall be my one and only correspondence. I appreciate the way you attempted to calm the fears of your countrymen. It was never my wish to invoke a panic or riots among our citizens, only a reasonable amount of intimidation. I have just one desire; I wish to restore our country to the just nation it once was. I have no other motives, no hidden agendas. Once I am certain we are headed in the right direction, I will simply disappear, and you will never hear from me again. It is my wish to make this a short war, but make no mistake, this is indeed a war.

I know you are a man of moral character. I know you can remember the days when there was genuine respect for a man's opinion, his property, the family, and most importantly, for human life. The word "respect," itself, seems to have lost its meaning. It certainly is difficult to apply the term in any context, to our current society. It must be difficult for you to understand how I can speak of respect for human life, and then turn around and kill Americans without mercy. I assure you, it is most difficult to do, but in the end, I will save countless lives.

I am not a religious zealot. I do not consider myself a fanatic of any kind. I am just a man who is tired of explaining who, what, when, where, why, and how to my children with regard to sex, corruption, and violence. In this evening's speech, you said that the only casualties we have seen so far are those of innocent people. I respectfully disagree. The House and Senate have become corrupt. Our representatives have forgotten about the American people. They are easily bribed. They pass legislation that allows immorality to flourish. They greedily attach pork initiatives to every bill, and make a mockery of the very freedom they swore to protect. We are not safe. We are being attacked from within our own borders, on our streets, and in our homes, and this must change.

Our children's lives have spun out of control. They join gangs and kill each other. Many steal to support their drug habits, but all of them lack respect for others. We have digressed from respect to total disrespect, and the journey began with the Supreme Court's ruling in the Roe vs. Wade case. Mind you, I couldn't care less what a woman does with her body. She can mangle it or take care of it, but anyone who takes the life of an unborn child is just plain wrong.

At last count, today's death toll stood at seventy-six. I have the power and resources to make this a daily event!!! If you wish to test me, go ahead, but I don't think you will. I believe you place a greater value on human life than do your congressmen and senators. I need you to hold private meetings with them, convince them to start acting on the list of demands I published last week. I have not made a single demand that will not make this country a better place to live. If they are worried about succumbing to a terrorist, then you must fight them until they surrender to you. If my demands are not met, I will triple the number of deaths in my next bombings. Your congressmen and senators should examine how their families would fare without them.

Finally, I ask that you do not attempt to use technology to resolve moral issues. It simply will not work. Your idea to mark inappropriate movie content with special coding, assumes that our nation's parents have the moral character and fortitude to use it properly. I assure you, they do not. Our parents have become weak and can no longer say "no" to their children. We must correct the problem at its core, not mask it with technology.

As I said at the start of this letter, I will not correspond with you again. I will not give you or anyone else the opportunity to attempt to reason with me. My identity cannot be discovered. My communications software is untraceable. Knowing this, you must ask yourself which is better: passing laws to make America a stronger nation, or watching as the governing body of our nation is torn apart? I will be vigilant, watching your actions and waiting for results, but I will not be patient. I need to see immediate action. You have the power to end this war. Good luck, and may God guide your hand.

—The Moral Mafia

Jim was an excellent writer. It had only taken him a few minutes to compose his message to the Commander-in-Chief. He pressed a combination of the *Control and Enter* keys," and the correspondence began its fractured journey through cyberspace.

He composed a similar message for Miguel Rodriguez at the Associated Press. It was for tomorrow's newspaper. As he sent the message on its way, he realized that he was still very tired. But before he made his way to the bedroom, he said a prayer to himself.

Forgive me, God, for what I have done today. I am a lowly sinner. I have killed in hopes of saving countless other lives, but I know the act itself is wrong. I am truly sorry for what I have done. Please forgive me, and then do with me what you will.

Jim found himself praying at odd times of the day. For weeks, a terrible guilt had been mounting within him. Today, it had climaxed. Jim spent more and more time reading his journal, trying to remember what he was thinking when he decided to take the law into his own hands. Sometimes he thought it was the only way to keep from going insane. Certain passages helped more than others, but it was the initial notes he had written describing the death of his daughter, Katie that helped to rekindle his determination to finish what he had started.

When he opened the bedroom door, Jim saw a pleasant and familiar sight. Peg was in bed devouring a paperback novel. Jim assumed it was probably another of her hopelessly romantic love stories. He laid his clothes across a chair and climbed into bed.

"What are you reading, Peg?"

She had to look at the cover to get the title. She read so many books she could hardly keep track.

"Love in the Spring," giving Jim a brief smile. "It's pretty much like the rest of them. In fact, I don't think I can read any more books from this author. Her love stories all seem to run together. It's like reading the same book over and over again."

Peg placed the book on her night stand and looked at Jim with hopeful eyes. "I'd rather we write a chapter of our own tonight."

Jim appeared almost frightened, or maybe it was a look of surprise. They hadn't made love since Katie's death. Peg noticed his expression and placed her hand on his shoulder.

"We don't have to if you aren't ready."

Jim recognized the gentle aroma of her perfume. He looked in her deep green eyes, and all at once he recalled everything he loved, everything he missed so much in his soul mate. He didn't hesitate a single moment, pulling her close and kissing her gently, passionately. How could they have stayed apart for so long? He rolled over to one side and put his arms around her, pulling her close, bringing their warm bodies together. The sensations of her smooth, soft skin against his created an immediate response. Peg raised her light silk gown. They continued to kiss passionately and reveled in the simple pleasures of holding and caressing each other. When his hand stroked her breast, she shifted slightly, creating a path for him to enter. As he did, she clasped both hands high on his shoulders, anxious and longing for what was to come. They moved together like young lovers, enjoying every motion, every nuance of the moment. Their bodies were precise, their timing exact, and when it was over, Jim kissed her once more with such fervency, that she began to cry softly.

She whispered, "I missed you, Jim—I missed you so much."

Peg fell asleep while Jim held her. He thought about the irony of it all. Today had been one of the best and worst days of his life. He spent a few late afternoon and evening hours with Peg, played games with his children, and made passionate love to his wife. In addition, he killed seventy-six people—not with his own hands, but certainly at his direction. When his quest began, there was clarity in his thinking, and solid reasoning for waging a war against his country. But now, the reasons seemed to have lost their luster. None of it made sense. He wondered if he had gone slightly mad and was only now coming to his senses. *I must end this!* a compelling voice cried within him.

38

AMERICA WAS PARALYZED. YESTERDAY'S BOMBINGS had taken a more serious toll than Jim could ever have imagined. Americans were panicking. Business trade had slowed and in many cases ceased altogether. The stock market tumbled to a record low. The country was in mourning, for the murdered government officials, now martyrs, Jim imagined, and he was terrified as to what might happen next. Although all of Jim's employees had shown up for work, he thought they must have been the only ones in Omaha to do so. There was no rush hour traffic. The streets of the city were almost desolate.

Listening to the news confirmed Jim's suspicions that Omaha had reacted no differently than the rest of the country. Yesterday, the President had dismissed all federal employees through the end of next week. Most governors and mayors followed his example by doing the same for state and city employees. Only an hour ago, Jim received a call from Federal Express. A package he was expecting today will not arrive because it was forced to travel by ground. All airline flights had been grounded.

Jim felt as though he was coming out of a stupor, a trance he had been in for months. He could hardly believe that he alone had brought the greatest country in the world to its knees. He felt no pride in the thought. Last night he had made some real progress. He spent a quality evening with his wife and children. The barriers he had put up after Katie's death were beginning to crumble, but something more unexpected was happening. Jim was questioning his own actions. Perhaps the realization that he had killed so many people was taking its toll. Viewing the videos allowed a deeply embedded empathy to surface. Seeing the people he hurt brought back memories of his own personal suffering. Jim was now preoccupied with a profound guilt like none he had ever felt before. The newspapers said the death toll increased by nine during the night to eighty-five.

Page one of the newspapers was always reserved for correspondence from the Moral Mafia, provided there was any. And today's story would indeed be controversial. Jim addressed the country with much of the same verbiage he sent to the President of the United States last night. However, his comments were much more threatening now. He wanted this nightmare to end, so he addressed both lawmaker s and the American people in a single response. He took a moment to skim the newspaper article, his letter to America.

> Fellow Americans:
> I appreciate the President's attempt to calm the fears of his countrymen. It was never my wish to invoke riots among our citizens. I ask all Americans to remain composed, and refrain from staging protests. Such actions will be futile and result in injuring innocent people. Instead, I ask that you help me to put an end to this madness now—today. Call your Congressman or Senator. Tell them to pass the legislation I outlined in my original demands. Tell them to do it immediately.

The President lied to you. The FBI has no leads in this case. It is more likely that I will be killed crossing the street than be captured by the FBI. I will continue to kill more lawmakers, more immoral activists, more immoral citizens, until these laws are passed, and I see positive results taking hold.

I have only one desire, I wish to restore our country to the just nation it once was. I have no other motives, no hidden agendas. Once I am certain we are headed in the right direction, I will simply disappear, and you will never hear from me again. It is my wish to make this a short war, but make no mistake, this is indeed a war.

I expect and insist that all my demands are met. The following issues could be changed within days:

1. Reverse of Roe vs. Wade.
2. Allow the Ten Commandments and religious displays from all religions to be exhibited in public institutions.
3. Outlaw gay marriage and special rights for gays.
4. Pass censorship of all forms of media that is sexually explicit, or contains unnecessary violence, or foul language.
5. Enact tougher penalties on drug crimes for users and dealers.
6. Pass legislation to limit elected officials to no more than two terms.

Next week, a set of reasonable censorship guidelines will be sent to Congress for a vote. Passing this legislation will demonstrate that our lawmakers care about the morals of our children. I have commented to the President with regard to the corruption of our lawmakers. They are dishonest, easily bribed, self seeking individuals, and I insist that we pass term limit legislation for everyone. In the future no one shall seek a third term for county, city, state, or national positions—ever!

At last count, yesterday's death toll stood at seventy-six. I have the power and resources to continue the bloodshed, daily if necessary! It would be wise not to test me. Congressmen and senators should examine how their families would fare without them. Their lives will be in constant jeopardy until my demands are met.

Finally, I would like to address the mothers and fathers of our nation's children, because our future depends on them. Our country became great because our forefathers instilled greatness in us— their children. Now it is time for us to concentrate on developing the moral character of our children, and stop worrying about how to entertain them. For God's sake—be parents!!!

The President recommended the use of technology to resolve our moral issues. This simply will not work. The idea of marking inappropriate movie content with special coding, assumes that our nation's parents themselves have the moral character and fortitude to use it properly. I assure you, they do not. Our parents have become weak and can no longer say "no" to their children. We must correct the problem at its core, not mask it with technology.

You have seen my power and determination. The next several rounds of bombs have been in position for weeks. I can escalate my actions, or delay them. I can cause infinitely more death and destruction.

Consider this carefully America—the next move is yours!

- The Moral Mafia

On page two of the morning paper, Jim found a transcript of the President's speech and a harsh commentary from an Omaha newspaper columnist. Jim was having problems concentrating on the story. More and more mental walls were crashing down in his head as he understood the ramifications of what he had done. He succeeded in pulling off his single-minded mission. But in his head it had become a shameful act, an act he regretted and couldn't reverse. He sat motionless behind his desk. The radio was piling more guilt on him by the minute. He could take no more. He stood up and turned it off.

Jim needed to focus on something else. He grabbed a legal pad and stepped into Scott Troia's office.

"Scott, can you gather everyone into the conference room? I want to see if we are making any headway on the Moral Mafia case."

Disappointedly, Scott said, "I can save you the trouble, Jim, we're completely stumped."

Anticipating such a comment, Jim said, "Let's have a whiteboard session. I'll meet you in the conference room."

Jim's whiteboard sessions were similar in nature to scientific think tanks. While conducting them, he would coax comments and theories from his employees to resolve difficult cases. He believed his whiteboard sessions helped them to open their minds to the impossible. Over time, they became accustomed to his style of holding these sometimes outrageous sessions. He taught them that there was no such thing as a stupid question or theory. In some of the early sessions, a few of the employees would smirk, or laugh out loud at an unlikely idea. But over and over, Jim proved the value of considering every premise, no matter how ridiculous it seemed.

The entire office converged on the conference room at once. The staff was somber. Even Randy Burks and Charlie Ford weren't engaged in one of their typical arguments. Jim sensed that yesterday's bombings had a demoralizing effect on the entire country.

"Scott tells me that everyone is stumped with regard to the Moral Mafia case, is that right?"

There were several murmurs and heads nodding up and down. Jim knew the consequences of being discovered, but he hated the fact that his employees were staring at defeat.

He said, "Well, it's time to catch these guys. Let's give this project everything we've got. Let's bring this murdering son-of-a-bitch to justice!"

The room got lively—instantly. To the employees of Computer Forensic Consultants, Jim was an icon, a hero who was bigger than life. If he thought it was possible—it was damn well possible. Just having a glimmer of hope in their hearts turned the murmurs into a full blown discussion. Scott was leaning against the wall on one side of the whiteboard. *God bless him—he never ceases to amaze me.*

The meeting lasted for two hours and fifty minutes, and no one looked the slightest bit tired when he dismissed them. They had a handful of theories to follow-up, some of them a little far-fetched, but Jim assured them that they needed to think outside the box.

Scott approached Jim, "For the first time ever, I thought even you couldn't possibly pull them out of their depressed state. I'm happy to say you proved me wrong. If I could bottle your leadership abilities, I'd be a billionaire."

I am a billionaire, Jim thought to himself, *and it doesn't help a bit.* "Thanks, Scott. What do you think of the theories we came up with?"

"I particularly liked the one you came up with, Jim. An e-mail that attaches itself randomly to hundreds of in-transit e-mails until it reaches the recipient. As crazy as it sounds, the idea has merit."

"It wouldn't be particularly difficult to design such a program, Scott. It's just a different delivery method than we are used to. The reason no one has thought of it before, is that it's inefficient. One always thinks of the fastest, most direct method of sending e-mail. If this is indeed the method the Moral Mafia is using, then we have only to decipher the ASCII string in the *'FROM:'* box to trace it back to the originator." Jim made it sound plausible, but he knew the odds were almost zero. "And since we know that the Moral Mafia is the originator of every e-mail, some of the work is already done for us."

"Even if we are successful in making sense of the ASCII code, how will that help us find Mr. M?"

"I have a hunch that the program takes the shortest random route possible. If this is true, its e-mails are leaving an exact address trail, based on geography. In other words, an e-mail sent from Chicago to Florida will choose to attach itself only to e-mails traveling between those two points and no others."

"Wait a minute, Jim, that's not exactly as the crow flies. Do you realize what this means in terms of research? We would have to examine every route an e-mail travels from telephone carriers, cable carriers, DSL carriers, and who knows what else? We don't have examples of the Moral Mafia's e-mails from different parts of the country. There is nothing to compare them to."

"No, but we have examples of e-mails sent from a single location in the country."

Troia shook his head like it was an impossible task.

Jim tried his best to comfort him. "I know, Scott, it seems unlikely that we could ever solve this case, but we have carte blanche according to Janet Stratman. All we are doing is coming up with the possible scenarios. Let's give the FBI some homework for a change."

Scott wanted to be supportive, but he never lied to Jim. "I think your chances of success are in the billions."

"Then you are much more optimistic than I am, Scott. Unfortunately, it's all we have."

The whiteboard session spawned a lot of traffic in and out of Jim's office throughout the rest of the day. Jim was impressed at how thoroughly his people took a handful of outrageous theories, and developed them into plausible scenarios. Miranda Peters had teamed up with Steve Wakeman. As a new employee, Steve had found Miranda to be somewhat intimidating. Her mind was so quick; she was often several steps ahead of him. Recently, Steve began to appreciate her keen senses. By partnering with her, maybe he could pick up some of her troubleshooting style and some of the latest techniques being taught in college.

In the mid-afternoon, Miranda dropped some notes off to Jim. She seemed excited, and said she wanted to discuss some new ideas that she and Steve had just come up with. He said he would review the notes before going home so they could discuss them Monday morning. Jim wondered why he saw her so differently today. Was it because he had rekindled his relationship with Peg? He didn't fail to notice the silky white see-through blouse Miranda was wearing. It was elegantly adorned with lace and complemented a matching lace bra that showed through in a provocative, but tasteful way. As of late, he had been feeling guilt for what he thought was an attraction to Miranda, but he did not seem to feel those attractions now. He was glad. It was already six o'clock. Jim had planned to make it home for dinner, but due to the flurry of activity, he decided to stay another hour or two. He called Peg. She was disappointed he would miss dinner, but was glad he would not be gone too late.

The office emptied out promptly at five. It was unusual, but yesterday's actions by the Moral Mafia had taken a toll on everyone. His employees, and probably most Americans, were fearful of what might happen next. Most of them were anxious to get to a television for a news fix. A small group was headed for Clancy's. Scott asked Jim if he would like to go, but he declined, saying only that he had some other commitments. Jim thought he was alone, when Miranda stepped into his office. Unaware of her presence, he was reading her notes intently. Suddenly, he sensed something moving. He jerked his head up, startled.

"My God, Miranda, I thought I was alone!"

39

"I'M SORRY, JIM, I DIDN'T MEAN TO FRIGHTEN YOU."

"That's okay; I was deep in thought when you came in."

Something looked different about her appearance from just a short while ago, but Jim didn't know what.

"What can I do for you?"

"I was just getting ready to go home, but I wanted to find out how you're doing."

"I'm doing fine, Miranda, why do you ask?"

"It's just been over a week since the riot at the courthouse, and you were moving a little slow for a while. I just wanted to make sure you were feeling all right."

Jim smiled, and pointed to his cheek. "The last bruise is nearly gone."

Miranda squinted to see it, and then rounded Jim's desk and turned on a small halogen lamp. She adjusted the lamp slightly and then took Jim's head in her hands stooping sharply over him.

Oh God, that's what's different!

As she leaned over, Jim had a clear view of her incredible breasts. His eyes only lingered a moment, but from the fully rounded contours, to her perfectly shaped nipples, it was a sight he was sure he would never forget.

But that would mean she had removed her bra—intentionally!

Jim's mind was stumbling awkwardly. He had no idea what to say, and then it happened. She took his hands and placed them on her breasts, and leaned over to kiss him. Hands still frozen on her breasts, he pushed her back, not too hard, but it was a definite push back. He quickly lowered his hands and said, "I'm so sorry, Miranda, I can't."

She stood up straight, appearing both hurt and confused, "Jim, I thought we—"

"No, Miranda, I'm happily married. If I ever gave you the impression that—"

"NO, STOP—LET ME JUST LEAVE! I'm very sorry. I thought you felt the same."

Jim had no idea why he just didn't let her go, but if nothing else, he was a compassionate man.

"Miranda, you are one of the most beautiful, intelligent, and exciting women I have ever met. If I wasn't married, I would go to hell and back to find someone like you."

The comment was a mistake.

Miranda came close again, "You always say nice things like that Jim. 'Miranda, you're a great catch—Miranda, you're going to make someone a great wife—'Miranda, you're beautiful and intelligent!' I think you have feelings for me, Jim."

Jim closed his eyes for a moment. *Jesus, I did say those things, didn't I? I need to stop this now.*

"I like you very much; Miranda, but I love my wife."

Her eyes were pleading, she had nothing to lose. The fingers of her right hand quickly looped around to separate the top two buttons of her blouse. She drew the edges of the blouses down over her shoulders and looking deep into Jim's eyes, spoke in pure desperation.

"No strings attached, Jim—I want you."

Jim's heart was breaking. In his sadness, he wanted to cry for her. Deep inside he knew he had been suppressing some feelings for her, but they were no match for those he had for Peg. He could never be unfaithful to her.

"Please, Miranda; don't make this harder, I could never betray Peg—never!"

He stood up and went to the door, "I have to go, please lock the door when you leave."

Miranda stood with her head down and arms crossed over her breasts, she didn't answer.

Jim started to go and then stopped cold, "I want you to take Monday off, with pay. I want you to think about your career with us. I don't want you to leave us—not because of this. When you come back on Tuesday this will all be forgotten, we don't have to speak about it ever."

Jim left the building.

Already on Jim's side of the desk, Miranda sat down in his chair and began to sob uncontrollably. She felt foolish now. She realized she may have misread Jim's kindness for love, yet he still seemed to—

"Nice tits lady."

Miranda's head shot up. "YOU!" she shrieked.

"I can't believe your boyfriend didn't take advantage of them. Really, they're a great pair. Any straight man would be glad to give em' a toss."

Miranda grasped her blouse and covered herself. She couldn't believe her eyes. Two familiar figures stood in the doorway. The thin, frail looking man, flaunted a horrid smile while repeatedly slapping a baton against the palm of his hand. The other man was a broad, foreboding figure with blond hair, and muscular arms.

"I promised you some fun with Billy, and I always keep my promises. Derek, introduce this pretty young lady to Billy—*BILLY CLUB*, that is—HA.

The two men moved swiftly around the desk. Aaron lifted Miranda out of the chair like she weighed nothing. His massive hand ripped her blouse off completely. He took her off balance and slammed her back against the floor, knocking the wind out of her. Miranda gasped for breath. Aaron began to fondle her breasts. As she caught her breath, she thought he looked repulsed at the very touch of them; his smile looked forced as he massaged them violently.

"Stop it! You're hurting me! I SAID STOP—"

Aaron placed one of his massive hands around her throat, squeezing just hard enough to keep her quiet. He wanted her awake for this; he wanted her to remember every detail of this night. With his free hand he squeezed her breasts harder. He knew he was hurting her. He turned his head toward Derek and quipped, "Well, what are you waiting for?"

Derek set the baton down beside her and unbuttoned her slacks. With eyes that seemed to be bulging out of their sockets, he pulled her slacks and panties off with a fluid yank. Miranda began to kick, but Aaron squeezed her throat harder. Derek spread her legs and on his knees scooted his torso between them. Miranda tried to scream, but couldn't. She knew what was going to happen. Grabbing the baton Derek looked down at the dark patch between her legs. "Lady, THIS IS BILLY!"

40

THE O'BRIEN PHONE RANG AT TEN MINUTES BEFORE seven. Shauna called, "Daaad, it's for you!" Jim and Peg were sitting together on the sofa for the second night in a row. They had just finished discussing arrangements for Tom's arrival home on Saturday. They agreed that Tom would be confined to the house for at least three months, and he would have no telephone privileges during that time. It wasn't a punishment, but rather a precaution and continuation of his treatment. They could not expect him to be completely cured after a ninety-day program, but at least they knew he would be drug-free. They intended to keep him that way. Peg reached for the phone on the end table, and handed it to Jim.

"Hello? Oh, hi Frank." Jim frowned, *What the hell is Saunders doing calling me at home?*

"You're where? YOU WHAT? Did you call an ambulance? What hospital are they taking her to? I'll meet you there."

Hearing only bits of the conversation, Peg was concerned, "What in the world was that all about—who's hurt?"

"It's Miranda, I gotta' go!"

Jim pushed through the door of Methodist Hospital's emergency room. He saw Saunders waiting for him.

"How is she?" Jim asked with great concern.

With a matter of fact intonation, he answered, "They're examining her right now. She's been badly beaten."

"Who would do this?"

"That's not a question for me, Jim. Say, while I've got you here, I want to ask you a few questions about Constantino's computer."

Jim stared at the uncaring bastard in disbelief, "You can ask me questions later Frank. Right now, I need to see how Miranda's doing."

"I just thought—"

"Go to hell Frank!"

Saunders already disliked Jim, who had just sunk a little lower on his hate list.

Someday, I'm going to give this guy a few broken bones, he thought, sneering at him.

Jim approached the admissions desk, "How is Miranda Peters?" he quipped, realizing he may have been rude. The woman behind the desk seemed not to notice his curt tone.

"Are you family, sir?"

"I'm her employer; she was attacked in my office."

"She arrived only moments ago, sir, if you'll have a seat, I'll let you know her condition as soon as possible."

Jim thanked her and saw Saunders fidgeting in the waiting area.

The sooner I get this over, cringing at the thought, *the sooner he can leave.*

"Okay, Frank, I'm all yours, but the second I get the green light to see Miranda, I'm out of here. But let me ask the first question. You said you found her—what were you doing in my office?"

"I'm on my way to Chicago to investigate the Constantino case. I thought I'd stop in Omaha on the way, and ask you some questions that might shed some light on the subject."

"Vince told me you were off the case."

Frank scowled, "Yes, thanks to you, Mr. O'Brien, but I'm doing this at my own expense, and on my own time. I think there's a connection between the Moral Mafia case, and Constantino's computer."

Jim raised his eyebrows, *Perhaps there is a shred of intelligence in Saunders after all.*

"Again, what were you doing in my office?"

"I checked into my hotel around six o'clock. I planned to see you tomorrow morning, but I know you often work late. I thought if I could see you tonight, I could get an early start on my way to Chicago. The office lights were on, so I went in. There was no one around. I walked to your office, and that's where I found the young lady—"

"Miranda," Jim said. Her name is Miranda."

"Yes, she was sprawled unconscious on the floor, naked and bleeding."

Jim's eyes fell, *My God, how bad is she hurt?* The image that came to mind was horrid. It made him shudder.

I left her there all alone, unprotected. He imagined the worst.

"She took a pretty good beating," said Saunders. "She was already bruising when I arrived. But whoever did this didn't want to kill her. He left her alive, like he wanted her to suffer. What time did you leave the office?"

"About ten past six."

"And I arrived at about six thirty. A lot can happen in twenty minutes. I'll bet the guy had his way with her in less than ten."

Jim hated the way Saunders said it, cold, heartless, without feeling.

"I called the ambulance and police, and then did a little detective work."

"What do you mean?"

"I thought you might be appreciative if I lent the police a hand—they aren't very bright, you know."

This son-of-a-bitch wouldn't help me in a million years; he must be desperate for my help on the Constantino case.

"What did you find, Frank?"

"Let's go with the obvious first," he said. "There was a police baton— you know the kind they use for crowd control, in her—well, let's just say it was *in her*. There was one of those yellow, sticky notes on it. Someone wrote, 'Compliments of the gay, sick, queer people.'"

Jim gagged involuntarily. He felt sick to his stomach as an image of the blond-haired man came to mind. He struggled for a moment.

What was his name?

Picturing his blond hair, square jaw, and handsome face, the name popped into his head.

"AARON!"

"Excuse me, Mr. O'Brien?"

"That's the name of the man who did this!"

"You know who did it?"

"I'm positive of it. He's a big burly gay man with the muscles of a body builder."

"That fits exactly with what I found."

"What do you mean?"

"Well, it makes sense that he's gay. The young lady was raped with that baton. There were no traces of semen at all. She had bright red marks around her throat, and wrists, her breasts are bruised, her face had been pummeled, and there is no telling what kind of vaginal tearing may have occurred."

Jim's heart was racked with pain, *I did this to her, it's my fault. I'm going to find that bastard, and when I do—I'm going to make him pay!*

Jim just realized he wasn't listening to a single word Saunders was saying. He had apparently asked him a question, and was waiting for an answer.

"Sorry Frank, I was preoccupied for a moment. What did you say?"

"I said, when we are finished here, you need to file another police report so they can pick this guy up."

"I don't know his last name, nor do I know where he lives," Jim said sheepishly. "I don't have a clue where to start looking for him."

"Well maybe this will help; I do remember an older Ford van leaving the parking lot as I was pulling in."

"What color?" Jim asked hopefully.

"I couldn't tell" Frank said. "It was dark. But it had one of those custom paint jobs with broad stripes, you know—the kind they used to do with an air brush. I'd say you should look for a full-size, mid-eighties Ford van, in a warm color scheme ranging from red to brown."

"Well, at least that eliminates blue or green." Jim's comment was laced with sarcasm.

"Best I can do under the circumstances, Mr. O'Brien. I've already reported all of this to the police. I hope they find the men who did this."

Jim looked genuinely contrite for his comment. "Yeah, Frank, me too. I appreciate what you've done. If you'd like, I can mention this to Vince—"

Saunders waved his hands, "FOR GOD'S SAKE—NO! Vince doesn't know I'm here. I'd rather you just not say anything at all."

"Done," Jim said. "Not a word," The way Saunders stared at Jim, it was obvious that he had shared all of the information he had. It was Jim's turn now.

"Alright," Jim said, "tell me your theory about the relationship between the Constantino and Moral Mafia cases."

As Saunders laid out his thoughts, Jim was impressed with the supporting logic on which his premise was based.

"I have to admit Frank, I think your theory merits some follow-up."

Jim was almost certain Saunders was standing a little taller now. "I'm glad you agree with me, Mr. O'Brien. If Constantino started using a new technology in June, it would certainly explain the lack of any correspondence from that date forward. If I can find a single e-mail to a family member or associate of Constantino's between June and November, and it matches the format of the correspondence sent from the Moral Mafia's, we can tie these cases together. Perhaps Constantino's mafia is also the Moral Mafia."

Jim thought it was a good plan—too good, in fact! He would have to warn the family that Saunders was snooping around. Make sure they destroyed all correspondence, both paper and electronic.

Jim's thoughts again turned to Miranda. He was anxious to see her, but the woman at the admissions desk had her head down, scribbling notes.

"You didn't come here to get my blessing on your theory, Frank. Do you have other questions?"

"That night in Chicago, Constantino told you some crazy story as to how he siphoned money from American Express card holders. I need you to repeat that story for me. It may not be so far-fetched, after all."

Jim had carefully crafted a response to this question months ago. He was glad he did.

"I'm glad to tell you everything I know," he lied convincingly. Then he protected himself a little, "Just keep in mind, it has been months since our conversation. I hope I can remember all the details." Jim contorted his facial features to convince Saunders he was reaching deep in his memory for particulars, and then he began to spin another lie. "Constantino kept telling me he had acquired some kind of software that he used for moving data to and from FTP sites. Apparently, there was one more use for the software. He could redirect POS funds to any account of his choosing."

"POS funds?" Frank looked puzzled.

"Point of Sale. That is what they call the transaction when money is transferred from a credit card holder to a merchant. A few seconds after a credit card is swiped in an electronic card reader, funds are verified by a credit card clearing house, and then deposited into the merchant's account. Constantino claimed that if he had the right data from a credit card company, he could intercept transactions, and redirect them to a bank account. I'm not certain of exactly how it works, but I suspect the data he refers to consist of some kind of origination coordinates."

Frank looked intense. There was no doubt he felt several steps closer to a glorious victory.

"Are you aware that we got a confession from the man who claims to have given Constantino this very information?"

Jim looked surprised, "No, I had no idea."

"It's true. But he couldn't tell us how he did it. Where is Constantino's computer now?"

"You picked it up a while back, Frank. I don't know what Vince did with it. If you're looking for software on the hard disk, there is none. We scoured the disk drive for days and came up empty."

"But Constantino told you there was software!"

"Yes, he did, but it wasn't on that computer. I planned to tell you too, until you came out of his room and told me the whole story had been manufactured just to waste our time. I took your word for it that the whole story was a hoax."

"Son-of-a-bitch!" said Saunders, whose face was turning a deeper shade of red by the second. "If the story he told you was true, why would he tell me it was a lie?"

"I don't know," Jim said in a puzzled voice. "He wasn't exactly fond of you, Frank."

"Or maybe there was some other reason," Saunders said scrutinizing Jim suspiciously.

"What do you mean by that?"

"I don't know—yet!" said Saunders, "but I'm sure I'll find out soon enough."

Jim didn't appreciate the implication, and finished by telling another lie. He said that Constantino told him the software resided in a small plug-in USB memory device. He claimed the FBI just wasn't smart enough to find it when they broke into his office and confiscated his computer.

"Well, at least now I know what I'm looking for."

Jim nodded, *You haven't the faintest idea, you dumb oaf.*

"Just one final thing, Frank—even though you told me that Constantino's story was just his idea of a joke, I applied similar concepts to the Moral Mafia case. All of my employees have been studying the odd ASCII data that seem to be characteristic of the Moral Mafia's e-mails. It appears to be random, and completely untraceable. The few theories we have come up with have already been communicated to Vince."

Saunders looked a little disappointed at hearing this. Jim knew he wanted to stay ahead of the rest of the FBI, and indeed, Frank

247

held a slight advantage. He was going in search of the one piece of evidence that could link the two cases together. Of course, he was also looking for something that didn't exist, software on a USB memory device. Jim hoped the diversion would dilute his efforts and prevent him from finding matching e-mails from Constantino from June through November.

"I wish you luck, Frank. We really need to solve both of these cases."

Saunders had gotten what he came for. Jim watched him leave through Methodist Hospital's emergency doors. He was relieved to see him go.

If he could see my face now, he might see my confidence waning.

More than ever, Jim wished this was all over.

41

FORTY-FIVE MINUTES HAD PASSED SINCE JIM HAD ARRIVED at Methodist Hospital. He had called Peg to tell her what had happened. She offered to come and wait with him, but Jim said he would be terrible company, and that he preferred to wait alone. Jim glanced at the woman at the admissions desk. She was still doing busy work.

"Excuse me. Do you have any word on Miranda Peters' condition?"

"Are you family, sir?"

"No, I told you before, I'm her employer. She was attacked in my office."

"I'm sorry, sir, but unless you are family, I can't give you any information."

Jim was becoming incensed.

"Look, ma'am, I just want to know that she is all right—can you tell me that much?"

"No, sir, I can't. I don't think they will allow anyone to see her either."

Those goddamn HIPAA regulations can go a little too far, Jim thought.

"Fine, I'll wait right here for her."

"I don't think that's a good idea, sir, she's been admitted to a room."

With modest relief, Jim asked, "I don't suppose you'll give me her room number?"

Although the admissions clerk managed a convincing look of empathy, she shook her head slowly and said, "I really do wish I could, sir."

Jim began walking. He had no idea which direction he was going. He only knew that he had to see her. Not that his apology would undo the damage that was done, and there was plenty of that. He left her broken-hearted, and only now realized that the way he had departed may have humiliated her as well. For her to be beaten and raped by those foul men with a police baton only minutes after he left—what psychological condition could she possibly be in? What could he possibly do to alleviate her mental anguish?

What is happening to me? he thought, stopping by a row of chairs in the waiting area. He plunked down in one of them. *Just a few months ago, I was the happiest man on earth. My biggest concern was hiring my next employee. Now, I'm a killer—a hunted man. I have ruined the lives of people all over the country for some crazy ideals that our country no longer shares. And now, I hurt one of the most wonderful people I have ever known.*

For a second, Jim experienced a moment of fuzziness in his thoughts. He saw Miranda's beautiful young face, and then Peg's soulful eyes. His head began to whirl with fragmented thoughts, hundreds of clips, images lasting only milliseconds, of the two most important women in his life. He began sobbing uncontrollably, and when he was done, he thanked God for the simple moment of clarity he was now experiencing.

There was absolutely no doubt he loved Miranda with his whole heart and soul. But he loved her as a person, in exactly the same way he loved his best friend, Scott Troia. Yes, she was beautiful, and yes, he found her attractive, but this love was not rooted in physical attraction, nor was it the same kind of love he had for his true soul mate, Peg. He knew he truly loved her as a friend.

The combination of high esteem and admiration he held for her confused him for a while, especially during the last few months, when he had immersed himself in caring for Constantino's family and controlling the Moral Mafia. Jim was feeling slightly better. But he also admitted to himself that he had known all along that Miranda had feelings for him.

But I ignored it.

He thought about her now. Jim loved her gentle heart, and admired her brilliant mind and character, but most of all he loved her kindness. Jim always admired kindness.

He swore that he would spend the rest of his life making it up to her. He could no longer imagine Computer Forensic Consultants without her. In seven months, Miranda had become as much a part of CFC as Scott Troia.

Somehow, I have to explain this to her, without leading her to believe I mean anything different. I can't let her read anything more into it.

Jim saw a woman using a pay phone on the far end of the waiting area. It gave him an idea. He walked to the adjoining phone and picked up the telephone book. He flipped its pages until he found the main number for Methodist Hospital. Inserting the correct change, he dialed it. Jim asked the operator for Miranda Peters' telephone extension. She said she didn't have it. He told her she was just admitted, and she told him to wait a moment. Seconds later, she gave him the number.

"That is extension 6729; would you like me to connect you?"

"No thank you," Jim replied, and he hung up.

Jim had visited friends and family at Methodist many times over the years. He knew that patient room numbers were contained in their telephone extensions. Extension 6729 translated to room 729.

The seventh floor was bustling with nurses. Just off the elevator, Jim turned and headed toward one of the patient hallways. A wall plaque indicated rooms 715 through 730 were to his left. As he neared her room, two police officers were just closing her door. The female officer was in civilian clothes. A portly nurse was pushing a cart into the room across the hall. Jim passed Miranda's room, walking to a window. He peered outside, east toward downtown Omaha. There was a lot of traffic, even for a Friday night. Miranda's room had a window on the south side of the building.

A more peaceful view, Jim thought, *especially with the light falling snow.*

He turned around to see that the police officers had disappeared around the corner, and for the moment, the hallway was empty. He gently pressed against Miranda's door, and slipped inside her room.

Jim stood quietly, new guilt mounting with every breath Miranda took. He wasn't sure if she was resting or sleeping. Her once perfect features were unrecognizable. Her high cheekbones were lost in a swollen mass, and bruised in a seemingly infinite pallet of blues and violets.

That son of a bitch!

The words crept into his mind easily and repeatedly, as he studied each new cut and bruise. Suddenly, the door opened and the portly nurse walked into the room. Jim put his index finger to his lips and made a shhhh sound, but she ignored it.

"I'm sorry, sir, this young lady requested no visitors; you'll have to leave."

"How is she?"

"Are you immediate family?"

"I am her employer."

"I'm sorry, sir, her information is private."

"I just want to know—"

"It's the law—I can't tell you a thing."

"Jim? Is that you?"

Hearing Miranda's voice, Jim ran a half circle around the nurse, "Yes, it's me!"

The nurse didn't appreciate Jim's evasive maneuver, and her curt tone told him so.

"Sir, I said you'll have to LEAVE!"

Miranda's right eye was almost swollen shut, but her left eye said she was both frightened, and glad he was there. She reached for his arm and squeezed it tightly.

"Its okay, nurse, he can stay."

The nurse watched Jim coldly as she took Miranda's vitals, something he was certain she had done only minutes ago, but Jim hardly knew she was there.

"Miranda, I'm so sorry—"

"Don't apologize Jim, it's not your fault."

"But it is, I left you alone—I should NEVER have left you alone."

"I work late all the time, this could have happened a dozen times by now."

"It's my company. I should have taken better security precautions, especially since Aaron's threat."

A look of shock overtook Miranda. "How did you know it was Aaron?"

The nurse was dawdling, trying to kill time so she could hear the whole story. In total silence, Jim stared at her until she became uncomfortable.

"I think I'm finished here," she said. "Just buzz me if you need anything."

Returning his attention to Miranda, Jim continued, "He left a sticky note. It said, *Compliments of the gay, sick, queer people.* Do you remember? That's what I called them that day at City Hall. I'm almost certain he was getting back at me by hurting you."

Miranda knew it was true, but she tried to ease his guilt.

"Neither of us took his threat seriously, and why would we? Who would have guessed they would stalk us over that scuffle?"

Did she say those guys? Jim thought.

"Was that other man there too?"

"DEREK? Yes, he was there. He's the scary one, Jim. He had a baton."

A tear rolled down Miranda's cheek. Jim looked deadly serious.

"I am going to find them. I won't rest until I do. Frank Saunders gave me a description of a van that left the parking lot at about six thirty. I'm going to give it to the police, but I hope I can find them first."

"Please don't Jim. I don't want to see you hurt."

"We can talk about that tomorrow, but right now, I have something very important to say."

Miranda looked hopeful, and Jim thought he could read her expression. It was as though she thought that Jim might confess a deep love for her after all.

"I've had some time to sort out my thoughts," Jim said, "and I owe you a grave apology. Since Katie's death, my relationship with Peg has been strained. It's not unusual for couples to get divorced after the death of a child. In fact, only the strongest marriages can survive such tragedies. Fortunately, Peg and I have such a relationship, and our marriage will endure."

Miranda closed her good eye, her swollen bottom lip quivered. Jim took her hand. "I do have feelings for you, Miranda. In fact I can honestly say I love you, but in the same way I love my dearest friend, Scott Troia. Aside from my family, you two mean more to me than anyone or anything. My life wouldn't be nearly so full without you."

Miranda began to cry softly. Jim continued, "A man needs friends Miranda—so does a woman. We need to know that we are loved and appreciated for who we are, apart from our physical looks. I said it before, and I'll say it now, if I wasn't married, I'd search the ends of the earth to find someone like you. There is no doubt in my mind, that you could fulfill my every need as a life partner and soul mate. But I already have one, and I am and will always remain, faithful to her."

Miranda's eyes were still closed. She was nodding to acknowledge what Jim was saying. Her anguish combined with her battered features, pierced his heart.

"I know it's very selfish of me, to expect you to continue to be a part of my life, Miranda, especially after what happened tonight. But aside from your value to the company, I want your friendship even more. I cherish the moments I spend with you and Scott, and in time, I was hoping you would feel the same and start spending time with us." Her tears were flowing a little faster now. "You need us, Miranda. You need best friends, and I swear to God, I'm up to the task. Let me help you through this difficult time, please—let me be there for you."

It wasn't at all what Miranda had hoped for. She loved Jim, and wondered if she could work for him under the circumstances. But she didn't want to let go of the best employer and friend she had ever had.

"Okay Jim, I'll stay for now, but I can't predict how I will feel in a month."

"That's all I can ask—now give your best buddy a hug!" Jim held Miranda in his arms for a long time. Before he left, they agreed that only Scott Troia would be told about the incident. Jim would give Miranda all the time she needed, with pay, to heal her wounds.

42

—*FEBRUARY 11, 2010*

I have decided to completely dismantle the Moral Mafia almost two months ahead of schedule, and return Tony Constantino's belongings to the family. I will keep two things, (1) the Ethernet cards containing the memory chips and software, which will be destroyed. These devices are simply too powerful a temptation to be used by an honest man, let alone a mafia don. (2) I will also keep Constantino's Swiss Bank Account. The money was obtained illegally, and I will use it as a financial tool to peacefully promote morally sound organizations.

I have notified David Manetti. He acknowledged my e-mail by placing an ad in the Chicago Tribune. He intends to make a trip to Omaha on Friday, February 24th, to pick up everything I mentioned. The two week lead time will give me a chance to outline the many business changes, and problems I have resolved for the family. Some of the changes will legitimize a number of their business dealings, but somehow, I doubt they will care. However, I will spend a few hours with David Manetti, and advise him on these issues. He will then make the intended deliveries to Jimmy Bonaiuto and Michael Lanza. He hopes to be promoted to a position of prominence for his part in helping Bonaiuto take his rightful position as don of the Constantino family.

I am anxious to end the madness that resulted from the creation of this organization. For a period of time, I was willing to kill anyone who got in my way, or stood between me, and my self-righteous views of morality. Although it is wrong, a part of me has a strong desire to finish what I have begun. After all, Congress just passed the censorship legislation I sent them, and same-sex marriage has just been declared unlawful. The American people have themselves, come out in support of term limits, and it is only a matter of time before the congress enacts even stronger limits than I had originally demanded. The Ten Commandments are now proudly displayed in every public place where they had been removed in the past few years. In fact, most of my demands have now been met, but at a great cost to our country.

In addition to the eighty-five lives that were lost on Black Thursday, over fourteen people have been killed as a result of violence during demonstrations that went awry. I'm afraid our country has become more deeply divided than ever over the issue of abortion. Congress has not yet submitted legislation to make it illegal. Demonstrations and riots have become almost a daily occurrence. The liberals are not looking at this as a moral issue, but have instead taken the opportunity to make this a "political last stand." It is simply the greatest emotional issue America has faced since the abolition of slavery.

I intend to address America one last time. I want to tell the people that as long as they continue to adopt ethical legislation regarding abortion; the Moral Mafia will not reappear. But I must make it a convincing bluff. Once I hand everything over to David Manetti, there will be no turning back. I will no longer have any control over the family. I have won many battles in the war against immorality, but I feel no joy from my victory. I will spend the rest of my life repenting, asking God to forgive me for my unholy deeds.

This will be one of the last journal entries I write. The war I waged did not bring my daughter, Katie back. And I do not know that my son *will ever recover from his drug addiction, but I cannot help but feel that millions of Americans will live safer, more fulfilling lives because the Moral Mafia has reduced the amount of sex, violence, and corruption our children will be subjected to. No one can extinguish it entirely, but our laws should promote moral behavior. I look forward to using Constantino's massive fortune to continue this fight in a positive and peaceful fashion.*

Jim backed up the data to his SD card, and deleted it from his Smart Phone, just as he had done many times before. It was nine o'clock on Saturday morning. In about a half hour, he and Peg would be leaving for Norfolk, Nebraska to bring Tom home. The three youngest O'Briens' were watching cartoons in the living room. Jim sat down with them for a few minutes. Danny climbed in his lap and snuggled his head in the crook of Jim's neck. Jim ruffled his hair.

"What time will you be home, Dad?"

"It's an hour and a half drive each way buddy. My guess is around one o'clock."

"I can't wait to see Tom; he hasn't even seen my turtle yet. Does he have to go back tomorrow?"

"No, Danny, he's home to stay," *I hope,* he thought.

About twenty minutes later, Peg appeared, rattling off instructions for Morgan, who was babysitting.

"There is almost a whole pizza you can warm up for the kids for lunch, and Dad's cell phone number is on the kitchen counter, if you need it. Any questions?"

"We'll be fine, Mom," Morgan insisted with a tone that said *"Don't worry, I'm fourteen years old."*

"Okay, that's everything—are you ready to go, Jim?"

Danny took his sweet time relinquishing possession of his father.

"We'll see you kids in a few hours."

Jim and Peg had a very serious discussion on the way to Norfolk. They were determined to avoid making any more mistakes with their children, and at this moment, Tom was fixed in their crosshairs. In their first counseling session, Peg admitted turning a blind eye to Jim's suspicions that Tom was using drugs. And now she lived in fear that at least some of her children would face adolescent problems that were equally as challenging.

They had already faced Tom's drug addiction and Katie's premature death. Drugs were still their biggest worry, but there was also smoking, alcohol, sexually transmitted diseases, and teenage pregnancy. They wondered if they would be lucky enough to escape these problems with the rest of the children. The best they could do was to maximize their awareness of the dangers, and minimize the children's exposure to them. Aside from praying, that was all any parent could do.

"Behavioral Health Specialists," was a non-profit drug and alcohol treatment center with multiple branches. The one in Norfolk, Nebraska was called Sunrise Place. Jim chose this institution because of their broad range of services. Detoxification was only the first of many steps in Tom's long-term rehabilitation program. They also offered a myriad of other services, including ongoing substance abuse treatment and psychological counseling.

Jim felt that Tom's problems were rooted far deeper than simple peer pressure or the desire to achieve a "high" from drugs. In the last year he had witnessed his son stealing to fund his addiction. This was not unusual, but Tom showed no signs of remorse for his actions. He had developed a cold, nonchalant attitude regarding his actions, and believed he had a right to take whatever he wanted. This was a mind-set he shared with his best friend Matt Bauer. The difference between the two boys was not so great, Jim thought. Matt was simply more honest, and outspoken about it.

Upon their arrival at Sunset Place, Jim and Peg were taken to the chief psychologist's office. About five minutes later, Dr. Edward Morton joined them. They smiled and shook hands, but the conversation went negative almost immediately. "Your son's case is most disturbing," he said rubbing his bald head. "While I cannot share the exact content of conversations I have had with your son, I can give you a diagnosis of his condition, and summarize my opinion of his current state-of-mind."

"We appreciate any information you can give us, Dr. Morton," Jim said apprehensively.

"Your son is delusional in many ways," the doctor began, as if he had quite a laundry list to recite. "From our recorded conversations and from what you told me about your family, I surmised that your son came from a loving home. Is that correct?"

Peg answered, "Yes, without question," wondering why there would be the slightest doubt.

"That is quite puzzling indeed," Dr. Morton continued. "In fact, he doesn't talk about his family much at all. It is as though your family is nothing more to him than a means of self preservation. In other words, you provide him food, shelter, and tend to his immediate needs, but I see an alarming lack of affection between the boy and his family."

Peg became defensive, "I can assure you, Doctor, Tom loves his fam—" Jim raised his hand to stop her in mid-sentence.

"Remember Peg, we agreed to listen to everything the doctor and his staff had to say. We need to keep an open mind about this. We need to remember who the experts are."

She was still stinging from the comment, but Peg apologized.

"I know this cannot be easy to hear," said the doctor with compassion, "but your son is quick to hurt other people. He only seems to cooperate when he wants something." A big light went off in Jim's head. *Had they been mistaking affection for something else, attention, cooperation perhaps?*

"You said he is quick to hurt people. What do you mean by that?"

"In my opinion, I think he hurts people before they can hurt him. It's an automatic defense mechanism, and he can no more help it than you can help having green eyes. He really doesn't care much about the feelings of others, Mr. O'Brien, but he wasn't born that way. No one is. Of course, he can be very cooperative, and very communicative, if it benefits him. For instance, we can easily bribe him with the promise of free time, or an extra long break. In those instances, he cooperates with us fully. But usually, he won't give us the time of day."

Jim looked at Peg and said, "I have seen these traits in him many times before, Peg. But because he is my son, I shrugged it off as something else. But to hear a professional say it—it all becomes much clearer now."

A tear rolled down Peg's cheek, "I've seen it too, I—I just never dreamed he didn't love us."

"I'm not saying he doesn't love you, Mrs. O'Brien. I am saying that he doesn't have a good grasp of his affections, like a normal child. His mannerisms are deliberate and manipulative, and you need to keep this in mind as you help him through his recovery. You can actually use these traits as a tool to control his behavior."

"There is one more thing you should know. In addition to his emotional immaturity, the boy shows a total lack of respect for women."

Jim watched Peg's expression as she opened her mouth in disbelief. If he had made the comment, she would have cut him off at the knees.

"Tom's first counselor was a woman, Susan Jensen. Your son was so disrespectful to her, that she abandoned his case. I had to assign him to a male counselor. In the end, he had three counselors in three months."

"In what way was he disrespectful, Doctor Morton?"

Doctor Morton broke eye contact with them as he struggled to find a way to say what he must. "He treats women as sexual objects. His conversations with them are laced with sexual undertones. He lingers on inappropriate topics until he gets the response he wants."

Jim was compelled to ask, "And what is that, Doctor Morton?"

"Shame, guilt, anger, I don't really know to be honest. I think the boy needs more help than we are capable of providing. I suggest you find a good psychologist in Omaha. I wouldn't waste any time either—he has a serious problem."

Peg tried to recall her initial conversation with Susan Jensen. She was a beautiful young woman, and highly intelligent too. Her exuberance to help her patients told Peg she was passionate about her work. They drifted off the topic of Tom several times and chatted about Erin's recent wedding and family events. Peg remembered liking this young woman a lot.

What did he do to make her abandon his case?

The question perplexed her.

Doctor Morton was still talking, "—and I will be happy to forward his records to his new doctor. Do you have anyone in mind, Mr. O'Brien?"

"No, not yet, but I'll begin looking on Monday."

"Fine, here is my card. Until you can find another doctor, please call or page me if you have any questions, or need advice."

Jim had additional questions, but he didn't want to ask them in front of Peg. He decided he could call Doctor Morton on Monday. They concluded their visit and were escorted back to the lobby where Tom was already waiting for them. Peg took him in her arms and embraced him like he were about to be escorted to the electric chair. Tom was truly glad to see them, and why not? He was being released from captivity.

43

JIM STUDIED THE LIST HE HAD JUST RESEARCHED AND compiled. He was unconsciously shaking his head. *Where do I begin?* he thought. The list was much larger than he imagined. It contained the names and locations of Omaha's gay organizations, clubs, and hangouts. *I only have one thing going for me,* Jim thought, *the van.* Saunders saw a mid-eighties Ford van with broad painted stripes leaving his parking lot the night Aaron attacked Miranda. *I need to find a striped van in warm color scheme.* The whole thing seemed a little improbable to him. This wasn't a TV detective show, where he can bust into a gay bar and force the bartender to give him the suspects address. And just because gay bars exist, doesn't mean Aaron frequents them.

For all I know, he could be a home body. Jim shuddered. The thought of Aaron snuggling up with another man made him a little nauseous.

Is Derek his significant other? Jim wondered.

Wait a minute! It was so obvious; he was almost embarrassed he hadn't thought of it before. *Who needs the van? How hard can it be to find a blond, muscle bound gay man, and his blond, skinny sidekick with an offset eye? Surely it would be difficult in New York City, or Chicago, but I won't have to dig too deep to find these guys in Omaha.*

Jim picked up the telephone and called Scott Troia. "Hey Buddy, can you meet me for an hour at the Pub?"

Jim arrived at Clancy's Pub at three thirty. He had just left Tom at the house, surrounded by his siblings. Even Erin and Trent were there. Peg was cooking a big welcome home dinner for him. They were catching up on all the events of the last ninety days, including Christmas. Tom had opened the gifts Peg had stored in her closet. Jim had given him a Smart Phone just like his. Although he wouldn't be activating the phone, or letting Tom leave the house for a while, Jim wanted to make certain he had a way to keep tabs on him, when the time arrived.

Jim waved to Sandy, and she approached the table with her usual warm smile. "Hi Jim, I almost didn't recognize you without the big guy."

Jim laughed, "Don't worry, Sandy, he'll be here any minute. We'll have the usual."

She whisked off saying, "A pitcher and two glasses coming up."

It was true. Jim couldn't remember the last time he was here without Scott. He had hopes that Miranda would someday become part of their after hours group. Clancy's Pub was the perfect place to talk shop. It wasn't too noisy, the food was good, and Jim and Scott liked to get a little raucous once in a while. On Saint Patrick's Day, Jim always took Troia and a group of employees to the Brazen Head, an authentic Irish Pub, for corned beef and cabbage, and a selection of fine Irish beers. At this moment, Jim longed to have some fun with his employees. The pressure of working on the Moral Mafia case had transformed his typically upbeat work family into a somewhat somber workforce. Jim checked his calendar. Saint Patrick's Day wasn't until March 17th.

We've got to have some fun before then, he thought.

"Looks like I'm just in time, Jim," Sandy said, as she spotted Scott approaching and set a pitcher on the table. "Do you think he smelled the aroma of beer?"

"I'm pretty sure of it, Sandy, with the size of that honker, he can smell the green cheese on the moon."

"Hey, I'm right here ya' know. Ain't you two got any feelings?"

Scott slapped Jim on the back and the two men exchanged a few comical jabs, as was typical of their relationship. A moment later, Jim explained what had happened to Miranda on Friday night. He continued with the details of how Saunders found Miranda, and that she would be taking a few weeks off to recover. When Jim finished, he placed his hand on Scott's shoulder.

"We've got to find these guys, Scott. We need to bring them to justice."

Jim knew that Scott wasn't afraid to go searching for Aaron, yet he hesitated, before answering. "I don't think it's a good idea."

"Why not?"

"If you had thought this through, you'd know why, Jim. This Aaron character knows where you work. You've got to assume he knows where you live as well. No doubt, he got your name from the newspaper article after the riot at City Hall. I'm sure he had no problem finding you in the phone book. You need to stay close to your family, Jim—keep watch over them. We can work through the police to find them."

"Perhaps you don't recall how ineffective the police were at finding Katie's killers?"

"Yeah, I remember, but it's still your best bet. Don't forget, Jim, Aaron threatened to kill you."

Jim started to disagree, but then remembered how Aaron fashioned a gun with his hand and pointed it at him just before pulling the trigger. It was in fact, a threat. And he probably intended to keep it, just as he had done with Miranda.

"The bastard's toying with me," Jim said in disgust. "He's taunting me, making me suffer before he comes in for the kill."

"Before Friday night, I'd have thought you were crazy for saying so, but now I'm not so sure."

"Then we can't wait, Scott. We've got to go after him now."

"And what do you expect to do when we find him?"

"No crazy stunts, if that's what you are thinking. We'll just locate him, and call the police—I promise."

With Jim's strict assurance, Scott reconsidered his position. He was concerned for Jim and his family. Anyone who would rape a woman so brutally was capable of anything.

"Alright, Jim, we'll ask around and see if we can find him, but that's all. The police take over from there. When do you want to start?"

"Monday. I've compiled a list of gay establishments."

Why doesn't that surprise me, Scott thought.

44

MONDAY MORNING CAME AND WENT IN THE USUAL fashion. Jim announced that Miranda Peters would be out of the office for the next few weeks. He said it in a casual way that drew no questions from anyone. Vince Mitchell stopped in to see what kind of progress Jim's staff was making on the Moral Mafia case. Scott Troia and Steve Wakeman joined him to brief Vince on their latest theories. Vince was savvy enough to understand their concepts, and congratulated them on their progress. When the briefing was over, he and Jim spoke privately in his office.

"The President has turned the heat up on this case, Jim. Never in our history have we been under such pressure to find someone."

"I can understand that, Vince. We have worked on little else since you first asked for our help. But even if we do discover how Mr. M is communicating, it would be impossible to duplicate the software, or the exact geography from which he is communicating. We have tried using every technology known to us to decipher the meaning of the ASCII characters in the *FROM:* field. We have no idea what they mean. And if they truly are random, they may never lead us anywhere."

Vince nodded, "Just keep plugging away, Jim. Your team is light years ahead of the bureau. At least you have come up with some plausible theories. As usual, the FBI is stumped. Do you remember when you asked me if I thought that the *Great Cyber Robbery* might be connected to this case?"

"Yes, I do. Why do you ask?"

"After a lot of thought, I think we should give the idea careful consideration. There are certain parallels I find suspicious," Vince said. "If Constantino started using some new software in June, it could explain why there was no trace of correspondence from that date forward. We are sending a small team of agents to Chicago to investigate. If I can find an e-mail from Constantino to one of his men, between June and November, and it matches the format of the Moral Mafia, we can tie the cases together. Perhaps the two organizations are one and the same."

Jim could hardly believe that Saunders had come to this conclusion before Vince, but he doubted that much would come of it. He had already contacted the members of the family and directed them to destroy all existing correspondence. Since Vince was getting a little closer to the truth, Jim thought he should make himself appear more concerned,

"Perhaps we should take another look at Constantino's computer."

"Funny you should mention it—it's in the car."

*   *   *

Everyone noticed that Jim was making an enormous effort to be home for dinner. He reduced the hours he spent at the office, and it showed in the children's behavior. They seemed to be less apprehensive and more relaxed whenever he was home. Last night, at his welcome home dinner, Tom was the center of attention. He seemed to have no problems readjusting to the familiar surroundings he grew up in. He spoke with his siblings like nothing had ever happened. When Danny asked him what it was like at the treatment facility, he just said there wasn't much to do. Tonight, he was still receiving lots of attention. Jim noticed he was fidgeting throughout the meal. He wondered if he was nervous, or if it had something to do with his addiction. He knew Tom would be asking to see his friends soon. He could not permit it. After all, these were the same friends that allowed him to become a drug user. Of course, he was certain Tom wouldn't see it that way.

After dinner, Jim took Tom into his study. He removed a tiny, postage stamp sized card from a zippered pocket in his brief case, and installed several games on Tom's Smart Phone telephone.

"There, Tom—this will help you pass the time until we are ready to send you back to school."

Tom was an expert with video games. Jim had never seen anything like it, or his aptitude for troubleshooting computers.

Perhaps there is still a chance he can work at Computer Forensic Consultants, Jim thought, but he had his doubts.

"By the way," Jim added, "your mother has made an appointment for you to meet with a counselor tomorrow."

"Dad is that really necessary—I'm doing fine."

"I'm afraid you are going to have to get used to it," Jim said firmly. "You'll be seeing counselors for quite some time."

While Jim referred to him as a counselor, Tom was scheduled to see a psychologist. The best one Jim could find. Tom didn't argue, and thanked his dad for the games. He headed toward the living room and Jim followed closely behind. He and Peg agreed that Tom was not to spend any idle time in his bedroom. They wanted him surrounded by family members at all times. Peg had her feet tucked under her on the sofa, and was arranging a warm fleece throw on her lap. Jim gave her a peck on the cheek, and said he was going to meet Scott for a few hours, and would be back between eight thirty and nine o'clock. Peg knew where they were going.

When she said, "Drive carefully!" he knew what she really meant.

Jim left through the garage and picked up a package wrapped in cellophane. He slipped a black, six inch tube out of the wrapper. Flinging it with a tight grip, Jim heard a "thwack" sound. The collapsible metal billy club locked in place. He slapped it across his hand. Decidedly the solidly built police baton would do the job. He retracted it and slipped the dense, heavy club in his coat pocket, backed out of the driveway and headed for Troia's house.

At seven o'clock Monday evening, Jim and Scott entered a parking lot at 15th and Jackson Streets. Both men were a little uncomfortable as they walked through the door of "The Max," the first gay bar either of them had ever seen. The sign on the wall, touted "The Max," as the best gay dance club in America. Jim had never heard of the club, yet it was a huge facility, complete with five theme bars and two dance floors. Even at seven o'clock there were quite a few people, mostly men, drinking and conversing from the large expanse of tables.

"I have a feeling this place does one helluva' business," Scott said with a smile. "With your ability to attract flight attendants, you could probably score in here, too."

Jim struggled not to laugh. "Don't get me started, Scott. We've got business to take care of."

It seemed like they crossed quite a stretch of real estate to reach the first bar. The barmaid, a stout, unshaven, dark-haired man, was just lifting a tray of drinks. He eyed the two outsiders with little interest. The bartender was occupied, looking for a bottle of liquor.

Jim called across the counter, "Excuse me, I wonder if you can help me?"

The bartender was about six foot two, with sandy blond hair. Interested women might describe him as "buff," Jim thought. He had an athletic build with wide shoulders and a tapered waist that was perfectly accentuated by his white sleeveless shirt and black slacks. The "Chippendales" look alike showed a beautiful smile that faltered only slightly when he glanced from Jim to Scott.

270 "How can I help you, sir?"

"I'm looking for a man who might frequent this club. He is about six-foot-three, extremely muscular—he could be a body builder. He has light blond hair, long on top and trimmed short on the sides. His first name is Aaron. Do you know where I can find him?"

"I couldn't say. There are quite a few muscle bound types that come in here." Jim was intrigued. The more he learned about the gay community, the more his stereotype impressions were shattered. "Well," he said, "this one has a companion, a blond slender man with a wandering eye." Jim realized his choice of words might not be appropriate, "That is, one of his eyes is offset."

"Oh, you mean Derek."

Trying to contain his excitement, Jim said, "Yes, that's his name! Do you know where I can find him?"

"No, I'm sorry, I don't even know his last name."

"What about the body builder?"

"I don't think I've ever seen him."

"What do you want with them?"

"I manufacture weight lifting equipment. I was hoping we could hire Aaron as a model for some magazine ads."

*   *   *

In Chicago, a black Lincoln Town Car pulled into a private lower level parking garage. Two men emerged from the vehicle and walked toward an elevator. Frank Saunders was amazed at the enormity of one of the men who had to duck to clear the elevator door. Saunders parked his car in a public parking lot over an hour ago, across the street and a half block east of the Farm Credit Building. He had been sitting on a concrete stoop, observing a paltry twenty parking spaces the building afforded its tenants. The Town Car was the sixth car to arrive this Wednesday morning. Saunders was thankful for the stall the driver chose. It was between two other cars and next to a wide support column. He would have plenty of cover while he did the job he came to do.

Saunders spent much of the night snooping through desk drawers and file cabinets in an old liquor warehouse that was owned by the Constantino family. He was looking for evidence that would link Constantino to the Moral Mafia. He found nothing. Even without sleep, Saunders was alert and focused. He spent the last hour doing exercises to keep his muscles toned. He had trained himself to do some form of exercise during every idle minute of the day. He was getting impatient. He had to find something soon, as his vacation was almost over.

His eyes swept the garage, making certain there was no one else present. He quickly strode to the Town Car. By the time he reached it, he had already removed a wedge tool from his jacket, and was fishing a strap tool from the same pocket. Like a seasoned locksmith, Saunders inserted the tools between the passenger glass and the window sash. After a few slight maneuvers, he tugged the tools upward and the door unlocked. He worked quickly, removing papers from the console and glove box. The name on the car's registration was Mario Manetti, a suspected hit man for the late Tony Constantino. He found a wide assortment of maps. His eyes widened when he noticed an Omaha city map. He unfolded it and saw several street markings near the Missouri River. He stuffed the map in his pocket and continued rummaging. Nothing. He turned around and leaned over the back seat. Barely visible was a thick accordion file protruding from under the drivers' seat. He snatched the file, opened it, and began reviewing groups of papers from a dozen pockets.

The fourth grouping of papers contained a large list of the names of Senators and Congressmen. Several of them had been killed in car bombings on Black Thursday. The accompanying e-mail contained instructions for a carefully timed assassination. Over a million dollars had been paid for the specialized explosives with synchronized calendars. All the assassin had to do was affix the bombs to the cars of their unsuspecting victims. It would be child's play for Constantino's men. When he reached the fifth group of documents, he froze momentarily. There were two hand written sheets with contacts from Omaha. Scanning the list, he recognized none of the names. The next sheet was a web page printout from the Embassy Suites Hotel, on South 10th Street in Omaha.

That is close to the street markings on the map, Saunders thought.

Reading the next sheet, Saunders was unaware that he held his breath for half a minute while his eyes raced from line to line. It was an e-mail, but not an ordinary e-mail. The *FROM*: field at the top of the page contained gibberish, a bunch of letters, numbers, and ASCII characters that had no apparent meaning. In the body of the e-mail were the names and physical descriptions of three boys. The physical descriptions were long and detailed, but two of them had no last names. The first boy was Deacon Reynolds, a black boy, sixteen or seventeen years of age. He was described five-foot-four inches tall, one hundred forty pounds, with broad shoulders and short matted hair, often covered with a women's nylon stocking. He had a deep two to three inch scar along one cheek. The other two boys, Mikey and Carlos, were vividly described as well. Following the boys descriptions were a few comments.

JOB 001 – HIT - $50,000 – ADVANCED EXPENSES - $5,000 – COMPLETION BONUS - $25,000.

The best information I have is that the boys live in South Omaha, close to the river, somewhere in the vicinity of 7th and Pierce Streets. The boys deal drugs and should not be difficult to find. All three must die together. Make it look like an accident. Spare no expense.

Place ad to notify when finished.

– Moral Mafia

Saunders had a feeling he was pushing his luck reading the memo in Manetti's car. He let out his breath, and keeping the stack of papers, placed the folder back where he found it, under the drivers' seat. After a last check that everything was in its place, Saunders locked the car and began walking toward the garage entrance.

I've got to get to the local office, Saunders thought smiling uncontrollably. *A little more research and its promotion time.*

*   *   *

Miranda was elated when Jim told her he found the name and address of one of Derek's acquaintances.

"This will, without a doubt, lead us to Aaron, and we can finally put these monsters away." She closed her eyes and tilted her head back.

Maybe that will put an end to my dreams, she thought wishfully.

Miranda had already experienced three nightmares in a row, and each was the same. She was naked, her wrists pinned down tightly by Aaron's knees. He squeezed her breasts hard, stopping occasionally to hit her in the face. A crazed looking man drove a baton into her harder and harder.

Those eyes, she thought, *those horrible eyes.*

*   *   *

Saunders had spent nearly four hours in the FBI's Chicago office. He was accessing reports from the bureau's computer link to the police database. His heart pounded as he read that the three boys described in the memo were suspected of shooting a little Omaha girl, Katie O'Brien, in early November. As he read the second report, Saunders became almost euphoric. The three boys were killed in a drunk driving accident in December. They drove a stolen car right into the Missouri River.

"I've got him!" Saunders said aloud.

Noticing a few agents staring at him, he said no more.

It was O'Brien all along! he thought.

While the police reports were printing, his imagination went wild.

He was avenging the death of his daughter, and he used Constantino's hit man, Manetti, to do it. But why would they cooperate? What does

O'Brien have on Manetti? And how did O'Brien get Constantino's software? Did he take it from the computer the FBI gave him? Had he known Constantino before that night in Chicago? Was any portion of the incredible story Constantino told O'Brien true?

Grabbing an envelope, he folded the hand written pages, the map, memo, and police reports, and shoved them inside.

Saunders drove to the western edge of Chicago and found a hotel. He was famished and in desperate need of sleep.

At least I can avoid the rush hour traffic from here, he thought. *I'll get an early start in the morning, and pick up O'Brien tomorrow evening. I wonder what Vince will say when he finds out his trusted friend is the head of the Moral Mafia.*

45

JIM CALLED PEG TO TELL HER HE WOULD BE LATE FOR
dinner. He and Troia were going to drive to the home of a man
who allegedly knew Derek. His name was Paul Schaefer. Jim was so
excited to get the man's name, he forgot to get a description of him,
but that didn't matter. Hopefully, Paul Schaefer would give them
Derek's last name, and maybe even his address.

Better yet, Jim thought, *maybe he knows Aaron, too.*

Jim was still troubled by the fact that no one had ever seen Aaron.
But finding Derek would certainly lead to Aaron's capture as well.

Troia recommended they leave the office at five o'clock. Perhaps
they could catch Mr. Schaefer coming home from work. Jim thought
it was an excellent idea. Most people came home from work between
five thirty and seven o'clock. Jim reached in his shirt pocket and
withdrew the slip of paper he had printed carefully eight hours ago.
The name and address read:

Paul A. Schaefer
922 South 38th Street

Scott poked his head into Jim's office. He held a large magnifying glass over one eye. "Are you ready to go Sherlock?"

Jim chuckled, shaking his head. As he walked to get his coat, he said in his best English brogue, "Let's get these bastards, Watson."

At five o'clock, a strapping and handsome blond-haired man unlocked the door to his residence at 922 South 38th Street. He threw his gym bag on an oak seat that was built into the side of the staircase by the telephone. He went directly to the kitchen and opened the oven door. He poked a pot roast with a fork, and then checked the carrots and potatoes. He figured it would be ready in about thirty minutes.

Too soon, he thought. *Derek won't be home until six.*

He turned the roast over and reduced the oven temperature by fifty degrees.

He went back to the hallway, and opened his gym bag. Pulling out the contents, he walked them to the laundry room, where he transferred wet clothes into the dryer, and threw his gym clothes in the washing machine. After adjusting the settings and starting the washer, he picked up the laundry basket and ran up the stairs to the bedroom. He spread the clothes out on the king size bed and began to fold them. Paul Aaron Schaefer was a meticulous housekeeper. He figured that was one of the things Derek liked most about him, his ability to keep a clean, orderly house.

Aaron put their clothes away and sprinted to the bathroom. He turned the shower faucet on and adjusted the temperature. He stepped in front of the bathroom mirror and undressed. His skin was still shiny with sweat from his daily workout. He studied his exquisitely rippled body. It took him years to achieve the muscle mass he currently admired in his reflection. Aaron was chiseled from head to toe, and there was little, if any, fat to be seen. A frown appeared when his glance drifted downward, as it did every day. No amount of exercise could improve the one part of his anatomy he desperately wanted to enlarge. Even shorter, less muscular men seemed to be better endowed than he. Perhaps he just looked smaller due to his disproportionately larger body, but he was always worried that his partner, Derek, would someday lose interest in him for a man of sexually larger proportions.

He showered quickly, and was toweling off when the doorbell rang. Still naked, he ran to the bedroom window and saw a silver, late model Honda Accord parked in the street. The car looked familiar, but he couldn't recall why. Something told him to use caution. Donning a long terrycloth robe, he descended the stairs, but avoided turning on any lights. Instead of going to the front door, he stepped into the recess of the living room bay window. He could see two figures on the front porch, one of them seemed very familiar. He approached the front door and peeked through the side lite window. Catching a glimpse of Jim and his distinct auburn hair, he jolted back behind the door.

That's the man from City Hall, the riot—that girl's boyfriend! he thought. *Jesus, he knows where we live!*

Aaron stood in a crouched position, frozen behind the door. He almost bolted when the doorbell rang again.

Oh God—I told Derek assaulting that girl was a bad idea, but he wouldn't listen.

Aaron could see the mantle clock. It was ten minutes before six. Derek would be home shortly. He had to warn him.

The two men waited another minute, and then headed to the car. Aaron could hear their voices growing fainter as they walked further away. He leaped at the stairs, taking them two at a time. On his bed, he found his cellular phone. Flipping it open, he quickly dialed Derek's number.

"Hi," Derek said in a sweet voice. "Is dinner ready?"

"Don't come home, Derek—stay away until I call you!"

"What do you mean? I'm only a half block away, what's wrong?"

"Stop the car! The man whose girlfriend we raped—a-assaulted the other night—he's out front. He knows where we live."

"O'Brien!" he said. "Jesus—hold on," Derek said, "don't hang up."

He set the cell phone on the passenger seat and pulled into a driveway about six houses up the street. He quickly backed the red Ford van out of the driveway, and headed in the opposite direction.

Picking up the phone, Derek asked, "Did you talk to him?"

"No, they came to the door. I didn't answer it."

"What do you mean, THEY?"

"There was another guy with him, a big guy."

"Bigger than you, Aaron?"

"No, but big enough. He looks like he can take care of himself just fine."

"Okay, I'm going to drive around for a while, or maybe stop at Club Joy for a drink."

"You said you were going to stop going there."

"This is no time for that discussion, Aaron. Call me when they've gone."

The van reached the stop sign at the far end of the block, and then continued making its way toward Leavenworth Street. Troia had seen it come toward them and turn around, but didn't give it a thought until now. Jim was talking, but he interrupted him in mid-sentence.

"Didn't you say Saunders saw a striped van leaving our parking lot just before he found Miranda?"

"Yes, a red, orange, or brown van, something like that—why?"

"A red striped van turned around down the street while we were talking. At least I think it was red, it's getting dark."

Jim started the car, shifted into gear, and started driving down the street. "Which way did he go?"

Derek's phone rang. The caller ID said it was Aaron, "What's up?"

"Those men just left. They must have seen you."

Derek nearly froze, "When did they leave?"

"Just a second ago, they are probably approaching Leavenworth now."

Derek was already on Leavenworth Street heading east toward downtown. He had at least a two block lead on them. He made a split second decision and turned right on 36th Street. "I'm coming back, Aaron. I want you to go outside and open the garage door. I'll be there in about a minute."

Jim and Scott tore down Leavenworth trying to close the gap between them, but it was too late. Derek had already doubled back. Jim's silver Accord passed the intersection where Derek turned right, and continued speeding east.

When Derek pulled into the driveway, he hardly slowed down until he reached the detached garage at the far end of the back yard. The two men closed the door and locked it. It was now pitch dark.

Noticing the glow from the windows, Derek said, "Come on, let's douse the lights."

The two men ate dinner by candle light. The pot roast was dry and overcooked. Both of them were chatting nervously.

"We can't sit in the dark every night," Aaron said. "I knew we shouldn't have molested that girl."

"It was the best way to punish O'Brien," said Derek with a vengeful glance. "He nearly crushed my cheekbone with that damned baton. I thought it was fitting to use it on the girl."

"Well, what do we do now that he knows who we are?"

"You've got to eliminate him, Aaron—tomorrow."

"Me?"

"Are you forgetting how he humiliated you? He had your arm pinned in a revolving door like an animal. Do you remember what he said about gays?" Derek took the opportunity to be dramatic, "You are sick people, gay, sick, queer people."

"We all went a little off the deep end that day, Derek, me included. It's no reason to kill him."

"How about going to prison for assaulting a police officer, or for raping a woman? Is that reason enough? If that happens, we'll be separated. There is no telling when we might see each other again."

Aaron looked distraught. Derek's features softened a bit.

"Come on, Aaron, let's go upstairs. We can soak in the tub and discuss the details. You haven't used the scented candles I bought you for Christmas. Now's a good time to try them out."

When Jim walked in the house it was nearly seven. His mood had been dampened by the fact that he may have let Derek slip through his fingers, without even knowing it. But he really couldn't be sure. Just because a red van turned around up the street from them, didn't mean it was Derek. Yet, he found it very suspicious. The van never came close enough to see him. If it was Derek, or Aaron, for that matter, he was unquestionably tipped off. Jim and Scott discussed the possibility that Paul Schaefer was home, and didn't answer the door.

But Paul Schaefer had never seen them before, had he?

Jim couldn't be certain of anything pertaining to the two men he despised so much. The greeting from his youngest children melted all of his concerns away.

"Daddy's home, Daddy's home! Daddy, want to play a game?" Molly said cheerfully.

"Me too, me too!" said Danny.

"Let your father eat his dinner first, okay kids?"

In a sing-song reply, Molly's voice floated up and down the musical scale, "Okay, Daddy—hurry up and eat—we'll be waiting for you."

Peg reached for the hot pads, and retrieved Jim's dinner, which was warming in the oven.

Setting the plate on the table, she said, "Have a seat dear, and give me your coat. I'll be right back and we can talk."

Jim sat down. He was mentally fatigued. He was hoping to have some good news for Miranda tonight, but now, the evening looked fruitless.

Peg listened to Jim's recollection of the evening. She could feel his frustration. He finished by saying how strange it was that Aaron had never been seen in any of the gay clubs, and that they still hadn't discovered his or Derek's last names.

"I agree, that is very odd. Where does this Paul Schaefer fellow live?"

Jim handed her the piece of paper from his shirt pocket.

"Oh my—that's not too far from my parents' house," Peg said, with a slight look of concern.

"Don't worry, Peg, they live far enough away from your folks."

"What does the "A" stand for?"

"What do you mean?"

"His name is Paul A. Schaefer—what does the "A" stand for?"

"I—I don't know," Jim said thoughtfully.

Peg's eyes grew wide. "Could it be 'A' as in Aaron?"

"O sweet Jesus," Jim leaned back in his chair in disbelief. "Why didn't I think of it?" He slapped his hand on the table. "He goes by his middle name! It all fits! He was home the whole time we were there. He recognized me and warned Derek to turn around. I've got to call Scott."

Jim stood up and started to leave the kitchen for the study.

"Not so fast, Mister!" Peg said in a teasing voice. "Two things—first, sit down and finish your meatloaf; second, I think I deserve a thank you."

Jim bent over and gave her a long, warm kiss. As he sat down and picked up his fork, she finished teasing, "That was just the down payment, right, honey?"

"You bet, Peg, and if it's alright with you, I'd like to make my first installment tonight." They both laughed, and Jim was smiling throughout the rest of his meal.

Scott was out when Jim finally called him. He told Joan not to have him return the call. They could talk in the morning. Jim kept his promise. He played two games with Danny and Molly, and later in the evening, he made his first installment to Peg.

46

SCOTT NEARLY BURST INTO JIM'S OFFICE ON THIS THURS-day morning. I've been thinking about it, Jim. "That Paul Schaefer fella' has got to be Derek's boyfriend—or partner—or significant other, or whatever the hell you call it."

"You're absolutely right, Scott."

"I am?"

Jim explained how Peg speculated that Paul Schaefer went by his middle name, Aaron. "The pieces all fit together perfectly. Having thought about it half the night, I'm more certain of it than ever. We have found Aaron, and if we play our hand right, we'll find Derek, too."

"How come we couldn't find anyone who knew Aaron in the gay bars?"

"I have several theories. Aaron is a body builder. Maybe he is health conscious and doesn't drink. Or maybe he plays the homemaker in their relationship. He stays home and is the faithful one, while his partner likes to get out and party."

"Boy, you really have given this some thought, haven't you?"

"Yeah, I guess I have. All we need to do now is to stake out the house long enough to make a positive ID, then we can call the police."

"I wanna be there with you, Jim. I want to see this queer body builder, and the skinny guy with the weird eye."

"You may regret it, Scott. Ever since I met those two, I feel like I've been sleeping with one eye open. They really give me the creeps."

"That's why it's gonna' be such a pleasure to put them away." Scott stared across the room and pondered out loud. "How do you wanna do this? They know you and your car. Why don't I stake the place out in my car and get a few digital pictures of 'em coming and going. Once you verify their identities, we'll turn the photos over to the police."

"Not bad, Scott, I like it, but you'll need to stay alert. Just promise me you'll not engage them in any way. They're dangerous."

"Hey, I'm the one who talked you into going to the police, remember?"

They planned a timetable for this evening. Scott would leave the office an hour earlier than yesterday, around four o'clock. Jim gave him the company's digital camera. He set the camera's resolution at its maximum, so he could easily enlarge the photos. "This camera has a 12X zoom Scott, that's the equivalent of 430mm. You should be able to get some excellent close-ups."

"Just tell me where to pop in the flash cube, Jim."

Scott fiddled with the camera, as Jim tried to stop laughing long enough to dial Miranda's telephone number on the speaker phone. She was elated to hear the news. Jim thought she actually sounded happy. She told them that most of the black and violet bruising on her face had gone away, but had been replaced by an ugly hue of yellow. The swelling over her right eye was only a fraction of what it was days ago, but still looked gruesome. "I really want to come back to work," she said. Jim could tell she was bored.

"Maybe if I apply some makeup—."

Jim tried to sound positive. "If you are healing that quickly, Miranda, I'd say we could see you in the office by the middle of next week, God knows we could really use you."

Miranda sounded a little disappointed, but deep inside she knew it was too soon to go back to work. The three discussed the plan to acquire some photos of Aaron and Derek. Miranda wished Jim and Scott good luck, and begged them to call her if successful.

At three o'clock in the afternoon, Peg O'Brien was putting on her coat. Picking up the kids from school was a part of her daily routine. Since Katie's death, there were only three O'Brien's and six neighborhood children in her car pool. By the time she dropped them at their doorsteps and returned home, it was usually around four o'clock. At Jim's pleading, Peg always took Tom and Molly with her. He still didn't trust Tom to be alone. This afternoon, they were engrossed in a video.

Buttoning the last button on her coat, she said, "Come on you two, we've got to pick up the kids from school."

Tom kept his eyes fixed on the television, "Do we have to go with you, Mom? It's cold outside, and we're just getting to the good part of the movie."

Molly was snuggled up to him.

They look so cozy, Peg thought, *and Tom has been behaving perfectly since he's come home.*

Hesitantly, she defied her better judgment. "I don't see why you two can't stay home. Just today, mind you. I'll be back in about an hour."

"We'll be fine, Mom, see you when you get back."

Peg had barely closed the door when Tom stood up and snagged Molly's blanket from off the floor. He covered her up and tucked the edges of the blanket beneath her. "There," he said, "that will keep you warm." *And confined,* he thought. "I'm going to go in the kitchen for a minute. I'll be right back, okay?"

Molly never looked up, "okay," she murmured.

Tom moved through the kitchen with the stealth of a cat. When he reached the back door, he quietly, he unlocked it and crossed the deck. Descending the steps, he quickly reached the air conditioning unit and the power box that was mounted to the house. He opened the metal door on the power box. He exhaled in relief to see the package he was waiting for had arrived. Slipping a plastic bag into his pocket, he backtracked into the house. He opened the silverware drawer, and removed a spoon. In a cabinet he found a book of matches. With the syringe that accompanied the white powder in the plastic bag, he had everything he needed.

Just a few more minutes, he thought, as he found his way to the bathroom and locked the door.

Jim watched out his office window as Scott Troia drove off. He was hopeful that Aaron and Derek would be in police custody before the day was over. All they needed was a positive ID to have them picked up. Jim couldn't help the nervous knot that was forming in his stomach. He had no idea how that knot would grow exponentially before the day was through.

The office seemed quiet, almost ghostly, in fact. Jim wondered if the same subdued spirit had dampened the hallways during his long absence after Katie's death. He strode down the main corridor to see if he could lend assistance to any of his employees. Most of them were still hard at work on the Moral Mafia case, but Jim was recently forced to resume work on other client projects as well. It was so quiet he could clearly hear the radio in Mike Arnold's office. A talk show host was describing the events unfolding at an abortion demonstration in front of the White House. It was becoming violent, the third such outbreak of violence this week. *Abortion,* Jim thought, *how could it ever have become an issue?* He understood the opposing perspective, and was respectful and sympathetic to the rights of all women. But his resolve on the issue never wavered.

Even if a woman's rights are somehow infringed by this issue, wouldn't the right to human life trump all others? It's a law and a commandment, "Thou shalt not kill." Reciting the words to himself, made him feel the familiar pangs of hypocrisy and guilt.

Linda found him about to enter Mike Arnold's office. "Jim," she said sternly, "Peg is on hold, she says it is urgent!"

Walking briskly to his office, he lifted the telephone receiver. "What's up Peg? Is everything okay?"

"It's Tom, he's high on something! I—I shouldn't have left him alone."

Alone?—Oh lord, tell me she didn't leave him alone!

But he knew it was true. There was clearly more than concern in Peg's voice, she was panicking, and didn't know what to do next.

"Stay calm, Peg. What does he look like?"

"He's pale. Ten minutes ago, he was vomiting terribly. Now, every few minutes, he goes from lucid to almost unconscious. His eyelids were fluttering and his eyes were rolled up in his head. I'm scared Jim, I think he may have overdosed!"

"I'm only two minutes away, Peg. I'll call you back in sixty seconds from my cell. Meanwhile, do two things. First, keep him awake, talk to him—slap him hard if you have to. Second, go through his pockets and see if you can find what kind of drug he took—and be careful not to get stuck by a needle, he was using heroin the last time."

Jim hung up the phone, grabbed his coat and headed to the front door. The thought of informing Linda that he was leaving, never entered his mind.

As Jim opened the car door, his cell phone rang.

"HELLO?" he said anxiously, as he sat behind the wheel. The voice on the other end was sobbing.

"I found a bag of white powder and a spoon, but no needle."

He probably hid the needle, Jim thought.

"Okay Peg, listen carefully. I'll call Dr. O'Neill from the car and ask him what we should do. Keep him awake, and send the kids to the basement. They don't need to see this!"

Finding Dr. O'Neill's number was difficult. Jim pressed several wrong keys on his Smart Phone before making a successful connection. Like Peg, he realized he was somewhat panicked as well. Finally, Dr. O'Neill's receptionist answered the phone.

*   *   *

Scott Troia passed the time taking photos of Aaron's home. Jim had mentioned the sizable memory card in the camera, so Scott decided to practice using it so he would be ready to capture images of their prey. The cameras lens was everything Jim said it was. He could zoom in close enough to see the hands of the clock that sat on the fireplace mantle. Scott had a good view through the bay window, but the day's light was beginning to fade. If Scott was to take any photos, it would have to be soon.

C'mon, damn it! he thought impatiently. *Jim and Miranda have had enough of this crap. Show your faces, you bastards!*

*   *   *

A small SUV was parked in the street one house away from the O'Brien home. Two figures occupied the front seats. They did not get out of the car. They appeared to be watching the O'Brien house. Frank Saunders, who was parked three houses away, found that intriguing.

It seems a lot of people are interested in Jim O'Brien, he thought. He reached for his binoculars, and focused on the driver of the car. He had blond hair and a very thick neck. Judging from his size, Saunders thought the man must have difficulty driving the small vehicle. The second man, also blond, was of a much smaller stature. Saunders began to contemplate how this might affect his plans to arrest O'Brien. He would have to watch the chain of events and see how they unfolded.

What do these men want with him, anyway?

Moments later, a silver Honda Accord pulled into the driveway, and rather quickly, Saunders mused. The front door of the house opened before Jim even came to a full stop. Mrs. O'Brien rushed a red haired youth to the car, and helped him into the passenger seat. She closed the door and spoke to Jim through the lowered window.

"How's he doing, Peg?"

"Better, I—I slapped him like you said. It brought him right back to consciousness. You may have to shake him once in a while to keep him awake. We talked a little. He admitted taking heroin. The needle was in the cabinet under the bathroom sink."

Jim looked relieved. "Dr. O'Neill recommended that we take him to the Emergency Room at Immanuel Medical Center if it was serious. Otherwise, he said we should take him to Alegent Health Behavioral Services. It's on the same campus as the Medical Center, but they are better suited to deal with this problem."

"Then take him to Behavioral Services," Peg said. "He'll make it, just keep him talking." Peg looked at her son with tears in her eyes. "I love you, Tom," she said with all the conviction a mother could muster.

"I love you, too, Mom."

His reply seemed to be more of a conditioned response. Jim backed out of the driveway as quickly as he had pulled in. He noticed neither of the cars that followed him.

Jim was at a loss for conversation, and asked the first question that came to mind. "Where did you get the heroin, Tom?"

"A friend of mine left it in the back yard."

"Matt?"

"Yes."

"Where in the back yard?"

"Inside the electrical box for the air conditioner."

Pretty cunning, Jim considered. *These boys know every trick.*

"Why did you do it? You were doing so well until now."

"I don't know. I guess I just made a mistake, that's all."

"You know," Jim said cynically, "that is exactly what you said last time."

"Well, it's true!"

"No, Tom, it's not true. A mistake is something that happens unintentionally. This, on the other hand, was as intentional and purposeful as it could possibly be."

289

Jim checked to see if Tom understood what he was saying. He was still going "on the nod," experiencing intervals of wakefulness, followed by periods of drowsiness. Right now his eyes were closed.

Jim shook his shoulder, "Tom—stay awake!"

Tom opened his eyes, but looked like he was in a stupor. Jim rolled the passenger window down half way. The cold air brought him back to the present moment.

"Where are you taking me?" he asked, like he had just realized they were in a moving vehicle.

"We are going to Alegent Health Behavioral Services, its part of Immanuel Medical Center. They can help you until we can get you into another program."

"I'm not going into another program—NO WAY!"

Tom began to flail his arms in every direction, hitting the dash, windows, and striking Jim in the face and chest. Jim fought to keep control of the car, which nearly veered off Interstate 80. He placed a hand on Tom's chest, trying to subdue him.

"THAT'S ENOUGH! DO YOU HEAR ME? THAT'S ENOUGH!"

"I'm not going into a program, Dad, those places are terrible!"

"How else can you expect to get better, Tom?"

"I can do it on my own. I don't need to go to one of those places!"

Jim was becoming angry, "You can do it on your own, huh? You proved that today, didn't you? If you could do it, Tom, you wouldn't have called Matt; you wouldn't have taken more heroin. If it takes a hundred programs to cure you, I'll see that you complete every damn one of them. I have no intention of seeing you rot away in some gutter. You are my son, and no matter what stupid things you do, I'm going to save your life."

Tom slid down in his seat. The cold air buffeted his face from his window. He knew there was no escaping his fate. He was going away and most likely, the duration would be longer than before. He grew listless, waiting to glimpse the facility where he would spend the night.

It was dark when Jim pulled into the nearly full parking lot of Immanuel Medical Center. Tom stared out the window as Jim closed it. He had passed these buildings from a distance hundreds of times. His school, Roncalli High, was only a few blocks away. He never dreamed he'd be admitted as a patient, in particular for drug addiction. Jim found a distant parking space at the far south end. Tom had lost any hope of avoiding confinement for the evening. Apprehension was overtaking him, and talking was only a stall tactic.

"Are you really going to leave me here?"

Jim sought to wear a face of concern and compassion, one that said he cared deeply for his son.

"I'll stay with you as long as I can, Tom, but I'm going to do whatever the doctor tells me to do. I trust them. You need to trust them, too."

Jim opened his door, but Tom didn't move at all. As Jim came around the car, he prayed under his breath.

"Give me strength, Lord."

Tom made no eye contact with his father when he opened the passenger door. He hesitated a final moment, and then emerged quietly from the car. The click of the electric door locks may as well have been prison doors slamming shut in some dark jail cell. When Tom faced his father, his gaze continued past him to something else. Jim turned to follow his son's stare. What he saw made him gnash his teeth.

"WHAT THE HELL ARE YOU DOING HERE?"

47

ALTHOUGH UNCERTAIN WHO THE MAN WAS, TOM COULD see his father seething with hatred. He looked once more at the immense muscular figure, and sensing trouble, froze in his tracks.

"We meet again," the broad shouldered man said, with an almost polite smile. With a touch of sarcasm he added, "It's been much too long, you know."

"I asked you a question. What you are doing here?" Jim said. "Why did you follow us?"

Aaron's eyes drifted to scrutinize the younger O'Brien as he answered the question. "We have unfinished business."

Jim was incensed, "I have no business with you at all."

"I wish that were true, but you have been following us, asking questions about us."

"You sexually assaulted one of my employees!"

"You mean your girlfriend?"

"She is not my girlfriend! But what difference would it make if she were?"

Aaron shrugged, as if he placed little value on Miranda or the violent act they committed. "In any case, you have been snooping around our private community. No doubt, you'd like to turn us in to the police, wouldn't you?"

"I plan to do just that, you heinous son-of-a-bitch!"

Ignoring Jim's answer, he asked, "And who's the handsome boy?"

The question angered Jim even more. "It's just someone I know, but you wouldn't like him—he's straight."

Aaron wore a polished smile. "He looks a lot like you, O'Brien, except for the fact that he can hardly stand up. What's he on?"

"NONE OF YOUR DAMNED BUSINESS!"

"Suit yourself. I guess I'll see how straight he is after I'm finished with you."

Jim knew a physical confrontation was unavoidable. It was probably only seconds away. He quickly scanned the parking lot, looking for Derek. He felt relieved to see no one else in sight.

"So what are you going to do, Aaron, kill us so you don't have to go to prison?"

"I have no intention of seeing the inside of a prison—not over the likes of you."

Jim had guessed correctly. He reached in his coat pocket and withdrew a small, black bar. He flicked his wrist and heard a "thwack" as the black steel billy club extended to its full length.

"I am much better prepared this time big man, and you don't have any of your gay buddies to help you now—do you?"

Aaron's smile subsided. "I don't need any help to take care of you," he uttered in a low voice. I can easily break you in two with my bare hands."

Aaron started toward them.

Jim whispered to Tom, "As soon as I engage him, run to the hospital for help."

Jim lunged and met Aaron half way. With all his might he arced the metal club across his cheek. The cracking of bone was audible. Aaron reeled back, holding his cheek and jaw in pain. Jim was ecstatic.

This is going to be a short fight, he thought.

He stepped closer to Aaron, and raised the club to plant another blow, but his wrist was caught by a massive hand. Aaron didn't speak, as if doing so would be painful. He cradled Jim's neck with his other hand, and effortlessly drove his wrist and arm back behind him. Jim wanted to scream in pain. He thought his shoulder might dislocate from its socket. Dropping the club, his face showed pure anguish. His only retaliation was a weak one. He grabbed Aaron's hair with his free hand, and pulled with all his might. The effort was useless. Aaron's head didn't budge.

Something, Jim thought, *I've got to do something.*

He tried a head butt. It was a pathetic effort, but he connected, and Aaron released him. Jim dove for the billy club. Only a weapon could even the odds against his stalwart opponent. Just as his hand clasped the baton, a foot came smashing down on it. Jim felt bones snap, yet somehow he managed to keep the club. It took all of his concentration to bring its shaft around to meet Aaron's knee cap. Aaron shrieked, and started to teeter. He tried to keep his balance, but couldn't. He fell next to Jim. Trying to get to his feet, Jim realized that something in his shoulder was torn. He was unable to imagine how he had successfully delivered the last blow. He rolled to his knees, and used his good arm to get up.

"This is for Miranda," he shouted as he landed a kick to Aaron's forehead. "And this one's for me," but the next kick never connected.

Aaron caught Jim's pants leg, and yanked, sending his entire body through the air and across his own. Jim's face skidded against concrete. Aaron rolled over him. He howled in pain when he tried to pin Jim down with his shattered knee. He sprawled out over him instead. Jim couldn't budge the heavy mass of muscle that lay on top of him. There was a long pause from Aaron. It seemed like he was just lying there, holding him at bay. Then it happened. Aaron hoisted himself to his good knee. His arm came down quickly. Jim barely saw the flash of the polished blade before it pierced his chest.

Tom's heart was pounding. He knew he was high, but he was hardly rational. He questioned whether he was seeing things correctly. Was this really happening? He should have run, but he was afraid and unable to move. It was shocking to see his father lying helplessly on the ground. His left hand was pressed against his wound, while his right arm lay limp at his side. He detected no fear in his father's eyes, and a few moments later he closed them. In the dark, his father almost looked like a stranger. But the man he admired and despised, and sometimes loved, was far from a stranger. This was the man who took care of him, gave him food, shelter, and money when he needed it.

He's going to die, Tom thought. *What will we do without him?*

Knife in hand, Aaron had a great deal of difficulty getting to his feet. Assuming Jim was dead, or near death, he started to leave the scene, moaning in agony as he hobbled. After a few steps, he remembered something and went rigid. He turned to see that Tom was watching him.

I can't have any witnesses, he thought. *Maybe Derek will take care of him for me.*

He waved his arm, signaling for someone to join him. There was no response.

Why do I put up with that man? Aaron thought. *He should have helped me. He should be helping me now.*

A pair of headlights flashed across his face as a vehicle turned into the parking lot. The car found an empty parking space somewhere downstream of their location.

We need to get out of here quickly, before someone sees us.

Tom was still standing motionless.

If he runs, Aaron thought, *I'll never catch him. But he's scared stiff. I've got to trick him, keep him there until I can get my hands on him.*

Aaron shifted the knife to his left hand and kept the blade behind him, out of sight.

"Sorry kid," he said motioning down at Jim. "I know he's got a family at home. Your dad and I had issues." He began limping toward him. "Before I go, I've got something of his I think you'll want to keep—you know, as a memento."

As he neared the petrified boy, he fished for something in his pocket. There was nothing there, but Tom didn't know it.

Just one more step, he thought.

"Oh, here it is," he said convincingly.

He withdrew his closed hand and started to hold it out, but the hand didn't stop. It went straight for Tom's throat. Tom couldn't scream. His senses came alive and he went rigid. Aaron delighted in the fear he saw in Tom's eyes. He raised the knife to shoulder height and—

Craack—a shot echoed through the parking lot. Aaron arched his back. The knife clanged on the asphalt, followed closely by the thud of his massive body. A man was standing at Jim's side. Tom could see a waft of smoke drifting from the gun in his hand.

"Its okay, son—Agent Saunders—FBI."

As the man holstered his gun, Tom flinched instinctively. For a split second, he thought he saw a figure moving between two cars. Looking again, he realized it must have been his imagination. After all, he was exhausted and shaken after the horrible things that had just happened. Saunders motioned him over. With legs like rubber, he cautiously approached Saunders and his father. Just being close to an FBI agent made him feel much safer. From his cell phone, Saunders called the police. He placed a hand on Jim's wound, applying pressure, as he identified himself to the dispatcher. He requested a cruiser and asked that they call the hospital and have them send a gurney to the south end of the parking lot.

Feeling the pressure on his chest, Jim was aroused. He opened his eyes. It took him a few seconds to recognize the man kneeling over him.

"Saunders," he murmured.

"Yes, Mr. O'Brien, it's me."

Jim was trying to figure out why he was looking up at Saunders. Was he lying down? When Tom neared him, he remembered where he was and what had happened.

"How did you find us?"

"I was on my way to take you into custody. I followed those men here."

Those men? Tom thought. He shot a glimpse over his shoulder.

Jim spoke softly, and with difficulty, "What do you mean—take me into custody?"

Saunders was studying Jim's condition, wondering if he would survive the stab wound. He hated Jim and had dreamed of getting even with him for months. If he should die, he would be cheated out of his revenge. Only half of what was happening was registering in Tom's mind. His confused thoughts were drifting to his current situation. He was once more dreading the thought of a treatment program at the hospital.

Can't go back to living in a treatment center, he thought. *Confinement! Doctors and counselors digging into my private affairs!*

He wondered if this turn of events might somehow change the outcome.

Answering Jim's question, Saunders said, "Yes, I was waiting for you to come home so I could arrest you. My trip to Chicago was successful."

With his free hand, he produced an envelope from the breast pocket of his coat and held it out for him to see.

"I found an e-mail written by you, placing a contract on the boys that killed your daughter. The header is similar to the e-mails sent by the Moral Mafia. You lead that organization, don't you?"

Jim looked past Saunders, to Tom. He was totally engulfed in shame and guilt. He wished Tom didn't have to witness his confession, but there had been enough lies and deceit. It was time to come clean.

"Yes, it's true. I created the Moral Mafia. But I did it to make the world a better place. I wanted to rid our country of the terrible influences that rip families apart. My son, Tom, is a drug addict, my daughter, Katie—gone."

Tom knelt on the other side of his father. He forgot about his predicament, his expression was mixed with pity and fascination.

"You killed all those people, Dad?"

"Yes, and even though we accomplished a great deal of good, I regret every death. I went about it the wrong way. I did bad things for a good cause. I was wrong. I can only hope that in the years to come, my actions will save many lives to make up for the ones I took. There are new laws—America is going to be a great nation again."

"Calm down, Mr. O'Brien, everything is going to be fine."

"Frank," Jim said gravely, "if I don't make it, you'll find a memory card in a zippered pocket of my brief case. It's compatible with my Smart Phone. In the Memo program, I have kept a log of all the Moral Mafia's business dealings, and a journal. You will find all the answers you need regarding Constantino's computer."

Saunders was smiling from ear to ear.

You sorry son-of-a-bitch—you can forget about a plea bargain, O'Brien!

Tom noticed Jim's eyes shift and grow wide. Saunders noticed it too. There was a muted, indistinguishable sound, and then Saunders slumped forward and hit the pavement.

Tom looked up, and saw a svelte, blond-haired man, holding a blood-stained knife. He was smiling wickedly, and one of his eyes was offset. Tom had never seen anything like them, and didn't know which eye to look into.

He must be the figure I thought I saw a second ago, Tom thought. *He must have picked up the knife used to stab my dad.*

The sound of police sirens approaching meant only one thing. *Confinement! Any minute now.*

Tom fought the notion as best he could. He stood up and faced the weird looking man.

With a voice devoid of emotion, Tom said, "You'd better get out of here fast; the police will be here any second."

"What are you saying, kid?" Derek asked, bewildered. "You want me to get away?"

Tom gazed at his father, motionless on the pavement. "I could care less either way, but you're wasting time."

Derek's eyes became more exaggerated, and so did his wicked smile. He tore off in the direction of Aaron's car.

The police will get him, Tom thought, as he picked up the envelope Saunders had dropped, and shoved it under his shirt.

Instinctively, Tom knelt over his father and placed his palm over the wound to stop the bleeding. With only bits of reality registering in his drug-ridden mind, he had barely a clear thought, except one; *Please God, help me keep him alive.*

48

OVER TWO HUNDRED TEENAGERS ATTENDED A PARTY organized by five graduating seniors from Roncalli High School. Many of them were friends of kids from other schools, or boys who heard that there would be lots of girls and free beer. The senior boys rented an old barn on a farm just outside of Wahoo, about twentyfive minutes west of Omaha. Tom O'Brien parked his father's Honda Accord along a gravel road that overlooked a clearing. He slammed the car door and squinted in the bright light of the setting sun. The view put an enormous smile on his face. There were kids everywhere. They were throwing Frisbees and footballs; boys were chasing girls in bikinis. A young girl was sprawled out in a chair with her mouth underneath a beer keg. She was gulping as fast as she could, but beer flowed from her mouth and across her t-shirt. As he strolled to the edge of the barn, Tom gauged the time to be just around eight o'clock on this mild May evening. The barn cast a perfect shadow over the sand volleyball court where a mixed game was in progress. No wonder this was such a popular party spot.

As Tom scrutinized the female players, he heard Matt call his name. He turned around to see his best friend approaching with his arm around a girl he did not recognize.

"Dude, look at all the people here," Matt said. "This party is awesome!"

Each boy made a fist. They tapped their knuckles together, in lieu of a handshake. Matt was pleased with himself.

"I told you, Tom. People are gonna talk about this party for a long time."

"Who's your friend?" Tom asked with a smile.

"Oh yeah, this is Rachel. We met at Krepp's party last Saturday."

Tom offered her a friendly greeting, "Hey Rachel, what's up?"

The young girl just smiled.

"So you went to Krepp's party?" Tom asked.

Rachel replied in a soft, pleasing voice, "Yes, we hang out sometimes. I don't remember seeing you there."

"That's because I wasn't," Tom said sarcastically. "I don't really get along too well with Jerry."

"Well, that's understandable. Jerry is a good guy to know, but sometimes he can be a rich brat."

"If you ask me," Tom said in agreement, "that guy wears his wealth on his sleeve, but it's his parent's money he's spending. I don't need to rely on my parent's money," Tom said smugly. "I earn enough on my own."

Matt caught Tom's eye, and frowned to signal he disapproved of his bragging. Rachel's eyes surveyed Tom closely.

"Matt has told me a lot about you. He says you're a real computer wizard. You don't look like a computer nerd to me."

She observed his reaction intently.

"Maybe it's because I'm not," Tom said, slightly offended. "We catch computer criminals, uncover digital evidence, and turn it in to the authorities. We have a contract with the FBI."

I'm bragging again, he thought.

"Wow," Rachel said, "it sounds interesting."

Tom studied Rachel a little closer.

She's cute as hell, he mused, *I wouldn't mind lying down with her.*

Rachel Stowe had very distinct, almost perfect features. In the center of her cheeks, there were pronounced dimples. She had short dark hair with a tossed look. Her skin had a beautiful tawny hue that looked like she had been tanning for weeks. Her eyes were dark in color, and they were indeed her best feature. They were very animated, very cute, and very sexy, all at the same time. Tom found them alluring. The more he looked in them, the more captivated he was. His gaze lingered with hers for a while longer.

"C'mon," Matt said, "let's get something to drink."

Putting his arm around Rachel's shoulder, Matt steered her in the direction of the beer kegs. Tom hadn't even noticed her shapely figure until they were walking away. Rachel was slender. Her waist was tiny, and Tom thought her hips were just right.

Then he realized, *Jesus, I never really saw her breasts. That's usually the first thing I check out.*

He decided he would have a beer as well.

On the way to the beer keg, Tom saw a young man staring at him with an unusual intensity. He looked about four or five years older than everyone else and certainly didn't fit in with the rest of the crowd. He was leaning against an oak tree drinking a beer from a clear plastic cup.

I wonder who he is? Tom thought.

Matt was just handing Rachel a beer as Tom approached the keg.

"Hey, Tom, did you see that guy over there? He's been staring at us."

"Yeah, I noticed. He looks a little out of place here."

"You'd think he could find a better place to pick up chicks than a high school graduation party," Matt grumbled. His expression showed disgust. He grabbed Rachel's wrist, and tugging her behind him muttered, "C'mon, let's mingle."

Tom watched as Matt led Rachel off. She turned around and looked at him like she didn't want to go. He glanced back toward the tree. The older boy was still staring. Tom ignored the uncomfortable feeling and poured himself a beer, trying carefully to minimize the amount of foam in his cup. As his eyes wandered back to Rachel, she looked back again.

She's interested, he thought.

The beer tasted great and the soft breeze was invigorating, but Tom's mood could only be described as melancholy. Matt struggled for days to convince him to come to the party. He boasted how this event had the potential to become a legend. Tom resisted the invitation, but in the end he gave in out of loyalty for their fading friendship. He pondered the real reason he wanted to avoid the party. The fact was he didn't know if he had the willpower to control his on again, off again, drug cravings. Although drugs prevented him from dwelling on the unpleasant events in his life, he realized that someday he would have to face them anyway. He saw some friends in the distance, but decided to walk in the direction of the pond. He was in no mood to talk. As he put some distance between himself and his classmates, his thoughts drifted to his family.

Tom had reached an old horse drawn cart that was rotting near the pond. He walked around to the open side of the cart and set his beer down. He could hear unfettered kids shrieking and laughing in the distance. The party would probably be everything Matt promised and more. He still struggled with his dilemma. Drugs of all kinds were abundantly available.

Maybe I can just get a little high, Tom thought. *It would sure kick this party in gear.*

An inner voice told him he was just kidding himself. Drugs had served only one purpose throughout his adolescence. They gave him temporary solace. They also drove a stake through his relationship with his parents. Having watched his father battle for his life, he desperately wanted to mend that relationship.

Tom's popularity had soared in recent months. Since his return to school, he seemed to be a changed person. He was more reserved, less self-centered, and far more kind than he used to be. His new found acceptance gave him some incentive to stay clean. A rumor circulated that he was working at his father's company to help his family make ends meet. His father had been attacked by the same two men he scuffled with at the courthouse during a riot a few months ago. The rumor was only half true. Tom was working for his father's company, but not because they needed the money. Tom was trying to make amends to his father. If he had not overdosed on heroin, he could have helped his father that night. Instead, he was a liability. He had drawn him into the open and made him vulnerable, while he stood by and watched in a drug induced stupor.

Jim had not worked since his injury. The knife wound had nicked the outer wall of his heart, but a skilled surgeon repaired the damage. A few days later, Jim contracted a staph infection, which nearly killed him. The doctor called it acute bacterial endocarditis. The source of the infection was unknown, but may have been caused by the knife that pierced his chest. Jim became ill quite quickly. By the time the doctors correctly diagnosed the problem, the condition was life threatening. Antibiotics were administered intravenously for several weeks, but the strain of bacteria that spread to his heart was highly drug-resistant. In all, it took nearly a month to treat. The bacterium damaged a heart valve, resulting in a second surgery, but only after Jim had regained enough strength to endure it.

As always, Peg O'Brien was the glue that held the family together. She spent countless hours at the hospital, in addition to keeping house and running the kids to their activities. Like Jim, Tom possessed a high degree of intelligence, and with the help of a tutor, had little problem accelerating his studies. Within thirty days after his father's attack, Tom had rejoined his classmates in school. Fortunately, Tom's most difficult requirements had already been completed by the end of his junior year. It would have been an impossible task if Peg had not enrolled him in a methadone treatment program. He was administered a controlled dosage of the drug each day after school. The synthetic narcotic suppressed his opioid withdrawal symptoms and reduced his physical craving for heroin. A month into the program, and against his doctor's advice, Tom reduced his dosage over a two week period and quit consuming the drug completely. He saw a psychiatrist weekly, and working at CFC helped provide a distraction from drugs, and from the disturbing things he had learned about his father.

Tom replayed the events of that night over and over in his head. He could still envision the blond-haired man with the crazy eyes, the FBI agent who saved his life, and the muscular man who almost killed his father. But it was Jim's confession that still intrigued and haunted him.

My father controls the Moral Mafia. Tom still had a difficult time coming to grips with the fact that his father gave commands to the nation, and they obeyed him—at least most of them did. Tom's mind was anything but clear that night, but he remembered a mention of a memory card in a zippered pocket of his father's brief case, where he kept a log and a journal. Tom had seen the card the night Jim had transferred some games to his Smart Phone a few days before the incident. The file Jim referred to was inconspicuously labeled "Birthday Gifts." It contained a complete journal of his father's dealings with a mafia organization in Chicago. Tom copied the file to his own Smart Phone. He read the entire journal twenty times or more. It painted a clear picture of the mental anguish his father suffered at the loss of his sister, Katie.

Tom stared across the pond's mildly rippled surface.

My father was killing people for the sake of morality. It's my fault, he thought. *If it hadn't been for me, Katie would still be alive, and none of this would have ever happened. Dad's cause was noble, but his method was wrong. How can I help him get out of this mess? What would I even say?*

Jim remembered confessing to his son, but he never mentioned it again. He probably hoped that Tom was too drug ridden to remember any details of the evening. Local FBI agents questioned them both, and seemed to be satisfied with their answers. Vince Mitchell flew in to see Jim between surgeries. He seemed quite perplexed as to why Frank Saunders would have followed him to the hospital in the first place. Jim explained that Saunders had stopped by on his way to Chicago to ask him for some help in the Moral Mafia case, a case he shouldn't have been working. Saunders had discovered Miranda unconscious in Jim's office. She had been beaten and sexually assaulted by the same men who killed him. Jim suggested that Saunders hit a dead end in Chicago, and simply had more questions regarding the case. Maybe he had seen the men following them and decided to tag along. Lots of theories surfaced, but none of them involved Tom's father being the head of the most feared organization in the country.

"You look like you're deep in thought," a voice said.

Tom spun around, startled. The older boy, who had been watching him, had approached unnoticed. He was tall and lanky; about twenty-two years old, with dark, neatly combed hair.

Tom's heart beat rapidly. "Who are you?" he asked.

"My name is David Manetti. I am an acquaintance of your father," he replied.

49

TOM STUDIED THE YOUNG ITALIAN MAN INTENTLY.
He recognized his name from his father's journal. The mere thought
that he was here, sent chills down his spine. He was surprised to
discover that Manetti was only a few years older than himself.

So this is the man we are so afraid of, Tom thought.

But he knew better than to judge a person by their appearance.
Looks can be deceiving. Power has more to do with money and
intellect than a man's outward appearance. Tom hoped to make
good use of his own intellect right now.

"You look a lot like your father," Manetti said with a dull smile.
"He's a good man, your father—we understand each other."

Tom took a step closer to him, "Well, let's hope you and I can
understand each other as well."

"Sit down," Manetti said, "we may be here for a while."

Tom sat on the edge of the old horse drawn cart. The wood was
splintered, soft, and damp. Having read about his father's encounter

with Manetti, Tom was suspicious. He looked for signs of a weapon bulging from Manetti's clothes. He saw none.

"Your father spoke to my uncle, Tony Constantino, on his death bed."

"I know who he is," Tom injected firmly.

"Tony told him the location of his personal files, which contained a phone book, bank accounts, and all of his assets. Your father promised to give them to me, but when I called him to set up a meeting place, I was told he was in the hospital, recovering from a serious injury."

"He was attacked by two men who stabbed him," Tom explained. "He almost died, once from the stab wound, and once from a staph infection. He's had one complication after another. Quite frankly, I think hospitals make healthy people sick. I can't wait to get him out of there."

David was strictly business, "What happened to your father is regretful, Tom, but those documents are vital to my family. I need them back."

Tom almost mentioned his father's journal, but checked himself and decided to play dumb.

"Why didn't your uncle just give them to you?" he asked.

David swirled the beer in his cup. "He didn't have time. His death took us all by surprise. Your father was one of the last people to see Uncle Tony alive. He trusted your dad to deliver the documents to Jimmy Bonaiuto as a last request, but for some reason, your dad held on to them." David was growing impatient. "None of this really matters, Tom. I didn't want to go to the hospital to see your father. He has a too many visitors from the police and FBI. I don't take those kinds of risks. I'm going to need your help."

"I don't know what I could do for you," Tom said anxiously, "and I sure as hell don't know where these documents are. They sound like the sort of thing he would keep in a safety deposit box, don't you agree?"

Manetti didn't care for the condescending tone of Tom's voice. He clenched his fists but kept his composure. "I figured you could talk to him for me—tell him I'm in town. Maybe I can pick them up while I'm in town."

"Sorry, David, I don't want anything to do with this. My dad has no idea that I know what's going on. If there are no more complications, my dad will be out of the hospital in a few weeks. Why don't you talk to him then?"

The lie was Tom's best effort to buy his father time. Jim was scheduled to come home tomorrow.

"You'll talk to him now!" David said with an intensity that was seared into Tom's memory. "If those documents get into the wrong hands, it could be tragic for you and your family."

"What do you mean, t—tragic?" Tom stuttered.

"What I mean is this; my family controls a powerful organization. The documents your father took include more than just our assets. They contain incriminating information as well. Some of our family members are sweating bullets because they don't know what happened to them. The FBI would love to nail us to the wall, and those documents would only make their job too easy. Jimmy Bonaiuto was designated to succeed Tony when he died, and even though he has taken the reigns, his power and authority have been severely diminished. These are ruthless men. They would kill your entire family to get Tony's money and assets back. All I would have to do is give the word—"

"Don't do that!" Tom spouted, hastily. "You'll get them back!"

It wasn't really a smile, Tom thought, but rather a satisfied look that spread to David's face.

"I knew you'd help."

Tom composed himself. He had taken the bait and spoke too soon.

"I'm happy to do whatever it takes, David. The trouble is my father has been very weak since his surgery. I can't talk to him about this until he's stronger."

"I understand that, Tom, and I believe you, but time is a luxury we no longer have. Your father hasn't been paying the bills. The family has been crippled without our assets. We have been reduced to a bit player, trying to compete against other families with sizable financial resources. We simply cannot afford to rebuild our organization from the ground up." Manetti gave Tom a serious look. "We need those bank accounts, and we need them now."

Tom looked despondent, "The pressure of all this could kill him, and then where would you be?"

Manetti gave him a sideways glance.

This fucking kid is just like his dad, a headstrong son-of-a-bitch.

"Okay, Tom, I'll give you a month to get everything in my hands—not a second longer. That's three weeks longer than you deserve."

Tom won a small battle, but he was visibly shaking as he contemplated what might happen by the end of the war. Manetti played the fear card, and it worked. His words were already ringing in Tom's head, *"All I would have to do is give the word—."* Tom tried to sound calm, but firm.

"I know I already agreed to help you, but before you leave here tonight, I want some assurances."

Manetti seemed to understand the concern in the boy's statement and nodded, "What do you need?"

"Safety—for myself and my family."

Slicing the air with a short wave of his hand, Manetti said, "Done!"

Completely unsatisfied with David's quick and casual response, Tom grew very intense.

"Look, David, I don't know what my father was doing with these documents, but I know about you and your family. Something tells me that once you have them, you might want to erase the trail that led you to them."

Leaning back as if he were surprised, Manetti replied, "Why would you even say that, Tom?"

"Just a feeling, David, but it's real, and for me, its gut wrenching. I need to know—I need your word of honor that you won't hurt me or my family."

"Perhaps you didn't hear me correctly the first time, when I said, 'done'. Don't mess with me, Tom! My word is my bond. And if you are one day late, just one, I will blow the whistle, and your family will suffer the consequences. I'll let the chips fall where they may, and Jimmy Bonaiuto can do whatever he deems fit."

Uh oh, Tom thought, *I think I insulted him. I need to fix this.*

"I'm sorry, David—I apologize. Maybe I'm being overprotective of my family. Can you understand that?"

David smiled, "I guess I can't blame you, Tom. Like Tony always said, 'Family is everything.' "

"Just one more thing, David, how will you explain the sudden appearance of these documents to the guy who took over the family? If you're not going to give us up, where will you say that you got them?"

"Your father said he would come up with a convincing story, something I can tell Jimmy Bonaiuto. It's up to him. You'd better talk to him soon," Manetti said coolly. "He only has four weeks to get his story together."

"Alright," Tom said, "it's a deal."

He offered his hand to shake on it, but David simply gazed out over the pond.

"Have you already forgotten? My word is my bond. No need for handshakes."

The two young men exchanged telephone numbers. David was leaving for Chicago in the morning, but promised to telephone Tom before making his return trip.

50

WILL THIBODEAU WAS A NEAR GENIUS. HE ONLY MISSED a perfect SAT score by one question. He and three other interns began working at CFC a week before Tom. With disheveled brown hair and mismatched clothes that were always in need of ironing, Will was far from a ladies man, but he had potential. That is, if such things as girls were important to him. But girls just interfered with the more important things in life, like mathematics and computer science.

Tom admired his intelligence, and the two young men struck an immediate friendship based on a common passion, computers. Will and Tom were assigned to Randy Burks and Charlie Ford as assistants. Will caught on to computer forensics quickly enough, but with all his intelligence, his skills were no match for Tom's. Years of watching his father and working with Troia paid tremendous dividends. Tom seemed to have an uncanny sense about troubleshooting computers and finding data in places that seemed unlikely to Will. Tom took Will under his wing and taught him everything he knew about logical troubleshooting techniques. But because data was sometimes concealed by humans, typical logic didn't always apply.

Tom found Charlie Ford to be very personable, and enjoyed working with him. At a height of about six-foot-three, he was a trim man in his mid-twenties, and had wavy, short black hair that was always a little frizzy. It was very curious to Tom that whenever they started a new project at the same time as Randy and Will, it immediately became a competition to see who could solve their case more quickly. Will joked about it for a while, but after six consecutive weeks of being thrashed by Charlie and Tom in nearly every instance, he grew irritable at the slightest mention of it. Tom chalked it up to bruising his intellectual ego.

About once a week, several of CFC's employees would go to Clancy's Pub for a beer. If Tom or Will decided to go, they had to order a soft drink, something they both found embarrassing. Randy or Charlie would slip them a beer on occasion. Neither boy realized that it was Troia who recommended they do it. If there was one thing Scott understood, it was camaraderie. To the employees of CFC, Clancy's was a social institution. It was where troubleshooting tips were shared, politics discussed, and lasting friendships forged.

On this second Monday in June, there was a lot of politics to discuss. The country was still incensed over the abortion issue. The Moral Mafia had forced the topic under the noses of Americans, and then completely disappeared. The newspapers hadn't heard from them in over three months. Politicians, on the other hand, argued both sides of the issue relentlessly. The country was so sharply split, the President was forced to install a military presence in many major cities. The strategy did not eliminate violence. In fact, it was sharply on the rise. As soon as an underground organization run by fanatics sprouted on right-to-life side, it was quickly met by a like organization on the pro-abortion side. Guerilla warfare was becoming a daily event. Two Congressmen and a Senator had been assassinated by the first week in June. This was followed by another but unsuccessful attempt. The police caught the perpetrator and quickly announced they had captured the head of the Moral

Mafia. It didn't take long to figure out that the man was simply a right-to-life zealot. Now politicians rarely appeared in public. They communicated with Americans through taped sound bites, or through newspaper snippets.

It was not even six o'clock when Tom announced he was leaving Clancy's to go home. He left behind a half-empty soft drink, and his fellow employees in mid-stream of a highly emotional debate. Although he rarely offered any youthful opinions, Tom enjoyed listening to his co-workers' spirited banter. He liked to ponder every side of an issue, but he wasn't mentally engaged tonight. A little more than two weeks ago, he had begun dating Rachel Stowe, the girl he met at a graduation party. He fell head-over-heels for her. He couldn't explain it, but after only six dates with Rachel, he was inexplicably preoccupied with her. When they were together, he was truly happy, but the minute they were apart, he felt lonely and withdrawn. Those feelings of emptiness were often the reason for Tom dwelling on unpleasant things—like his father, for instance.

On this evening, Tom was especially down-in-the-dumps. His father had been home for two weeks. Watching him labor to get around the house was depressing, at best. The doctor said Jim would experience a near full recovery, but to-date, he didn't seem interested in exercise or physical therapy. He appeared to be deeply troubled about something. Peg thought he was afraid to stress his heart, afraid of leaving her a widow. He used to walk around the lake in the evenings, but he had hardly been out of his chair all week. Jim had lost weight. He looked frail, haggard, and years older than before his injury.

Perhaps it was the fear of upsetting his father that kept Tom from telling him about his encounter with David Manetti. But he needed to do it soon. Time was running out and young Manetti seemed damned impatient. If he didn't recover his uncle's possessions soon, he threatened to expose Jim's identity to the "family."

What was it he said? Tom thought, *"I'll let the chips fall where they may."*

Tom was going out with Rachel tonight. The thought of seeing her lightened his mood. He promised to bring her home after dinner to meet his parents.

Dad's going to love her, he thought. *If this doesn't lift his spirits, nothing will. I'm working, I'm drug-free, and I found a great girl. Meeting her has got to cheer him up.*

During dinner Tom was still distracted, thinking about how he would approach his father about Manetti. The Moral Mafia was a subject he had once hoped to avoid forever. But now it seemed he had no choice in the matter. He took Rachel to the Spaghetti Works, a restaurant in Omaha's Old Market, a popular section of the downtown area full of quaint restaurants, pubs, shops, and galleries. After eating, they walked hand in hand as they browsed the shops and strolled along the streams in the downtown parks.

"You seem preoccupied tonight, Tom. Is anything wrong?"

"Not really," he lied. "I'm probably just tired. I guess I'm just not used to working full-time hours yet."

"Do you know what you need? You need a fun weekend."

Tom looked at her with a cautious grin. "What do you have in mind?"

"Worlds of Fun—it would be great! We can stay the weekend in Kansas City."

Tom's mind didn't hesitate to read between the lines.

Stay the weekend? In the same hotel? In the same room? Does she like me that much?

"Do you think your parents would allow it, Rachel? I know mine wouldn't."

Her smile accentuated her dimples, "They'll allow it if we go with a group of friends. I'll invite Stacy and Theresa. You invite two of your friends. We can go this weekend."

Nervous and overwhelmed, Tom let go of her hand. "Are you talking about staying in the same room?" he uttered cautiously.

Her eyes gazed deeply into his, "I wasn't—I didn't—well, someday I want to, Tom, that is—if you do."

He realized that she did not intend for them to share a room.

He drew her near and whispered softly, "I didn't mean to suggest that we sleep together, Rachel. But just so you know, there's no one else I'd rather be with—no one in the world."

He kissed her and all the problems in the world seemed to evaporate into thin air.

"Hey, it's almost nine o'clock. We need to get to my house if we are going to see Dad before he goes to bed."

51

JIMMY BONAIUTO WAS DOING HIS BEST TO LEAD TODAY'S meeting with the same confidence his predecessor might have exuded, but he couldn't quite hide his despondence. As of late, things looked grim for the head of the family. The Moral Mafia had stopped transferring money into their bank accounts. The last deposit was received in February. The business units had been making ends meet, but just barely. Rumors spread like wildfire that the Chicago family was broke. They could hardly acquire a decent shipment of drugs any more. Other families were stepping up, picking up the slack to provide the supply the market demanded. Jimmy was trying to sell two of the family's business units, but that took time. They needed the money now.

"Is everything in place, Mario?"

"They will never know what hit them, Jimmy."

"Old man Scarpello's birthday party is gonna' end with a bang—right, guys?"

The conference room erupted with laughter, but subsided quickly when Jimmy shot a cross look at the man who made the comment.

Bonaiuto's eyes narrowed, "You had all better be ready to do your part this evening. If we screw this up, we're finished!" He returned his attention to Manetti, "How many bombs did you plant on the premises?"

"Thirteen—three in the basement, five on the main level, and five on the veranda. That's where the family will be gathered for the party. I will detonate all of them at seven o'clock sharp. Carlo's men will storm their warehouse at the same time—I suggest we synchronize our watches now. I have six minutes after ten."

Bonaiuto continued as the men set their watches, "You guys at the warehouse gotta work fast. The cocaine is in plain wooden crates marked 'Fragile'. I figure there oughta be about fifty bags, or so. Get in and get out! Mannie will drive it to the docks to meet Angelo. His connection will take everything we have. For the rest of the evening, I want all of you to hunt down any stragglers—take em' out. By tomorrow morning, I don't want there to be a single member of the Scarpello family alive."

David Manetti noticed how the room went suddenly still. It was like a morgue. David had never witnessed bad times for the family. The devastation of watching this once powerful family stoop to robbing another family's drug cargo, made his head hurt. Bonaiuto still thought the Moral Mafia was headed by the Corsetto or Scarpello family, but David knew differently. He had come so close to retrieving Constantino's wealth and belongings, but Jim O'Brien had been injured just before their rendezvous date. He wanted to divulge everything to Jimmy, but it was too late. He should have done that months ago. Admitting it now would be a mistake, one from which he might never recover. Besides, tonight's operation would buy him time and provide the family some desperately needed cash.

Young Manetti was intelligent. His plan was back on track, but due to unforeseen circumstances, it was moving at a snail's pace. But now that Jim O'Brien was out of the hospital, he would finally get his due. He could change the facts about how he recovered

Constantino's fortune and documents. He frowned unconsciously. He could still hear Bonaiuto ranting in the background, but he wasn't paying attention.

Just one more week and I'll get back to Omaha. O'Brien's son will help me bring this nightmare to an end.

52

TOM ASKED, "DO YOU NEED SOMETHING, SCOTT, OR DID you just miss me?"

Troia leaned against Tom's front cubicle wall, his arms resting on the top rail. His chin rested on his hands as he watched Tom type on his keyboard.

"I just came by to say morning, boss," he said teasingly. "Any words of wisdom for us blue collar folk?"

"Yes," Tom said shaking his head with a smile, "don't call me boss."

"Well, at the pace you're learning this business; it won't be long before you'll be my boss. Anyway, I'm just ribbin' ya, ya know."

"I know, Scott, and I understand—it's your way."

Troia didn't exactly know what to make of the comment. Then he understood, when he caught Tom's backward glance and grin.

Over the past two months, Tom and Scott were developing a banter similar to the one Scott had enjoyed with Jim. It was slightly different, due to the span in their ages, but both of them enjoyed "dishing out the goods" whenever they had the opportunity. Scott often mused about how much Tom reminded him of Jim when he was younger, except that Tom seemed to be a little guarded and a little sad sometimes. But he had definite leadership qualities, and they were blossoming right before his eyes. Scott entered the cubicle and sat down.

"How's your dad feeling this morning?"

"About the same, I guess. He's still talking about coming back to work, but on the other hand, he doesn't stray far from his recliner. Mom thinks he's afraid of stressing his heart."

"Yeah, I know," Scott said. "He told me he was concerned about leaving your mother a widow."

"It's not like Dad to be afraid of anything," Tom said in a firm voice.

Scott nodded, "You know, he's not afraid for himself. It's Peg and the kids he's worried about. They have already lost a daughter and sister, he doesn't want them to lose a husband and father, too."

Tom felt a familiar pang of guilt, "I don't blame him, Scott. He's had a lot to deal with the past few months. I just want to see him get back to normal."

"Don't worry about your dad, Tom. I think he's about ready to come back to work. I'll see to it that he does."

Scott tapped the face of his watch, "Aren't you taking off, soon?"

"Yeah, I'm leaving for Kansas City at noon."

Scott smiled and raised his eyebrows, "Jim says you're taking Rachel with you."

Tom tried not to make a big deal of it. In a dry tone, he said, "Yes, a group of us are going to Worlds of Fun."

"That's wonderful, Tom, you've been working hard, and you deserve some fun."

Tom nodded, "I can't remember the last time I took a vacation. Of course, there are probably lots of things I don't remember over the last three years."

Although he said it jokingly, Scott could sense a little pain, perhaps a little remorse in the comment.

"Well, you've done a damn fine job here over the past two months," Scott said cheerfully. "I wasn't kidding when I said it won't be long before you'll be my boss. And from what I can see, you'll make a good one, just like your father."

Tom grew a little somber. "I know everyone compares me to my father. I'm really not certain I could ever measure up to him."

"Forget it, Tom. You already have. You are twice the troubleshooter he was at your age. This business is in your blood. As for everything else, just give it time. You've got a helluva' lotta' potential, kid."

"Thanks, Scott. I probably needed to hear that."

"I'm not gonna' say you're welcome, cause' the compliment wasn't a gift—you earned it."

"Well, I'd better wrap things up here so I can go."

"Yeah, I'll get out of your hair now. Have a great weekend, Tom. You kids have some fun."

"We will, Scott."

As Scott walked off, Tom wondered what he would think if he knew how he had stolen Rachel from his best friend, Matt Bauer. Of course, Tom and Matt had been drifting apart for months. Tom realized that getting high was the only real bond they ever shared, and since his father's attack, he had only traces of the once serious cravings that had ravaged him.

Tom recalled how Matt had casually introduced Rachel at Roncalli High School's graduation party. His attraction to her was immediate. After a long discussion with David Manetti, Tom was visibly upset. When he returned to the party to find Matt and Rachel cuddled together, he was even more so. Rachel didn't appear to be much of a willing participant. Tom couldn't explain it, but he was repulsed at the sight of Rachel sitting with Matt. He located Jessica Cole, a busty Burke High School student with a reputation. He paid her fifty dollars to get Matt away from Rachel. He told her if she kept him away for the rest of the evening, he would give her fifty more. He said that Matt was a sucker for a girl in a bikini. He knew that she would sleep with him. He mused at the similarity of hiring a prostitute for his friend.

The plan worked perfectly. Matt was predictably all party and no business. Jessica came to him, dressed in a tight bikini. She stooped over him, pulled his face toward her breasts, and kissed him on the top of his head. Her fingers lingered momentarily on his cheeks, and then she slowly walked to the barn. Matt was already enjoying a cocaine high. He didn't even bother to make any excuses. He abandoned Rachel without saying a word. Tom slipped beside her before Matt was even out-of-sight.

After his talk with Manetti, Tom had felt the familiar temptation to bury his fears in a good high of his own, but Rachel was captivating, and they talked all night long. By morning, Tom was still clean and sober. To Rachel's surprise, he retrieved a small cooler of soft drinks from his car. That impressed her. From that night forward, their relationship blossomed much further than either imagined it would. Since meeting Rachel, he was experiencing wonderful things. It was like the years of living without a purpose had ended, and a fog had suddenly lifted. He smiled as he recalled the details of that evening.

The hundred dollars I paid Jessica Cole was the best money I have ever spent, he thought.

Tom introduced Rachel to his parents earlier in the week. Jim was so impressed by the young woman; he couldn't stop talking about her. Watching the two kids together made him see Tom in a completely different light. He really had changed. He was becoming the son Jim had always hoped for. Scott said he was already outperforming half of their employees. Miranda agreed. Some of his coworkers were referring to him as "Tommy," in reference to the blind pinball wizard, who possessed extraordinarily keen senses. Jim couldn't be prouder. And now he had met a beautiful young woman. And whether Tom had admitted it or not, Jim could see they were deeply in love.

To Tom, she was sensual in every way. Even in conversation, he was immersed in Rachel's jewel-like eyes, her tawny skin, and her dimpled smile. Tom wasn't one to daydream, but his anticipation to see her was so great, he lost complete track of what he was doing.

I might as well get going, he thought. *I can finish this project on Monday.*

.

53

SCOTT STOPPED AT MIRANDA'S OFFICE. "CAN I BUY YOU a cup of coffee?"

Miranda smiled when she sensed Scott's upbeat mood and said, "No, Scott, but I could use a refill of water."

When Scott and Miranda reached the break room, they were shocked by the conversation they were hearing. Almost daily during the past month, there was media talk about the possibility of a civil war in America. One analyst was already on record stating that it was inevitable. Demonstrations had become a daily occurrence, and so had violence. Hate crimes were gaining popularity and talking heads on both sides of the issue were subject to attacks. A pro-abortion Congressman from Philadelphia was kidnapped and beaten to within an inch of his life. Retaliation from the other side resulted in the stabbing of a right-to-life advocate. Both men survived, but an explosion of death threats sent politicians into complete hiding. Neither side had any intention of yielding on abortion. The violence seemed to fortify their resolve on the issue. The President of the

United States was asking for a peaceful resolution, but his pleas fell on deaf ears. America appeared to be bracing itself for the worst.

After hiring Will Thibodeau in June, Troia had offered three more intern positions. The three young college kids sat at a break room table, laying out hypothetical strategies for which politicians they would kill, and in what order, to end the fighting and resolve the issue. It appeared that it was no more than a chess game to them. Scott filled his coffee cup, and Miranda stopped at the water cooler, when a young intern named Sophie pondered out loud, "I think killing Senator Williams would take all the wind out of their sails. Without him, the right-to-lifers would become fragmented." Justin disagreed. "There will always be someone to step in and take his place. Therefore, the side with the most supporters will win. It's that simple." Evan agreed. Scott looked at Miranda.

"I can't pass this up," he whispered. Turning around, he clanged a spoon on his coffee cup.

"DO YOU PEOPLE HEAR YOURSELVES?" Scott boomed. "Do you have any idea what you are saying?"

The young girl just stared at him. Her expression screamed, *What did I do?*

"This is not a game," Scott said. "People are being beaten and violated because of their beliefs. Soon they—or we—may be killing each other. This is a serious matter, and the three of you are having fun with it. Well, I don't want to hear any more talk of it within these walls, DO YOU UNDERSTAND?"

The young girl took the scolding seriously and answered sheepishly, "Yes."

"Back to work—everyone. And let's leave that television off."

The congregation of young people scattered quickly. Troia didn't look like the kind of man they wanted to anger.

"Let's go to my office for a little while," Scott said to Miranda. "I need to talk to you."

Scott had a small table like Jim's in the corner of his office. He and Miranda took chairs and got comfortable.

"What do you think of the company's recent progress?" Scott asked, framing the question with an obvious probing tone.

Scott and Miranda had become very close since Jim's injury. Jim never told Scott about Miranda's crush on him.

"It's a mixed bag, Scott," Miranda said cautiously.

"On one hand, we seem to be doing very well financially. The Microsoft contract, combined with our new agreement with Hallmark Cards, will keep us flush with cash for many years. My only concern lies with the talent and quality of people we have been hiring lately."

"Bingo!" Scott said, "I couldn't have put it better myself. It's not that these young kids aren't intelligent. You only have to look as far as Tom and Will to see that. They all seem bright enough, but I wonder about their maturity and ethics. You just witnessed a sample of what I am referring to in the break room a moment ago."

Miranda's features were somber, "They certainly have no genuine appreciation for our company. They have no idea how fortunate they are to be working here," she added.

"Agreed," he said softly. "I think the intern program has merit, but there is no question, we are going to have to be much more selective about who we choose to hire in the future."

Miranda brandished a half smile, "I certainly have seen a positive change in Tom since he started dating Rachel. Do you think she's the one?"

"It's hard to say, but you're right. I'm starting to see some of Jim's better qualities surface in the kid."

The mention of Jim's name gave Miranda a dour expression. It slowly melted to sadness. "I miss Jim. He makes this company extraordinary."

"I miss him too, Miranda—but don't you worry. Come Monday, I'm dragging his butt in here."

The two friends were quiet for a moment, each of them recalling fond images of a man who made a profound impact on their lives.

54

TOM KNOCKED ON STACY BRODY'S FRONT DOOR AT precisely twelve thirty, Friday afternoon. Rachel spent the night at Stacy's house. They told Mr. and Mrs. Stowe they were going to Worlds of Fun with some school friends. Tom didn't invite anyone. He liked Will a lot, but he didn't think he would mesh well with the group. And Matt was simply out of the question, as he would undoubtedly show up high on his "drug of the day". Theresa couldn't go, but Stacy invited Brian Woodhouse to come along. They were just good friends. Rachel greeted Tom with an overfilled duffle bag and a beautiful smile.

"Let's go," she shrieked in anticipation, "this is going to be soooo much fun!"

Stacy waved goodbye, "Have fun you two—we'll meet you at the hotel in a few hours!"

Rachel threw her bag at Tom, and raced to the car. Tom didn't chase after her. He carried the bag, pretending to struggle under the weight. The top was down on his new red Mustang convertible, a reward he bought himself last week. Jim and Peg had no objection, now that he was working steady.

"The car is just beautiful, Tom. That blue really sparkles in the sun."

He tossed her duffle bag in the back seat and opened Rachel's door. Tom had never in his life opened a door for a girl. In fact, he felt a little silly doing it now, but then again, he found himself doing a lot of silly things these days. As he sat down beside her, he took in the fullness of her presence. Her cute brown eyes and well-defined dimples, her tan supple skin and amazing smile. As he gazed at her, he saw nothing but good in the world. A world that had nearly passed him by in a drug-induced stupor. But few old things, including old friends were on his mind these days. Indeed, everything was new, and work, study, and play were all bearable because of this wonderful creature—Rachel Stowe.

The hot, humid weather didn't sap any of the fun from the drive to Kansas City. The young couple enjoyed the sunshine and the wind-in-the face experience. Tom had a brief thought about Manetti, but Rachel's singing interrupted it. He was beginning to get used to the country music Rachel insisted on playing, and even learned the words to a song or two. He thought it was funny to over accentuate the southern drawl most country singers seemed to have, even those who weren't really from the South. They stopped to get something cold to drink in St. Joseph, Missouri. Tom went in the store alone, and when he came back to the car, Rachel was clearly mortified by something she was listening to on the radio, a live broadcast. He sat down and listened with her.

"—and gunfire seems to be coming from every direction as demonstrators scatter in search of cover! The police have arrived, but the panicked crowds continue to trample them, as well as protesters and onlookers. There is total chaos in the streets of San Francisco. People are running for their lives. Sharp shooters are beginning to appear on the rooftops of local shops, but they are not firing. Who is the enemy, America? Just who are we fighting? Picket signs have become weapons. There are no clear cut sides, no battle lines drawn. It's just people hurting people. A screaming mother is holding her young daughter—MY GOD—SHE'S BEEN SHOT! I can't tell which direction the shot came from! There are too many people in the streets. They have no sense of direction, and nowhere to go. The streets are turning red—there are bodies everywhere!"

"That's enough!" Tom shuddered. His heart raced, and he clicked off the radio, "We don't need to listen to this!"

"Did you hear that?" Rachel cried, trembling. "That was another riot over abortion. Those people are killing each other!"

"It's okay," Tom said putting his arm around her, "you're here with me."

"I have a cousin in San Francisco!" Rachel said. "She's my age."

"I'm sure your cousin is all right. Why would she put herself in the middle of something like that, anyway?"

"I don't know, but I've got to call her, make sure she's okay."

I wish my father could have finished the job he started, Tom thought. *He brought the country to a pinnacle. If he hadn't been injured—if I hadn't allowed it, he could have finished it!*

Tom handed his phone to Rachel, and she called her sister, Kayla, to look up her cousin's phone number. A call to San Francisco provided her relief, when she discovered that her cousin was safe and at home. But she, too, was shaken by the unbelievable outbreak of violence. Rachel wondered if they shouldn't turn around and go back home, but Tom convinced her that they were only an hour from their destination, and she would feel differently in a little while. Their mood was somber as they continued their trip. Rachel rested with her head on Tom's shoulder. He gently stroked her hair, while he heard snippets of the radio broadcast replay over and over in his head.

The world is going insane, he thought, *are we all going to kill each other over a stupid disagreement?*

They arrived at the Fairfield Inn & Suites around three thirty. They had planned a lazy Friday evening, which included dinner and an in-room movie at the hotel. Tomorrow, they would go to Oceans of Fun, a water resort, and on Sunday, Worlds of Fun, a neighboring popular amusement park.

Approaching the car where Rachel waited, he held up two sets of room keys. "TA DA! We've got adjoining rooms," he exclaimed.

Rachel smiled for the first time since they left St. Joseph. "Well, well, don't you have a devilish look in your eyes!"

"You can't blame me for that, I've got the prettiest girl in Omaha all to myself for the weekend, and I'm going to make sure it's the best weekend she's ever had."

They drove to the side entrance, and Tom raised the convertible top and grabbed their bags. Their rooms were on the third floor. They could see the colorfully painted Worlds of Fun water tower from their room windows. They sat by the pool until Brian and Stacy arrived around seven o'clock. The four of them talked and laughed until three in the morning.

Rachel woke up at about eight o'clock on Saturday morning. The television was still on from the in-room movie they never finished watching. She nudged Tom, who was still sleeping on the love seat with his feet propped on the coffee table. Tom scanned the room. It looked like a disaster. In addition to pizza boxes and candy wrappers, there were soda bottles, and glasses, sofa pillows, clothes, and towels strewn everywhere they looked.

"Did we make all this mess?" Tom snickered.

Rachel's eyes glimmered with their characteristic twinkle. "You started the pillow fight, Mister!"

Tom and Rachel took turns in the bathroom, getting dressed and ready to go, but Brian and Stacy wanted to sleep in.

"We'll meet you there after lunch," Stacy said.

Breakfast was Tom's favorite meal. They found a restaurant serving a brunch buffet, and sampled nearly everything. Their table talk began with sweet comments. When Tom looked into Rachel's eyes, he realized all at once how much he had changed in the last few months—and why. As of late, he had been experiencing more and more recollections of how he once used people for his own selfish gains. He had been manipulative and cruel. Now he found himself questioning why he had been such a callous person. Was it the drugs? He didn't think so or at least it wasn't the entire reason. Tom had been thinking a lot lately about Christina Mackenzie, a girl that had taunted him relentlessly in his early teenage years. Christina was his first love, or so he thought, until she betrayed him. He couldn't help but think that his early disdain for women was because of her.

Much of his past was still foggy, unclear. It took months for Tom to develop a different perspective about his father. He was very close to his dad when he was young. It was only when he started getting into trouble that their relationship had soured.

"I'm glad you met my mom and dad, Rachel."

She gave him an adoring look, "I'm glad I met them, too. They are amazing people."

Tom nodded. "I'll bet Dad never dreamed I could find someone as good as you."

"Oh, that's so sweet," she said. Tom almost slipped and said the words he really wanted to say, but he couldn't. He had taken too many big steps lately, and telling a girl that he loved her was just too big a step, at least for now.

Rachel had a sudden thought. "Is it safe to go swimming right after eating? I was always taught to wait for an hour after you eat."

"I'm pretty sure that's an old wives tale, Rachel, but I'm in no hurry to leave. We can talk awhile."

"Good, because I want to ask you something. What do you think of what happened in San Francisco yesterday?"

"Well, it was horrible, of course."

"And which side of the abortion issue do you support?"

Tom froze, *Oh, dear lord, don't let me answer this question wrong!*

Tom skirted the answer, "My father and mother support the right-to-life. My dad always said that the right-to-life automatically trumps all other rights."

"And what is your opinion, Tom?"

"I'm not sure I have one."

"Of course you do, but you're afraid your opinion may oppose mine, aren't you?"

"I'm not sure it matters."

"Everything matters, Tom. I won't think any less of you if some of your beliefs are contrary to mine, but it is important that I know what you stand for. You know I'm going to find out sooner or later—why not now?"

Tom continued to resist answering the question. "Why does everyone have to choose one side or the other? Why can't people just be neutral on a subject?"

Rachel placed her hand on his, "There is no such thing as neutral, Tom. There are two sides to every issue. You may be sympathetic to both sides, but somewhere in your heart, one side weighs heavier than the other. That's how you know, that's how you decide."

Tom never considered himself a man of values. He evaded responsibilities for years. But since he met Rachel, he had begun to ponder life, and thus, form firm opinions on many issues. It was becoming difficult to avoid contemplating the red hot topics currently being debated everywhere, from Congress to the local bars. Rachel was right, with the nation's political factions tearing each other apart, it was important to know who stood with you on the issues.

Tom looked concerned, "But if we don't agree," he said, "how could we love each other? After all, people are being killed over these issues."

Rachel's eyes lit up, "Are you saying you love me?"

Tom sighed, *At least this question is easy to answer,* he thought. *At least I know the answer.*

"Yes," he said firmly. "I'm crazy about you."

Rachel threw her arms around him, "Oh, thank God!" she said, "I wasn't sure you felt the same about me."

"I'm sorry I didn't say it sooner, Rachel. I'm not very good at expressing my feelings. But since I'm on the topic, I want to thank you for saving my life."

She looked puzzled. "What do you mean, 'saving your life'?"

Tom avoided Rachel's eyes, scribbling with his fork in maple syrup. He fought back tears, but he couldn't stop his eyes from watering a little. It was difficult not to choke on his words. "A few months ago, I was on a path of self destruction. I didn't realize it at the time, but all I could think about was getting high. With the money I now earn, I could easily buy all the drugs I want, and probably would have overdosed by now. Something bad happened the night we met. I was beginning to lose my grip, feeling the old temptation again. I thought about finding Matt to help me score, but then I saw you. Once Matt left, we talked all night long. I had no desire to get high. I just wanted to be with you. You literally saved my life."

They embraced tightly. Rachel stroked Tom's cheek with the back of her fingers. Tom was overwhelmed with emotion. To his surprise, there were tears flowing down his cheeks. He was a little embarrassed at his sudden outpouring of emotion, but there was something more he wanted to say.

"You might hear things about me, Rachel, awful things. Besides the drugs, I wasn't a very good person for a few years."

Rachel looked at him lovingly, "I can't imagine that, and even if it were true, I don't care about the past, Tom. I know who you are now. Every bone in my body can feel your goodness, your kindness. Whatever happened in the past is over and done." Her words made it easier for him to continue.

"My psychiatrist thinks I treated people badly, as a defense mechanism so I wouldn't get close to them. After some bad experiences with my first girlfriend, Christina Mackenzie, I really didn't want another. I was fourteen when we met. She was a demented person. She made me do crazy things. I was so deeply in love with her, or so I thought, that I would do anything she asked. She knew it, too. She played with my emotions like a toy, taunted me with her beauty. She said she only let me come over because she felt sorry for me. She told me that I wasn't as good as the other boys." A glint of anger pooled in his eyes as he continued, "God knows she compared me to every damn kid at school. She seemed to enjoy telling me, 'You're not as handsome, not as smart, or not as fun as so and so.'"

"She ruined my self esteem. She did it so slowly, I didn't realize what was happening. At least that's what my psychiatrist told me. But she wouldn't let me go either. That's what is so twisted about this story. Her mom and dad both worked. Christina invited me to her house almost every day after school, and I was so infatuated with her, that I went without the slightest hesitation. I was lovesick, and stuck in a relationship with someone who literally used me to make herself feel superior. She taught me how to kiss, and even let me feel her breasts a few times, but said I wasn't good enough to make love to her."

Rachel couldn't believe what she was hearing.

"She said that someday, she might mold me into someone that she could make love to. One afternoon, we got out of school early. She invited some friends to her house to watch a video. She left the basement, and about fifteen minutes later, I noticed several of the guys had left, too. I went to find her, and do you know where she was? In her bedroom with her pants off and her top hiked up to her neck. She was letting all the guys take turns with her. They were all watching each other, laughing, and having a great time. When they saw me, they laughed even harder; they knew what she was doing to me."

Tom gritted his teeth, "That was the last time I spoke to her, although I saw her around school for two more years, until her folks moved to Dallas. I hated her. I hated all women. She broke my heart and didn't even care. I've never treated another girl with decency since—that is, until I met you."

Tom felt like a great burden had been lifted from his shoulders. It was even better than when he had first told his psychologist.

"One night Matt offered me some heroin. I said no, but when he told me it would help me forget about Christina, I changed my mind. I forgot about her alright, but I never forgot how much I hated women. I've treated them like crap ever since. When we first met, I thought you were just a good-looking girl. I imagined about how great it would be to get you in bed. I didn't really care about you personally. But once we started talking, I knew you were different. I knew I could trust you."

He looked away from Rachel, wiping his cheeks with his sleeve.

"If I were to lose you—I'm afraid I would go back to drugs. I've never been so afraid of anything. I've lost three years of my life taking drugs. I still have hazy moments when I can't think straight or recall the details of past events, but I'm over the worst. Things are becoming clearer to me every day. With you in my life, I know I can succeed. I know I can be someone respectable."

He bit the insides of his cheeks and fought to regain his composure. "I'm sorry, Rachel. I know we came here to have fun. I don't want to ruin your weekend with depressing talk. I just thought you should know this about me."

Rachel looked at him affectionately. "Tom, I've never loved anyone so much in my life. You don't have to worry about losing me—ever."

She took his hand and squeezed it firmly. He had no difficulty believing her.

"Well then," he said with a little more confidence, "let's go swimming!"

55

TOM LOOKED FORWARD TO OCEANS OF FUN. IT WAS a giant water park owned and operated by the popular Worlds of Fun amusement park company. As a child, he loved to swim, but he had never even seen a water park. Oceans of Fun boasted sixty acres and a million gallons of water. It was the 29th of July, and sweltering heat plagued the Midwest. It was almost unbearable walking across the blacktop of the parking lot to the water park's entrance.

The crowd at the Oceans of Fun entrance seemed enormous, even for a day this blistering hot. Tom estimated it would take twenty minutes or so just to get inside the gate. He and Rachel talked about some of the rides and attractions they had read about. One of the pools featured a wave-making machine. Tom couldn't imagine how it worked. Fifteen minutes had passed, and the line hadn't moved an inch. Tom stood on his tip toes and tried to peer at the gate. The crowd blocked his view.

"Maybe we should reverse the order," he said, "go to Worlds of Fun today, and come back here tomorrow."

"Let's give it a few more minutes," Rachel said. "Just think how good that water will feel."

"Actually," he said grinning, "I was thinking how good a bath for two would feel right now."

"I can see we are going to be spending a little time in the deep water," she teased.

Glancing behind him, Tom noticed a KCTV 5 News van. He recognized the WB station affiliation and wondered what it was doing there. Maybe the temperature is going to break a record, he thought. Another five minutes passed. The line still hadn't moved. The park opened at ten o'clock, forty-five minutes ago. He was growing impatient.

With an almost comical expression, he said, "I've got an idea, Rachel!"

He reached in his back pocket and produced his wallet, from which he withdrew his company photo ID. He went to one knee and removed the shoe lace from one of his tennis shoes.

"What are you doing?" Rachel asked.

"You'll see in a second."

Threading the shoe lace through the punched hole in the laminated card, Tom placed the shoe lace around his neck, tying the ends in a knot.

"There," he said proudly, "do I look official?"

Rachel didn't understand, "What is it?"

"It's my Channel 5 News Reporter ID. C'mon, hang on to my shirt and follow my lead."

"Excuse me, Channel 5 News! Pardon me, sir, Channel 5 News!"

Tom parted the crowd with authority. He held out his photo ID from the lace around his neck, and forged ahead like he had a story to cover. Grasping his shirt tail, Rachel noticed a few people weren't totally convinced the young man was part of the news organization, but they let him pass. When they reached the front of the line, they were witness to some pushing and shoving on the other side of the entrance gate.

"What's going on?" Tom asked one of the bystanders.

A plump older lady in a flowery swim suit answered, "A bunch of pro-abortionists got in the park ahead of us and were passing out pamphlets to people coming in. The park's security guards are trying to get them to leave peacefully. Freaking zealots!" she added.

"I don't like this, Tom. Remember what happened in San Francisco yesterday?"

Trying to assess the situation, Tom couldn't sense the slightest threat of danger looming. He continued observing the group of people inside the gate. The shoving had stopped, and the security guard was on his phone. Tom was convinced there was nothing to worry about—for now. He put his arm around Rachel, "If things look like they are going to go bad Rachel, we're out of here."

Tom counted eight middle-aged people and a wiry older woman, holding armloads of pamphlets. The security guard was now trying to reason with her calmly, but she wasn't responding to his logic.

"Look, ma'am, I believe in the right to choose, just like you, but this is private property. You can't hand those pamphlets out here."

"Nonsense," the woman shrugged, "it's a free country. We're exercising our right to free speech and to peaceably assemble."

"Look lady, the police have been notified. If you don't move your butts outta' here, you're gonna' be getting your Miranda rights, too. Now I don't think you want that."

The crowd was growing angry. The direct sun was heating the blacktop to unbearable temperatures.

"Get the hell out of there, so we can get in the park, lady!" one man yelled.

Others began to grumble too. "Where's the manager? Tell him to let us in!" screamed a woman with three children.

Tom approached the gate and called to the security guard, "Excuse me, sir, is there any way you can let us in, and remove these people afterward?"

The guard looked indifferent, "Sorry, kid, we can't let our customers be hassled by these people."

Tom frowned, "It seems to me we are being hassled more by standing out here in the heat."

DAN REYNOLDS

"Company policy," he said curtly, "the police will be here in a minute."

Three strongly built men were standing directly behind Rachel. One of them said, "Let's do everybody a favor, and toss these pamphlet pushers out of here!"

Those within earshot cheered. The endorsement was all the three men needed. They started through the gate.

"Rachel, maybe we should come back"— but before Tom could finish his sentence, the crowd started pushing toward the entrance, filling the empty gap vacated by the three men. A few young kids pushed through the gate, and then a few more. Suddenly the trickle of people pushing through the gates exploded into a stampede. Tom took Rachel's hand, but the woman with three children slipped between them separating their grip. Rachel flowed toward the entrance like a spec of sand through an hourglass. People accelerated from the crowd's center. Tom continued moving forward, but his direction was forced slightly askew of the mainstream crowd.

"Jesus, I've lost her—Rachel! Where the hell are you?"

Many in the crowd clearly saw the opportunity to gain entrance without paying.

"Slow down," Tom screamed, "someone's gonna get hurt!"

As he fought his way through the small opening, he tripped on something, and almost lost his balance. A moment later, he was on the other side, still being knocked and jarred by others coming through. He looked to his right; the three burly men were escorting the pro-abortion supporters to an exit. One of them had the wiry old woman by the waistband of her skirt. Looking to his left, Tom saw no sign of Rachel. There were streams of people pouring through three gate openings.

His shoulder was being pounded by shoving customers again and again, 'HEY, WATCH IT!" he growled.

Looking directly behind him, he saw several people on the ground, and more people tripping, falling over them. Good God, they are being trampled. And then a frightening thought occurred to him.

340   *What or who did I trip over coming through the entrance?*

He fought his way back to the gate, helping two people get up as he went. This was no longer a crowd, it was a mob. Unexpectedly, he was knocked off his feet by the impact of two boys smashing against both of his shoulders at once. As he struggled to get up, he felt a hard shoe strike his temple. His head seared with pain. Dizzy, he tried to get up, but no sooner than he would raise his torso, than he would be knocked down again. More pain to his head and groin. Lying on his side, he realized his face was unprotected. He covered it with his hands just as another shoe connected. The impact snapped one of the fingers covering his left eye. He felt something crack, as someone kicked his ribs. He rolled his body in the opposite direction. There was a kick to the small of his back, and then someone fell on him. He was hopelessly pinned to the ground. He felt the weight on him increase again, *another body,* he thought. It was hard to breathe. His hands still over his face, he saw stars, like bright pinpoints of light, and then nothing at all.

56

AT TWO O'CLOCK ON SATURDAY AFTERNOON, JIM O'BRIEN called Scott Troia at home. His wife, Joan, answered.

"Joan, this is Jim, is Scott home?"

"You sound upset, Jim. Is everything alright?"

"No, Tom has been hurt badly, I need Scott."

"Oh my, hold on dear, I'll get him."

A few seconds later, Scott picked up the receiver. "Jim—what's this about Tom gettin' hurt?"

"There was a stampede at Oceans of Fun. Several people were trampled by a crowd trying to get in to the park."

Scott was stunned, "How is he?" he asked.

"He's in serious condition."

"Good God!—and Rachel?"

"They wouldn't tell me."

Silence fell on both sides of the call. Finally Scott spoke, "There are two explanations as to why they wouldn't tell you," Scott said. "I hope to hell it's because of the privacy laws. Have her parents been notified?"

"I don't know. I tried to reach Rachel's folks, but no one is home. I don't know if they have a cell phone number."

"For God's sake, how could something like this happen?"

"I don't know, Scott—it sounds unbelievable. I'm going down there."

Scott huffed, "I'm going with you, buddy. I'm gonna' throw a few things in a bag. I'll be ready in five minutes."

"I was hoping you'd say that. Tom won't be in any shape to drive back. Oh—I need driving directions to North Kansas City Hospital, can you get them on the internet?"

"You bet I'll be ready when you get here."

"JOAN!" Scott barked, "I'm going to Kansas City!"

Scott was waiting at the curb when Jim arrived. He threw a small duffel in the back seat and plunked down beside Jim.

"I got the directions, Jim, let's go."

The Honda's tires chirped as the car lunged forward. Jim made a beeline toward the interstate. Scott was clipping a radar detector to the windshield visor.

"I thought you might be inclined to take some liberties with Missouri's speed limits."

A row of lights lit and the unit began to shriek as Scott plugged it into the cigarette lighter receptacle.

"I'm glad one of us is thinking rationally, Scott, thanks."

Scott continued, "Have you heard anything further about Tom or Rachel?"

"Nothing," Jim said. "I doubt we'll get any more information by telephone."

"A stampede?" Scott asked, fidgeting. "Like at a rock concert?"

"That's what I was told," Jim replied. "I don't know much more than that. Both Tom and Rachel were trampled by patrons trying to get in to Oceans of Fun. Tom is unconscious and has several broken bones. I have no idea how Rachel is doing."

Jim had been to Kansas City dozens of times. From Omaha, it was a leisurely three hour trip, two and a half at a brisk clip. He planned to shave a considerable amount of time from his personal best. Jim handed Scott his cell phone.

"Here, Scott, press the talk button twice. If Mr. or Mrs. Stowe answer, hand it back to me."

Scott tried the number. No one picked up the phone. Jim was careful not to drive too fast on I-80 East through Omaha and Council Bluffs, but as soon as he hit the open road, his speed varied between ten and twenty miles an hour over the speed limit. Scott could sense that Jim was terrified. And why shouldn't he be? After years of disappointments, Tom's life had just come back together. His future couldn't have looked any brighter and now this, a freak accident.

"How did Peg take the news?" Jim.

"She's worried sick. She insisted that I call you and ask you to come with me. I never had to ask. Thanks, Scott."

"You'd do the same, Jim; I never gave it a thought."

"She wanted you to drive, but if anyone is going to get a ticket, it should be me."

"I know you're okay to drive, Jim. But you should save your strength. It's going to be a long night."

Jim agreed and steered to the side of the road. Within a minute, they were traveling I-29 South, a little faster than they were before.

Jim stared out the window, "I just met Rachel this week," he said, absently. "She's such a lovely girl. She's warm, intelligent, and interesting, and on top of all that, she's very pretty. I couldn't have found him a more perfect match."

"I only met her briefly," Scott said. "Tom brought her in to tour the office one afternoon. I'll be damned if I didn't hear some pride in his voice as he gave her the tour, Jim."

"They're in love," Jim continued. "I can tell by the way they look at each other. Tom treats her like a princess. I've never seen him so happy." A quick glance at Jim, and Scott noticed the same thing Tom had observed earlier. Jim was underweight. His face was drawn and sullen. Scott noticed a few gray hairs had sprouted at Jim's temples.

344 Jim's cell rang, interrupting them.

"Hi Peg, did you reach them? Oh, my God," he mumbled. "This is going to crush him."

Jim listened quietly for a minute. When he hung up the phone, he set it in a recess in the console.

"What was it, Jim?"

"Rachel didn't make it, Scott, she's dead."

By six o'clock, Jim and Scott had just left the information desk at North Kansas City Hospital. Tom's condition had stabilized, and he was moved from intensive care to a private room only twenty minutes ago.

Jim wondered *Is he conscious? Does he know?*

The two men hurried to the elevator as fast as they could. When they arrived at Tom's room, the door was closed. Scott quickly waved a nurse down.

"We need to see Tom O'Brien. Is it okay to go in?"

"Are you family?"

"I'm the boy's uncle," Scott lied, "that's his father by the door. We just arrived from Omaha."

"He's not awake yet," the nurse said as she studied him, "I don't know if you should go in or not. I should probably ask the doctor."

"Look," Scott said in a testy voice, "that boy doesn't know it yet, but his girlfriend died in an accident at Oceans of Fun. When he wakes up, he's gonna' need his father an' me right there by his side."

The nurse looked sympathetic, "Okay, sir, you can go in. But don't wake him. He's been hurt pretty badly."

"Thank you," Scott said gratefully. "Would you please tell the doctor we'd like to see him when he has a moment?"

Jim slowly opened the door, and walked to the side of Tom's bed. He was searching for some part of his body that wasn't wrapped in bandages. There were few. He began to weep. He was glad Peg was not here to see this.

She has suffered enough sorrow with respect to her son, Jim thought. *Why did this have to happen now? Everything was going so well for him. He'd put drugs behind him and was beginning to mature and take responsibility for himself. Just last week, Peg had commented how the kids were starting to look up to him, like the big brother he always wanted to be. He's been a perfect fit for the company, and for Rachel.*

The room door opened. The man who entered didn't wear a white coat, but Jim still assumed it might be the doctor. "Are you his doctor?" Jim whispered.

"No, I am Charles Stowe, Rachel's father. How is Tom doing?"

Jim noticed his red eyes and figured he'd been crying.

But who wouldn't? he thought. *There is no greater tragedy than to lose a child.*

"He's doing better; he just came off the critical list about a half hour ago. Look, Mr. Stowe, I'm very sorry about your daughter."

Stowe nodded, "She was a wonderful girl, Mr. O'Brien. Hardly a day would pass when I didn't thank God for blessing me with two wonderful daughters." He choked as he struggled to continue, "Raising them has been effortless; never a problem for their mother and me."

His eyes were welling with tears again.

"Come on, Mr. Stowe; let's go sit down for a few minutes."

Jim glanced sideways at Troia as he put an arm around Stowe, and guided him to the door. Scott nodded and moved a chair to the head of Tom's bed.

In the hallway, the two men resumed their conversation, "We are all shocked by the news, Mr. Stowe. I can't imagine how such a thing happened."

"The news reports vary widely," Stowe said. "I saw some footage on the local news a minute ago. There must have been a thousand people storming the gates to get into that park. I just can't figure out why."

"Is there anything I can do for you, Mr. Stowe? Anything at all?"

"Please, call me Charles." He hesitated a moment and said, "I really don't have anywhere to go. It's late, and I can't finish making arrangements to have Rachel brought home until tomorrow. Would you mind if I waited with you until Tom wakes? I'd like to know that he is well, and maybe he can shed some light on what happened."

"You're welcome to stay with us, Charles. I could use the company, and I'm sure Tom will appreciate your concern. Did you say there was television footage of people storming the gates?"

"Yes, it was pretty senseless, to say the least. I can't imagine what possibly set it off."

The two men decided to sit in the waiting lounge for a while. The accident wasn't even mentioned on FOX or CNN. Apparently, the headline paled in comparison to the riots occurring all across the nation. The top national news story was about a protest march gone badly in San Francisco yesterday. About two hundred right-to-life supporters were marching along Fisherman's Wharf when they were attacked by an angry pro-choice group. It began with heckling and progressed to rock throwing and finally pushing and shoving. Hundreds more joined the violence on both sides. Shots were fired, killing a man named Alan Anniston, a right-to-life leader. What followed turned into a full blown riot. Several more guns surfaced during the fighting, sparking an unprecedented spree of violence. In the aftermath, police found hundreds of weapons, including clubs, knives, glass bottles, bricks, and even a pair of brass knuckles. There was little doubt to the authorities that these people intended to fight, or at the very least, protect themselves. Thirty-two people were killed, seventeen remained in critical condition, and over two hundred others were injured. The report mentioned that many bystanders were trampled by the scattering crowds. Hearing that, Stowe shook his head in disbelief.

KCTV Channel 5 had aired the Oceans of Fun footage several times during the newscast. In the incident, two people were killed, and forty-two people were injured, many seriously. There was no mention of the delay caused by the pro-abortion group. The entire incident was under investigation.

Stowe spoke softly, staring at the floor, "Rachel said she was coming here with Tom and some other friends. Stacy Brodie was one of them. Are they all right?"

"I'm sorry, Charles, I just arrived here. I haven't heard anything more. As far as I know, only Rachel and Tom were hurt."

Jim's heart went out to him, *I know how he feels,* he thought. *I know exactly how he feels.*

Jim spoke softly, "I think they were in love, Charles."

"Yes, they were. She told me so. To be honest, I'm really fond of Tom. I think he was good for Rachel. I think she was good for him, too."

"I only met Rachel earlier in the week. I was very taken with her. I thought she was a very sweet young lady."

Replays of the footage continued to interrupt the regular broadcasts. It was difficult for Stowe to watch. Jim decided they would be better off in Tom's room.

*　　*　　*

The Tuesday morning drive from Kansas City to Omaha was difficult for both Tom and his father. During the three hour trip, there were only brief periods of conversation. Tom kept his eyes closed most of the time. Jim suspected that he feigned sleep to avoid talking about Rachel. He didn't blame him. Scott left on Sunday evening to drive Tom's car back to town. When Tom awoke around seven thirty Saturday evening, he was still groggy from sedation when he learned of Rachel's death. Falling in and out of consciousness, Jim had to break the news to him several times before he understood that she was really gone.

Tom's reaction wasn't at all what Jim expected. He hardly spoke a word, but from that moment, there was a steady stream of tears rolling down his cheeks. Charles Stowe stayed for a few hours. He wanted Tom to know how Rachel had confided to him that he was the one, her true love, her soul mate. Tom was gripped by guilt. "I'm so sorry this happened, Mr. Stowe, we just wanted to have a fun weekend together. We never expected anything like this to happen."

"I know son," Stowe replied with empathy. "I know exactly how you felt about Rachel. It's not your fault."

Driving north on I-29, Jim continued to glance at Tom from time to time. He had partially reclined the passenger seat to take the pressure off of two broken ribs. Seeing him so solemn was depressing for Jim. *What can the poor kid be thinking? He's not lost his temper, never asked, why me? But maybe he needs to let some steam off. At the very least, he needs someone he can talk to. I hope Peg has succeeded in scheduling some appointments with his psychiatrist. He's going to need them.*

Jim and Peg had spoken several times a day since the accident. He warned her that Tom was likely to be facing a serious bout with depression, even if he did get some help. Their greatest concern was whether Tom would try to dull his emotions by self-medicating with drugs. They would have to keep a close eye on him. Peg planned to have all the children attend Rachel's wake tonight. Tom would need their support. Jim stopped about half way to Omaha for gas. When he asked Tom if he wanted to stop and eat, he declined the offer, saying that he didn't want to be seen like this. Was he referring to his bandages, his tears, or his state of mind?

Jesus, Jim thought, *what's he going to be like at the wake and funeral?*

The question Jim pondered was answered that evening at six-thirty. The wake did not start until seven, but Tom asked Peg if they could arrive a half hour early. He offered his condolences to Charles and Brenda Stowe, and Rachel's younger sister, Kayla. Seeing Tom's bruised face and the remaining bandages around his temple and hand, made Brenda Stowe burst into tears. She knew that Rachel must have looked much worse than him. At Charles request, she never viewed the body. The casket was closed, and would remain so forever.

The bronze casket was surrounded by flowers. Tom signaled to Molly, who came running to him with a rose he asked his mother to purchase earlier. He placed the rose on the casket, and winced in pain as he lowered himself onto the kneeler before it. He bowed his head and began to pray, remaining perfectly still for almost twenty minutes. Toward the end of that time, his thoughts drifted to images of Rachel. He imagined her in a wedding gown. He saw them both smiling and laughing as he carried her over a threshold. He laid her on a bed and caressed her face in his hands. He could see every detail of her perfect features, her smooth, tawny skin, the pronounced dimples in her cheeks, her dark eyes sparkling in the light.

He felt a hand on his shoulder, "Tom, people are coming in for the wake." He recognized his mother's voice.

"Mom," he said in embarrassment, "I can't get up—can you help me?"

During the Catholic prayer service, the priest led the rosary. Just before they left the house, Jim gave Tom a rosary that had belonged to his father and told him to keep it. Tom didn't remember all of the steps involved, but he said every Hail Mary and Our Father with fervor and sincerity. At the end of the service, a few friends and family members stood up and shared fond recollections of Rachel. Tom wanted to do the same, but he knew the words wouldn't come. He would surely break down and cry. With every shared memory, he could picture her clearly. Rachel was depicted as a gentle soul; a warm intelligent young woman who enjoyed every moment life had to offer. Tom thought about how true that was.

He spotted Scott and Miranda. Randy, Charlie, and Will were there as well. He was only half surprised that Matt wasn't present. It was probably for the best. Their friendship was nothing more than memories, or the lack of them, depending how you looked at it. When the service concluded, he thanked his friends for coming. As they were leaving, Rachel's younger sister Kayla caught him at the door, and gave him a hug.

"Tom," she said, "I know you could really use a friend right now. I think I could, too. Maybe we could get together sometime and talk."

"Sure, I'd like that," Tom said, as he held the exit door for his siblings. Then he followed them outside.

57

UGLY—THAT'S HOW TOM FELT IN HIS SOUL. AND THAT'S HOW others would look at him without Rachel. He was certain of it. It was Friday. He saw his psychiatrist two days in a row, but that didn't stop thoughts of Rachel from clawing at him relentlessly. Tom didn't want to forget about her, but on the other hand, the very thought of her, pierced his heart, leaving him empty and forlorn. It was similar to the unnerving agony he had experienced years ago, when he saw those high school boys taking turns with Christina Mackenzie. Without drugs to numb the heartache, he was ready to climb the walls.

Maybe it would help if I went to work. Dad is there today he thought in desperation.

He ambled to his car, but the attempt to get behind the wheel of the low slung Mustang proved to be too painful. Although his wounds were beginning to heal, his bruises were still tender, especially his ribs.

I guess I'd better stay home. Tom went to the kitchen and poured a cup of coffee. He avoided sitting on the picnic style benches at the table and instead, eased into his father's chair.

The next thing he knew, he heard his mother's voice, "TOM?— TOM! Are you alright?"

Peg's voice startled him. Tom realized he was sweating; his teeth clenched so hard his head hurt. When Peg's words jolted him back to reality, his surroundings materialized quickly. He was at the kitchen table, his hands clasping a cold cup of coffee. Relaxing his jaw, a wave of pain swept across his skull.

"I—I must have been daydreaming. I need to just sit here for a minute."

He didn't know what else to do. He wanted to cry, but he couldn't. There were no more tears left; he was emotionally spent. Tom felt his mother staring at him. He didn't budge. He didn't know what reaction he should have, what muscle to move.

A finger? A toe? Should I stand, sit, walk, WHAT?

Tom remained still, almost expecting the next tragedy to walk through the door at any second.

Peg could bear no more, "You've been sitting there for an hour, Tom. I'm going to put you to bed. You look like you could use some sleep."

It was true. Tom had not slept much since Rachel's death almost a week ago. He couldn't stop thinking about her, not even for a moment. To make matters worse, he was plagued by guilt from another tragedy.

This is how Mom and Dad must have felt when Katie died.

Anxiety ridden, bruised and sore, he could barely sleep for more than a few minutes at a time. Most of his bandages had been discarded throughout the week, with the exception of a patch on his forehead and the splint protecting a broken finger on his left hand. His eyes were red and weary.

Maybe I can sleep now, he more hoped than believed. *I need to forget for a while.* A brief image of a heroin syringe flashed in his mind. *I need to forget.*

Peg sat down beside him, "I'm really concerned about you, Tom. Too many things have happened in a short time. Do you want to talk about it?"

Tom managed a small smile, "Thanks, Mom. I appreciate what you're doing and I understand your concern, but I'm all talked out. Dr. Fenton saw to that. I'm scheduled to spend three more sessions with him next week."

Peg's voice cast an emotional tone, "It's just that I know how you are hurting. I know how you feel."

Tom leaned back against his chair and closed his eyes. "I was just thinking the same thing. You must have felt this way when Katie died."

Peg's green eyes were radiant with compassion, "Her death was difficult, Tom, and we'll miss her always, but the pain will ease with time."

Tom nodded and then hesitated, like there was something else on his mind. Peg noticed. "Is something else wrong?"

With a look of deep appreciation, Tom said, "I never thanked you for not sending me back to that drug treatment program, Mom. If you had, I'm not certain I could have recovered from my addiction. You'll never know how grateful I am."

"I've always had faith in you, Tom. I never saw anything but the good in you. You just lost your way for a while."

"To be honest, I'm pretty lost right now. First Katie, then Dad, and now Rachel; I can't focus on much else."

"If it weren't difficult, you wouldn't be human. Your father had a hard time going back to work after Katie's death."

"You're right Mom, and on top of everything else, he had to deal with my drug addiction at the same time. How did he ever do it?"

"He's a strong man, Tom, but so are you. You'll get through this— and you'll be a better person in the end."

Tom doubted it, but he replied, "I hope so. I owe Dad a great debt. I can't think of a better way of repaying him, than to help him grow the company."

"I need to tell you something, Tom. In addition to your giving up drugs, your father and I have seen so many wonderful changes in you. Scott Troia told him how hard you've worked to become a valuable part of the company. He's so proud of you."

Tom didn't think he had any tears left, but Peg's comment forced one down his cheek.

"Maybe so, but what took me so long? Why was I such a terrible son? I've put you both through so much."

"You weren't a terrible son, Tom. You developed a terrible habit, and that's quite different. Your father knew that you loved him—and he's always loved you. That's why he never gave up on your rehabilitation. He saw the good in you, too—even through the drugs, he knew you better than you knew yourself."

Tom avoided Peg's gaze. He looked incredibly sad, his eyes still watery.

"Thanks, Mom, thanks for everything." Peg hugged him gently, but he still grimaced in pain.

Tom walked into the living room and saw Molly playing "Chutes and Ladders" by herself. "Hey, kiddo, what do you say we play a game together after my nap?"

"Okay," she was sing-songing in her familiar musical voice. "We can play a game after our naps."

It was almost eleven.

"Let me get you something to eat first," Peg shouted from the kitchen. "I have a feeling you'll be out for the entire day."

Tom mentioned how he had been unable to sleep much all week. While he ate a sandwich, Peg scoured the medicine cabinet and returned with two capsules.

"Here, Tom, these are only Benadryl, but they will make you drowsy," she said.

In total darkness, Tom climbed into bed and gently rolled to his good side. His soft pillow felt like heaven against his face. Several thoughts still hung in his mind.

If I hadn't taken Rachel to the front of the line, she would still be alive—if I had stayed away from drugs, Katie would still be here—if I hadn't been high that night, Dad wouldn't have been hurt.

Tom tried to clear his head.

Jesus, he thought, cynically, *with all the shame, guilt, and sadness, it hardly leaves me any room for self-pity.*

Tom tried to imagine a white board, the kind you draw on with dry erase markers. It was a trick he learned while he was in treatment. He would just stare at the center of the white board, purging his mind of everything else. Even at the brink of total exhaustion, it wasn't working; his busy thoughts were fighting sleep.

Unexpectedly, an image of David Manetti flashed in his mind. When he jerked upright, a sharp pain shot across his ribs.

Clutching his side, he asked himself, *What's today's date?* He didn't know, but he remembered promising David Manetti delivery of Constantino's documents. *Was it by today? I haven't even talked to Dad about it yet. I've got to help him get out of the mess he's in. Maybe that's my penance.*

It was suddenly clear what he had to do. When his dad came home from the office, he would confront him; show him the envelope Frank Saunders was carrying the night he was killed. It contained evidence linking his father to the Moral Mafia. He would convince him to turn everything over to David Manetti. After rethinking things a bit, Tom realized that it would take no convincing at all. His father had planned to turn everything over to Manetti all along. He had just been interrupted by the men who attacked him. The Moral Mafia was as good as dead, anyway. The organization's long absence had made it defunct.

If it kills me, I'll make sure Manetti never hurts my family, and when it's over, I'll help Dad to end this madness over abortion. We can use the Swiss bank account just like he planned, and find a peaceful means to stop the violence. Even if it kills me, he thought.

A moment later, he was sound asleep.

58

SATURDAY MORNING WAS NEARLY OVER WHEN TOM awoke. He sat with his feet dangling over the edge of his bed for about five minutes.

Mom was right, he thought. *I must have slept at least twenty-four hours.*

He recalled yesterday's events and those of the entire week. A few moments later, he remembered what he was thinking, just before he fell asleep.

Manetti.

And then he recalled Rachel's voice saying, *"It's important to know what you stand for."*

For the first time in a week, Tom was no longer at the brink of exhaustion. Yesterday, his physical condition had magnified his emotions to the point of rendering him completely helpless.

I can't let myself get that tired again, he thought. *I need to be at my mental peak when I speak with Dad and deliver the documents to Manetti.*

Tom spent about an hour with Shauna, Danny, and Molly. It was amazing the healing effect they had on him.

He grabbed an apple and headed for the study. Between the books on the book shelf, he withdrew a large manila envelope. It was the one Saunders was carrying the night his father was stabbed. It supposedly contained enough evidence for the FBI agent to arrest his dad. Tom had shoved it down his shirt and hid it as soon as he got home.

Tilting the envelope sharply, he slid the documents into his hand, and began to examine them for the first time in months. They looked much different than he remembered. He observed the gibberish in the header section of the e-mails. It was something he hadn't noticed before. It looked just like the e-mails the Moral Mafia had sent to the Associated Press, the ones Scott Troia had show him. One of the documents orchestrated a hit on Deacon Reynolds and the other two boys who killed Katie.

This is the evidence that FBI agent was talking about, Tom thought.

Tom deplored violence, but he couldn't help feeling some consolation in the act of vengeance his father had taken against them. After all, Katie was just an innocent little girl of nine; she didn't deserve to have her life snuffed out so abruptly.

Tom tore the page into pieces and stuffed them in his back pocket. He did the same with some maps and a newspaper article depicting the death of three teenagers in a reckless drunken driving incident that plunged them into the Missouri River.

The small pieces will flush down the toilet easily, he thought.

Studying another e-mail, he immediately recognized the authoritative style in which it was written. It contained detailed instructions to assassinate a list of senators and congressmen. It read with the similarity and commanding presence of the newspaper communications written by the leader of the Moral Mafia. A part of Tom was still in denial that his father could give such commands.

What will he say when I confront him? I wonder if Constantino's documents are hidden in his safe. It's more likely they are in a safety deposit box somewhere, he thought.

Once again, he ripped documents into pieces. Peg told him his father had gone to the office. Since it was Saturday, there shouldn't be anyone else working besides him and Troia. They could talk calmly, and in private.

Getting behind the wheel of the Mustang was nearly as painful as yesterday's attempt, but once inside, driving wasn't much of a chore. His finger splint made it clumsy to turn corners, but he managed. It was almost noon when he arrived at the office. Bracing his hands on the car's window frame, he hoisted himself from the driver's seat. He winced and groaned in unison. He only took a few steps when he was greeted by three men standing by a black Lincoln Town Car.

A freakishly large man held the rear door open and gestured, saying, "This way, Mr. O'Brien." Tom saw a mustached man withdraw his hand from his pocket just enough so that he could catch a glimpse of his gun. Tom got in the car.

*   *   *

Scott and Miranda sat at the small round table in the corner of Jim's office. It was just like old times. They were briefing Jim, bringing him up to speed on several business issues, when his cell phone rang. He answered the phone.

"DAD, ARE YOU ALONE?"

Tom sounded frantic, "No, Tom, I'm here with Scott and Miranda—are you all right?"

"Ask them to leave, Dad, and hurry! I need to speak to you in private. It's an emergency!"

Scott didn't miss the concerned look on Jim's face when he asked them to give him a moment alone. "Is everything okay, Jim?"

"Yeah, everything's fine; I just need to talk to Tom for a few minutes." Jim did his best to conceal his fear as he added, "Why don't you two grab us a cup of coffee. We'll pick up where we left off, shortly."

Miranda's eyes lingered on Jim as she closed his door. "He looks worried, Scott, I hope there's no problem."

"You got that right, kiddo. Problems are something the O'Brien family can do without."

Alone now, Jim's query was intense and to the point. "What's the matter, Tom?"

"I have a message from Jimmy Bonaiuto, Dad. He says if you want to see me alive, you'd better bring Constantino's bank books and documents down here within the hour."

Jim's mind exploded in a flash of emotions and questions. *Bonaiuto? He's here? He knows? Did David Manetti tell him? Would he hurt Tom?*

He already knew the answer to the last question. Even if he complied with Bonaiuto's wishes, more than likely he and Tom would both be killed. If not for their knowledge of the family's dealings, then as sheer retribution for what he had done.

"Where are you, son?"

"I don't know, exactly; I'm in a warehouse down by the river. Someone is going to give you directions. Dad, I'm sorry. I was supposed to talk to you this week; get the documents, and give them to David Manetti. After Rachel's death, I was so absorbed in self-pity, I forgot all about it. It's all my fault."

Jim tried to shift the guilt where it belonged, "Don't say that, Tom, you shouldn't even be involved in this. I started this mess, I should be there, not you. Whatever you do—don't panic. Try to stay cool. I'm coming to get you."

"I'm counting on that—YOU FUCK!" The voice was only vaguely familiar, but Jim surmised that it was Jimmy Bonaiuto.

"Don't hurt my son," Jim pleaded. "I'll do anything you ask, just don't hurt him!"

"I've waited a long time for this, Mr. O'Brien. I've dreamed about the day I would come face to face with the man who betrayed us. You made Tony Constantino look like a fool. David told me you did all of this just so you could play some moral fucking saint. You put my family through hell, and now I'm gonna' return the favor."

Jim's gut churned. Bonaiuto's point was accurate.

I took what wasn't mine, I had no right. "Listen, Jimmy, I was going to give it all back. David and I arranged for a meeting, but I was seriously injured before we could get together. I spent several months in the hospital. I had to wait until I recovered, but don't worry—I'll return everything and no one knows anything about it."

The explanation seemed weak. Jim felt like a child being scolded for having his hand in the cookie jar, but no one was ever killed for stealing cookies. There was little question in Jim's mind, the man he was speaking to wanted revenge.

To what degree? Jim wondered, anguishing over the fact that Tom was being held captive, by a man whose voice was rancid with hate.

"You'd better hope so, or I'll wipe your entire family out before the day is over."

Jim wasn't breathing. He didn't doubt Bonaiuto's sincerity for a moment. *The family is ruthless.* After all, they carried out the commands of the Moral Mafia and committed murder for much less than was at stake now.

They're going to kill us both, he thought, suddenly stricken with panic. *No matter what I do, they'll kill us both.*

Bonaiuto gave him an address and told him he had one hour to arrive. For every minute he was late, he said that Tom would lose a finger. Jim tried to protest, reason with him, but he suddenly realized there was no one on the other end of the phone. Bonaiuto had hung up on him. Incensed and fearful, Jim sprang to his feet and darted down the hall. Scott and Miranda heard the muted echoes of his footsteps slapping against the short loop carpet.

Scott called after him, "Where ya' going, Jim?" but it was too late. Jim was already out the front door. Scott gave Miranda a sideways glance, "This can't be good."

Jim only lived a few miles from the office, but by the time he retrieved the accordion style folder and address book from his safe, he had burned more than twenty precious minutes. He needed a little time to study the Bersa Thunder .380 pistol he kept for self-protection. It had never been fired, and Jim was only vaguely familiar

360

with its operation. The clip held nine rounds, and Jim shoved a spare clip in his pocket. He pulled the nickel plated slide back, chambering a round. The mechanical sound made him shudder, as he realized he had every intention of using it within the next half hour. After moving the safety lever to the off position, Jim carefully slid it in with the papers which added substantial girth to the folder. He moved to his computer and opened a DOS window, and typed a series of nonsensical characters. Then he typed a short memo:

We have confirmed that Jim O'Brien is close to discovering the secret of our "stealth software". Take him out immediately. Don't hesitate to kill anyone else with knowledge of the software.

—The Moral Mafia

Jim addressed the correspondence to Mario Manetti. Seconds later, he printed a copy with the odd ASCII characters in the *FROM:* box. He wondered if he'd have the chance to plant it on Jimmy Bonaiuto or leave it at the premises to frame him as being the head of the Moral Mafia. Of course, that might mean he'd have to kill him first. Jim grabbed the correspondence and darted from the den. Danny said something to his father as he whisked through the living room and toward the door, but the words didn't register. "Was that your father?" Peg asked, as she poked her head out of the kitchen. Shauna replied, "Yeah, Mom, he was in a real hurry."

Tangled thoughts hampered Jim's driving concentration. He cursed when he missed the I-80 turn. A few more missed turns could cost Tom a finger—or two. It didn't help that his phone kept ringing. Both Scott and Peg were trying to reach him. Jim's face contorted as he recalled the image of Tom's abandoned Mustang in the parking lot. His mind kept racing and his thoughts were jumbled. He had to make a critical decision.

Do I call Vince Mitchell, or not?

It wasn't the mere fact that he would reveal himself as the leader of the Moral Mafia that concerned him. He would gladly turn himself in to save his son. But Vince could be anywhere. Could he get FBI agents to him on time? He wondered if doing so would place Tom's life in greater jeopardy. For some reason, Jim thought he had a better chance of rescuing Tom without interference from the FBI or police. He hoped he would be lucky enough to avoid a shoot-out, but his intuition told him a confrontation was unavoidable. But who will end up dead? How many men did Bonaiuto have with him? How outnumbered was he?

Jim made his way east on Dodge Street through Saturday's busy traffic. He regretted not taking the interstate, but his preoccupation with Jimmy Bonaiuto had betrayed his clarity of thinking. He was juggling thoughts of a faster route and a plan of action once he arrived. Jim had little confidence that he would ever plant the phony e-mail he had just written on Bonaiuto or one of his men. That would assume that he and Tom could escape the family's clutches, but the very thought seemed unrealistic at the moment. While delayed at a stop light at Tenth and Dodge Street, a better plan was materializing in Jim's mind; a plan he hoped would save their lives. Noticing a police cruiser approaching from oncoming traffic, Jim questioned the wisdom of his decision. Soon traffic resumed and the cruiser disappeared in his rearview mirror. Jim began to think about dying. Jim quickly asked for God's forgiveness, and also that He protect his son.

Jim had circled the abandoned coffee warehouse twice. A raised garage door suggested that he enter on the east end of the building. However, the west end of the building would work better for his plan. A glance at his watch confirmed he had about seven or eight minutes to set things up. He parked the car about twenty yards up the hill on Pierce Street. Running to the back of the building, Jim's eyes scoured the premises. There were crumbling bricks at the building's edge. A few of them were missing.

Perfect, Jim thought.

He panted, out of breath from the short sprint, as he set his plan in motion. It was then he realized how fragile he still was.

I should have gone to physical therapy, he thought. *I'm terribly out of shape.*

The four men carried on a conversation as though Tom wasn't there. He was glad. He didn't want to talk anymore. He'd had enough questioning. When Tom had arrived with his captors, Bonaiuto was interrogating David Manetti calmly, from across the table. The giant man walked Tom to the table and sat him down beside David. The two young men acknowledged each other with a silent nod. Bonaiuto looked at the man with a thick black mustache.

With his hand outstretched, Bonaiuto had said, "Mario, let me have your gun."

The pistol Mario produced was odd looking. There was something attached to the barrel's end. It looked unnaturally long.

Bonaiuto had pointed the gun at Tom's forehead. Shocked, and overtaken with fear, Tom inhaled sharply and held his breath. He was no less afraid as Bonaiuto's arm swung a few inches left and he squeezed the trigger. There was no noisy explosion, just a muted "phum" sound, and a thin waft of smoke. David Manetti's body lost its rigid posture, slumping forward. His head crashed to the table with a thud louder than the shot itself.

Mario Manetti was clearly shocked by the shooting. He just stared at David's lifeless corpse until John Henry carried him away. That was the instant Tom's interrogation began. Bonaiuto fondled the gun throughout his interview. He seemed to savor every moment he spent grilling the boy. But Tom held steadfast in his responses to the questions. He had his father's quiet strength. No, he did not know the whereabouts of Constantino's documents. No, he had never heard mention of them, except from David Manetti. No, he couldn't say for certain if his father was the head of the Moral Mafia. He said he couldn't imagine it being true.

But Jimmy Bonaiuto knew the answers. David Manetti had already confessed, confirming his earlier suspicions. Jimmy knew that Tony Constantino's ring was on his finger the night he had been rushed to the hospital. In fact, he was certain that Constantino never took it off. If the FBI hadn't confiscated it, there could only be two possibilities. Either David Manetti obtained it during one of his visits to his room, or it was given to the stranger who had interviewed Constantino late that night.

A handsome man with auburn hair had left the hospital through the main entrance, led by the same FBI agent he arrived with. Constantino's men tailed him to a hanger at Midway Airport, where he met a private plane and flew to Omaha. There was no flight roster, no record of the man's identity, and therefore, no way to track him down. But when Mario Manetti received orders from the Moral Mafia to kill three teenage boys in Omaha, Bonaiuto became suspicious. David Manetti's trips to Omaha clinched his theory. There had to be a link between David and the man who interviewed Constantino that night.

Bonaiuto began keeping David under constant surveillance. When David claimed to be taking a few days off to attend a security symposium in Kansas City, it was quickly discovered that there was no such event taking place. Three of his men followed him to Omaha. David was apprehended while staking out Jim O'Brien's home. The three men picked him up and escorted him to the old coffee warehouse, and within two hours, Bonaiuto had arrived via the family's own private jet.

David Manetti confessed to discovering Jim's identity several months ago. He swore to Jimmy that he only wanted to return the documents and bank accounts to the family. Bonaiuto cursed at him, told him his father would be disappointed to know that he'd held O'Brien's identity a secret. When asked why he didn't come to him for help, David replied sheepishly, "I just wanted to make you proud of me, Jimmy." Now his body was in a plastic bag and lay near the loading dock, and Tom waited impatiently for his father to arrive and take him away from this dreadful place.

For the last fifteen minutes, Tom had tried to imagine that this nightmare was over. He stared blankly at the floor, and envisioned his dad coming for him, exchanging the documents for his freedom. The daydream spawned thoughts of the future. He visualized the two of them working together to undo some of the damage done by the Moral Mafia. He could almost hear his father giving inspirational speeches to rally the country toward peace. Unfortunately, those hopes seemed just as likely as escaping his captors alive.

It's a simple matter to stop one fight, he thought. *But how do you stop millions of people from fighting?*

Months ago, the situation could have been resolved much easier, but now, the hatred had escalated to catastrophic proportions. Tom wasn't sure a solution even existed. He was appalled by the endless demonstrations and riots, the needless killing. Violence over the abortion issue had grown to be so commonplace, that Americans had become desensitized to it. The headlines no longer carried the impact and shock value they once did. Americans no longer huddled around their radios and televisions. Many countries were now predicting that America was on the very brink of a civil war.

There's got to be a way to make people see where we are headed, he thought. *We are gravitating toward unimaginable bloodshed. I owe it to Dad and Rachel to help stop the mayhem. But I'm just a kid—a thousand kids just like me couldn't stop this freight train from running its course.* He closed his eyes. *Pray for me, Rachel. Right or wrong, I'm taking a moral stand. If I get out of this alive, people will know where I stand on everything.*

59

"WHAT DO YOU WANT?" THE GRUFF VOICE SCOWLED.

The man wore a thin overcoat in the searing summer heat. His hands were in his pockets, and his black hair was matted with sweat. It took little imagination for Jim to figure out he was clutching a gun.

"I need to see Jimmy Bonaiuto. He's holding my son."

Mike Sloan scrutinized Jim and motioned him to go through the raised garage door.

"Keep your hands in front of you and walk slowly," he said.

Jim held the accordion file out in front of him and walked straight ahead. As soon as they were inside, Sloan brandished his pistol using it to gesture ahead.

"Keep going," he said, "I'll tell you when to stop."

Jim studied every detail of his surroundings, as if memorizing them might save his life. There wasn't much to study. Two stalls over, there was an ancient delivery truck that looked like it had been untouched since the building was abandoned. Jim noticed every doorway and window. There were several. They reached some rickety steps leading to a raised glass enclosure overlooking the freight storage facility and loading docks. Again the man waved the gun prompting Jim to climb the steps.

Inside the warehouse's dispatch room, Jim glimpsed a silver-haired man posed with his hands clasped behind his back. Unlike Constantino, he looked physically fit for his age. Wearing finely tailored black slacks and a white polo shirt, he flaunted a look of distain as he watched Jim enter the room. Directly behind him was a table where Tom was seated. Two more men surveyed him from dark recesses of the room. One of them was incredibly big. Jim's eyes wanted to linger on him, but he was more concerned for his son.

"Are you alright, Tom?"

Tom looked up with apologetic eyes. The very sight of his father made them moist. He suddenly felt like a little boy, who desperately craved the reassuring strength of his father.

Tom looked a little ashamed when his voice cracked, "I'm okay, Dad."

Bonaiuto wasted no time.

"Did you bring me everything, Mr. O'Brien?"

"I did," Jim said, "and if you don't mind, I don't care to know anything more about you, or your family. I just want to take my son and go."

Bonaiuto broke into a booming belly laugh. "I see. You steal our assets, take over my organization, and put us through hell for nine months, and then you just want to waltz outta' here with your son?" With that comment, Jim's worst fears materialized.

We're not leaving here alive.

With great effort, Jim forced a stoic glance. "Yes, we'd like to go now," he said flatly.

"I'll say this for you, Mr. O'Brien; you've got balls," he steamed. "Just about the biggest pair of balls I've ever seen."

Jim set the accordion folder on a dust ridden file cabinet, "Let's go son, these gentlemen have a long trip ahead of them."   **367**

Tom started to stand, but the long and unusual looking barrel of Mario Manetti's gun met his gaze. He sat back down. Jim's eyes turned to slits, "I thought you were an honorable man, Mr. Bonaiuto. Are you going back on your word?"

"Not at all," he said coolly. "I never said I'd let you go, or live for that matter. I merely said if you weren't here within an hour, your son would begin to lose his fingers. Well, you've seen him, Mr. O'Brien, and all of his digits are accounted for. Now it's time for you both to die."

Adrenaline coursed through Jim's veins. He realized his right leg was shaking. He fought hard to control it. It was becoming increasingly difficult to remain composed as he calculated their unlikely odds of survival.

"I see," Jim seethed. "Is your play on words supposed to make you honorable, as opposed to a liar?"

Bonaiuto began to open his mouth to speak, but Jim cut him off.

"You know what you implied, Jimmy. You know goddamned well what you implied."

"You're a business man, Mr. O'Brien; you know better than most, the value of specifying the fine details of a contract. I'm afraid I was a bit vague, and we made no bargain—none at all."

"Then perhaps we can make one now," Jim said, sweeping the room with careful eyes. "I brought you everything, as promised, but I didn't bring it all inside with me."

The rage in Bonaiuto came to life as quickly as a struck match. He grabbed the accordion style folder and ripped it open. A two inch stack of documents filled the folder's recess, but the book, Tony's black book, was missing.

"Where is it, you son-of-a-bitch? Where's Tony's black book?"

Jim could see pinpoints of light everywhere he looked, the kind you see just before passing out.

Setting his jaw, he thought, *Here it goes; if this doesn't work we've bought the farm.*

"Which one, Jimmy, the copy I gave my attorney with a note for the FBI, or the original?"

"You fuck! You goddamned FUCK! I'M GONNA' KILL EVERY MEMBER OF YOUR FAMILY, O'BRIEN, BUT NOT BEFORE I TORTURE EACH AND EVERY ONE OF EM'!"

Bonaiuto screamed the threat wildly. Spittle covered his bottom lip, but he didn't notice. His temper had risen to an uncontrollable level. With clenched fists, he took an intimidating step toward Jim, like he was going to punch him. And then he stopped cold and spun around.

"John Henry, come over here!"

From the shadows, the gargantuan figure emerged. The thudding of his lumbering footsteps said he was three hundred-fifty pounds or more. And through the dingy windows, the feeble light lent itself to expose the magnitude of his uncanny size and features.

"Hold him still," Bonaiuto said with a deranged look.

Jim shuddered, as the mammoth figure stepped behind him and reached his arm across his chest. He felt as fragile as a pretzel as John Henry locked his hold on him. He braced himself for a brutal beating. But Bonaiuto turned and went in the direction of the table, toward Tom.

"Mario, hold the boy's hand to the table."

Jim's eyes widened. He thought his heart might stop. He recognized Mario Manetti's name, having enlisted his help on several occasions. He was still holding his gun. With the silencer attached to the barrel, it was much too large to be holstered. He set it on a nearby desk, and went to Tom.

Manetti knew what would happen next. He grabbed Tom's arm in two locations and forced it down to keep his hand flat on the table.

"What are you doing?" Jim asked. Bonaiuto saw the splint on Tom's broken finger.

"Gimme' the other hand," he said, glancing back at Jim.

He reached in his pocket and withdrew a slender stiletto. With a muted click, the narrow blade snapped in place. Its long tapering shape reflected bits of light.

"WHAT ARE YOU GOING TO DO?" Jim demanded.

"I'm going to get your cooperation, Mr. O'Brien. Maybe then you'll quit fucking with me."

Bonaiuto raised the knife. Tom's eyes pleaded for his father's help.

"There's no need for this, Jimmy, I'll get you the book!"

Bonaiuto's eyes glimmered, tainted with a crazed look of vengeance. Jim had never been more desperate for forgiveness than he was at this moment.

This is going to hurt, Tom—I'm so sorry, son.

Bonaiuto's arm swung down hard. Tom screamed. His eyes bulged and he turned white when he saw that the blade had pierced his hand, pinning his palm to the table. The pain was worse for Jim. Watching his son's horrified expression was unbearable. A thin trail of blood ran from the back of Tom's hand to the table. He remained motionless, afraid to move. He stared in disbelief at what had just happened. Bonaiuto grinned. He looked like a man who had finally won a round in a boxing match after losing several in a row. Only for a split-second did Jim taste the blood in his mouth from biting his cheek. The thought was already gone. Jim had a difficult bluff ahead of him, he wondered if he could pull it off. What he was about to say would sound harsh and uncaring to Tom. He hoped Tom would realize what he was doing.

"Do you think this will make me cooperate with you, Jimmy?"

Jimmy shot back ferociously, "It had better, or we'll start chopping off the kid's fingers!"

Jim fought back the instinct to plead with him. "I wasn't kidding about the copies I gave my attorney, Jimmy. If anything happens to us, he will turn them over to the FBI."

"Do you really expect me to believe that bullshit story?"

"Try me, Jimmy! You must think I'm pretty stupid not to have some kind of insurance in place. I know all about your drug dealing and the crooked businesses your family owns. I know as much about your businesses as you do. Those documents will bring the FBI right to your door. Is that what you want?"

Bonaiuto studied Jim carefully. Jim's green eyes were fearless. But even worse, they were convincing. They stared each other down for about ten seconds. "So, how do I know you won't turn them over anyway?"

"You must be kidding?" Jim said sarcastically. "I'm the leader of the Moral Mafia. The FBI wants me a hell of a lot more than they want you. If those documents find their way into the FBI's hands, it will be your doing, not mine."

The look of disgust Bonaiuto gave Jim was intense. His eyes turned to slits as he removed a handkerchief from his back pocket. He clasped the stiletto still pinning Tom's hand to the table, and yanked it upward. Tom winced and immediately tried closing his hand. Drops of blood spattered on the table, but Jim felt a sigh of relief as he watched Tom open and close it repeatedly.

"Where's the fucking address book?" Bonaiuto asked. He controlled his anger by wiping down the stiletto's blade.

"I left it outside, around the back of the building. We can all go get it together. Tom and I will leave from there."

Bonaiuto checked his temper. "No, Mike and John Henry will take you to get it. Bring it back to me, and then you and your son can go." Jim worried that Bonaiuto was lying, but there was no other alternative. Jim gave his son a parting glance. He hoped like hell his plan would work. So far, so good.

"Tom, I'll be back in a few minutes. Everything is going to be fine. Will you be alright?"

Tom glimpsed at his father's stance. Even after all of the trauma Jim had been through, he still looked like a man of great strength. Unfortunately, appearances can lie, and physically, his father was certainly not the man he used to be. Maybe it was Jim's confidence or character that put Tom at ease. Tom did his best to sound composed. He was pinching the gash that pierced the center of his hand. The splint on his other hand hindered his efforts.

Nodding his head, Tom replied, "I'll be okay, Dad."

Good, Jim thought. *Tom believes they are going to set us free. I wish I felt the same.*

Jim led Mike Sloan and John Henry along the north side of the warehouse at a slow pace. Once more, he studied his surroundings in silence.

Although Jimmy might let us go, he thought, *I still can't trust him. If I were dealing with Constantino, it would be different, but Jimmy hates me too much to let me live.*

Jim stumbled on a stubby plant sprouting from the broken concrete, but managed not to fall. As he maneuvered past other obstacles jutting from the quagmire of concrete, all he could think about was the plan he'd conceived in haste.

This is just Jimmy's ruse to get the book back, Jim decided. *He's still planning to do away with us.*

The men following Jim couldn't see his face. His features had grown intense. He felt like a caged animal awaiting slaughter.

I've lost one child; I won't chance losing another. There is no other choice; I've got to go through with this.

His heart began to pound. He hoped it would be strong enough to sustain him through the next fifteen minutes, or so. But earlier, he had been winded by an insignificant jog from his car to the building.

Jim asked himself, *What if something goes wrong? Can I endure a prolonged struggle?*

He had serious doubts. Nervously, he picked up his pace. As they neared the west end of the building, he looked to his right. Through the tall chain link fence, Jim noticed a few residential homes across the street. Two young boys were chasing after a dog.

They turned the corner at the building's west end. There was a grinding sound of gravel and broken glass under their shoes. Jim looked up at office windows; many were shattered with rocks thrown by neighboring juveniles. Most were boarded up.

What a terrible playground to grow up with, he thought, sadly.

"It's just a few feet more," Jim offered, trying to sound calm.

They reached the spot. Jim took a position between Mike Sloan and John Henry, and pointed to the recess where he planted the phone book.

Shrugging his shoulders, Jim said, "It's in there."

Assured that John Henry had his back, Sloan removed his hand from his pocket and bent down to peer into the deep cavity. John

Henry must not have felt any reason to fear Jim because he had stooped over to watch Sloan retrieve the address book he had only heard about. That was all the distraction Jim needed to slip his hand into the small of his back and withdraw the retractable billy club he'd come to depend on since his skirmish at City Hall. It fit perfectly with his belt tightly cinched.

Hearing an odd metallic "thwack", Sloan glanced behind him at Jim, but he never saw the billy club. The next sound was that of breaking bone. Jim crushed Sloan's skull with a blow that was driven by fear and pure adrenaline. He spun quickly to see where the monster was.

John Henry knew that Sloan was dead. He narrowed his eyes and showed his teeth. "That skinny little stick won't hurt me so bad," John Henry said in a voice that wasn't all too confident. He had to know that it wielded a lot more power in the hands of a desperate man. Jim took a few steps toward a flattened cardboard box and kicked it away. Adeptly, he scooped up a satin nickel plated pistol. "Maybe not," he said, coarsely, "but this will hurt you plenty."

"Pick your feet up, John Henry; you make too much noise when you walk." It was the third time Jim had warned John Henry to move quietly. Jim was attempting to reverse navigate his way through the building to the room where Tom was being held.

Its probably futile to warn him, Jim thought. *This guy is no ballerina dancer, that's for sure.*

They came in on the third floor, which was on higher ground than the building's east end. It was dark, so Jim had John Henry rip the plywood from a boarded up window near the main entrance. IIis massive hands peeled the sheets away like tissue paper.

Thank God he's slow, Jim thought. *If this guy had any reflexes at all, I'd be dead by now.*

Jim concentrated on hugging the north side of the building as they headed east. They needed the windows for light in order to maneuver around the trash and discarded furniture left behind. Jim never had to ask John Henry to pull any more plywood off the windows. He did it like it was his job. If everything worked out, they could take Jimmy Bonaiuto by surprise.

Bonaiuto and Manetti stared across the expansive garage to the loading docks. Even though the windows were filthy, they could see every inch from their glass enclosed vantage point. Manetti rested his arm on the dusty file cabinet while pointing the gun in the direction they expected Jim to appear. Tom was seated again at the table, but his hands had been tied behind his back.

"As soon as we get the book, Mario, I want you to kill them both," Bonaiuto said. He turned to Tom and smiled wickedly.

You lying bastard, Tom thought. *He's still going to kill us. What about the rest of our family? Is he going after them, too? God, there's nothing we can do to stop him.*

"What about the copies O'Brien claims he gave his attorney?" Manetti asked. "Aren't you afraid he'll turn them over to the FBI?"

Bonaiuto stepped forward peering into Manetti's eyes, "O'Brien is bluffing. It's a damn good bluff, too, but he would never turn himself in. He's too smart for that."

"MY DAD DOESN'T LIE!" Tom injected furiously. "If he says his attorney has a copy of the documents, you can bet he does."

Bonaiuto gave Tom a repugnant look and walked over to his chair. He grabbed a handful of Tom's hair and jerked it back. "You know, it's gonna' be a pleasure to kill you, kid—in fact, I may just pull the trigger myself." A small grin spread across Bonaiuto's face, and it continued to widen until Tom felt repulsed and surprised by his desire to put a gun to Bonaiuto's head and reciprocate.

"I may just do you both," Bonaiuto finished.

Tom's vision of his dad rescuing him had all but disappeared. The situation was bleak. By the time his dad got close enough to hear a scream of warning, it would be too late.

Manetti's gun was still trained on the east entrance. Unsatisfied by Bonaiuto's answer to his prior question, Manetti was starting to fidget.

"If you're wrong about this, Jimmy, it'll bring the whole family down—all of us." Bonaiuto began pacing the floor, "Well then," he retorted with a scowl, "I guess it's a good thing I'm right."

His tone of voice said the matter wasn't up for discussion. He stopped mid-pace and kicked a small box of trash across the room.

"They should have been back by now, Mario. Go see what's taking them so long."

Manetti took a moment to remove the silencer from his gun. He placed it in his left pocket, the gun in his right. He went to the rickety staircase.

As he took his first step, he turned and said reassuringly, "I'll only be a minute, Jimmy."

Bonaiuto leaned against the file cabinet to keep watch, but quickly backed away, as he realized it left a large print of dirt on his polo shirt. He noticed Tom eyeing the dirt.

"Are we amused—you little shit? I'm glad you've found something humorous in your last minutes of life. Let's see if you are still amused when I blow your brains out."

Tom shifted his gaze back to a safe spot on the floor. He didn't want to incite any further anger from a man who was obviously losing control.

"If there are any brains blown out, Jimmy, they'll be yours, not his."

Tom jerked his head up in sheer disbelief, "DAD, YOU'RE OKAY!"

Jim waved his gun, motioning John Henry to move from the rear doorway toward Bonaiuto. He threw the black book on the file cabinet with the other documents, and edged toward Tom, keeping his distance from the two men; a difficult task in the cramped, shallow room.

"I'm fine, Tom, let me untie you and we'll call the police."

Jim tugged and fidgeted with the cords used to tie Tom's hands.

Tom looked more afraid than ever, "But, Dad, if you call the police, they'll find out who you are—they'll arrest you."

"It's a small price to pay to ensure our family's safety, Tom. This man is a lunatic; he'll stop at nothing until he's killed us all."

The cords that bound Tom's wrists were tied too snugly to loosen with one hand. Jim looked up, "I'll need your knife, Jimmy."

Bonaiuto seemed irritated at having to withdraw his attention from John Henry. He had been giving him an expression that indicated just how badly he'd screwed things up.

Reluctantly, he looked at Jim, "FUCK YOU, O'BRIEN! You want the knife? Come and get it"

Jim had no intention of taking the bait. "I'm not playing that game, Jimmy, I can do without it."

While Jim struggled to free Tom, Bonaiuto asked John Henry what happened to Mike Sloan.

"He's dead, boss. O'Brien crushed his skull with a metal stick. He planted a gun nearby and took me by surprise."

Tom gave his father a look of admiration.

Bonaiuto fumed, "Jesus, you're so slow, a snail could take you by surprise."

"I'm sorry boss."

"Yeah, well you can write me an apology from prison, shit head."

Bonaiuto looked over his shoulder. Mario had just entered the garage. He was reattaching the silencer to his gun.

Jim gave up trying to untie Tom with one hand. He pulled the table a few feet away from them, and set his gun on top. "Don't try anything, Jimmy. I can get to this gun a lot faster than you can."

Bonaiuto didn't answer; he just stood there seething at him. The cording around Tom's wrists was made of a vinyl material that made it easy to tighten, and difficult to untie. Jim wasn't sure he could even remove the knots using both hands. Bonaiuto elbowed John Henry and nodded toward the table. John Henry understood, and wasted no time carrying out his implied instructions. He wasn't fast, but his stride was incredibly long. With a fluid motion, John Henry took a giant step and kicked the table hard into Jim and Tom, toppling them both. The gun slid off the table. Bonaiuto moved for it quickly, and while Jim moved faster, he was also farther away. Bonaiuto had it in his grasp a split second before Jim grabbed his arm. The two men struggled on the floor.

The massive dose of adrenaline that infused Jim's body, more than compensated for his weakened condition. He bent Bonaiuto's fingers back hardly noticing his scream of pain. Just as he was about to rip the gun from his hand, he felt a sensation of weightlessness, quickly followed by a heavy dose of gravity. John Henry had picked him up and thrown him to the other end of the room. He crashed against a desk. The resulting pain that rifled up his back told him he was done. He could hardly move. He looked for Tom and watched him roll over to meet his gaze.

I failed, Jim thought. *I had them in my grasp and I failed.*

Jim didn't take his eyes off of Tom as Bonaiuto moved in on him. He wondered which of them he would kill first. The answer came quickly, as his own gun was thrust firmly against his cheek.

Kneeling in front of Jim was a man whose facial expression defined the word "demented." Bonaiuto's eyes were wild with a mixture of anger and delight.

"I'm going to enjoy this, O'Brien. Your boy is next, and who knows? Maybe there will be a fire in the O'Brien home tonight."

No! Jim thought, *I can't let him—I've got to try—*

Blood spattered Jim's shirt. The eyes that had been mauling him lost their intensity and Bonaiuto's body fell on top of Jim. Jim pushed off, guiding the limp mass to his right side. He didn't even hear the thud. The world had gone quiet. He was now gaping at Manetti who stood on the stairs, his hand still outstretched from the deadly shot. The mafia assassin climbed the last stair slowly. As he entered the room, John Henry inquired in a low lumbering voice, "Mario, why?"

"Listen carefully, John Henry. Mr. O'Brien fulfilled his end of the bargain. Tony would have let him go. He would never have gambled with his family's fate like Jimmy did. We have to assume that Mr. O'Brien's attorney has a copy of all the documents. That means that both of us have insurance. Neither of us stands to gain a thing by turning them over to the FBI. As always, Jimmy let his temper get the best of him, just like he did when he killed David a half hour ago. The kid may have gone about things the wrong way, but he was only trying to help. You know as well as I do, that Angelo would have killed Jimmy as soon as he heard the news about David. I only saved him the trouble, that's all."

Jim looked dumfounded.

"Who is Angelo?" Jim asked, confused. Mario grabbed Jim's arm and helped him to his feet.

"Angelo is my brother, David's father. He should have succeeded Tony, but over the last five years, Cousin Jimmy got closer to him. Tony never saw his recklessness, or his lack of loyalty to the family, but we did. Jimmy only cared about himself."

Jim's thoughts were clearing. He now recalled Angelo Manetti's role in the family. He was the one who had established international contacts in the drug trade. Jim assumed that he couldn't have been more than a notch below the family's leader in rank. Jim made his way to where Tom was lying on the floor. A sharp pain shot up his back as he lifted Tom to his feet. Once more, Jim began to tug and twist at the tight cording around his wrists. Concentrating, he spoke as he worked.

"You did the right thing, Mario. I never wanted to bring down your family. I only wanted to ensure the safety of mine. I had a lot of respect for Tony. Whatever else he may have done in his life, he always took care of his family."

Jim finally managed to thread the vinyl cord through the last loop responsible for restricting Tom's hands. Tom brought them to his front side and studied the wound in his right hand. Miraculously, the blood was clotting.

"Can you still open and close it, Tom?" He gently opened and closed it several times. "I'm sorry you had to be a part of this, son." Jim hugged him fiercely. "We'll go to the hospital from here."

"I have to ask you, Mr. O'Brien, is this everything you promised to return to us?" Manetti was pointing to the torn accordion folder and Tony Constantino's black book.

"Yes," Jim said, "that folder contains all of the family's assets, including all of the family's bank accounts. You should be able to get back to business in high style."

Jim had kept the Swiss numbered account, because it never belonged to the family. It was Tony's personal account and unknown to them.

Jim looked into Manetti's emotionless brown eyes. "I have a request of you, Mario. I don't think you realize how close the FBI came to catching us—all of us. I sent you an e-mail requesting that you destroy all the correspondence with regard to the Moral Mafia.

An FBI agent made a trip to Chicago, and somehow managed to confiscate a handful of correspondence that incriminated all of us. Will you search for any remaining documents and destroy them?"

Manetti looked distraught. "Of course, I had no idea the FBI was on our trail." Then he paused, "What happened to those documents?"

Jim eyed Tom, "The FBI agent came to Omaha to arrest me. I was attacked by two men, and he was killed while trying to save my life. Thank God my son retrieved the documents. If he hadn't, we would all be in prison today."

"I destroyed them, Dad. I flushed them down the toilet."

"I'll relay that to Angelo, Mr. O'Brien. I'm sure he'll be grateful."

"Thanks, Mario. And by all means, please give him my condolences. David was only trying to help; he certainly didn't deserve to die."

Manetti nodded, "You are well aware of my profession, Mr. O'Brien, and yet death is hard to accept when it is a family member."

Manetti's eyes flashed a momentary look of sorrow.

Jim placed a firm grip on Tom's shoulder. "We'd like to go now, Mario, is that alright?"

Mario held his hand out, and Jim shook it. "It was a pleasure working for you, Mr. O'Brien. What will happen to the Moral Mafia?"

"I don't know. We still have a lot more work to do before we can call it quits, but I want to find a peaceful solution. The country is tearing itself apart, and I'm responsible for it."

"I wish you luck, Mr. O'Brien." Mario gave a nod of respect to the man whose orders he had followed for several months.

"Me, too," John Henry added. He held his hand out and Jim was in awe, as it completely engulfed his own.

Jim and Tom walked hurriedly up the hill to the silver Honda Accord. Each of them was hurting physically and emotionally. As they passed the west end of the building, Jim looked back at the window that he and John Henry had entered. Mike Sloan's body still lay just outside that window. He was covered with plywood. Jim would have to tell Tom how he killed him, and then led John Henry through the length of the building to rescue him. At least this death could be attributed to self preservation. The many others in recent months could not.

"Let's get you to the doctor, Tom, and then I think we need to go to the office and talk for a while."

60

JIM AND TOM NEVER RETURNED TO THE OFFICE. BY THE time they got home from the emergency room, it was a quarter to five. They did find time to talk while driving to and from the hospital. Jim explained to Tom how the Moral Mafia got its start. Tom expressed his desire to help Jim repair the fractured country. Neither knew how they would do it, but they both agreed that they had to try to unify the people again. Jim suggested they spend an hour each night in his study. There, they would figure out their next steps.

The aroma of Peg's Hungarian Goulash and garlic bread filled the house. Jim was on Tom's heels when he strolled into the kitchen. Tom started to ask how long it would be before dinner. He stopped mid-sentence when he saw Kayla Stowe sitting at the kitchen table with Peg and the children. For a split second, Tom thought it was Rachel, but that was impossible. In fact, he had mistaken Kayla for Rachel several times in the past. The resemblance that was once a novelty was now a painful reminder of his loss. Kayla was about an inch shorter and ten pounds lighter than her sister, but she had Rachel's eyes, dimples, and deep skin tone. Her hair possessed the same tossed appearance, but it was a few inches longer. Danny and Molly were kneeling on the picnic style benches, their hands loaded with photographs. It looked as though they were passing them around the table.

"Hi, boys," Peg said warmly. "Look who stopped by to visit."

"Well hi," Tom said. "I sure didn't expect to see you here. How are you?"

"I'm doing fine," she said with a slight look of concern. "H-how are you?"

Tom looked away and forced a casual tone in his response, "I'm doing my best to keep busy. It helps. I'm sure you know what I mean."

"I do," Kayla replied. "My parents and I are trying to keep busy, too."

Kayla changed the subject, "Your bruises, Tom, they're almost gone."

"Yeah, I'm healing pretty well—still pretty sore in the ribs though, and typing is a chore." He held up his finger splint.

Peg noticed the bandage on Tom's right hand, "What happened to your other hand, Tom?"

Jim jumped in, "You're son, the klutz, tripped in the break room and fell on his coffee cup—unfortunately, it was a glass cup. We just got back from the emergency room." Jim grinned, "I think this is Tom's way of getting a few days off work," Tom's hand was wrapped in gauze and the wound itself was indiscernible.

Peg wrinkled her facial features as if she was thinking, *Ouch, that must have hurt.* "Are you okay, Tom?" she asked.

"I'm fine, Mom; just a few stitches, that's all."

"And what's with the jacket, Jim? It's a little warm for one, don't you think?"

Jim stuttered slightly, "Oh yeah, I—I almost forgot. I left this jacket at the office, and didn't want to forget to bring it home, so I just put it on."

Actually, he'd grabbed a wind breaker from his trunk to conceal his blood spattered shirt.

Peg looked at Kayla and rolled her eyes, "Men, they don't always make sense, do they?" Kayla just laughed.

Reminded that he had a bloody shirt to dispose of, Jim excused himself. "I'm going to go clean up for dinner. Kayla, why don't you join us for supper?"

Kayla peered up at Tom. "No, I couldn't."

"Sure you can," Tom said politely. "We'd love to have you. I'll get the phone so you can call your parents."

Jim headed for the bedroom and Tom retrieved the phone from the kitchen counter.

"Kayla brought over some pictures of you and Rachel," Peg said. "Wasn't that thoughtful?"

Great, he thought, *photos of the girl I can't get out of my mind.*

"Yes, thank you, Kayla. I appreciate it."

"Goodness, look at the time," Peg said, "I've got to get dinner on the table. Why don't you two look at the pictures in the living room while I get everything ready."

The dinner table was a hotbed of noise and laughter, as was typical in the O'Brien home. The kids kept Kayla engaged in small talk, and there were multiple conversations occurring at once. A few months ago, Erin's husband, Trent, had admitted how intimidated he'd felt the first few times he had dinner with the O'Brien family. Unaccustomed to the roar of children's laughter, and conversations ranging from Barbie Dolls and Spiderman, to cute boys and volleyball, Tom could understand how daunting the experience might be to a newcomer. He studied Kayla. She laughed and spoke as though she were completely at home in the chaotic setting.

God, she looks like Rachel, Tom mused sadly. *Even her mannerisms are similar.* He felt uncomfortably foolish and unfaithful when he realized his gaze had drifted to Kayla's breasts.

Sorry Rachel, that was wrong, he thought.

Kayla's eyes caught the light in a familiar way. They sparkled in a manner that made Tom catch his breath.

He was nearly gawking at her when she pointed to the red-orange sauce over flat noodles and said, "The dinner is fantastic, Mrs. O'Brien. What do you call it?"

Peg set her fork down. "We call it Hungarian Goulash. I believe it is an authentic Hungarian dish, but I'm not really certain. The recipe has been in my family for generations. My mother used to make it with hamburger, but along the way we substituted cubed steak."

"It's very spicy," Kayla said, "but not too hot."

"That's the Cayenne Pepper," Peg added. "Jim usually sneaks in a dash more pepper than the recipe calls for. He says he knows he's enjoying it when his cheeks begin to perspire."

Jim interjected, "Peg browns the cubed steak, and then it simmers in a red broth all day long. You thicken it by mixing in some flour just before serving it."

"I have never tasted anything like it," Kayla confessed. "I don't think I could accurately describe the flavor."

"Do you think your folks would like it?" Peg asked

"Oh yes! My dad would love it."

"Good, I'll send the recipe home with you."

"Who cuts your hair?" Eileen asked.

Well, that's it. Tom thought. *The conversation on hairstyles should take us through the rest of dinner.*

Indeed it did. Tom was kind of glad, as it took the pressure off of Kayla's awkward visit. The less he had to participate, the better. Megan, Eileen, and Morgan went on about hairstyles and then proceeded to makeup. Shauna even injected a few comments, although she was a few years shy of obtaining permission to wear it.

Tom and Kayla were seated at the center of the long bench. Danny occupied the position just left of Jim's chair at the head of the table. Above the roar, he was demonstrating his latest magic trick.

"—and voila, the ball is gone! What do you think, Dad?"

Jim was about to answer, when he heard Megan ask Kayla an interesting question. "Are you dating anyone at Westside?" she asked.

"No, I haven't found anyone I want to go out with."

"You're kidding? Westside has some of the cutest boys in town. You're a senior, right?"

"Yes, but I'm graduating early, next December. I have way more credits than I need. I'll probably start college in January."

"Me, too," said Tom.

"What do you mean?" asked Peg. "Your classes begin on August 28th, don't they?"

"I postponed my classes until next semester," Tom said in a soft, firm voice.

"I want to learn all I can about Dad's business—hit it hard for a few months, and then I'll have some time to decide how to tailor my classes to best meet the company's needs. Besides, with everything that has happened, I think I could use a short break from school. I'll start next semester, I promise."

Jim nodded his approval at Peg, and Peg looked at her son with understanding eyes. "I think you made a good decision, Tom. A good, mature decision, I might add." Tom's cheeks reddened.

"So I guess we'll be going together then," Kayla said smiling. "It will be good to know someone at college."

"What do you say we celebrate with dessert," Peg said, as she started clearing plates from the table. Morgan and Eileen began to help, and Peg removed a large plastic container of ice cream from the freezer. Megan reached up high to slide a large pan of brownies from the top of the refrigerator. As the girls made brownie sundaes, Jim's thoughts were wandering in every direction. It wasn't difficult to see that Kayla was smitten with Tom. Although Tom didn't seem to return her affection, maybe things would change over time. The clanging of dishes and commotion of children soothed Jim's nerves. He felt his family was truly safe for the first time in months. But still he faced the matter of resolving the nation's unrest over the issues of the day—including abortion.

Next Tuesday is the Fourth of July, he thought. *What kind of celebration can we expect when our hearts are filled with hate and despair?*

385

After dessert, Peg supervised the kids until they got a good start on the dishes. Tom and Kayla could hear the clashing of pots and dishes all the way to the den.

"This is my father's study," Tom said. "Funny, I rarely came into this room when I was a kid."

"It's gorgeous," Kayla replied. "I can picture you working in a room like this."

"It fits my dad like a glove. He spends hours in here, honing his craft, working on cases that would baffle most men."

"You are very proud of your dad, aren't you?"

"I am," Tom replied with certainty.

They sat on a love seat by the window. "Rachel said your relationship with your father wasn't too good for a while."

"That's true, but that was my fault," Tom said regretfully. "He was the best father anyone could hope for, and that goes double for Mom. But it took me a long time to recognize it. He put up with a lot of crap from me, and although I could sometimes fool Mom, I never fooled Dad. I don't know why or how he was ever able to forgive me."

Kayla seemed puzzled, "Certainly you couldn't have done anything so bad your parent's couldn't forgive you?"

"Don't count on it," Tom said. "At fifteen I started using drugs, and drug users are not nice people. I was cold and bitter and never thought about anyone but myself. I was selfish and self-centered, and only lived for the next chance to get high. I had to steal to support my habit. At Erin's wedding reception, Dad had a run-in with the kids I was buying my drugs from. They killed my sister, Katie—shot her down in the reception hall parking lot. That's when Dad put me in a treatment program. Even ninety days later, I hated him for it. I would have gone back to drugs again, and in fact, Matt almost talked me into getting high for old times sake the night I met Rachel. But we talked all night, and by morning, I'd lost any desire to get high. Rachel saved my life."

Kayla could sense the torture he was feeling. "I never knew that, Tom. I'm so sorry about your sister, but I'm glad you never went back to using. Drugs have a way of destroying so many lives."

Tom nodded, "As for my father, I can hardly remember him during the years I was using. When you are high, everything is hazy and distorted. Thank God I have so many childhood memories to sustain me. They are good memories, and now I'm getting to know him all over again. It's made me realize just how much I missed in those three short years."

Kayla's eyes were tearing. Tom could sense her empathy. It was as strong as Rachel's. He quickly changed the direction of their conversation.

"Well, anyway," he said with finality, "my family means a lot to me, and I plan to watch out for them as long as I live." Pausing a moment, he admitted one more thing. "If I could do everything all over again, I would. But the only thing I want to do now is live up to my dad's expectations."

"And you will," Kayla said. "I'm sure of it."

"I'm going to try—but he sets a pretty high bar."

The two teenagers talked for an hour more. A few times Tom had to remind himself he wasn't speaking to Rachel. Kayla's eyes were alluring too, but he realized any feelings he might have for her really belonged to Rachel. He decided it would be best to say good night.

"Kayla," he said, "I can't thank you enough for the photographs. I'm glad you came by. Would you tell your mom and dad I said hello?"

Kayla looked a little disappointed. She knew Tom was trying to end their conversation.

"Sure, Tom, they will be glad to hear you are doing well. They were very upset to see you hurt so badly. They like you a lot."

"They're good people, Kayla. You're lucky to have such great parents."

Tom looked at his watch. "I'm sorry we can't visit longer, but I've had a pounding headache all day. I'd like to get some rest tonight."

"I understand," Kayla said sincerely. "Maybe we can do this again sometime."

She looked at Tom as though she could see right inside him. Her eyes said that she liked him. Despite all of the wrongs he had done in his life, she liked him.

"I'd like that," Tom said, in awe of her trusting nature, but as pleasant as she was, he had no intention of seeing her again.

It just wouldn't be right, he thought.

61

LATER THAT EVENING, JIM WITHDREW A FOLDING keyboard from his brief case. In seconds it was connected to his Smart Phone. Inserting the postage stamp size memory card, he transferred and opened the journal he had begun writing almost eight months ago. Scrolling to the bottom of the document, he entered the date and a new entry.

– *July 1, 2010*

Today, I nearly lost my son, Tom. I could never have sustained the loss of another child. Katie's death drove me to the brink of insanity and Tom's would surely have nudged me over the edge. David Manetti wasn't as lucky. Jimmy Bonaiuto killed him for not coming to him with the facts that I had the family's documents and bank accounts. I only hope that the memory of seeing another person killed will not create an endless stream of nightmares for Tom. He has endured far too much pain for a young man of eighteen.

Much of our nightmare has ended. I managed to rescue Tom from the clutches of Bonaiuto and his men, but not before killing one of them. Mario Manetti saved my life only a split second before Bonaiuto intended to pull the trigger of a gun he held to my head. Manetti believed that I had given a complete set of their documents to my attorney with instructions to hand them over to the FBI upon my death. Mario killed Jimmy to protect the family, something it seems we have all been trying to do. Jimmy gave no credence to my story and he was correct, but now that I understand the protection it affords us, I will take copies to my attorney and instruct him to turn them over if and when it becomes necessary.

Tomorrow, I will resurrect the Moral Mafia for one last time. Tom and I discussed it this evening and neither of us have the desire to promote violence in any way. We still possess Constantino's Swiss numbered account, and we intend to use the money to find a peaceful end to this unholy state of affairs. However, the nation needs to hear from me one last time. I have prepared my final correspondence and will release it to the Associated Press tomorrow. As always, they will recognize my characteristic signature and print the letter without question. I want the demonstrations, riots, and killings to stop. I did not intend for the country to be so severely split by the abortion issue. I certainly never intended to see the day when Americans would kill each other. I only hope the memory of the Moral Mafia remains intimidating enough in the minds of the American people to stop it. If not, there will undoubtedly be a second civil war, and I will be forced to conduct a bigger demonstration of power than I did on Black Thursday. I pray that this show of force never becomes necessary.

I have logged many entries in this journal, semi-confident that they would never be read by another soul. If indeed these passages are discovered and read, I hope I will be remembered not as the monster that contrived and controlled the Moral Mafia, but as a man who loved his country and the people who made it great. I realize now, it was the murder of my daughter and the addictions of my son that drove me to believe the world was hopelessly infested with corruption. It was these things that compelled me to wage a war that no sane person would believe they could win. Yet I believe there was a degree of justice achieved in my attempt to correct a problem that no one else was willing to confront. Perhaps there is still a chance that Americans can forgive one another for having differing opinions. Maybe it is still possible that we can be a nation of tolerance. I pray this to be true.

Tony Constantino loved his God, his family, and his friends. He once told me that God would forgive him for his sins. I hope He will forgive me as well. The war I waged against our country was not a war of vengeance, or revenge, but rather a war to preserve morality and justice. I believe that God knows this and will consider my intentions on the day of my judgment. Meanwhile, I will spend my remaining days on earth in the service of my fellow man.

– Jim O'Brien

Jim went through the mundane steps of saving the appended journal. Contemplating what he had just written, he imagined himself standing at heaven's gates. *Will God forgive me for what I have done?* he pondered. *I have always been taught that God is compassionate and if I am truly sorry for my sins, they will be forgiven.* Jim felt a burning desire to go to confession as soon as possible. But he would have to find a church that still used confessionals. The sins he would declare were far too great to chance a face-to-face confession. Behind a curtain he could bear his soul and still remain anonymous.

No more of this tonight, he thought, pulling himself from the dank mire of his thoughts. *It's eight o'clock, I think I'll spend some time with Peg and the kids.*

62

AS JIM ENTERED THE OFFICE EARLY MONDAY MORNING, he was full of mixed emotions. For the first time in weeks, he felt safe. He slept soundly, knowing that his family was no longer in danger. On the other hand, he had once more killed another human being. A hit man, but a human being, nonetheless. He took no satisfaction in what he had done, but he found solace in the fact that Tom was alive and most of this nightmare was over.

Sunday night, Jim had written two brief letters. The first was a letter of condolences to Angelo Manetti for the loss of his son, David, and Mike Sloan, a valued member of the family. He restated his wish that no harm befall his family, and that as long as he was safe, the copied documents would never fall into the wrong hands. He conveyed the same message in a second letter, addressed to Constantino's attorney, Michael Lanza. In addition, he pointed out that the balance of the three bank accounts had been untouched and totaled more than fifty-six million.

Jim waited for Tom to get some coffee and meet him in his office.

The poor kid, he thought. *He's hardly been able to drive that new car of his. It will be a few days before his hands have healed enough to drive to work.*

In addition, he wouldn't be able to type either, but that didn't matter. Jim promised to teach him some administrative duties to keep him busy. When Tom arrived, Jim removed the morning paper from his briefcase and handed it to him. The front page contained a familiar large, bold type. Tom sipped his coffee as he read the message:

Read this carefully America and heed my warning! The next time you hear from me, there will be a rampage of death and destruction like you have never seen. A few months ago, I bid you farewell. The Congress and Senate passed almost all of the legislation I demanded. Abortion was the sole remaining issue. Acknowledging the importance and complexity of the topic, I left it up to the American people to finalize legislation to outlaw abortion once and for all, but you have failed me—miserably.

The United States is more deeply divided than ever over an issue so weak, it doesn't deserve to be called an "issue." Abortion is wrong!—period!—end of discussion! I will not debate the topic, nor will you! I have watched my fellow Americans kill each other. There has been slaying upon slaying of innocent people in demonstrations and riots that have become almost a daily occurrence. The liberals are not looking at this as a moral issue, but have instead taken the opportunity to make this a "political last stand." The conservatives have been cowards, taunting their opponents instead of leading the way with hard hitting legislation. Well, I've had enough!

Other nations scoff at us as we travel down a dangerous road that will undoubtedly lead to a civil war. I will not allow it. As of today, the Moral Mafia is outlawing abortion. We declare it illegal. Any doctor performing an abortion will be tracked down like an animal and killed. Politicians proposing legislation supporting abortion, will be killed. Any judge handing down an opposing decision or ruling will be killed. Demonstrations pro or con will not be allowed. All violence will cease. Abortion is a past tense word. The practice itself no longer exists. Heed my words, America. Heed my words!

– The Moral Mafia

Tom was somber as he peered across the table at his father, "I'll say one thing for the leader of the Moral Mafia, Dad—he got his point across."

"Menacing and to the point is the best way to do it, son."

Tom fell silent. Expecting a response of some kind, Jim was disappointed.

He prompted him for his opinion, "Don't look so glum, Tom. It's just an idle threat—a bluff. What do you think? Will this threat be more successful than the others?"

"Oh, I'm certain that ninety-nine percent of Americans will heed the warning, Dad. It's the one percent I'm worried about. You know as well as I do that no one wants to live under the tyranny of a dictator. What the leader of the Moral Mafia just said makes him a dictator."

"You're wrong, Tom. Americans are free to live the life they choose. They can work and live where they want, they just can't kill unborn babies. It's already against the law to kill adults, so why isn't this wrong?"

"I know what you are trying to do here, Dad, but there's a law against killing adults. It sounds like the Moral Mafia wants to take away the people's right to choose."

Jim looked surprised and a little upset. He tried to remain understanding and respectful as he said, "Substitute the word 'kill' for the word 'choose' and repeat that sentence. Since when do people have the right to kill?"

Tom felt a little hypocritical. "We are the ones who have been doing the killing."

"You mean that I am the one who has been doing the killing, don't you?"

"I didn't mean it that way, Dad. I'm just saying that the tone of the message may conjure up some die-hard abortionists, unwilling to follow the orders of the Moral Mafia. What will we do if Americans decide not to cooperate? Quite frankly, I'd be surprised if they do."

"Listen, Tom, I agree the Moral Mafia's methods have been heavy-handed, but it's the only way to stop the rioting and senseless violence."

"Then why didn't we! Why didn't we simply threaten reprisals to anyone involved in demonstrations or violence? Why did we dictate the law? I think you went too far."

Jim pondered what Tom just said. When he first began writing his address to America, he had a single goal in mind. He wanted to stop the rioting and violence. That's all.

Good Lord, Tom is right! Maybe I shouldn't have gone so far. I injected my opinion. But abortion is the root of the problem, he thought. *Stopping abortion will automatically end the violence. But can anyone really stop it? Is there enough reason or compassion in the world to stop it?* He didn't know, but now he was regretting what he had written.

Jim tried to reassess the likelihood of success. "If left unchecked, this insane, inhuman act called abortion will drive our country to the brink of a much larger war. Have you considered that?"

Tom grimaced, "Of course I have, Dad, but you are asking Americans to embrace intimidation, and the dictatorship of someone they feel is a killer. I don't think they'll do that."

Tom's words stung. "Maybe I did go too far," Jim said, "but maybe not. I made extremely powerful threats, gambling that Americans don't want to see another demonstration of the Moral Mafia's power. And yes, it is intimidation in its purest form, but it is better to intimidate than to kill."

"I hope we don't have to back up our words with actions," Tom said. "I hope it ends, here and now."

Jim looked at him with desperate eyes. "No one wants to see it end more than me, son. Anyway, I don't think you'll find many Americans who want a war on their neighborhood streets. They'll come around."

When Miranda appeared with her copy of the morning paper, Tom knew they would be discussing it for a while. He went to the break room to warm up his coffee. He really didn't like coffee that much, but it was a hot soothing drink and coffee breaks became a daily ritual he depended on to keep tabs on what others were doing in the company. As usual, the new interns were standing around the television listening to FOX News.

Don't these people ever work, Tom thought.

Evan, one of the interns, was in the middle of a commentary.

"Aww, someone's gonna' try it, but when they get their head blown off by the Moral Mafia, everyone else will stop doing em' altogether."

"Stop doing what?" Tom asked.

"Abortions, dude, the Moral Mafia said they would blow the head off of anyone caught doin' one."

"You're wrong on two counts," Tom said. "The Moral Mafia never mentioned blowing heads off, and my name is not dude. Now, let's all get back to work, okay?"

Tom watched the threesome disperse. When he turned to exit through the rear break room door, he saw Scott Troia leaning against it with a huge smile.

"THAT—Thomas, was one of the most beautiful things I have ever seen—ever, ever, ever!"

Tom couldn't help but to return the smile. "Don't these kids ever work?"

"Most of our employees work damn hard, Tom, but I'm afraid those three may have been a mistake. What do you think?"

"I guess so, Scott. We'll probably have to address that sooner or later."

"Well, it was my idea to start this silly internship program; I guess it's my job to let them go."

"The program isn't silly, Scott. In fact, I like it. Look how well our genius, Will Thibodeau, has worked out. We just need to find more candidates like him—screen the younger candidates more thoroughly, that's all."

"Well, maybe recruiting the younger crowd should be your enchilada. You'll probably meet a lot of good candidates in college. What do you think?"

No wonder Dad loves this guy, Tom thought.

"It sounds good to me, Scott. Of course, Dad may have something to say about it."

"Jim is desperate for new talent. If you can find good people, he'll support you."

63

CLANCY'S PUB SAW SCOTT TROIA AT LEAST ONCE A week and sometimes more. It was only Monday, but Scott was more than happy to grace the establishment with his presence. He grabbed Jim and Miranda a full hour earlier than usual, and since he wasn't driving his car, Tom made the group a foursome.

"We're gonna' be talking business anyway, right? Might as well be at Clancy's," Scott said. But that wasn't the reason Scott wanted to leave early. This was the first time Jim had been at Clancy's since the stabbing. Scott and Miranda had continued the weekly tradition without him, but it wasn't the same. Tonight, they were all together, and each of them felt a genuine giddiness to be reunited. Scott was anxious to tell Jim what he overheard Tom say to the interns.

Sandy never questioned Tom's age. She just brought a pitcher and four glasses. Scott raised his eyebrows and shrugged, and Jim got the idea this wasn't Tom's first beer at Clancy's. As she filled the last of four frosted mugs, Scott was already constructing a proper toast.

Raising his glass he said, "Welcome back, Jim. Computer Forensic Consultants is finally 'whole' again."

Miranda chimed in, "To the 'whole' company."

Tom raised his glass to his father, adding, "To our ace in the 'whole.'"

Jim returned Tom's grin, toasting, "May you never drink so much that you fall in a 'whole.'"

At that, Scott guffawed and added, 'I think you should call Peg and let her know where you two are 'wholed' up." Laughing heartily, the four clanged beer mugs and drank.

It didn't take Scott long to explain how he overheard Tom telling the interns to get back to work after listening to their juvenile comments regarding the Moral Mafia. Miranda was entertained by the story, while Jim shook his head in disgust.

"I think Tom should take over recruiting for the intern program," Scott suggested. "He'll run into a lot of talented kids in college." Jim fully agreed.

"I'm so proud of you, Tom," Scott beamed. "You're quite a lot like your old man."

"Yes, there is something very different about you, Tom," Miranda said. "I like it."

"Thanks," Tom said, blushing a little.

Scott nodded, "Something tells me you're going to be a big contributor to the company, Tom."

Tom noticed Miranda observing him intently. She had always been brisk with him in the past. But now her eyes had a softer look.

She sure is beautiful, he thought.

But reaching for his beer, he considered her age.

She is five or six years older than me. I would never stand a chance with her.

As business topics gradually faded to current events, Scott glanced at one of the pub's televisions and spotted a report on the Moral Mafia.

He said, "Hold on guys, I wanna' hear this."

Tom turned around to see a split TV screen. The news commentator occupied the left side, a graphic occupied the right. Above the words Moral Mafia, Tom saw an icon consisting of a sword, two daggers, and four hand guns arranged in the shape of a crucifix. The menacing image sent chills down his spine. *Jesus,* he thought, *look how they're depicting us.* He caught a little of the news bite:

—It has been six months since the world has heard from the organization, and their threats have never been more severe. However, one doctor refuses to cooperate with the Moral Mafia's edict. For more on the story, we go live to our reporter in Memphis, Tennessee.

The footage showed a man engulfed in a swarm of reporters and cameramen who crowded him all the way to a waiting taxi, which whisked him away. The next film clip covered a statement he had made earlier in the day.

"I will not cower to the Moral Mafia. A woman has a God given right to choose every aspect of her destiny, including whether or not she wants to bear children. Our country may not have the guts to stand up to these lunatics, but I do. In my clinic tomorrow and every day thereafter, it will be business as usual."

Jim saw the man's name; Doctor Dean Powers, appear on the screen. *The crazy son of a bitch,* he thought. *He's committing suicide.*

Troia turned around shaking his head, "I guess this guy didn't notice the eighty-five people who were killed on Black Thursday. If he performs a single abortion, he's as good as dead."

"Why would he do this?" Miranda said. "What makes him think the Moral Mafia won't get to him? He won't have the same protection our congressmen and senators had."

"Maybe he will," said Jim. "Maybe the FBI will be watching him like a hawk."

"That's a good point," Scott mused. "But if you can figure that out, so can the Moral Mafia. I think he's a goner."

Jim's evening was ruined, his mood soured, as he came to the realization that the battle was still in progress, the war was not won. He remembered Tom's comment earlier in the day.

"I'm certain that ninety-nine percent of Americans will heed the warning. It's the one percent I'm worried about."

Scott continued talking, "I know this sounds crazy, but I was almost relieved this morning when I read the message from the Moral Mafia. It gave me hope that we might actually stop killing each other for a while, and that maybe I wouldn't have to listen to those damn kids make bets on which right-to-choose or right-to-life leader they would assassinate to stop the fighting. Well, at least there haven't been any demonstrations today."

Jim perked up a little. *That's right!* he thought. *There were no demonstrations today, no riots, and no killings. If he were to demonstrate the Moral Mafia's sincere intentions, with regard to his threats, it might just end the violence as he had planned. I need to get home and think this through.*

64

FROM BEHIND HIS COMPUTER, JIM REVIEWED THE message he had just typed to Mario Manetti. He wasn't certain he would cooperate, or that Angelo Manetti would allow it, but if he didn't want the job, he would not rest until he found someone who did. He substantially increased the payment he had offered him in the past, hoping he would take the job, even though he no longer controlled the family.

JOB   096—HIT—DEAN   POWERS—COMPENSATION—$1,000,000—ADVANCED EXPENSES—$10,000—COMPLETION BONUS—$100,000.

Office Address:

Dr. Dean Powers

Unity Women's Clinic

401 S. Bellevue Blvd.

Memphis, TN 38104

This man has appeared on national news, and you will find his photograph in several newspapers. Be extremely careful with this job. Powers is probably under surveillance by the FBI, as they will expect us to make a move on him. It may be wise to draw him to a spot where you can detonate a remote explosive, or arrange an accident. It's your decision. Spare no expense.

You are under no obligation to accept this job, but I ask you to consider taking it to prevent a civil war in this country. Also consider the enormous amount I am willing to pay.

Place two ads. One of acceptance, the other to notify when finished.

—Moral Mafia

I could walk away, Jim thought. *Ignore all of this, and simplify my life forever.* Before the thought could solidify in his mind, he looked at the keyboard and in unison, pressed the Control and Enter keys. The e-mail was on its way.

"Ingeniously diabolical!"
—Sean Doolittle, author of *Safer*

danger
ous
DNA

a novel

DAN
REYNOLDS

kindle version available!

As Detective John Dietrich delves into a series of seemingly unrelated crimes, he realizes that he should be content that these cases are open and shut. However, something seems terribly wrong. In every case there is too much evidence—easy evidence that will surely convict five highly respected citizens. All of the suspects have iron-clad alibis, and no apparent motives, but the videos, fingerprints, and DNA will surely convict them. When the mayor of Kansas City is linked to the crimes, Dietrich investigates the cases more closely. Recent clues suggest that the mayor's friend, hailed as the wealthiest bachelor in the city, is in danger. Can Dietrich save his life?

Available online at www.RNRPublishingCo.com!

www.ingramcontent.com/pod-product-compliance
Lightning Source LLC
Chambersburg PA
CBHW051545250626
47157CB00001B/195